A SHADOW.

TRUMPS.

A Novel.

By GEORGE WILLIAM CURTIS,

AUTHOR OF

"NILE NOTES OF A HOWADJI," "THE HOWADJI IN SYRIA,"
"THE POTIPHAR PAPERS," PRUE AND I," ETC.

ILLUSTRATED BY AUGUSTUS HOPPIN.

NEW YORK:

HARPER & BROTHERS, PUBLISHERS,

FRANKLIN SQUARE.

CONTENTS.

CONTENTS.

TRUMPS.

CHAPTER I.

SCHOOL BEGINS.

FORTY years ago Mr. Savory Gray was a prosperous merchant. No gentleman on 'Change wore more spotless linen
or blacker broadcloth. His ample white cravat had an air of
absolute wisdom and honesty. It was so very white that his
fellow-merchants could not avoid a vague impression that he
had taken the church on his way down town, and had so puri-
fied himself for business. Indeed a white cravat is strongly
to be recommended as a corrective and sedative of the public
mind. Its advantages have long been familiar to the clergy;
and even, in some desperate cases, politicians have found a re-
sort to it of signal benefit. There are instructive instances,
also, in banks and insurance offices of the comfort and value
of spotless linen. Combined with highly-polished shoes, it is
of inestimable mercantile advantage.

Mr. Gray prospered in business, and nobody was sorry. He
enjoyed his practical joke and his glass of Madeira, which had
made at least three voyages round the Cape. His temperament, like his person, was just unctuous enough to enable him
to slip comfortably through life.

Happily for his own comfort, he had but a speaking acquaintance with politics. He was not a blue Federalist, and
he never d'd the Democrats. With unconscious skill he shot
the angry rapids of discussion, and swept, by a sure instinct,
toward the quiet water on which he liked to ride. In the

counting-room or the meeting of directors, when his neighbors waxed furious upon raking over some outrage of that old French infidel, Tom Jefferson, as they called him, sending him and his gun-boats where no man or boat wants to go, Mr. Gray rolled his neck in his white cravat, crossed his legs, and shook his black-gaitered shoe, and beamed, and smiled, and blew his nose, and hum'd, and ha'd, and said, " Ah, yes !" " Ah, indeed ?" " Quite so !" and held his tongue.

Mr. Savory Gray minded his own business ; but his business did not mind him. There came a sudden crash—one of the commercial earthquakes that shake fortunes to their foundations and scatter failure on every side. One day he sat in his office consoling his friend Jowlson, who had been ruined. Mr. Jowlson was terribly agitated—credit gone—fortune wrecked —no prospects—" O wife and children !" he cried, rocking to and fro as he sat.

" My dear Jowlson, you must not give way in this manner. You must control your feelings. Have we not always been taught," said Mr. Gray, as a clerk brought in a letter, the seal of which the merchant broke leisurely, and then skimmed the contents as he continued, " that riches have wings and—my God !" he ejaculated, springing up, " I am a ruined man !"

So he was. Every thing was gone. Those pretty riches that chirped and sang to him as he fed them ; they had all spread their bright plumage, like a troop of singing birds— have we not always been taught that they might, Mr. Jowlson ?—and had flown away.

To undertake business anew was out of the question. His friends said, " Poor Gray ! what shall be done ?"

The friendly merchants pondered and pondered. The worthy Jowlson, who had meanwhile engaged as book-keeper upon a salary of seven hundred dollars a year—one of the rare prizes—was busy enough for his friend, consulting, wondering, planning. Mr. Gray could not preach, nor practice medicine, nor surgery, nor law, because men must be instructed in those professions ; and people will not trust a suit of a thousand dollars, or a sore throat, or a broken thumb, in the hands of a man who has not fitted himself carefully for the responsibility. He could not make boots, nor build houses, nor shoe horses, nor lay stone wall, nor bake bread, nor bind books. Men must be educated to be shoemakers, carpenters, blacksmiths, bakers, masons, or book-binders. What *could* be done? Nobody suggested an insurance office, or an agency for diamond mines on Newport beach; for, although it was the era of good feeling, those ingenious infirmaries for commercial invalids were not yet invented.

"I have it!" cried Jowlson, one day, rushing in, out of breath, among several gentlemen who were holding a council about their friend Gray—that is, who had met in a bank parlor, and were talking about his prospects—"I have it! and how dull we all are! What shall he do? Why, keep a school, to be sure!—a school!—a school! Take children, and be a parent to them!"

"How dull we all were!" cried the gentlemen in chorus. "A school is the very thing! A school it shall be!" And a school it was.

Upon the main street of the pleasant village of Delafield Savory Gray, Esq., hired a large house, with an avenue of young lindens in front, a garden on one side, and a spacious play-ground in the rear. The pretty pond was not far away, with its sloping shores and neat villas, and a distant spire upon the opposite bank—the whole like the vignette of an English pastoral poem. Here the merchant turned from importing pongees to inculcating principles. His old friends sent some of their children to the new school, and persuaded their friends to send others. Some of his former correspondents in other parts of the world, not entirely satisfied with the Asian and East Indian systems of education, shipped their sons to Mr. Gray. The good man was glad to see them. He was not very learned, and therefore could not communicate knowledge. But he did his best, and tried very hard to be respected. The boys did not learn any thing; but they had plenty of good beef, and Mr. Gray played practical jokes upon them; and on Sundays they all went to hear Dr. Peewee preach.

CHAPTER II.

HOPE WAYNE.

WHEN there was a report that Mr. Savory Gray was coming to Delafield to establish a school for boys, Dr. Peewee, the minister of the village, called to communicate the news to Mr. Christopher Burt, his oldest and richest parishioner, at Pinewood, his country seat. When Mr. Burt heard the news, he foresaw trouble without end; for his orphan grand-daughter, Hope Wayne, who lived with him, was nearly eighteen years old; and it had been his fixed resolution that she should be protected from the wicked world of youth that is always going up and down in the earth seeking whom it may marry. If incessant care, and invention, and management could secure it, she should arrive safely where Grandpa Burt was determined she should arrive ultimately, at the head of her husband's dinner-table, Mrs. Simcoe, ma'am.

Mrs. Simcoe was Mr. Burt's housekeeper. So far as any body could say, Mrs. Burt died at a period of which the memory of man runneth not to the contrary. There were traditions of other housekeepers. But since the death of Hope's mother Mrs. Simcoe was the only incumbent. She had been Mrs. Wayne's nurse in her last moments, and had rocked the little Hope to sleep the night after her mother's burial. She was always tidy, erect, imperturbable. She pervaded the house; and her eye was upon a table-cloth, a pane of glass, or a carpet, almost as soon as the spot which arrested it. Housekeeper *nascitur non fit.* She was so silent and shadowy that the whole house sympathized with her, until it became extremely uncomfortable to the servants, who constantly went away; and a story that the house was haunted became immensely popular and credible the moment it was told.

There had been no visiting at Pinewood for a long time, because of the want of a mistress and of the unsocial habits of Mr. Burt. But the neighboring ladies were just beginning to call upon Miss Wayne. When she returned the visits Mrs. Simcoe accompanied her in the carriage, and sat there while Miss Wayne performed the parlor ceremony. Then they drove home. Mr. Burt dined at two, and Miss Hope sat opposite her grandfather at table; Hiram waited. Mrs. Simcoe dined alone in her room.

MRS. SIMCOE, MA'AM.

There, too, she sat alone in the long summer afternoons, when the work of the house was over for the day. She held a book by the open window, or gazed for a very long time out upon the landscape. There were pine-trees near her window; but beyond she could see green meadows, and blue hills, and a glittering river, and rounded reaches of woods. She watched the clouds, or, at least, looked at the sky. She heard the birds in spring days, and the dry hot locusts on sultry afternoons; and she looked with the same unchanging eyes upon the

opening buds and blooming flowers, as upon the worms that
swung themselves on filaments and ate the leaves and ruined
the trees, or the autumnal hectic which Death painted upon
the leaves that escaped the worms.

Sometimes on these still, warm afternoons her lips parted,
as if she were singing. But it was a very grave, quiet performance. There was none of the gush and warmth of song,
although the words she uttered were always those of the
hymns of Charles Wesley—those passionate, religious songs of
the New Jerusalem. For Mrs. Simcoe was a Methodist, and
with Methodist hymns she had sung Hope to sleep in the days
when she was a baby; so that the young woman often listened
to the music in church with a heart full of vague feelings, and
dim, inexplicable memories, not knowing that she was hearing, though with different words, the strains that her nurse
had whispered over her crib in the hymns of Wesley.

It is to be presumed that at some period Mrs. Simcoe, whom
Mr. Burt always addressed in the same manner as " Mrs. Simcoe, ma'am," had received a general system of instruction to
the effect that " My grand-daughter, Miss Wayne—Mrs. Simcoe, ma'am—will marry a gentleman of wealth and position ;
and I expect her to be fitted to preside over his household.
Yes, Mrs. Simcoe, ma'am."

What on earth is a girl sent into this world for but to make
a proper match, and not disgrace her husband—to keep his
house, either directly or by a deputy—to take care of his children, to see that his slippers are warm and his Madeira cold,
and his beef not burned to a cinder, Mrs. Simcoe, ma'am?
Christopher Burt believed that a man's wife was a more sacred piece of private property than his sheep-pasture, and
when he delivered the deed of any such property he meant
that it should be in perfect order.

"Hope may marry a foreign minister, Mrs. Simcoe, ma'am.
Who knows? She may marry a large merchant in town or a
large planter at the South, who will be obliged to entertain a
great deal, and from all parts of the world. I intend that she

shall be fit for the situation, that she shall preside at her husband's table in a superior manner."

So Hope, as a child, had played with little girls, who were invited to Pinewood—select little girls, who came in the prettiest frocks and behaved in the prettiest way, superintended by nurses and ladies' maids. They tended their dolls peaceably in the nursery; they played clean little games upon the lawn. Not too noisy, Ellen! Mary, gently, gently, dear! Julia, carefully! you are tumbling your frock. They were not chattery French nurses who presided over these solemnities; they were grave, housekeeping, Mrs. Simcoe-kind of people. Julia and Mary were exhorted to behave themselves like little ladies, and the frolic ended by their all taking books from the library shelves and sitting properly in a large chair, or on the sofa, or even upon the piazza, if it had been nicely dusted and inspected, until the setting sun sent them away with the calmest kisses at parting.

As Hope grew older she had teachers at home—recluse old scholars, decayed clergymen in shiny black coats, who taught her Latin, and looked at her through round spectacles, and, as they looked, remembered that they were once young. She had teachers of history, of grammar, of arithmetic—of all English studies. Some of these Mentors were weak-eyed fathers of ten children, who spoke so softly that their wives must have had loud voices. Others were young college graduates, with low collars and long hair, who read with Miss Wayne in English literature, while Mrs. Simcoe sat knitting in the next chair. Then there had been the Italian music-masters, and the French teachers, very devoted, never missing a lesson, but also never missing Mrs. Simcoe, who presided over all instruction which was imparted by any Mentor under sixty.

But when Hope grew older still and found Byron upon the shelves of the Library, his romantic sadness responded to the vague longing of her heart. Instinctively she avoided all that repels a woman in his verses, as she would have avoided the unsound parts of a fruit. But the solitary, secluded girl lived unconsciously and inevitably in a dream world, for she had no knowledge of any other, nor contact with it. Proud and shy, her heart was restless, her imagination morbid, and she believed in heroes.

When Dr. Peewee had told Mr. Burt all that he knew about the project of the school, Mr. Burt rang the bell violently.

"Send Miss Hope to me."

The servant disappeared, and in a few moments Hope Wayne entered the room. To Dr. Peewee's eyes she seemed wrapped only in a cloud of delicate muslin, and the wind had evidently been playing with her golden hair, for she had been lying upon the lawn reading Byron.

"Did you want me, grandfather?"

"Yes, my dear. Mr. Gray, a respectable person, is coming here to set up a school. There will be a great many young men and boys. I shall never ask them to the house. I hate boys. I expect you to hate them too."

"Yes—yes, my dear," said Dr. Peewee; "hate the boys? Yes; we must hate the boys."

Hope Wayne looked at the two old gentlemen, and answered,

"I don't think you need have warned me, grandfather; I'm not so apt to fall in love with boys."

"No, no, Hope; I know. Ever since you have lived with me—how long is it, my dear, since your mother died?"

"I don't know, grandfather; I never saw her," replied Hope, gravely.

"Yes, yes; well, ever since then you have been a good, quiet little girl with grandpapa. Here, Cossy, come and give grandpa a kiss. And mind the boys! No speaking, no looking—we are never to know them. You understand? Now go, dear."

As she closed the door, Dr. Peewee also rose to take leave.

"Doctor," said Mr. Burt, as the other pushed back his chair, "it is a very warm day. Let me advise you to guard against any sudden debility or effect of the heat by a little cordial."

As he spoke he led the way into the dining-room, and fumbled slowly over a bunch of keys which he drew from his pocket. Finding the proper key, he put it into the door of the side-board. "In this side-board, Dr. Peewee, I keep a bottle of old Jamaica, which was sent me by a former correspondent in the West Indies." As Dr. Peewee had heard the same remark at least fifty times before, the kindly glistening of his nose must be attributed to some other cause than excitement at this intelligence.

"I like to preserve my friendly relations with my old commercial friends," continued Mr. Burt, speaking very pompously, and slowly pouring from a half-empty decanter into a tumbler. "I rarely drink any thing myself—"

"H'm, ha!" grunted the Doctor.

"—except a glass of port at dinner. Yet, not to be impolite, Doctor, not to be impolite, I could not refuse to drink to your very good health and safe return to the bosom of your family."

And Mr. Burt drained the glass, quite unobservant of the fact that the Rev. Dr. Peewee was standing beside him without glass or old Jamaica. In truth Mr. Burt had previously been alarmed about the effect of the bottle of port—which he metaphorically called a glass—that he had drunk at dinner, and to guard against evil results he had already, that very afternoon, as he was accustomed to say with an excellent humor, been to the West Indies for his health.

"Bless my soul, Doctor, you haven't filled your glass! Permit me."

And the old gentleman poured into the one glass and then into the other.

"And now, Sir," he added, "now, Sir, let us drink to the health of Mr. Gray, but not of the boys—ha! ha!"

"No, no, not of the boys? No, not of the boys. Thank you, Sir—thank you. That is a pleasant liquor, Mr. Burt. H'm, ha! a very pleasant liquor. Good-afternoon, Mr. Burt; a very good day, Sir. H'm, ha!"

As Hope left her grandfather, Mrs. Simcoe was sitting at her window, which looked over the lawn in front of the house upon which Hope presently appeared. It was already toward sunset, and the tender golden light streamed upon the landscape like a visible benediction. A few rosy clouds lay in long, tranquil lines across the west, and the great trees bathed in the sweet air with conscious pleasure.

As Hope stood with folded hands looking toward the sunset, she began unconsciously to repeat some of the lines that always lay in her mind like invisible writing, waiting only for the warmth of a strong emotion to bring them legibly out:

"Though the rock of my last hope is shivered,
    And its fragments are sunk in the wave;
Though I feel that my soul is delivered
    To pain, it shall not be its slave.
There is many a pang to pursue me;
    They may crush, but they shall not contemn;
They may torture, but shall not subdue me;
    'Tis of thee that I think, not of them."

At the same moment Mrs. Simcoe was closing her window high over Hope's head. Her face was turned toward the sunset with the usual calm impassive look, and as she gazed at the darkening landscape she was singing, in her murmuring way,

"I rest upon thy word;
    Thy promise is for me:
My succor and salvation, Lord,
    Shall surely come from thee.
But let me still abide,
    Nor from my hope remove,
Till thou my patient spirit guide
    Into thy perfect love."

CHAPTER III.

AVE MARIA!

MR. GRAY's boys sat in several pews, which he could command with his eye from his own seat in the broad aisle. Every Sunday morning at the first stroke of the bell the boys began to stroll toward the church. But after they were seated, and the congregation had assembled, and Dr. Peewee had gone up into the pulpit, the wheels of a carriage were heard outside —steps were let down—there was an opening of doors, a slight scuffling and treading, and old Christopher Burt entered. His head was powdered, and he wore a queue. His coat collar was slightly whitened with powder, and he carried a gold-headed cane.

The boys looked in admiration upon so much respectability, powder, age, and gold cane united in one person.

But all the boys were in love with the golden-haired grand-daughter. They went home to talk about her. They went to bed to dream of her. They read Mary Lamb's stories from Shakespeare, and Hope Wayne was Ophelia, and Desdemona, and Imogen—above all others, she was Juliet. They read the "Arabian Nights," and she was all the Arabian Princesses with unpronounceable names. They read Miss Edgeworth— "Helen," "Belinda."—"Oh, thunder!" they cried, and dropped the book to think of Hope.

Hope Wayne was not unconscious of the adoration she excited. If a swarm of school-boys can not enter a country church without turning all their eyes toward one pew, is it not possible that, when a girl comes in and seats herself in that pew, the very focus of those burning glances, even Dr. Peewee may not entirely distract her mind, however he may rivet her eyes? As she takes her last glance at the Sunday toilet in her sunny dressing-room at home, and half turns to be

SUNDAY MORNING.

sure that the collar is smooth, and that the golden curl nestles precisely as it should under the moss rose-bud that blushes modestly by the side of a lovelier bloom—is it not just supposable that she thinks, for a wayward instant, of other eyes that will presently scan that figure and face, and feels, with a half-flush, that they will not be shocked nor disappointed?

There was not a boy in Mr. Gray's school who would have dared to dream that Hope Wayne ever had such a thought.

When she appeared behind Grandfather Burt and the gold-headed cane she had no more antecedents in their imaginations than a rose or a rainbow. They no more thought of little human weaknesses and mundane influences in regard to her than they thought of cold vapor when they looked at sunset clouds.

During the service Hope sat stately in the pew, with her eyes fixed upon Dr. Peewee. She knew the boys were there. From time to time she observed that new boys had arrived, and that older ones had left. But how she discovered it, who could say? There was never one of Mr. Gray's boys who could honestly declare that he had seen Hope Wayne looking at either of the pews in which they sat. Perhaps she did not hear what Dr. Peewee said, although she looked at him so steadily. Perhaps her heart did not look out of her eyes, but was busy with a hundred sweet fancies in which some one of those fascinated boys had a larger share than he knew. Perhaps, when she covered her eyes in an attitude of devotion, she did not thereby exclude all thoughts of the outer and lower world. Perhaps the Being for whose worship they were assembled was no more displeased with the innocent reveries and fancies which floated through that young heart than with the soft air and sweet song of birds that played through the open windows of the church on some warm June Sunday morning.

But when the shrill-voiced leader of the choir sounded the key-note of the hymn-tune through his nose, and the growling bass-viol joined in unison, while the congregation rose, and Dr. Peewee surveyed his people to mark who had staid away from service, then Hope Wayne looked at the choir as if her whole soul were singing; and young Gabriel Bennet, younger than Hope, had a choking feeling as he gazed at her—an involuntary sense of unworthiness and shame before such purity and grace. He counted every line of the hymn grudgingly, and loved the tunes that went back and repeated and prolonged—the tunes endlessly *da capo*—and the hymns that he heard as he looked at her he never forgot.

But there were other eyes than Gabriel Bennet's that watched Hope Wayne, and for many months had watched her—the flashing black eyes of Abel Newt. Handsome, strong, graceful, he was one of the oldest boys, and a leader at Mr. Gray's school. Like every handsome, bold boy or young man, for he was fully eighteen, and seemed much older, Abel Newt had plenty of allies at school—they could hardly be called friends. There was many a boy who thought with the one nicknamed Little Malacca, although, more prudently than he, he might not say it: "Abe gives me gingerbread; but I guess I don't like him!" If a boy interfered with Abe he was always punished. The laugh was turned on him; there was ceaseless ridicule and taunting. Then if it grew insupportable, and came to fighting, Abel Newt was strong in muscle and furious in wrath, and the recusant was generally pommeled.

Reposing upon his easy, conscious superiority, Abel had long worshiped Hope Wayne. They were nearly of the same age—she a few months the younger. But as the regulations of the school confined every boy, without especial permission of absence, to the school grounds, and as Abel had no acquaintance with Mr. Burt and no excuse for calling, his worship had been silent and distant. He was the more satisfied that it should be so, because it had never occurred to him that any of the other boys could be a serious rival for her regard. He was also obliged to be the more satisfied with his silent devotion, because never, by a glance, did she betray any consciousness of his particular observation, or afford him the least opportunity for saying or doing any thing that would betray it. If he hastened to the front door of the church he could only stand upon the steps, and as she passed out she nodded to her few friends, and immediately followed her grandfather into the carriage.

When Gabriel Bennet came to Mr. Gray's, Abel did not like him. He laughed at him. He made the other boys laugh at him whenever he could. He bullied him in the play-ground. He proposed to introduce fagging at Mr. Gray's. He praised it as a splendid institution of the British schools, simply because he wanted Gabriel as his fag. He wanted to fling his boots at Gabriel's head that he might black them. He wanted to send him down stairs in his shirt on winter nights. He wanted to have Gabriel get up in the cold mornings and bring him his breakfast in bed. He wanted to chain Gabriel to the car of his triumphal progress through school-life. He wanted to debase and degrade him altogether.

"What is it," Abel exclaimed one day to the large boys assembled in solemn conclave in the school-room, "that takes all the boorishness and brutishness out of the English character? What is it that prevents the Britishers from being servile and obsequious—traits, I tell you, boys, unknown in England—but this splendid system of fagging? Did you ever hear of an insolent Englishman, a despotic Englishman, a surly Englishman, a selfish Englishman, an obstinate Englishman, a domineering Englishman, a dogmatic Englishman? Never, boys, never. These things are all taken out of them by fagging. It stands to reason they should be. If I shy my boots at a fellow's head, is he likely to domineer? If I kick a small boy who contradicts me, is he likely to be opinionated and dogmatic? If I eat up my fag's plum-cake just sent by his mamma, hot, as it were, from the maternal heart, and moist with a mother's tears, is that fag likely to be selfish? Not at all. The boots, and the kicking, and the general walloping make him manly. It teaches him to govern his temper and hold his tongue. I swear I should like to have a fag!" perorated Abel, meaning that he should like to be the holy office, and to have Gabriel Bennet immediately delivered up to him for discipline.

Once Gabriel overheard this kind of conversation in the play-ground, as Abel Newt and some of the other boys were resting after a game at ball. There were no personal allusions in what Abel had said, but Gabriel took him up a little curtly:

"Pooh! Abel, how would you like to have Gyles Blanding shy his boots at your head?"

Abel looked at him a moment, sarcastically. Then he replied:

THE FAGGING QUESTION.

"My young friend, I should like to see him try it. But fagging concerns small boys, not large ones."

"Yes!" retorted Gabriel, his eyes flashing, as he kept tossing the ball nervously, and catching it; "yes, that's the meanness of it: the little boy can't help himself."

"By golly, I'd kick!" put in Little Malacca.

"Then you'd be licked till you dropped, my small Sir," said Abel, sneeringly.

"Yes, Abel," replied Gabriel, "but it's a mean thing for an American boy to want fagging."

"Not at all," he answered; "there are some young American gentlemen I know who would be greatly benefited by being well fagged; yes, made to lie down in the dirt and lick a little of it, and fetch and carry. And to be kicked out of bed every morning and into bed every night would be the very best thing that could happen to 'em. By George, I should like to have the kicking and licking begin now!"

Gabriel had the same dislike of Abel which the latter felt for him, but they had never had any open quarrel. Even thus far in the present conversation there had been nothing personal said. It was only a warm general discussion. Gabriel merely asked, when the other stopped,

"What good does the fagging do the fellow that flings the boots and bullies the little one?"

"Good?" answered Abel—"what good does it do? Why, he has been through it all himself, and he's just paying it off."

Abel smiled grimly as he looked round upon the boys, who did not seem at all enthusiastic for his suggestion.

"Well," said he, "I'm afraid I shall have to postpone my millennium of fagging. But I don't know what else will make men of you. And mark you, my merry men, there's more than one kind of fagging;" and he looked in a droll way—a droll way that was not in the least funny, but made the boys all wonder what Abel Newt was up to now.

CHAPTER IV.

NIGHT.

IT was already dusk, but the summer evening is the best time for play. The sport in the play-ground at Mr. Gray's was at its height, and the hot, eager, panting boys were shout-

ing and scampering in every direction, when a man ran in from
the road and cried out, breathless,

"Where's Mr. Gray?"

"In his study," answered twenty voices at once. The man
darted toward the house and went in; the next moment he
reappeared with Mr. Gray, both of them running.

"Get out the boat!" cried Mr. Gray, "and call the big
boys. There's a man drowning in the pond!"

The game was over at once, and each young heart thrilled
with vague horror. Abel Newt, Muddock, Blanding, Tom
Galt, Jim Greenidge, and the rest of the older boys, came rushing out of the school-room, and ran toward the barn, in which
the boat was kept upon a truck. In a moment the door was
open, the truck run out, and all the boys took hold of the
rope. Mr. Gray and the stranger led the way. The throng
swept out of the gate, and as they hastened silently along, the
axles of the truck kindled with the friction and began to
smoke.

"Carefully! steadily!" cried the boys all together.

They slackened speed a little, but, happily, the pond was
but a short distance from the school. It was a circular sheet
of water, perhaps a mile in width.

"Boys, he is nearly on the other side," said Mr. Gray, as the
crowd reached the shore.

In an instant the boat was afloat. Mr. Gray, the stranger,
and the six stoutest boys in the school, stepped into it. The
boys lifted their oars. "Let fall! give way!" cried Mr. Gray,
and the boat moved off, glimmering away into the darkness.

The younger boys remained hushed and awe-stricken upon
the shore. The stars were just coming out, the wind had
fallen, and the smooth, black pond lay silent at their feet.
They could see the vague, dark outline of the opposite shore,
but none of the pretty villas that stood in graceful groves
upon the banks—none of the little lawns that sloped, with a
feeling of human sympathy, to the water. The treachery of
that glassy surface was all they thought of. They shuddered

to remember that they had so often bathed in the pond, and recoiled as if they had been friends of a murderer. None of them spoke. They clustered closely together, listening intently. Nothing was audible but the hum of the evening insects and the regular muffled beat of the oars over the water. The boys strained their ears and held their breath as the sound suddenly stopped. But they listened in vain. The lazy tree-toads sang, the monotonous hum of the night went on.

Gabriel Bennet held the hand of Little Malacca—a dark-eyed boy, who was supposed in the school to have had no father or mother, and who had instinctively attached himself to Gabriel from the moment they met.

"Isn't it dreadful?" whispered the latter.

"Yes," said Gabriel, "it's dreadful to be young when a man's drowning, for you can't do any thing. Hist!"

There was not a movement, as they heard a dull, distant sound.

"I guess that's Jim Greenidge," whispered Little Malacca, under his breath; "he's the best diver."

Nobody answered. The slow minutes passed. Some of the boys peered timidly into the dark, and clung closer to their neighbors.

"There they come!" said Gabriel suddenly, in a low voice, and in a few moments the beat of the oars was heard again. Still nobody spoke. Most of the boys were afraid that when the boat appeared they should see a dead body, and they dreaded it. Some felt homesick, and began to cry. The throb of oars came nearer and nearer. The boat glimmered out of the darkness, and almost at the same moment slid up the shore. The solemn undertone in which the rowers spoke told all. Death was in the boat.

Gabriel Bennet could see the rowers step quickly out, and with great care run the boat upon the truck. He said, "Come, boys!" and they all moved together and grasped the rope.

"Forward!" said Mr. Gray.

Something lay across the seats covered with a large cloak.

The boys did not look behind, but they all knew what they
were dragging. The homely funeral-car rolled slowly along
under the stars. The crickets chirped; the multitudinous
voice of the summer night murmured on every side, mingling
with the hollow rumble of the truck. In a few moments the
procession turned into the grounds, and the boat was drawn
to the platform.

"The little boys may go," said Mr. Gray.

They dropped the rope and turned away. They did not
even try to see what was done with the body; but when
Blanding came out of the house afterward, they asked him
who found the drowned man.

"Jim Greenidge," said he. "He stripped as soon as we
were well out on the pond, and asked the stranger gentleman
to show him about where his friend sank. The moment the
place was pointed out he dove. The first time he found nothing. The second time he touched him"—the boys shuddered—"and he actually brought him up to the surface. But
he was quite dead. Then we took him into the boat and
covered him over. That's all."

There were no more games, there was no other talk, that
evening. When the boys were going to bed, Gabriel asked
Little Malacca in which room Jim Greenidge slept.

"He sleeps in Number Seven. Why?"

"Oh! I only wanted to know."

Gabriel Bennet could not sleep. His mind was too busy
with the events of the day. All night long he could think of
nothing but the strong figure of Jim Greenidge erect in the
summer night, then plunging silently into the black water.
When it was fairly light he hurried on his clothes, and passing
quietly along the hall, knocked at the door of Number Seven.

"Who's there?" cried a voice within.

"It's only me."

"Who's me?"

"Gabriel Bennet."

"Come in, then."

It was Abel Newt who spoke; and as Gabriel stepped in, Newt asked, abruptly,

"What do you want?"

"I want to speak to Jim Greenidge."

"Well, there he is," replied Newt, pointing to another bed.

"Jim! Jim!"

Greenidge roused himself.

"What's the matter?" said his cheery voice, as he rose upon his elbow and looked at Gabriel with his kind eyes. "Come here, Gabriel. What is it?"

Gabriel hesitated, for Abel Newt was looking sharply at him. But in a moment he went to Greenidge's bedside, and said, shyly, in a low voice,

"Shall I black your boots for you?"

"Black my boots! Why, Gabriel, what on earth do you mean? No, of course you shall not."

And the strong youth looked pleasantly on the boy who stood by his bedside, and then put out his hand to him.

"Can't I brush your clothes then, or do any thing for you?" persisted Gabriel, softly.

"Certainly not. Why do you want to?" replied Greenidge.

"Oh! I only thought it would be pleasant if I could do something—that's all," said Gabriel, as he moved slowly away. "I'm sorry to have waked you."

He closed the door gently as he went out. Jim Greenidge lay for some time resting upon his elbow, wondering why a boy who had scarcely ever spoken a word to him before should suddenly want to be his servant. He could make nothing of it, and, tired with the excitement of the previous evening, he lay down again for a morning nap.

CHAPTER V.

PEEWEE PREACHING.

UPON the following Sunday the Rev, Amos Peewee, D.D., made a suitable improvement of the melancholy event of the week. He enlarged upon the uncertainty of life. He said that in the midst of life we are in death. He said that we are shadows and pursue shades. He added that we are here to-day and gone to-morrow.

During the long prayer before the sermon a violent thunder-gust swept from the west and dashed against the old wooden church. As the Doctor poured forth his petitions he made the most extraordinary movements with his right hand. He waved it up and down rapidly. He opened his eyes for an instant as if to find somebody. He seemed to be closing imaginary windows—and so he was. It leaked out the next day at Mr. Gray's that Dr. Peewee was telegraphing the sexton at random—for he did not know where to look for him—to close the windows. Nobody better understood the danger of draughts from windows, during thunder-storms, than the Doctor; nobody knew better than he that the lightning-rod upon the spire was no protection at all, but that the iron staples with which it was clamped to the building would serve, in case of a bolt's striking the church, to drive its whole force into the building. As a loud crash burst over the village in the midst of his sermon, and showed how frightfully near the storm was, his voice broke into a shrill quaver, as he faltered out, "Yes, my brethren, let us be calm under all circumstances, and Death will have no terrors."

The Rev. Amos Peewee had been settled in the village of Delafield since a long period before the Revolution, according to the boys. But the parish register carried the date only to the beginning of this century. He wore a silken gown in summer, and a woolen gown in winter, and black worsted gloves, always with the middle finger of the right-hand glove slit, that he might more conveniently turn the leaves of the Bible, and the hymn-book, and his own sermons.

The pews of the old meeting-house were high, and many of them square. The heads of the people of consideration in the congregation were mostly bald, as beseems respectable age, and as the smooth, shiny line of pates appeared above the wooden line of the pews they somehow sympathetically blended into one gleaming surface of worn wood and skull, until it seemed as if the Doctor's theological battles were all fought upon the heads of his people.

But the Doctor was by no means altogether polemical. After defeating and utterly confounding the fathers who fired their last shot a thousand years ago, and who had not a word to say against his remaining master of the field, he was wont to unbend his mind and recreate his fancy by practical discourses. His sermons upon lying were celebrated all through the village. He gave the insidious vice no quarter. He charged upon it from all sides at once. Lying couldn't stand for a moment. White lies, black lies, blue lies, and green lies, lies of ceremony, of charity, and of good intention disappeared before the lightning of his wrath. They are all children of the Devil, with different complexions, said Dr. Peewee.

But if lying be a vice, surely, said he, discretion is a virtue. "My dear Mr. Gray," said Dr. Peewee to that gentleman when he was about establishing his school in the village, and was consulting with the Doctor about bringing his boys to church—"my dear Mr. Gray," said the Doctor, putting down his cigar and stirring his toddy (he was of an earlier day), "above all things a clergyman should be discreet. In fact, Christianity is discretion. A man must preach at sins, not sinners. Where would society be if the sins of individuals were to be rudely assaulted?—one more lump, if you please. A man's sins are like his corns. Neither the shoe nor the sermon must fit too snugly. I am a clergyman, but I hope I am also

a man of common sense—a practical man, Mr. Gray.   The general moral law and the means of grace, those are the proper
themes of the preacher.   And the pastor ought to understand
the individual characters and pursuits of his parishioners, that
he may avoid all personality in applying the truth."

"Clearly," said Mr. Gray.

"For instance," reasoned the Doctor, as he slowly stirred
his toddy, and gesticulated with one skinny forefinger, occasionally sipping as he went on, "if I have a deacon in my
church who is a notorious miser, is it not plain that, if I preach
a strong sermon upon covetousness, every body in the church
will think of my deacon—will, in fact, apply the sermon to
him?   The deacon, of course, will be the first to do it.   And
then, why, good gracious! he might even take his hat and
cane and stalk heavily down the broad aisle, under my very
nose, before my very eyes, and slam the church door after
him in my very face!   Here at once is difficulty in the
church; hard feeling; perhaps even swearing.   Am I, as a
Christian clergyman, to give occasion to uncharitable emotions, even to actual profanity?   Is not a Christian congregation, was not every early Christian community, a society of
brothers?   Of course they were; of course we must be.   Little children, love one another.   Let us dwell together, my
brethren, in amity," said the Doctor, putting down his glass,
and forgetting that he was in Mr. Gray's study; "and please
give me your ears while I show you this morning the enormi-
ty of burning widows upon the funeral pyres of their husbands."

This was the Peewee Christianity; and after such a sermon
the deacon has been known to say to his wife—thin she was
in the face, which had a settled shade, like the sober twilight
of valleys from which the sun has long been gone, though it
has not yet set—

"What shocking people the Hindoos are!   They actually
burn widows!   My dear, how grateful we ought to be that
we live in a Christian country where wives are not burned!—

Abraham! if you put another stick of wood into that stove I'll skin you alive, Sir. Go to bed this instant, you wicked boy!—It must be bad enough to be a widow, my dear, let alone the burning. Shall we have evening prayers, Mrs. Deacon?"

In the evening of the day on which the Doctor improved the drowning, and exhorted his hearers to be brave, Mr. Gray asked Gabriel Bennet, "Where was the text?"

"I don't know, Sir," replied Gabriel. As he spoke there was the sound of warm discussion on the other side of the dining-room, in which the boys sat during the evening.

"What is it, Gyles?" asked Mr. Gray.

"Why, Sir," replied he, "it's nothing. We were talking about a ribbon, Sir."

"What ribbon?"

"A ribbon we saw at church, Sir."

"Well, whose was it?" asked Mr. Gray.

"I believe it was Miss Hope Wayne's."

"You believe, Gyles? Why don't you speak out?"

"Well, Sir, the fact is that Abel Newt says she had a purple ribbon on her bonnet—"

"She hadn't," said Gabriel, breaking in, impetuously. "She had a beautiful blue ribbon, and lilies of the valley inside, and a white lace vail, and—"

Gabriel stopped and turned very red, for he caught Abel Newt's eyes fixed sharply upon him.

"Oh ho! the text was there, was it?" asked Mr. Gray, smiling.

But Abel Newt only said, quietly:

"Oh well! I guess it *was* a blue ribbon after all."

CHAPTER VI.

EXPERIMENTUM CRUCIS.

"The truth is, Gyles," said Abel to Blanding, his chum, "Gabriel Bennet's mother ought to come and take him home for the summer to play with the other calves in the country. People shouldn't leave their spoons about."

The two boys went in to tea.

In the evening, as the pupils were sitting in the dining-room, as usual, some chatting, some reading, others quite ready to go to bed,

"Mr. Gray," said Abel to Uncle Savory, who was sitting talking with Mrs. Gray, whose hands, which were never idle, were now busily knitting.

"Well, Abel."

"Suppose we have some game."

"Certainly. Boys, what shall we do? Let us see. There's the Grand Mufti, and the Elements, and My ship's come loaded with—and—well, what shall it be?"

"Mr. Gray, it's a good while since we've tried all calling out together. We haven't done it since Gabriel Bennet came."

"No, we haven't," answered Mr. Gray, as his small eyes twinkled at the prospect of a little fun; "no, we haven't. Now, boys, of course a good many of you have played the game before. But you, new boys, attend! the thing is this. When I say three—*one, two, three!*—every body is to shout out the name of his sweet-heart. The fun is that nobody hears any thing, because every body bawls so loud. You see?" asked he, apparently feeling for his handkerchief. "Gabriel, before we begin, just run into the study and get my handker-chief."

Gabriel, full of expectation of the fun, ran out of the room.

The moment he closed the door Mr. Gray lifted his finger and said,

"Now, boys! every body remain perfectly quiet when I say three."

It was needless to explain why, for every body saw the intended joke, and Gabriel returned instantly from the study saying that the handkerchief was not there.

"No matter," said Mr. Gray. "Are you all ready, boys. Now, then—*one, two, three !*"

As the word left Mr. Gray's lips, Gabriel, candid, full of spirit, jumped up from his seat with the energy of his effort, and shouted out at the top of his voice,

"Hope Wayne!"

—It was cruel. That name alone broke the silence, ringing out in enthusiastic music.

Gabriel's face instantly changed. Still standing erect and dismayed, he looked rapidly around the room from boy to boy, and at Mr. Gray. There was just a moment of utter silence, and then a loud peal of laughter.

Gabriel's color came and went. His heart winced, but not his eye. Young hearts are tender, and a joke like this cuts deeply. But just as he was about to yield, and drop the telltale tear of a sensitive, mortified boy, he caught the eye of Abel Newt. It was calmly studying him as a Roman surgeon may have watched the gladiator in the arena, while his life-blood ebbed away. Gabriel remembered Abel's words in the play-ground—"There's more than one kind of fagging."

When the laugh was over, Gabriel's had been loudest of all.

CHAPTER VII.

CASTLE DANGEROUS.

THE next day when school was dismissed, Abel asked leave to stroll out of bounds. He pushed along the road, whistling cheerily, whipping the road-side grass and weeds with his little ratan, and all the while approaching the foot of the hill up which the road wound through the estate of Pinewood. As he turned up the hill he walked more slowly, and presently stopped and leaned upon a pair of bars which guarded the entrance of one of Mr. Burt's pastures. He gazed for some time down into the rich green field that sloped away from the road toward a little bowery stream, but still whistled, as if he were looking into his mind rather than at the landscape.

After leaning and musing and vaguely whistling, he turned up the hill again and continued his walk.

At length he reached the entrance of Pinewood—a high iron gate, between huge stone posts, on the tops of which were urns overflowing with vines, that hung down and partly tapestried the columns. Immediately upon entering the grounds the carriage avenue wound away from the gate, so that the passer-by could see nothing as he looked through but the hedge which skirted and concealed the lawn. The fence upon the road was a high, solid stone wall, along whose top clustered a dense shrubbery, so that, although the land rose from the road toward the house, the lawn was entirely sequestered; and you might sit upon it and enjoy the pleasant rural prospect of fields, woods, and hills, without being seen from the road. The house itself was a stately, formal mansion. Its light color contrasted well with the lofty pine-trees around it. But they, in turn, invested it with an air of secrecy and gloom, unrelieved by flowers or blossoming shrubs, of which there were no traces near the house, although in the rear there was a garden so formally regular that it looked like a penitentiary for flowers.

These were the pine-trees that Hope Wayne had heard sing all her life—but sing like the ocean, not like birds or human voices. In the black autumn midnights they struggled with the north winds that smote them fiercely and filled the night with uproar, while the child cowering in her bed thought of wrecks on pitiless shores—of drowning mothers and hapless children. Through the summer nights they sighed. But it was not a lullaby—it was not a serenade. It was the croning of a Norland enchantress, and young Hope sat at her open window, looking out into the moonlight, and listening.

Abel Newt opened the gate and passed in. He walked along the avenue, from which the lawn was still hidden by the skirting hedge, went up the steps, and rang the bell.

"Is Mr. Burt at home?" he asked, quietly.

"This way, Sir," said the nimble Hiram, going before, but half turning and studying the visitor as he spoke, and quite unable to comprehend him at a glance. "I will speak to him."

Abel Newt was shown into a large drawing-room. The furniture was draped for the season in cool-colored chintz. There was a straw matting upon the floor. The chandeliers and candelabras were covered with muslin, and heavy muslin curtains hung over the windows. The tables and chairs were of a clumsy old-fashioned pattern, with feet in the form of claws clasping balls, and a generally stiff, stately, and uncomfortable air. The fire-place was covered by a heavy painted fire-board. The polished brass andirons, which seemed to feel the whole weight of responsibility in supporting the family dignity, stood across the hearth, belligerently bright, and there were sprays of asparagus in a china vase in front of them. A few pictures hung upon the wall—family portraits, Abel thought; at least old Christopher was there, painted at the age of ten, standing in very clean attire, holding a book in one hand and a hoop in the other. The picture was amusing, and looked to Abel symbolical, representing the model boy, equally devoted to study and play. That singular sneering smile flitted over his face as he muttered, "The Reverend Gabriel Bennet!"

There were a few books upon the centre-table, carefully placed and balanced as if they had been porcelain ornaments. The bindings and the edges of the leaves had a fresh, unworn look. The outer window-blinds were closed, and the whole room had a chilly formality and dimness which was not hospitable nor by any means inspiring.

Abel seated himself in an easy-chair, and was still smiling at the portrait of Master Christopher Burt at the age of ten, when that gentleman, at the age of seventy-three, was heard in the hall. Hiram had left the door open, so that Abel had full notice of his approach, and rose just before the old gentleman entered, and stood with his cap in his hand and his head slightly bent.

Old Burt came into the room, and said, a little fiercely, as he saw the visitor,

"Well, Sir!"

Abel bowed.

"Well, Sir!" he repeated, more blandly, apparently mollified by something in the appearance of the youth.

"Mr. Burt," said Abel, "I am sure you will excuse me when you understand the object of my call; although I am fully aware of the liberty I am taking in intruding upon your valuable time and the many important cares which must occupy the attention of a gentleman so universally known, honored, and loved in the community as you are, Sir."

"Did you come here to compliment me, Sir?" asked Mr. Burt. "You've got some kind of subscription paper, I suppose." The old gentleman began to warm up as he thought of it. "But I can't give any thing. I never do—I never will. It's an infernal swindle. Some deuced Missionary Society, or Tract Society, or Bible Society, some damnable doing-good society, that bleeds the entire community, has sent you

up here, Sir, to suck money out of me with your smooth face.
They're always at it.   They're always sending boys, and min-
isters in the milk, by Jove! and women that talk in a way to
turn the milk sour in the cellar, Sir, and who have already
turned themselves sour in the face, Sir, and whom a man can't
turn out of doors, Sir, to swindle money out of innocent people! I tell you, young man, 'twon't work! I'll be whipped
if I give you a solitary red cent!" And Christopher Burt, in
a fine wrath, seated himself by the table and wiped his forehead.

Abel stood patiently and meekly under this gust of fury,
and when it was ended, and Mr. Burt was a little composed,
he began quietly, as if the indignation were the most natural
thing in the world:

"No, Sir; it is not a subscription paper—"

· "Not a subscription paper!" interrupted the old gentleman,
lifting his head and staring at him. "Why, what the deuce
is it, then?"

"Why, Sir, as I was just saying," calmly returned Abel,
"it is a personal matter altogether."

"Eh! eh! what?" cried Mr. Burt, on the edge of another
paroxysm, "what the deuce does that mean?   Who are you,
Sir?"

"I am one of Mr. Gray's boys, Sir," replied Abel.

"What! what!" thundered Grandpa Burt, springing up
suddenly, his mind opening upon a fresh scent.   "One of Mr.
Gray's boys? How dare you, Sir, come into my house?
Who sent you here, Sir? What right have you to intrude
into this place, Sir?   Hiram! Hiram!"

"Yes, Sir," answered the man, as he came across the hall.

"Show this young man out."

"He may have some message, Sir," said Hiram, who had
heard the preceding conversation.

"Have you got any message?" asked Mr. Burt.

"No, Sir; but I—"

"Then why, in Heaven's name, don't you go?"

"Mr. Burt," said Abel, with placid persistence, "being one of Mr. Gray's boys, I go of course to Dr. Peewee's Church, and there I have so often seen—"

"Come, come, Sir, this is a little too much. Hiram, put this boy out," said the old gentleman, quite beside himself as he thought of his grand-daughter. "Seen, indeed! What business have you to see, Sir?"

"So often seen your venerable figure," resumed Abel in the same tone as before, while Mr. Burt turned suddenly and looked at him closely, "that I naturally asked who you were. I was told, Sir; and hearing of your wealth and old family, and so on, Sir, I was interested—it was only natural, Sir—in all that belongs to you."

"Eh! eh! what?" said Mr. Burt, quickly.

"Particularly, Mr. Burt, in your—"

"By Jove! young man, you'd better go if you don't want to have your head broken. D'ye come here to beard me in my own house? By George! your impudence stupefies me, Sir. I tell you go this minute!"

But Abel continued:

"In your beautiful—"

"Don't dare to say it, Sir!" cried the old man, shaking his finger.

"Place," said Abel, quietly.

The old gentleman glared at him with a look of mixed surprise and suspicion. But the boy wore the same look of candor. He held his cap in his hand. His black hair fell around his handsome face. He was entirely calm, and behaved in the most respectful manner.

"What do you mean, Sir?" said Christopher Burt, in great perplexity, as he seated himself again, and drew a long breath.

"Simply, Sir, that I am very fond of sketching. My teacher says I draw very well, and I have had a great desire to draw your place, but I did not dare to ask permission. It is said in school, Sir, that you don't like Mr. Gray's boys, and I knew nobody who could introduce me. But to-day, as I came by, every thing looked so beautifully, and I was so sure that I could make a pretty picture if I could only get leave to come inside the grounds, that almost unconsciously I found myself coming up the avenue and ringing the bell. That's all, Sir; and I'm sure I beg your pardon for troubling you so much."

Mr. Burt listened to this speech with a pacified air. He was perhaps a little ashamed of his furious onslaughts and interruptions, and therefore the more graciously inclined toward the request of the young man.

So the old man said, with tolerable grace,

" Well, Sir, I am willing you should draw my house. Will you do it this afternoon ?"

" Really, Sir," replied Abel, " I had no intention of asking you to-day; and as I strolled out merely for a walk, I did not bring my drawing materials with me. But if you would allow me to come at any time, Sir, I should be very deeply obliged. I am devoted to my art, Sir."

" Oh! you mean to be an artist ?"

" Perhaps, Sir."

" Phit! phit! Don't do any such silly thing, Sir. An artist! Why how much does an artist make in a year?"

" Well, Sir, the money I don't know about, but the fame !"

" Oh! the fame! The fiddle, Sir! You are capable of better things."

" For instance, Mr. Burt—"

" Trade, Sir, trade—trade. That is the way to fortune in this country. Enterprise, activity, shrewdness, industry, that's what a young man wants. Get rid of your fol-de-rol notions about art. Benjamin West was a great man, Sir; but he was an exception, and besides he lived in England. I respect Benjamin West, Sir, of course. We all do. He made a good thing of it. Take the word of an old man who has seen life and knows the world, and remember that, with all your fine fiddling, it is money makes the mare go. Old men like me don't mince matters, Sir. It's money—money !"

Abel thought old men sometimes minced grammar a little,

but he did not say so. He only looked respectful, and said,
" Yes, Sir."

" About drawing the house, come when you choose," said
Mr. Burt, rising.

" It may take more than one, or even three or four afternoons, Sir, to do it properly."

" Well, well. If I'm not at home ask for Mrs. Simcoe, d'ye
hear? Mrs. Simcoe. She will attend to you."

Abel bowed very respectfully and as if he were controlling
a strong desire to kneel and kiss the foot of his Holiness, Christopher Burt, but he mastered himself, and Hiram opened the
front door.

" Good-by, Hiram," said Abel, putting a piece of money into
his hand.

" Oh no, Sir," said Hiram, pocketing the coin.

Abel walked sedately down the steps, and looked carefully
around him. He scanned the windows; he glanced under the
trees; but he saw nothing. He did every thing, in fact, but
study the house which he had been asking permission to draw.
He looked as if for something or somebody who did not appear. But as Hiram still stood watching him, he moved
away.

He walked faster as he approached the gate. He opened
it; flung it to behind him, broke into a little trot, and almost
tumbled over Gabriel Bennet and Little Malacca as he did so.

The collision was rude, and the three boys stopped.

" You'd better look where you're going," said Gabriel,
sharply, his cheeks reddening and swelling.

Abel's first impulse was to strike; but he restrained himself,
and in the most contemptuous way said merely,

" Ah, the Reverend Gabriel Bennet!"

He had scarcely spoken when Gabriel fell upon him like a
young lion. So sudden and impetuous was his attack that for
a moment Abel was confounded. He gave way a little, and
was well battered almost before he could strike in return.
Then his strong arms began to tell. He was confident of vic-

THE BATTLE.

tory, and calmer than his antagonist; but it was like fighting
a flame, so fierce and rapid were Gabriel's strokes.

Little Malacca looked on in amazement and terror.
"Don't! don't!" cried he, as he saw the faces of the fighters.
"Oh, don't! Abel, you'll kill him!" For Abel was now fully
aroused. He was seriously hurt by Gabriel's blows.

"Don't! there's somebody coming!" cried Little Malacca,

with the tears in his eyes, as the sound of a carriage was heard driving down the hill.

The combatants said nothing. The faces of both of them were bruised, and the blood was flowing. Gabriel was clearly flagging; and Abel's face was furious as he struck his heavy blows, under which the smaller boy staggered, but did not yet succumb.

"Oh, please! please!" cried Little Malacca, imploringly, the tears streaming down his face.

At that moment Abel Newt drew back, aimed a tremendous blow at Gabriel, and delivered it with fearful force upon his head. The smaller boy staggered, reeled, threw up his arms, and fell heavily forward into the road, senseless.

"You've killed him! You've killed him!" sobbed Little Malacca, piteously, kneeling down and bending over Gabriel.

Abel Newt stood bareheaded, frowning under his heavy hair, his hands clenched, his face bruised and bleeding, his mouth sternly set as he looked down upon his opponent. Suddenly he heard a sound close by him—a half-smothered cry. He looked up. It was the Burt carriage, and Hope Wayne was gazing in terror from the window.

CHAPTER VIII.

AFTER THE BATTLE.

Hiram was summoned to the door by a violent ringing of the bell. Visions of apoplexy—of—in fact, of any thing that might befall a testy gentleman of seventy-three, inclined to make incessant trips to the West Indies—rushed to his mind as he rushed to the door. He opened it in hot haste.

There stood Hope Wayne, pale, her eyes flashing, her hand ungloved. At the foot of the steps was the carriage, and in the carriage sat Mrs. Simcoe, with a bleeding boy's head resting upon her shoulder. The coachman stood at the carriage door.

"Here, Hiram, help James to bring in this poor boy."

"Yes, miss," replied the man, as he ran down the steps.

The door was opened, and the coachman and Hiram lifted out Gabriel.

They carried him, still unconscious, up stairs and laid him on a couch. Old Burt could not refuse an act of mere humanity, but he said in a loud voice,

"It's all a conspiracy to get into the house, Mrs. Simcoe, ma'am. I'll have bull-dogs — I'll have blunderbusses and spring-guns, Mrs. Simcoe, ma'am! And what do you mean by fighting at my gate, Sir?" he said, turning upon Little Malacca, who quivered under his wrath. "What are you doing at my gate? Can't Mr. Gray keep his boys at home? Hope, go up stairs!" said the old gentleman, as he reached the foot of the staircase.

But Hope Wayne and Mrs. Simcoe remained with the patient.—Hope rubbed the boy's hands, and put her own hand upon his forehead from time to time, until he sighed heavily and opened his eyes. But before he could recognize her she went out to send Hiram to him, while Mrs. Simcoe sat quietly by him.

"We must put you to bed," she said, gently, "and to-morrow you may go. But why do you fight?"

Gabriel turned toward her with a piteous look.

"No matter," replied Mrs. Simcoe. "Don't talk. You shall tell all about it some other time. Come in, Hiram," she added, as she heard a knock.

The man entered, and Mrs. Simcoe left the room after having told him to undress the boy carefully and bathe his face and hands. Gabriel was perfectly passive, Hiram was silent, quick, and careful, and in a few moments he closed the door softly behind him, and left Gabriel alone.

He was now entirely conscious, but very weak. His face was turned toward the window, which was open, and he watched the pine-trees that rustled gently in the afternoon breeze. It was profoundly still out of doors and in the house;

and as he lay exhausted, the events of the last few days and months swam through his mind in misty confusion. Half-dozing, half-sleeping, every thing glimmered before him, and the still hours stole by.

When he opened his eyes again it was twilight, and he was lying on his back looking up at the heavy tester of the great bedstead from which hung the curtains, so that he had only glimpses into the chamber. It was large and lofty, and the paper on the wall told the story of Telemachus. His eyes wandered over it dreamily.

He could dimly see the beautiful Calypso—the sage Mentor—the eager pupil—pallid phantoms floating around him. He seemed to hear the beating of the sea upon the shore. The tears came to his eyes. The ghostly Calypso put aside the curtain of the bed. Gabriel stretched out his hands.

" I must go," he murmured, as if he too were a phantom.

The lips of Calypso moved.

" Are you better ?"

Gabriel was awake in a moment. It was Hope Wayne who spoke to him.

About ten o'clock in the evening she knocked again gently at Gabriel's door. There was no reply. She opened the door softly and went in. A night-lamp was burning, and threw a pleasant light through the room. The windows were open, and the night-air sighed among the pine-trees near them.

Gabriel's face was turned toward the door, so that Hope saw it as she entered. He was sleeping peacefully. At that very moment he was dreaming of her. In dreams Hope Wayne was walking with him by the sea, her hand in his: her heart his own.

She stood motionless lest she might wake him. He did not stir, and she heard his low, regular breathing, and knew that all was well. Then she turned as noiselessly as she had entered, and went out, leaving him to peaceful sleep—to dreams —to the sighing of the pines.

Hope Wayne went quietly to her room, which was next to

the one in which Gabriel lay. Her kind heart had sent her to
see that he wanted nothing. She thought of him only as a
boy who had had the worst of a quarrel, and she pitied him.
Was it then, indeed, only pity for the victim that knocked
gently at his door? Was she really thinking of the conqueror
when she went to comfort the conquered? Was she not trying somehow to help Abel by doing all she could to alleviate
the harm he had done?

Hope Wayne asked herself no questions. She was conscious of a curious excitement, and the sighing of the pines
lulled her to sleep. But all night long she dreamed of Abel
Newt, with bare head and clustering black hair, gracefully
bowing, and murmuring excuses; and oh! so manly, oh! so
heroic he looked as he carefully helped to lay Gabriel in the
carriage.

CHAPTER IX.

NEWS FROM HOME.

ABEL found a letter waiting for him when he returned to
the school. He tore it open and read it:

"MY DEAR ABEL,—You have now nearly reached the age
at which, by your grandfather's direction, you were to leave
school and enter upon active life. Your grandfather, who
had known and respected Mr. Gray in former years, left you,
as you know, a sum sufficient for your education, upon condition of your being placed at Mr. Gray's until your nineteenth
birthday. That time is approaching. Upon your nineteenth
birthday you will leave school. Mr. Gray gives me the best
accounts of you. My plans for you are not quite settled.
What are your own wishes? It is late for you to think of
college; and as you will undoubtedly be a business man, I see

no need of your learning Greek or writing Latin poetry. At your age I was earning my own living. Your mother and the family are well. Your affectionate father,

"BONIFACE NEWT.

"P.S.—Your mother wishes to add a line."

"DEAR ABEL,—I am very glad to hear from Mr. Gray of your fine progress in study, and your general good character and deportment. I trust you give some of your leisure to solid reading. It is very necessary to improve the mind. I hope you attend to religion. It will help you if you keep a record of Dr. Peewee's texts, and write abstracts of his sermons. Grammar, too, and general manners. I hear that you are very self-possessed, which is really good news. My friend Mrs. Beacon was here last week, and she says you *bow beautifully!* That is a great deal for her to admit, for her son Bowdoin is one of the most elegant and presentable young men I have ever seen. He is very gentlemanly indeed. He and Alfred Dinks have been here for some time. My dear son, could you not learn to waltz before you come home? It is considered very bad by some people, because you have to put your arm round the lady's waist. But I think it is very foolish for any body to set themselves up against the customs of society. I think if it is permitted in Paris and London, we needn't be so very particular about it in New York. Mr. Dinks and Mr. Beacon both waltz, and I assure you it is very *distingué* indeed. But be careful in learning. Your sister Fanny says the Boston young men stick out their elbows dreadfully when they waltz, and look like owls spinning on invisible teetotums. She declares, too, that all the Boston girls are dowdy. But she is obliged to confess that Mr. Beacon and Mr. Dinks are as well dressed and gentlemanly and dance as well as our young men here. And as for the Boston ladies, Mr. Dinks tells Fanny that he has a cousin, a Miss Wayne, who lives in Delafield, who might alter her opinion of the dowdiness of Boston girls. It seems she is a great heiress, and very beautiful; and it is said here (but you know how idle such gossip is) that she is going to marry her cousin, Alfred Dinks. He does not deny it. He merely laughs and shakes his head—the truth is, he hasn't much to say for himself. Bless me! I've got to take another sheet.

"Now, Abel, my dear, do you know Miss Wayne? I have never heard you speak of her, and yet, if she lives in Delafield, you must know something about her. Your father is working hard at his business, but it is shocking how much money we have to spend to keep up our place in society properly. I know that he spends all his income every year; and if any thing should happen— I cry my eyes out to think of it. Miss Wayne, I hear, is very beautiful, and about your age. Is it true about her being an heiress?

"What is the news—let me see. Oh! your cousin, Laura Magot, is engaged, and she has made a capital match. She will be eighteen on her next birthday; and the happy man is Mellish Whitloe. It is the fine old Knickerbocker family. Fanny says she knows all about them—that she has the Whitloes all at her fingers' ends. You see she is as bright as ever. It is a capital match. Mr. Whitloe has at least five thousand dollars a year from his business now; and his aunt, Patience Doolittle, widow of the old merchant, who has no children, is understood to prefer him to all her relations. Laura will have a little something; so there could be nothing better. We are naturally delighted. But what a pity Laura is not a little taller—about Fanny's height; and as I was looking at Fanny the other day, I thought how sorry I was for Mr. Whitloe that Laura was not just a little prettier. She has *such* a nose; and then her complexion! However, my dear Abel of course cares nothing about such things, and, I have no doubt, is wickedly laughing at his mamma at this very moment for scribbling him such a long, rambling letter. What is Miss Wayne's first name? Is she fair or brunette? Don't forget to write me all you know. I am going to Saratoga in a few days—I think Fanny ought to drink the waters.

I told Dr. Lush I was perfectly sure of it; so he told your father, and he has consented.

"Do you remember Mrs. Plumer, the large, handsome woman from New Orleans, whom you saw when we dined at your Uncle Magot's last summer? She has come on, and will be at the Springs this year. I am told Mr. Plumer is a very large planter—the largest, some people say, in the country. Their oldest daughter, Grace, is at school in town. She is only fourteen, I believe. What an heiress she will be! The Moultries, from South Carolina, will be there too, I suppose. By-the-by, how old is Sligo Moultrie? Then there are some of those rich Havana people coming. What diamonds they wear! It will be very pleasant at the Springs; and I hope the little visit will do Fanny good. Dr. Maundy is giving us a series of sermons upon the different kinds of wood used in building Solomon's Temple. They are very interesting; and he has such a flow of beautiful words and such wavy gestures, and he looks so gentlemanly in the pulpit, that I have no doubt he does a great deal of good. The church is always full. Your Uncle Lawrence has been to hear a preacher from Boston, by the name of Channing, and is very much pleased. Have you ever heard him? It seems he is very famous in his own sect, who are infidels, or deists, or pollywogs, or atheists —I don't know which it is. I believe they preach mere morality, and read essays instead of sermons. I hope you go regularly to church; and from what I have heard of Dr. Peewee, I respect him very highly. Perhaps you had better make abstracts of his sermons, and I can look over them some time when you come home.

"Speaking of religion, I must tell you a little story which Fanny told me the other day. She was coming home from church with Mr. Dinks, and he said to her, 'Miss Newt, what do you do when you go into church and put your head down?' Fanny did not understand him, and asked him what he meant. 'Why,' said he, 'when we go into church, you know, we all put our heads down in front of the pew, or in our hands, for a little while, and Dr. Maundy spreads his handkerchief on the desk and puts his face into it for quite a long time. What do *you* do?' he asked, in a really perplexed way, Fanny says. 'Why,' said she, gravely, 'Mr. Dinks, it is to say a short prayer.' 'Bless my soul!' said he; 'I never thought of that.' 'Why, what do you do, then?' asked Fanny, curiously. 'Well,' answered Dinks, 'you know I think it's a capital thing to do; it's proper, and so forth; but I never knew what people were really at when they did it; so I always put my head into my hat and count ten. I find it comes to about the same thing—I get through at the same time with other people.' He isn't very bright, but he is a good-hearted fellow, and very gentlemanly, and I am told he is very rich. Fanny laughs at him; but I think she likes him very well. I wish you would find out whether Miss Wayne really is engaged to him. Here I am at the very end of my paper. Take care of yourself, my dear Abel, and remember the religion and the solid reading.

" Your affectionate mother,

" NANCY NEWT."

Abel read the letters, and stood looking at the floor, musingly. His school days, then, were numbered; the stage was to be deepened and widened—the scenery and the figures so wonderfully changed! He was to step in a moment from school into the world. He was to lie down one night a boy, and wake up a man the next morning.

The cloud of thoughts and fancies that filled his mind all drifted toward one point—all floated below a summit upon which stood the only thing he could discern clearly, and that was the figure of Hope Wayne. Just as he thought he could reach her, was he to be torn away?

And who was Mr. Alfred Dinks?

CHAPTER X.

BEGINNING TO SKETCH.

THE next morning when Gabriel declared that he was perfectly well and had better return, nobody opposed his departure. Hope Wayne, indeed, ordered the carriage so readily that the poor boy's heart sank. Yet Hope pitied Gabriel sincerely. She wished he had not been injured, because then there would have been nobody guilty of injuring him; and she was quite willing he should go, because his presence reminded her too forcibly of what she wanted to forget.

The poor boy drove dismally away, thinking what a dreadful thing it is to be young.

After he had gone Hope Wayne sat upon the lawn reading. Suddenly a shadow fell across the page, and looking up she saw Abel Newt standing beside her. He had his cap in one hand and a port-folio in the other. The blood rushed from Hope's cheek to her heart; then rushed back again. Abel saw it.

Rising from the lawn and bowing gravely, she turned toward the house.

"Miss Wayne," said Abel, in a voice which was very musical and very low—she stopped—"I hope you have not already convicted and sentenced me."

He smiled a little as he spoke, not familiarly, not presumptuously, but with an air which indicated his entire ability to justify himself. Hope said:

"I have no wish to be unjust."

"May I then plead my own cause?"

"I must go into the house—I will call my grandfather, whom I suppose you wish to see."

"I am here by his permission, and I hope you will not regard me as an intruder."

"Certainly not, if he knows you are here;" and Hope lingered to hear if he had any thing more to say.

"It was a very sudden affair. We were both hot and angry; but he is smaller than I, and I should have done nothing had he not struck me, and fallen upon me so that I was obliged to defend myself."

"Yes—to be sure—in that case," said Hope, still lingering, and remarking the music of his voice. Abel continued—while the girl's eyes saw how well he looked upon that lawn—the clustering black hair—the rich eyes—the dark complexion—the light of intelligence playing upon his face—his dress careful but graceful—and the port-folio which showed this interview to be no design or expectation, but a mere chance—

"I am very sorry you should have had the pain of seeing such a spectacle, and I am ashamed my first introduction to you should have been at such a time."

Hope Wayne lingered, looking on the ground.

"I think, indeed," continued Abel, "that you owe me an opportunity of making a better impression."

"Hope! Hope!" came floating the sound of a distant voice calling in the garden.

Hope Wayne turned her head toward the voice, but her eyes looked upon the ground, and her feet still lingered.

"I have known you so long, and yet have never spoken to you," said the musical voice at her side; "I have seen you so constantly in church, and I have even tried sometimes—I confess it—to catch a glance from you as you came out. But I am not sorry, for now—"

"Hope! Hope!" called the voice from the garden.

Hope looked dreamily in that direction, not as if she heard it, but as if she were listening to something in her mind.

"Now I meet you here on this lovely lawn in your own beautiful home. Do you know that your grandfather permits me to sketch the place?"

"Do you draw, Mr. Newt?" asked Hope Wayne, in a tone which seemed to Abel to trickle along his nerves, so exquisite and prolonged was the pleasure it gave him to hear her call him by name. How did she know it? thought he.

"Yes, I draw, and am very fond of it," he answered, as he untied his port-folio. "I do not dare to say that I am proud of my drawing—and yet you may perhaps recognize this, if you will look a moment."

"Hope! Hope!" came the voice again from the garden. Abel heard it—perhaps Hope did not. He was busily opening his port-folio and turning over the drawings, and stepped closer to her, as he said:

"There! now, what is that?" and he handed her a sketch.

Hope looked at it and smiled.

"That is the farther shore of the pond with the spire; how very pretty it is!"

"And this?"

"Oh! that is the old church, and there is Mr. Gray's face at the window. How good they are! You draw very well, Mr. Newt."

"Do you draw, Miss Wayne?"

"I've had plenty of lessons," replied Hope, smiling; "but I can't draw from nature very well."

"What do you sketch, then?"

"Well, scenes and figures out of books."

"How very pleasant that must be! That's a better style than mine."

"Why so?"

"Because we can never draw any thing as handsome as it seems to us. You can go and see the pond with your own eyes, and then no picture will seem worth having." He paused. "There is another reason, too, I suppose."

"What is that?" asked Hope, looking at her companion.

"Well," he answered, smiling, "because life in books is always so much better than real life!"

"Is it so?" said Hope, musingly.

"Yes, certainly. People are always brave, and beautiful, and good, in books. An author may make them do and say just what he and all the world want them to, and it all seems right. And then they do such splendidly impossible things!"

"How do they?"

"Why, now, if you and I were in a book at this moment, instead of standing on this lawn, I might be a knight slaying a great dragon that was just coming to destroy you, and you—"

"Hope, Hope!" rang the voice from the garden, nearer and more imperiously.

"And I—might be saved by another knight dashing in upon you, like that voice upon your sentence," said Hope, smiling.

"No, no," answered Abel, laughing, "that shouldn't be in the book. I should slay the great dragon who would desolate all Delafield with the swishing of his scaly tail; then you would place a wreath upon my head, and all the people would come out and salute me for saving the Princess whom they loved, and I"—said Abel, after a momentary pause, a shade more gravely, and in a tone a little lower—"and I, as I rode away, should not wonder that they loved her."

He looked across the lawn under the pine-trees as if he were thinking of some story that he had been actually reading. Hope smiled no longer, but said, quietly,

"Mr. Newt, I am wanted. I must go in. Good-morning!" And she moved away.

"Perhaps your cousin Alfred Dinks has arrived," said Abel, carelessly, as he closed his port-folio.

Hope Wayne stopped, and, standing very erect, turned and looked at him.

"Do you know my cousin, Mr. Dinks?"

"Not at all."

"How did you know that I had such a cousin?"

"I heard it somewhere," answered Abel, gently and respectfully, but looking at Hope with a curious glance which seemed to her to penetrate every pore in her body. That glance said as plainly as words could have said, "And I heard you were engaged to him."

Hope Wayne looked serious for a moment; then she said, with a half smile,

"I suppose it is no secret that Alfred Dinks is my cousin;" and, bowing to Abel, she went swiftly over the lawn toward the house.

CHAPTER XI.

A VERDICT AND A SENTENCE.

HOPE WAYNE did not agree with Abel Newt that life was so much better in books. There was nothing better in any book she had ever read than the little conversation with the handsome youth which she had had that morning upon the lawn. When she went into the house she found no one until she knocked at Mrs. Simcoe's door.

"Aunty, did you call me?"

"Yes, Hope."

"I was on the lawn, Aunty."

"I know it, Hope."

The young lady did not ask her why she had not sought her there, but she asked, "What do you want, Aunty?"

The older woman looked quietly out of the window. Neither spoke for a long time.

"I saw you talking with Abel Newt on the lawn. Why did he strike that boy?" asked Mrs. Simcoe at length, still gazing at the distant hills.

"He had to defend himself," said Hope, rapidly.

"Couldn't a young man protect himself against a boy without stunning him? He might easily have killed him," said Mrs. Simcoe, in the same dry tone.

"It was very unfortunate, and Mr. Newt says so; but I don't think he is to bear every thing."

"What did the other do?"

"He insulted him."

"Indeed!"

The tone in which the elderly woman spoke was trying. Hope was flushed, and warm, and disconcerted. There was so much skepticism and contempt in the single word "indeed!" as Mrs. Simcoe pronounced it, that Hope was really angry with her.

"I don't see why you should treat Mr. Newt in that manner," said she, haughtily.

"In what manner, Hope?" asked the other, calmly, fixing her eyes upon her companion.

"In that sneering, contemptuous manner," replied Hope, loftily. "Here is a young man who falls into an unfortunate quarrel, in which he happens to get the better of his opponent, who chances to be younger. He helps him carefully into the carriage. He explains upon the spot as well as he can, and to-day he comes to explain further; and you will not believe him; you misunderstand and misrepresent him. It is unkind, Aunty—unkind."

Hope was almost sobbing.

"Has he once said he was sorry?" asked Mrs. Simcoe. "Has he told you so this morning?"

"Of course he is sorry, Aunty. How could he help it? Do you suppose he is a brute? Do you suppose he hasn't ordinary human feeling? Why do you treat him so?"

Hope asked the question almost fiercely.

Mrs. Simcoe sat profoundly still, and said nothing. Her face seemed to grow even more rigid as she sat. But suddenly turning to the proud young girl who stood at her side, her bosom heaving with passion, she drew her toward her by both hands, pulled her face down close to hers, and kissed her.

Hope sank on her knees by the side of Mrs. Simcoe's chair. All the pride in her heart was melted, and poured out of her eyes. She buried her face upon Mrs. Simcoe's shoulder, and her passion wept and sobbed itself away. She did not understand what it was, nor why. A little while before, upon the lawn, she had been so happy. Now it seemed as if her heart

were breaking. When she grew calmer, Mrs. Simcoe, holding
the fair face between her hands, and tenderly kissing it once
more, said, slowly,

"Hope, my child, we must all walk the path alone. But
you, too, will learn that our human affections are but tents of
a night."

"Aunty, Aunty, what do you mean?" asked Hope, who had
risen as the other was speaking, and now stood beside her,
pale and proud.

"I mean, Hope, that you are in love with Abel Newt."

Hope's hands dropped by her side. She stepped back a little. A feeling of inexpressible solitude fell upon her—of alien-
ation from her grandfather, and of an inexplicable separation
from her old nurse—a feeling as if she suddenly stood alone
in the world—as if she had ceased to be a girl.

"Aunty, is it wrong to love him?"

Before Mrs. Simcoe could answer there was a knock at the
door. It was Hiram, who announced the victim of yesterday's
battle, waiting in the parlor to say a word to Miss Wayne.

"Yes, Hiram." He bowed and withdrew. Hope Wayne
stood at the window silent for a little while, then, with the
calm, lofty air—calmer and loftier than ever—she went down
and found Gabriel Bennet. He had come to thank her—to
say how much better he was—how sorry that he should have
been so disgraced as to have been fighting almost before her
very eyes.

"I suppose I was very foolish and furious," said he. "Abel
ran against me, and I got very angry and struck him. It was
wrong; I know it was, and I am very sorry. But, ma'am, I
hope you won't—ch—ch—I mean, won't—"

That unlucky "ma'am" had choked all his other words.
Hope was so lofty and splendid in his eyes as she stood before him that he was impressed with a kind of awe. But the
moment he had spoken to her as if he were only a little boy
and she a woman, he was utterly confused. He staggered
and stumbled in his sentence until Hope graciously said,

"I blame nobody."

But poor Gabriel's speech was gone. His mouth was parched and his mind dry. He could not think of a word to say; and, twisting and fumbling his cap, did not know how to go.

"There, Miss Wayne!" suddenly said a voice at the door.

Hope and Gabriel turned at the same moment, and beheld Abel Newt entering the room gayly, with a sketch in his hand. He nodded to Gabriel without speaking, but went directly to Hope and showed her the drawing.

"There, that will do for a beginning, will it not?"

It was a bold, dashing sketch. The pine-trees, the windows, the piazzas—yes, she saw them all. They had a new charm in her eyes.

"That tree comes a little nearer that window," said she.

"How do you know it does?" he replied. "You, who only draw from books?"

"I think I ought to know the tree that I see every day at my own window!"

"Oh! that is your window!"

Gabriel was confounded at this sudden incursion and apparent resumption of a previous conversation. As he ran up the avenue he had not remarked Abel sketching on the lawn. But Abel, sketching on the lawn, had observed Gabriel running up the avenue, and therefore happened in to ask Miss Wayne's opinion of his drawing. He chatted merrily on:

"Why, there's your grandpapa when he was a little grandbaby and had an old grandpapa in his turn," said he, pointing at the portrait he had remarked upon his previous visit in that parlor. "What a funny little old fellow! Let me see. Gracious! 'twas before the Revolution. Ah! now, if he could only speak and tell us just what he saw in the room where they were painting him—what he had for breakfast, for instance—what those dear little ridiculous waistcoats, with all their flowery embroidery, cost a yard, say—yes, yes, and what book that is—and who gave him the hoop—"

He rattled on. Never in Hope's lifetime had such sounds of gay speech been heard in that well-arranged and well-behaved parlor. They seemed to light it up. The rapid talk bubbled like music.

"Hoop and book—book and hoop! Oh yes. Good boy, very good boy," said Abel, laughing. "I should think it was a portrait of the young Dr. Peewee—the wee Peewee, Miss Hope," said the audacious youth, sliding, as it were, unconsciously and naturally into greater familiarity. "Ah! I know you know all his sermons by heart, for you never look away from him. What on earth are they all about?"

What a contrast to Gabriel's awkward silence of the moment before! Such a handsome face! such a musical voice!

In the midst of it all Hiram was heard remonstrating out side:

"Don't, Sir, don't! You'll—you'll—something will happen, Sir."

There was a moment's scuffling and trampling, and Christopher Burt, restrained by Hiram, burst into the room. The old man was white with wrath. He had his cane in one hand, and Hiram held the other hand and arm.

He had come in from the garden, and as he stopped in the dining-room to take a little trip to the West Indies, he had heard voices in the drawing-room. Summoning Hiram to know if they were visitors, he had learned the awful truth which apprised him that his Hesperidian wall was down, and that the robbers at that very moment might be shaking his precious fruit from the boughs. To be sure he had himself left the gate open. Do you think, then, it helps a man's temper to be as furious with himself as with other people? He burst into the room.

There stood Hope: Abel at her side, in the merry midst of his talk, with his sketch in his hand, his port-folio under his arm, and his finger pointed toward the portrait; Gabriel, at a little distance, confounded and abashed by an acquaintance between Hope and Abel of which he had no previous suspicion.

The poor boy! forgotten by Hope, and purposely trampled down by the eager talk of Abel.

"Hope, go up stairs!" shouted the old gentleman. "And what are you doing in my house, you scamps?"

He lifted his cane as he came toward them. "I knew all this fighting business yesterday was a conspiracy—a swindling cheat to get into this house! I've a mind to break your impudent bones!"

"Why, Sir," said Abel, "you gave me leave to come here and sketch."

"Did I give you leave to come into my parlor and bring boys with you, Sir, and take up the time of my grand-daughter? Hope, I say, go up stairs!"

"I only thought, Sir—" began Abel.

"Now, in Heaven's name, don't make me angry, Sir!" burst in the old gentleman, almost foaming at the mouth. "Why should you think, Sir? What business have you to think, Sir? You're a boy, Sir—a school-boy, Sir! Are you going to dispute with me in my own house? I take back my permission. Go, both of you! and never let me see your faces again!"

The old man stood pointing with his cane toward the door.

"Go, both of you!" repeated he, fiercely. It was impossible to resist; and Abel and Gabriel moved slowly toward the door. The former was furious at finding himself doomed in company with Gabriel. But he betrayed nothing. He was preternaturally calm. Hope, dismayed and pale, stood looking on, but saying nothing. Gabriel went quietly out of the room. Abel turned to the door, and bowed gravely to Hope.

"Remember, Sir," cried the old man, "I take back my permission!"

"I understand, Sir," replied Abel, bowing to him also.

He closed the door; and as he did so it seemed to Hope Wayne as if the sunshine were extinguished.

CHAPTER XII.

HELP, HO!

ABEL NEWT was fully aware that his time was short. His father's letter had apprised him of his presently leaving school. To leave school—was it not to quit Delafield? Might it not be to lose Hope Wayne? He was banished from Pinewood. There were flaming swords of suspicion waving over that flowery gate. The days were passing. The summer is ending, thought he, and I am by no means saved.

Neither he nor Gabriel had mentioned their last visit to Pinewood and its catastrophe. It was a secret better buried in their own bosoms. Abel's dislike of the other was deepened and imbittered by the ignominy of the expulsion by Mr. Burt, of which Gabriel had been not only a companion but a witness. It was an indignity that made Abel tingle whenever he thought of it. He fancied Gabriel thinking of it too, and laughing at him in his sleeve, and he longed to thrash him. But Gabriel had much better business. He was thinking only of Hope Wayne, and laughing at himself for thinking of her.

The boys were strolling in different parts of the village. Abel, into whose mind had stolen that thought of the possible laughter in Gabriel's sleeve, pulled out his handkerchief suddenly, and waved it with an indignant movement in the air. At the same moment a carriage had overtaken him and was passing. The horses, startled by the shock of the waving handkerchief, shied and broke into a run. The coachman tried in vain to control them. They sprang forward and had their heads in a moment.

Abel looked up, and saw that it was the Burt carriage dashing down the road. He flew after, and every boy followed. The horses, maddened by the cries of the coachman and pass-

ers-by, by the rattling of the carriage, and their own excitement and speed, plunged on with fearful swiftness. As the
carriage flew by, two faces were seen at the window—both
calm, but one terrified. They were those of Hope and Mrs.
Simcoe.

"Stop 'em! stop 'em!" rang the cry along the village street;
and the idling villagers looked from the windows or came to
the doors—the women exclaiming and holding up their hands,
the men leaving whatever they were doing and joining the
chase.

The whole village was in motion. Every body knew Hope
Wayne—every body loved her.

Both she and Mrs. Simcoe sat quietly in the carriage. They
knew it was madness to leap—that their only chance lay in remaining perfectly quiet. They both knew the danger—they
knew that every instant they were hovering on the edge of
death or accident. How strange to Hope's eyes, in those
swift moments, looked the familiar houses—the trees—the
signs—the fences—as they swept by! How peaceful and secure they were! How far away they seemed! She read the
names distinctly. She thought of little incidents connected
with all the places. Her mind, and memory, and perception
were perfectly clear; but her hands were clenched, and her
cheek cold and pale with vague terror. Mrs. Simcoe sat beside her, calmly holding one of Hope's hands, but neither of
them spoke.

The carriage struck a stone, and the crowd shuddered as
they saw it rock and swing in its furious course. The mad
horses but flew more wildly. Mrs. Simcoe pressed Hope's
hand, and murmured, almost inaudibly,

> "'Christ shall bless thy going out,
> Shall bless thy coming in;
> Kindly compass thee about,
> Till thou art saved from sin.'"

"That corner! that corner!" shouted the throng, as the
horses neared a sudden turn into a side-road, toward which

they seemed to be making, frightened by the persons who came running toward them on the main street. Among these was Gabriel, who, hearing the confused murmur that rang down the road, turned and recognized the carriage that was whirled along at the mercy of wild horses. He seemed to his companions to fly as he went—to himself he seemed to be standing still.

"Carefully, carefully!" cried the others, as they saw his impetuosity. "Don't be trampled!"

Gabriel did not hear. He only saw the fatal corner. He only knew that Hope Wayne was in danger—that the carriage, already swaying, would be overturned—might be dashed in pieces, and Hope—

He came near as the horses were about turning. The street toward which they were heading was narrow, and on the other corner from him there was a wall. They were running toward Gabriel down the main road; but just as he came up with them he flung himself with all his might toward the animals' heads. The startled horses half-recoiled, turned sharply and suddenly—dashed themselves against the wall—and the carriage stood still. In a moment a dozen men had secured them, and the danger was past.

The door was opened, and the ladies stepped out. Mrs. Simcoe was pale, but her heart had not quailed. The faith that sustains a woman's heart in life does not fail when death brushes her with his finger-tips.

"Dear child!" she said to Hope, when they both knew that the crisis was over, and her lips moved in silent prayer and thanksgiving.

Hope herself was trembling and silent. In her inmost heart she hoped it was Abel Newt who had saved them. But in all the throng she did not see his face. She felt a secret disappointment.

"Here is your preserver, ma'am," said one of the villagers, pushing Gabriel forward. Mrs. Simcoe actually smiled. She put out her hand to him kindly; and Hope, with grave sweet-

ness, told him how great was their obligation. The boy bowed
and looked at her earnestly.

"Are you hurt?"

"Oh! no, not at all," replied Hope, smiling, and not without some effort, because she fancied that Gabriel looked at
her as if she showed some sign of pain—or disappointment—
or what?

"We are perfectly well, thanks to you."

"What started the horses?" asked Gabriel.

"I'm sure I don't know," replied Hope.

"Abel Newt started them," said Mrs. Simcoe.

Hope reddened and looked at her companion. "What do
you mean, Aunty?" asked she, haughtily.

Mrs. Simcoe was explaining, when Abel came up out of
breath and alarmed. In a moment he saw that there had been
no injury. Hope's eyes met his, and the color slowly died
away from her cheeks. He eagerly asked how it happened,
and was confounded by hearing that he was the cause.

"How strange it is," said he, in a low voice, to Hope, as
the people busied themselves in looking after the horses and
carriage, and Gabriel talked to Mrs. Simcoe, with whom he
found conversation so much easier than with Hope—"how
strange it is that just as I was wondering when and where
and how I should see you again, I should meet you in this
way, Miss Wayne!"

Pleased, still weak and trembling, pale and flushed by turns,
Hope listened to him.

"Where *can* I see you?" he continued; "certainly your
grandfather was unkind—"

Hope shook her head slowly. Abel watched every movement—every look—every fluctuating change of manner and
color, as if he knew its most hidden meaning.

"I can see you nowhere but at home," she answered.

He did not reply. She stood silent. She wished he would
speak. The silence was dreadful. She could not bear it.

"I am very sorry," said she, in a whisper, her eyes fastened upon the ground, her hands playing with her handker-chief.

"I hope you are," he said, quietly, with a tone of sadness, not of reproach. There was another painful pause.

"I hope so, because I am going away," said Abel.

"Where are you going?"

"Home."

"When?"

"In a few weeks."

"Where is your home?"

"In New York."

It was very much to the point. Yet both of them wanted to say so much more; and neither of them dared!

"Miss Hope!" whispered Abel.

Hope heard the musical whisper. She perceived the audacity of the familiarity, but she did not wish it were otherwise. She bent her head a little lower, as if listening more intently.

"May I see you before I go?"

Hope was silent. Dr. Livingstone relates that when the lion had struck him with his paw, upon a certain occasion, he lay in a kind of paralysis, of which he would have been cured in a moment more by being devoured.

"Hope," said Mrs. Simcoe, "the horses will be brought up. We had better walk home. Here, my dear!"

"I can only see you at home," Hope said, in a low voice, as she rose.

"Then we part here forever," he replied. "I am sorry."

Still there was no reproach; it was only a deep sadness which softened that musical voice.

"Forever!" he repeated slowly, with low, remorseless music.

Hope Wayne trembled, but he did not see it.

"I am sorry, too," she said, in a hurried whisper, as she moved slowly toward Mrs. Simcoe. Abel Newt was disappointed.

"Good-by forever, Miss Wayne!" he said. He could not

" GOOD-BY ! "

see Hope's paler face as she heard the more formal address, and knew by it that he was offended.

"Good-by!" was all he caught as Hope Wayne took Mrs. Simcoe's arm and walked away.

CHAPTER XIII.

SOCIETY.

TRADITION declares that the family of Newt has been uni· formly respectable but honest — so respectable, indeed, that Mr. Boniface Newt, the father of Abel, a celebrated New York merchant and a Tammany Sachem, had a crest. He had even buttons for his coachman's coat with a stag's head engraved upon them. The same device was upon his seal-ring. It appeared upon his carriage door. It figured on the edges of his dinner-service. It was worked into the ground glass of the door that led from his dining-room to the back stairs. He had his paper stamped with it; and a great many of his neighbors, thinking it a neat and becoming ornament, imitated him in its generous use.

Mrs. Newt's family had a crest also. She was a Magot—another of the fine old families. which came to this country at the earliest possible period. The Magots, however, had no buttons upon their coachman's coat; one reason of which omission was, perhaps, that they had no coachman. But when the ladies of the Magot family went visiting or shopping they hired a carriage, and insisted that the driver should brush his hat and black his boots; so that it was not every body who knew that it was a livery equipage.

Their friends did, of course; but there were a great many people from the country who gazed at it, in passing, with the same emotion with which they would have contemplated a private carriage; which was highly gratifying to the feelings of the Magots.

Their friends knew it, but friends never remark upon such things. There was old Mrs. Beriah Dagon—dowager Mrs. Dagon, she was called—aunt of Mr. Newt, who never said, "I see the Magots have hired a hackney-coach from Jobbers

to make calls in. They quarreled with Gudging over his last
bill. Medora Magot has turned her last year's silk, which is
a little stained and worn; but then it does just as well."

By-and-by her nephew Boniface married Medora's sister,
Nancy.

It was Mrs. Dagon who sat with Mrs. Newt in her parlor,
and said to her,

"So your son Abel is coming home. I'm glad to hear it.
I hope he knows how to waltz, and isn't awkward. There are
some very good matches to be made; and I like to have a
young man settle early. It's better for his morals. Men are
bad people, my dear. I think Maria Chubleigh would do very
well for Abel. She had a foolish affair with that Colonel Or-
son, but it's all over. Why on earth do girls fall in love with
officers? They never have any pay worth speaking of, and a
girl must tramp all over the land, and live I don't know how.
Pshaw! it's a wretched business. How's Mr. Dinks? I saw
him and Fanny waltzing last month at the Shrimps'. Who are
the Shrimps? Somebody says something about the immense
fortune Mr. Shrimp has made in the oil trade. You should
have seen Mrs. Winslow Orry peering about at the Shrimps.
I really believe she counted the spoons. What an eye that
woman has, and what a tongue! Are you really going to
Saratoga? Will Boniface let you? He is the kindest man!
He is so generous that I sometimes fear somebody'll be taking
advantage of him. Gracious me! how hot it is!"

It was warm, and Mrs. Dagon fanned herself. When she
and Mrs. Newt met there was a tremendous struggle to get
the first innings of the conversation, and neither surrendered
the ground until fairly forced off by breathlessness and ex-
haustion.

"Yes, we shall go to Saratoga," began Mrs. Newt; "and I
want Abel to come, so as to take him. There'll be a very
pleasant season. What a pity you can't go! However, people must regard their time of life, and take care of their health.
There's old Mrs. Octoyne says she shall never give up. She

hopes to bring out her great-grand-daughter next winter, and says she has no life but in society. I suppose you know Herbert Octoyne is engaged to one of the Shrimps. They keep their carriage, and the girls dress very prettily. Herbert tells the young men that the Shrimps are a fine old family, which has been long out of society, having no daughters to marry; so they have not been obliged to appear. But I don't know about visiting them. However, I suppose we shall. Herbert Octoyne will give 'em family, if they really haven't it; and the Octoynes won't be sorry for her money. What a pretty shawl! Did you hear that Mellish Whitloe has given Laura a diamond pin which cost five hundred dollars? Extravagant fellow! Yet I like to have young men do these things handsomely. I do think it's such a pity about Laura's nose—"

"She can smell with it, I suppose, mother; and what else do you want of a nose?"

It was Miss Fanny Newt who spoke, and who had entered the room during the conversation. She was a tall young woman of about twenty, with firm, dark eyes, and abundant dark hair, and that kind of composure of manner which is called repose in drawing-rooms and boldness in bar-rooms.

"Gracious, Fanny, how you do disturb one! I didn't know you were there. Don't be ridiculous. Of course she can smell with it. But that isn't all you want of a nose."

"I suppose you want it to turn up at some people," replied Miss Fanny, smoothing her dress, and looking in the glass. "Well, Aunt Dagon, who've you been lunching on?"

Aunt Dagon looked a little appalled.

"My dear, what do you mean?" she said, fanning herself violently. "I hope I never say any thing that isn't true about people. I'm sure I should be very sorry to hurt any body's feelings. There's Mrs. Kite—you know, Joseph Kite's wife, the man they said really did cheat his creditors, only none of 'em would swear to it; well, Kitty Kite, my dear, does do and say the most abominable things about people. At the Shrimps' ball, when you were waltzing with Mr. Dinks, I heard her say

to Mrs. Orry, 'Do look at Fanny Newt hug that man!' It
was dreadful to hear her say such things, my dear; and then
to see the whole room stare at you! It was cruel—it was
really unfeeling."

Fanny did not wince. She merely said,

"How old is Mrs. Kite, Aunt Dagon?"

"Well, let me see; she's about my age, I suppose."

"Oh! well, Aunt, people at her time of life can't see or hear
much, you know. They ought to be in their beds with hot
bottles at their feet, and not obtrude themselves among people who are young enough to enjoy life with all their senses,"
replied Miss Fanny, carelessly arranging a stray lock of hair.

"Indeed, Miss, you would like to shove all the married people into the wall, or into their graves," retorted Mrs. Dagon,
warmly.

"Oh no, dear Aunt, only into their beds—and that not until they are superannuated, which, you know, old people never
find out for themselves," answered Fanny, smiling sweetly and
calmly upon Mrs. Dagon.

"What a country it is, Aunt!" said Mrs. Newt, looking at
Fanny with a kind of admiration. "How the young people
take every thing into their own hands! Dear me! dear me!
how they do rule us!"

Miss Newt made no observation, but took up a gayly-bound
book from the table and looked carelessly into it. Mrs. Dagon rose to go. She had somewhat recovered her composure.

"Don't think I believed it, dear," said she to Fanny, in
whom, perhaps, she recognized some of the family character.
"No, no—not at all! I said to every body in the room that I
didn't believe what Mrs. Kite said, that you were hugging Mr.
Dinks in the waltz. I believe I spoke to every body I knew,
and they all said they didn't believe it either."

"How kind it was of you, dear Aunt Dagon!" said Fanny,
as she rose to salute her departing relative, "and how generous people were not to believe it! But I couldn't persuade
them that that beautiful lace-edging on your dress was real

Mechlin, although I tried very hard. They said it was natural in me to insist upon it, because I was your grand-niece;
and it was no matter at all, because old ladies could do just
as they pleased; but for all that it was not Mechlin. I must
have told as many as thirty people that they were wrong.
But people's eyes are so sharp—it's really dreadful. Good-
morning, darling Aunt Dagon!"

"Fanny dear," said her mother, as the door closed upon
Mrs. Dagon, who departed speechless and in what may be
called a simmering state of mind, "Abel will be here in a day
or two. I really hope to hear something about this Miss
Wayne. Do you suppose Alfred Dinks is actually engaged
to her?"

"How should I know, mother?"

"Why, my dear, you have been so intimate with him."

"My dear mother, how *can* any body be intimate with Alfred Dinks? You might as well talk of breathing in a vac-
uum."

"But, Fanny, he is a very good sort of young man—so respectable, and with such good manners, and he has a very
pretty fortune—"

Mrs. Newt was interrupted by the servant, who announced
Mr. Wetherley.

Poor Mr. Zephyr Wetherley! He was one of the rank and
file of society—one of the privates, so to speak, who are mentioned in a mass after a ball, as common soldiers are mentioned
after a battle. He entered the room and bowed. Mrs. Newt
seeing that it was one of her daughter's visitors, left the room.
Miss Fanny sat looking at the young man with her black eyes
so calmly that she seemed to him to be sitting a great way off
in a cool darkness. Miss Fanny was not fond of Mr. Wetherley, although she had seen plainly enough the indications of
his feeling for her. This morning he was well gloved and
booted. His costume was unexceptionable. Society of that
day boasted few better-dressed men than Zephyr Wetherley.
His judgment in a case of cravat was unerring. He had been

in Europe, and was quoted when waistcoats were in debate. He had been very attentive to Mr. Alfred Dinks and Mr. Bowdoin Beacon, the two Boston youths who had been charming society during the season that was now over. He was even a little jealous of Mr. Dinks.

After Mrs. Newt had left the room Mr. Wetherley fell into confusion. He immediately embarked, of course, upon the weather; while Fanny, taking up a book, looked casually into it with a slight air of *ennui*.

"Have you read this?" said she to Mr. Wetherley.

"No, I suppose not; eh! what is it?" replied Zephyr, who was not a reading man.

"It is John Neal's 'Rachel Dyer.'"

"Oh, indeed! No, indeed. I have not read it!"

"What have you read, Mr. Wetherley?" inquired Fanny, glancing through the book which she held in her hand.

"Oh, indeed!—" he began. Then he seemed to undergo some internal spasm. He dropped his hat, slid his chair to the side of Fanny's, and said, "Ah, Miss Newt, how can you ask me at such a moment?"

Miss Fanny looked at him with a perfectly unruffled face.

"Why not at this moment, Mr. Wetherley?"

"Ah, Miss Newt, how can you when you know my feelings? Did you not carry my bouquet at the theatre last evening? Have you not long authorized me by your treatment to declare—"

"Stop, Mr. Wetherley," said Fanny, calmly. "The day is warm—let us be cool. Don't say any thing which you will regret to remember. Don't mistake any thing that I have done as an indication of—"

"Oh, Miss Newt," interrupted Zephyr, "how can you say such things? Hear me but one word. I assure you that I most deeply, tenderly, truly—"

"Mr. Wetherley," said Fanny, putting down the book and speaking very firmly, "I really can not sit still and hear you proceed. You are laboring under a great misapprehension.

D

You must be aware that I have never in the slightest way given you occasion to believe that I—"

"I must speak!" burst in the impetuous Zephyr. "My feelings forbid silence! Great Heavens! Miss Newt, you really have no idea—I am sure you have no idea—you can not have any idea of the ardor with which for a long, long time I have—"

"Mr. Wetherley," said Fanny Newt, darker and cooler than ever, "it is useless to prolong this conversation. I can not consent to hear you declare that—"

"But you haven't heard me declare it," replied Zephyr, vehemently. "It's the very thing I am trying to do, and you won't let me. You keep cutting me off just as I am saying how I—"

"You need go no further, Sir," said Miss Newt, coldly, rising and standing by the table; while Zephyr Wetherley, red and hot and confused, crushed his handkerchief into a ball, and swept his hand through his hair, wagging his foot, and rubbing his fingers together. "I understand, Sir, what you wish to say, and I desire to tell you only—"

"Just what I don't want to hear! Oh dear me! Please, please, Miss Newt!" entreated Zephyr Wetherley.

"Mr. Wetherley," interrupted the other, imperiously, "you wish to ask me to marry you. I desire to spare you the pain of my answer to that question by preventing your asking it."

Mr. Wetherley was confounded. He wrinkled his brows doubtfully a moment—he stared at the floor and at Miss Newt —he looked foolish and mortified. "But—but—but—" stammered he. "Well—but—why—but—haven't you somehow answered the question?" inquired he, with gleams of doubtful intelligence shooting across his face.

Fanny Newt smiled icily.

"As you please," said she.

Poor Zephyr was bewildered.

"It is very confusing, somehow, Miss Newt, isn't it?" said he, wiping his face.

"Yes, Mr. Wetherley; one should always look before he leaps."

"Yes, yes; oh, indeed, yes. A man had better look out, or—"

"Or he'll catch a Tartar!" said a clear, strange voice.

Fanny Newt and Wetherley turned simultaneously toward the speaker. It was a young man, with clustering black hair and sparkling eyes, in a traveling dress. He stood in the back room, which he had entered through the conservatory.

"Abel!" said his sister, running toward him, and pulling him forward.

"Mr. Wetherley, this is my brother, Mr. Abel Newt."

The young men bowed.

"Oh, indeed!" said Zephyr. "How'd he come here listening?"

"Chance, chance, Mr. Wetherley. I have just returned from school. Pretty tough old school-boy, hey? Well, it's all the grandpa's doing. Grandpas are extraordinary beings, Mr. Wetherley. Now there was—"

"Oh, indeed! Really, I must go. Good-morning, Miss Newt. Good-morning, Sir." And Mr. Zephyr Wetherley departed.

The brother and sister laughed.

"Sensible fellow," said Abel; "he flies the grandpas."

"How did you come here, you wretch!" asked Fanny, "listening to my secrets?"

"My dear, I arrived this morning, only half an hour ago. I let myself in by my pass-key, and, hearing voices in the parlor, I went round by the conservatory to spy out the land. Then and there I beheld this spectacle. Fanny, you're wonderful."

Miss Newt made a demure courtesy.

"So you've really come home for good? Well, Abel, I'm glad. Now you're here I shall have a man of my own to attend me next winter. And there's to be the handsome Boston bride here, you know, next season."

"Who is she?" said Abel, laughing, sinking into a chair. "Mother wrote me you said that all Boston girls are dowdy. Who is the dowdy of next winter?"

"Mrs. Alfred Dinks," replied Fanny, carelessly, but looking with her keenest glance at Abel.

He sprang up and began to say something; but his sister's eye arrested him.

"Oh yes," said he, hurriedly—"Dinks, I've heard about Alfred Dinks. What a devil of a name!"

"Come, dear, you'd better go up stairs and see mamma," said Fanny; "and I'm so sorry you missed Aunt Dagon. She was here this morning, lovely as ever. But I think the velvet is·wearing off her claws."

Fanny Newt laughed a cold little laugh. Abel went out of the room.

"Master Abel, then, does know Miss Hope Wayne," said she to herself. "He more than knows her—he loves her—or thinks he does. Wouldn't he have known if she had been engaged to her cousin?"

She pondered a little while.

"I don't believe," thought Miss Fanny, "that she is engaged to him."

Miss Fanny was pleased with that thought, because she meant to be engaged to him herself, if it proved to be true, as every body declared, that he had ten or fifteen thousand a year.

CHAPTER XIV.

A NEW YORK MERCHANT.

MR. LAWRENCE NEWT, the brother of Boniface, sat in his office. It was upon South Street, and the windows looked out upon the shipping in the East River—upon the ferry-boats incessantly crossing—upon the lofty city of Brooklyn opposite, with its spires. He heard the sailors sing—the oaths of the stevedores—the bustle of the carts, and the hum and scuffle of the passers-by. As he sat at his table he saw the ships haul into the stream—the little steamers that puffed alongside bringing the passengers; then, if the wind were not fair, pulling and shoving the huge hulks into a space large enough for them to manage themselves in.

Sometimes he watched the parting of passengers at the wharf when the wind was fair, and the ship could sail from her berth. The vast sails were slowly unfurled, were shaken out, hung for a few moments, then shook lazily, then filled round and full with the gentle, steady wind. Mr. Lawrence Newt laughed as he watched, for he thought of fine ladies taking their hair out of curl-papers, and patting and smoothing and rolling it upon little sticks and over little fingers until the curls stood round and full, and ready for action.

Then the ship moved slowly, almost imperceptibly, from the wharf—so slowly, so imperceptibly, that the people on board thought the city was sliding away from them. The merchant saw the solid, trim, beautiful vessel turn her bow southward and outward, and glide gently down the river. Her hull was soon lost to his eyes, but he could see the streamer fluttering at the mast-head over the masts of the other vessels. While he looked it vanished—the ship was gone.

Often enough Mr. Lawrence Newt stood leaning his head against the window-frame of his office after the ship had disappeared, and seemed to be looking at the ferry-boats or at the lofty city of Brooklyn. But he saw neither. Faster than ship ever sailed, or wind blew, or light flashed, the thought of Lawrence Newt darted, and the merchant, seemingly leaning against his office-window in South Street, was really sitting under palm-trees, or dandling in a palanquin, or chatting in a strange tongue, or gazing in awe upon snowier summits than the villagers of Chamouni have ever seen.

And what was that dark little hand he seemed to himself to press?—and what were those eyes, soft depths of exquisite darkness, into which through his own eyes his soul seemed to be sinking?

There were clerks busily writing in the outer office. It was dark in that office when Mr. Newt first occupied the rooms, and Thomas Tray, the book-keeper, who had the lightest place, said that the eyes of Venables, the youngest clerk, were giving out. Young Venables, a lad of sixteen, supported a mother and sister and infirm father upon his five hundred dollars a year.

"Eyes giving out in my service, Thomas Tray! I am ashamed of myself."

And Lawrence Newt hired the adjoining office, knocked down all the walls, and introduced so much daylight that it shone not only into the eyes of young Venables, but into those of his mother and sister and infirm father.

It was scratch, scratch, scratch, all day long in the clerks' office. Messengers were coming and going. Samples were brought in. Draymen came for orders. Apple-women and pie-men dropped in about noon, and there were plenty of cheap apples and cheap jokes when the peddlers were young and pretty. Customers came and brother merchants, who went into Mr. Lawrence Newt's room. They talked China news, and South American news, and Mediterranean news. Their conversation was full of the names of places of which poems and histories have been written. The merchants joked complacent jokes. They gossiped a little when business had been discussed. So young Whitloe was really to marry Magot's daughter, and the Doolittle money would go to the Magots after all! And old Jacob Van Boozenberg had actually left off knee-breeches and white cravats, and none of his directors knew him when he came into the Bank in modern costume. And there was no doubt that Mrs. Dagon wore cotton lace at the Orrys', for Winslow's wife said she saw it with her own eyes.

Mr. Lawrence Newt's talk ceased with that about business. When the scandal set in, his mind seemed to set out. He stirred the fire if it were winter. He stepped into the outer office. He had a word for Venables. Had Miss Venables seen the new novel by Mr. Bulwer? It is called "Pelham," and will be amusing to read aloud in the family. Will Mr. Venables call at Carville's on his way up, have the book charged to Mr. Lawrence Newt, and present it, with Mr. Newt's compliments, to his sister? If it were summer he opened the window, when it happened to be closed, and stood by it, or drew his chair to it and looked at the ships and the streets, and listened to the sailors swearing when he might have heard merchants, worth two or three hundred thousand dollars apiece, talking about Mrs. Dagon's cotton lace.

One day he sat at his table writing letters. He was alone in the inner room; but the sun that morning did not see a row of pleasanter faces than were bending over large books in odoriferous red Russia binding, and little books in leather covers, and invoices and sheets of· letter paper, in the outer office of Lawrence Newt.

A lad entered the office and stood at the door, impressed by the silent activity he beheld. He did not speak; the younger clerks looked up a moment, then went on with their work. It was clearly packet-day.

The lad remained silent for so long a time, as if his profound respect for the industry he saw before him would not allow him to speak, that Thomas Tray looked up at last, and said,

"Well, Sir?"

"May I see Mr. Newt, Sir?"

"In the other room," said Mr. Tray, with his goose-quill in his mouth, nodding his head toward the inner office, and turning over with both hands a solid mass of leaves in his great, odoriferous red Russia book, and letting them gently down— proud of being the author of that clearly-written, massive work, containing an accurate biography of Lawrence Newt's business.

The youth tapped at the glass door. Mr. Newt said, "Come in," and, when the door opened, looked up, and still holding his pen with the ink in it poised above the paper, he said, kindly, "Well, Sir? Be short. It's packet-day."

"I want a place, Sir."

"What kind of a place?"

"In a store, Sir."

"I'm sorry I'm all full. But sit down while I finish these letters; then we'll talk about it."

CHAPTER XV.

A SCHOOL-BOY NO LONGER.

A SCHOOL-BOY NO LONGER.

THE lad seated himself by the window. Scratch — scratch — scratch. The sun sparkled in the river. The sails, after yesterday's rain, were loosened to dry, and were white as if it had rained milk upon them instead of water. Every thing looked cheerful and bright from Lawrence Newt's window. The lad saw with delight how much sunshine there was in the office.

"I don't believe it would hurt my health to work here," thought he.

Mr. Lawrence Newt rang a little bell. Venables entered quietly.

"Most ready out there?" asked Mr. Newt.

"Most ready, Sir."

"Brisk's the word this morning, you know. Please to copy these letters."

Venables said nothing, took the letters, and went out.

"Now, young man," said the merchant, "tell me what you want."

The lad's heart turned toward him like a fallow-field to the May sun.

"My father's been unfortunate, Sir, and I want to do something for myself. He advised me to come to you."

"Why?"

"Because he said you would give me good advice if you couldn't give me employment."

"Well, Sir, you seem a strong, likely lad. Have you ever been in a store?"

"No, Sir. I left school last week."

Mr. Newt looked out of the window.

"Your father's been unfortunate?"

"Yes, Sir."

"How's that? Has he told a lie, or lost his eyes, or his health, or has his daughter married a drunkard?" asked Mr. Lawrence Newt, looking at the lad with a kindly humor in his eyes.

"Oh no, Sir," replied the boy, surprised. "He's lost his money."

"Oh ho! his money! And it is the loss of money which you call 'unfortunate.' Now, my boy, think a moment. Is there any thing belonging to your father which he could so well spare? Has he any superfluous boy or girl? any useless arm or leg? any unnecessary good temper or honesty? any taste for books, or pictures, or the country, that he would part with? Is there any thing which he owns that it would not be a greater misfortune to him to lose than his money? Honor bright, my boy. If you think there is, say so!"

The youth smiled.

" Well, Sir, I suppose worse things could happen to us than poverty," said he.

Mr. Lawrence Newt interrupted him by remarks which were belied by his beaming face.

" Worse things than poverty! Why, my boy, what are you thinking of? Do you not know that it is written in the largest efforts upon the hearts of all Americans, 'Resist poverty, and it will flee from you?' If you do not begin by considering poverty the root of all evil, where on earth do you expect to end? Cease to be poor, learn to be rich. I'm afraid you don't read the good book. So your father has health"— the boy nodded—" and a whole body, a good temper, an affectionate family, generous and refined tastes, pleasant relations with others, a warm heart, a clear conscience"—the boy nodded with an increasing enthusiasm of assent—" and yet you call him unfortunate—ruined! Why, look here, my son; there's an old apple-woman at the corner of Burling Slip, where I stop every day and buy apples; she's sixty years old, and through thick and thin, under a dripping wreck of an umbrella when it rains, under the sky when it shines—warming herself by a foot-stove in winter, by the sun in summer— there the old creature sits. She has an old, sick, querulous husband at home, who tries to beat her. Her daughters are all out at service—let us hope, in kind families—her sons are dull, ignorant men; her home is solitary and forlorn; she can not read much, nor does she want to; she is coughing her life away, and succeeds in selling apples enough to pay her rent and buy food for her old man and herself. She told me yesterday that she was a most fortunate woman. What does the word mean? I give it up."

The lad looked around the spacious office, on every table and desk and chair of which was written Prosperity as plainly as the name of Lawrence Newt upon the little tin sign by the door. Except for the singular magnetism of the merchant's presence, which dissipated such a suggestion as rapidly as it rose, the youth would have said aloud what was in his heart.

"How easy 'tis for a rich man to smile at poverty!"

The man watched the boy, and knew exactly what he was thinking. As the eyes of the younger involuntarily glanced about the office and presently returned to the merchant, they found the merchant's gazing so keenly that they seemed to be mere windows through which his soul was looking. But the keen earnestness melted imperceptibly into the usual sweetness as Lawrence Newt said,

"You think I can talk prettily about misfortune because I know nothing about it. You make a great mistake. No man, even in jest, can talk well of what he doesn't understand. So don't misunderstand me. I am rich, but I am not fortunate."

He said it in the same tone as before.

"If you wanted a rose and got only a butter-cup, should you think yourself fortunate?" asked Mr. Newt.

"Why, yes, Sir. A man can't expect to have every thing precisely as he wants it," replied the boy.

"My young friend, you are of opinion that a half loaf is better than no bread. True—so am I. But never make the mistake of supposing a half to be the whole. Content is a good thing. When the man sent for cake, and said, 'John, if you can't get cake, get smelts,' he did wisely. But smelts are not cake for all that. What's your name?" asked Mr. Newt, abruptly.

"Gabriel Bennet," replied the boy.

"Bennet—Bennet—what Bennet?"

"I don't know, Sir."

Lawrence Newt was apparently satisfied with this answer. He only said:

"Well, my son, you do wisely to say at once you don't know, instead of going back to somebody a few centuries ago, of whose father you have to make the same answer. The Newts, however, you must be aware, are a very old family." The merchant smiled. "They came into England with the Normans; but who they came into Normandy with I don't know. Do you?"

Gabriel laughed, with a pleasant feeling of confidence in his companion.

"Have you been at school in the city?" asked the merchant.

Gabriel told him that he had been at Mr. Gray's.

"Oh ho! then you know my nephew Abel?"

"Yes, Sir," replied Gabriel, coloring.

"Abel is a smart boy," said Mr. Newt.

Gabriel made no reply.

"Do you like Abel?"

Gabriel paused a moment; then said,

"No, Sir."

The merchant looked at the boy for a few moments.

"Who did you like at school?"

"Oh, I liked Jim Greenidge and Little Malacca best," replied Gabriel, as if the whole world must be familiar with those names.

At the mention of the latter Lawrence Newt looked interested, and, after talking a little more, said,

"Gabriel, I take you into my office."

He called Mr. Tray.

"Thomas Tray, this is the youngest clerk, Gabriel Bennet. Gabriel, this is the head of the outer office, Mr. Thomas Tray. Thomas, ask Venables to step this way."

That young man appeared immediately.

"Mr. Venables, you are promoted. You have seven hundred dollars a year, and are no longer youngest clerk. Gabriel Bennet, this is Frank Venables. Be friends. Now go to work."

There was a general bowing, and Thomas Tray and the two young men retired.

As they went out Mr. Newt opened a letter which had been brought in from the Post during the interview.

"DEAR SIR,—I trust you will pardon this intrusion. It is a long time since I have had the honor of writing to you; but I thought you would wish to know that Miss Wayne will be in New York, for the first time, within a day or two after you receive this letter. She is with her aunt, Mrs. Dinks, who will stay at Bunker's.

"Respectfully yours,

"JANE SIMCOE."

Lawrence Newt's head drooped as he sat. Presently he arose and walked up and down the office.

Meanwhile Gabriel was installed. That ceremony consisted of offering him a high stool with a leathern seat. Mr. Tray remarked that he should have a drawer in the high desk, on both sides of which the clerks were seated. The installation was completed by Mr. Tray's formally introducing the new-comer to the older clerks.

The scratching began again. Gabriel looked curiously upon the work in which he was now to share. The young men had no words for him. Mr. Newt was engaged within. The boy had a vague feeling that he must shift for himself—that every body was busy—that play in this life had ended and work begun. The thought tasted to him much more like smelts than cake. And while he was wisely left by Thomas Tray to familiarize himself with the entire novelty of the situation his mind flashed back to Delafield with an aching longing, and the boy would willingly have put his face in his hands and wept. But he sat quietly looking at his companions—until Mr. Tray said,

"Gabriel, I want you to copy this invoice."

And Gabriel was a school-boy no longer.

CHAPTER XVI.

PHILOSOPHY.

ABEL NEWT believed in his lucky star. He had managed Uncle Savory—couldn't he manage the world?

"My son," said Mr. Boniface Newt, "you are now about to begin the world." (Begin? thought Abel.) "You are now coming into my house as a merchant. In this world we must do the best we can. It is a great pity that men are not considerate, and all that. But they are not. They are selfish. You must take them as you find them. *You*, my son, think they are all honest and good."—Do I? quoth son, in his soul. —"It is the bitter task of experience to undeceive youth from its romantic dreams. As a rule, Abel, men are rascals; that is to say, they pursue their own interests. How sad! True; how sad! Where was I? Oh! men are scamps—with some exceptions; but you must go by the rule. Life is a scrub-race—melancholy, Abel, but true. I talk plainly to you, but I do it for your good. If we were all angels, things would be different. If this were the Millennium, every thing would doubtless be agreeable to every body. But it is not—how very sad! True, how very sad! Where was I? Oh! it's all devil take the hindmost. And because your neighbors are dishonest, why should you starve? You see, Abel?"

It was in Mr. Boniface Newt's counting-room that he preached this gospel. A boy entered and announced that Mr. Hadley was outside looking at some cases of dry goods.

"Now, Abel," said his father, "I'll return in a moment."

He stepped out, smiling and rubbing his hands. Mr. Hadley was stooping over a case of calicoes; Blackstone, Hadley, & Merrimack—no safer purchasers in the world. The countenance of Boniface Newt beamed upon the customer as if he saw good notes at six months exuding from every part of his person.

"Good-morning, Mr. Hadley. Charming morning, Sir— beautiful day, Sir. What's the word this morning, Sir?"

"Nothing, nothing," returned the customer. "Pretty print that. Just what I've been looking for" (renewed rubbing of hands on the part of Mr. Newt)—"very pretty. If it's the right width, it's just the thing. Let me see—that's about seven-eighths." He shook his head negatively. "No, not wide enough. If that print were a yard wide, I should take all you have."

"Oh, that's a yard," replied Mr. Newt; "certainly a full yard." He looked around inquiringly, as if for a yard-stick.

"Where is the yard-stick?" asked Mr. Hadley.

"Timothy!" said Mr. Newt to the boy, with a peculiar look.

The boy disappeared and reappeared with a yard-stick, while Mr. Newt's face underwent a series of expressions of subdued anger and disgust.

"Now, then," said Mr. Hadley, laying the yard-stick upon the calicoes; "yes, as I thought, seven-eighths; too narrow— sorry."

There were thirty cases of those goods in the loft. Boniface Newt groaned in soul. The unconscious small boy, who had not understood the peculiar look, and had brought the yard-stick, stood by.

"Mr. Newt," said Hadley, stopping at another case, "that is very handsome."

"Very, very; and that is the last case."

"You have no other cases?"

"No."

"Oh! well, send it round at once; for I am sure—"

"Mr. Newt," said the unconscious boy, smiling with the satisfaction of one who is able to correct an error, "you are mistaken, Sir. There are a dozen more cases just like that up stairs."

"Ah! then I don't care about it," said Mr. Hadley, passing on. The head of the large commission-house of Boniface Newt & Co. looked upon the point of apoplexy.

"Good-morning, Mr. Newt; sorry that I see nothing far-ther," said Mr. Hadley, and he went out.

Mr. Newt turned fiercely to the unconscious boy.

"What do you mean, Sir, by saying and doing such things?" asked he, sharply.

"What things, Sir?" demanded the appalled boy.

"Why, getting the yard-stick when I winked to you not to find it, and telling of other cases when I said that one was the last."

"Why, Sir, because it wasn't the last," said the boy.

"For business purposes it *was* the last, Sir," replied Mr. Newt. "You don't know the first principles of business. The tongue is always the mischief-maker. Hold your tongue, Sir, hold your tongue, or you'll lose your place, Sir."

Mr. Boniface Newt, ruffled and red, went into his office, where he found Abel reading the newspaper and smoking a cigar. The clerks outside were pale at the audacity of Newt, Jun. The young man was dressed extremely well. He had improved the few weeks of his residence in the city by visits to Frost the tailor, in Maiden Lane; and had sent his measure to Forr, the bootmaker in Paris, artists who turned out the prettiest figures that decorated the Broadway of those days. Mr. Abel Newt, to his father's eyes, had the air of a man of superb leisure; and as he sat reading the paper, with one leg thrown over the arm of the office-chair, and the smoke languidly curling from his lips, Mr. Boniface Newt felt profoundly, but vaguely, uncomfortable, as if he had some slight pre-science of a future of indolence for the hope of the house of Newt.

As his father entered, Mr. Abel dropped by his side the hand still holding the newspaper, and, without removing the cigar, said, through the cloud of smoke he blew,

"Father, you were imparting your philosophy of life."

The older gentleman, somewhat discomposed, answered,

"Yes, I was saying what a pity it is that men are such d—d rascals, because they force every body else to be so too.

THE GOSPEL OF MAMMON.

But what can you do? It's all very fine to talk, but we've
got to live. I sha'n't be such an ass as to run into the street
and say, 'I gave ten cents a yard for those goods, but you
must pay me twenty.' Not at all. It's other men's business
to find that out if they can. It's a great game, business is,
and the smartest chap wins. Every body knows we are going
to get the largest price we can. People are gouging, and
shinning, and sucking all round. It's give and take. I am

not here to look out for other men, I'm here to take care of
myself—for nobody else will.   It's very sad, I know; it's very
sad, indeed.   It's absolutely melancholy.   Ah, yes! where was
I?   Oh! I was saying that a lie well stuck to is better than
the truth wavering.   It's perfectly dreadful, my son, from some
points of view—Christianity, for instance.   But what on earth
are you going to do?   The only happy people are the rich
people, for they don't have this eternal bother how to make
money.   Don't misunderstand me, my son; I do not say that
you must always tell stories.   Heaven forbid!   But a man is
not bound always to tell the whole truth.   The very law itself
says that no man need give evidence against himself.   Besides,
business is no worse than every other calling.   Do you suppose a lawyer never defends a man whom he knows to be
guilty?   He says he does it to give the culprit a fair trial.
Fiddle-de-dee!   He strains every nerve to get the man off.
A lawyer is hired to take the side of a company or a corpora-
tion in every quarrel.   He's paid by the year or by the case.
He probably stops to consider whether his company is right,
doesn't he?   he works for justice, not for victory?   Oh, yes!
stuff!   He works for fees.   What's the meaning of a retainer?
That if, upon examination, the lawyer finds the retaining party
to be in the right, he will undertake the case?   Fiddle! no!
but that he will undertake the case any how and fight it
through.   So 'tis all round.   I wish I was rich, and I'd be out
of it."

Mr. Boniface Newt discoursed warmly; Mr. Abel Newt
listened with extreme coolness.   He whiffed his cigar, and
leaned his head on one side as he hearkened to the wisdom
of experience; observing that his father put his practice into
words and called it philosophy.

CHAPTER XVII.

OF GIRLS AND FLOWERS.

MR. ABEL NEWT was not a philosopher; he was a man of action.

He told his mother that he could not accompany her to the Springs, because he must prepare himself to enter the counting-room of his father. But the evening before she left, Mrs. Newt gave a little party for Mrs. Plumer, of New Orleans. So Miss Grace, of whom his mother had written Abel, and who was just about leaving school, left school and entered society, simultaneously, by taking leave of Madame de Feuille and making her courtesy at Mrs. Boniface Newt's.

Madame de Feuille's was a "finishing" school. An extreme polish was given to young ladies by Madame de Feuille. By her generous system they were fitted to be wives of men of even the largest fortune. There was not one of her pupils who would not have been equal to the addresses of a millionaire. It is the profound conviction of all who were familiar with that seminary that the pupils would not have shrunk from marrying a crown-prince, or any king in any country who confined himself to Christian wedlock with one wife, or even the son of an English duke—so perfect was the polish, so liberal the education.

Mrs. Newt's party was select. Mrs. Plumer, Miss Grace Plumer and the Magots, with Mellish Whitloe, of course; and Mrs. Osborne Moultrie, a lovely woman from Georgia, and her son Sligo, a slim, graceful gentleman, with fair hair and eyes; Dr. and Mrs. Lush. Rev. Dr. and Mrs. Maundy, who came only upon the express understanding that there was to be no dancing, and a few other agreeable people. It was a Summer party, Abel said—mere low-necked muslin, strawberries and ice-cream.

The eyes of the strangers of the gentler sex soon discovered the dark, rich face of Abel, who moved among the groups with the grace and ease of an accomplished man of society, smiling brightly upon his friends, bowing gravely to those of his mother's guests whom he did not personally know.

"Who is that?" asked Mrs. Whetwood Tully, who had recently returned with her daughter, one of Madame de Feuille's finest successes, from a foreign tour.

"That is my brother Abel," replied Miss Fanny.

"Your brother Abel? how charming! How very like he is to Viscount Tattersalls. You've not been in England, I believe, Miss Newt?"

Fanny bowed negatively.

"Ah! then you have never seen Lord Tattersalls. He is a very superior young man. We were very intimate with him indeed. Dolly, dear!"

"Yes, ma."

"You remember our particular friend Lord Viscount Tattersalls?"

"Was he a bishop?" asked Miss Fanny Newt.

"Law! no, my dear. He was a—he was a—why, he was a Viscount, you know—a Viscount."

"Oh! a Viscount?"

"Yes, a Viscount."

"Ah! a Viscount."

"Well, Dolly dear, do you see how much Mr. Abel Newt resembles Lord Tattersalls?"

"Yes, ma."

"It's very striking, isn't it?"

"Yes, ma."

"Or now I look, I think he is even more like the Marquis of Crockford. Don't you think so?"

"Yes, ma?"

"Very like indeed."

"Yes, ma."

"Dolly, dear, don't you think his nose is like the Duke of

Wellington's? You remember the Wellington nose, my child?"

"Yes, ma."

"Or is it Lord Brougham's that I mean?"

"Yes, ma."

"Yes, dear."

"May I present my brother Abel, Miss Tully?" asked Fanny Newt.

"Yes, I'm sure," said Miss Tully.

Fanny Newt turned just as a song began in the other room, out of which opened the conservatory.

> "Last May a braw wooer cam down the lang glen,
>   And sair wi' his love he did deave me:
> I said there was naething I hated like men—
>   The deuce gae wi'm to believe me, believe me,
>   The deuce gae wi'm to believe me."

The rooms were hushed as the merry song rang out. The voice of the singer was arch, and her eye flashed slyly on Abel Newt as she finished, and a murmur of pleasure rose around her.

Abel leaned upon the piano, with his eyes fixed upon the singer. He was fully conscious of the surprise he had betrayed to sister Fanny when she spoke suddenly of Mrs. Alfred Dinks. It was necessary to remove any suspicion that she might entertain in consequence. If Mr. Abel Newt had intentions in which Miss Hope Wayne was interested, was there any reason why Miss Fanny Newt should mingle in the matter?

As Miss Plumer finished the song Abel saw his sister coming toward him through the little crowd, although his eyes seemed to be constantly fixed upon the singer.

"How beautiful!" said he, ardently, in a low voice, looking Grace Plumer directly in the eyes.

"Yes, it is a pretty song."

"Oh! you mean the song?" said Abel.

The singer blushed, and took up a bunch of roses that she had laid upon the piano and began to play with them.

"How very warm it is!" said she.

"Yes," said Abel. "Let us take a turn in the conservatory—it is both darker and cooler; and I think your eyes will give light and warmth enough to our conversation."

"Dear me! if you depend upon me it will be the Arctic zone in the conservatory," said Miss Grace Plumer, as she rose from the piano. (Mrs. Newt had written Abel she was fourteen! She was seventeen in May.)

"No, no," said Abel, "we shall find the tropics in that conservatory."

"Then look out for storms!" replied Miss Plumer, laughing.

Abel offered his arm, and the young couple moved through the humming room. The arch eyes were cast down. The voice of the youth was very low.

He felt a touch, and turned. He knew very well who it was. It was his sister.

"Abel, I want to present you to Miss Whetwood Tully."

"My dear Fanny, I can not turn from roses to violets. Miss Tully, I am sure, is charming. I would go with you with all my heart if I could," said he, smiling and looking at Miss Plumer; "but, you see, all my heart is going here."

Grace Plumer blushed again. He was certainly a charming young man.

Fanny Newt, with lips parted, looked at him a moment and shook her head gently. Abel was sure she would happen to find herself in the conservatory presently, whither he and his companion slowly passed. It was prettily illuminated with a few candles, but was left purposely dim.

"How lovely it is here! Oh! how fond I am of flowers!" said Miss Plumer, with the prettiest little rapture, and such a little spring that Abel was obliged to hold her arm more closely.

"Are you fond of flowers, Mr. Newt?"

"Yes; but I prefer them living."

"Living flowers—what a poetic idea! But what do you mean?" asked Grace Plumer, hanging her head.

Abel saw somebody on the cane sofa under the great orange-tree, almost hidden in the shade. Dear Fanny! thought he.

"My dear Grace," began Abel, in his lowest, sweetest voice; but the conservatory was so still that the words could have been easily heard by any one sitting upon the sofa.

Some one was sitting there—some one did hear. Abel smiled in his heart, and bent more closely to his companion. His manner was full of tender devotion. He and Grace came nearer. Some one not only heard, but started. Abel raised his eyes smilingly to meet Fanny's. Somebody else started then; for under the great orange-tree, on the cane sofa, sat Lawrence Newt and Hope Wayne.

CHAPTER XVIII.

OLD FRIENDS AND NEW.

LAWRENCE NEWT had called at Bunker's, and found Mrs. Dinks and Miss Hope Wayne. They were sitting at the window upon Broadway watching the promenaders along that famous thoroughfare; for thirty years ago the fashionable walk was between the Park and the Battery, and Bunker's was close to Morris Street, a little above the Bowling Green.

When Mr. Newt was announced Hope Wayne felt as if she were suffocating. She knew but one person of that name. Her aunt supposed it to be the husband of her friend, Mrs. Nancy Newt, whom she had seen upon a previous visit to New York this same summer. They both looked up and saw a gentleman they had never seen before. He bowed pleasantly, and said,

"Ladies, my name is Lawrence Newt."

There was a touch of quaintness in his manner, as in his dress.

"You will find the city quite deserted," said he. "But I have called with an invitation from my sister, Mrs. Boniface

Newt, for this evening to a small party. She incloses her card, and begs you to waive the formality of a call."

That was the way that Lawrence Newt and Hope Wayne came to be sitting on the cane sofa under the great orange-tree in Boniface Newt's conservatory.

They had entered the room and made their bows to Mrs. Nancy; and Mr. Lawrence, wishing to talk to Miss Hope, had led her by another way to the conservatory, and so Mr. Abel had failed to see them.

As they sat under the tree Lawrence Newt conversed with Hope in a tone of earnest and respectful tenderness that touched her heart. She could not understand the winning kindliness of his manner, nor could she resist it. He spoke of her home with an accuracy of detail that surprised her.

"It was not the same house in my day, and you, perhaps, hardly remember much of the old one. The house is changed, but nothing else; no, nothing else," he added, musingly, and with the same dreamy expression in his eyes that was in them when he leaned against his office window and watched the ships—while his mind sailed swifter and farther than they.

"They can not touch the waving outline of the hills that you see from the lawn, nor the pine-trees that shade the windows. Does the little brook still flow in the meadow below? And do you understand the pine-trees? Do they tell any tales?"

He asked it with a half-mournful gayety. He asked as if he both longed and feared that she should say, "Yes, they have told me: I know all."

The murmurs of the singing came floating out to them as they sat. Hope was happy and trustful. She was in the house of Abel—she should see him—she should hear him! And this dear gentleman—not exactly like a father nor an uncle—well, yes, perhaps a young uncle—he is brother of Abel's mother, and he mysteriously knows so much about Pinewood, and his smiling voice has a tear in it as he speaks of old days. I love him already—I trust him entirely—I have found a friend.

"Shall we go in again?" said Lawrence Newt. But they saw some one approaching, and before they arose, while they were still silent, and Hope's heart was like the dawning summer heaven, she suddenly heard Abel Newt's words, and watched him, speechlessly, as he and his companion glided by her into the darkness. It was the vision of a moment; but in the attitude, the tone, the whole impression, Hope Wayne instinctively felt treachery.

"Yes, let us go in!" she said to Lawrence Newt, as she rose calmly.

Abel had passed. He could no more have stopped and shaken hands with Hope Wayne than he could have sung like a nightingale. He could not even raise his head erect as he went by—something very stern and very strong seemed to hold it down.

Miss Plumer's head was also bent; she was waiting to hear the end of that sentence. She thought society opened beautifully. Such a handsome fellow in such a romantic spot, beginning his compliments in such a low, rich voice, with his hair almost brushing hers. But he did not finish. Abel Newt was perfectly silent. He glided away with Grace Plumer into grateful gloom, and her ears, exquisitely apprehensive, caught from his lips not a word further.

Lawrence Newt rose as Hope requested, and they moved away. She found her aunt, and stood by her side. The young men were brought up and presented, and submitted their observations upon the weather, asked her how she liked New York—were delighted to hear that she would pass the next winter in the city—would show her then that New York had some claim to attention even from a Bostonian—were charmed, really, with Mr. Bowdoin Beacon and—and—Mr. Alfred Dinks; at mention of which name they looked in her face in the most gentlemanly manner to see the red result, as if the remark had been a blister, but they saw only an unconscious abstraction in her own thoughts, mingled with an air of attention to what they were saying.

E

"Miss Hope," said Lawrence Newt, who approached her with a young woman by his side, " I want you to know my friend Amy Waring."

The two girls looked at each other and bowed. Then they shook hands with a curious cordiality.

Amy Waring had dark eyes—not round and hard and black —not ebony eyes, but soft, sympathetic eyes, in which you expect to see images as lovely as the Eastern traveler sees when he remembers home and looks in the drop held in the palm of the hand of the magician's boy. They had the fresh, unworn, moist light of flowers early in June mornings, when they are full of sun and dew. And there was the same transparent, rich, pure darkness in her complexion. It was not swarthy, nor black, nor gloomy. It did not look half Indian, nor even olive. It was an illuminated shadow.

The two girls—they were women, rather—went together to a sofa and sat down. Hope Wayne's impulse was to lay her head upon her new friend's shoulder and cry; for Hope was prostrated by the unexpected vision of Abel, as a strong man is unnerved by sudden physical pain. She felt the over- whelming grief of a child, and longed to give way to it ut- terly.

"I am glad to know you, Miss Wayne!" said Amy Waring, in a cordial, cheerful voice, with a pleasant smile.

Hope bowed, and thanked her.

"I find that Mr. Newt's friends always prove to be mine," continued Amy.

"I am glad of it ; but I don't know why I am his friend," said Hope. "I never saw him until to-day. He must have lived in Delafield. Do you know how that is ?"

She found conversation a great relief, and longed to give way to a kind of proud, indignant volubility.

"No ; but he seems to have lived every where, to have seen every thing, and to have known every body. A very useful acquaintance, I assure you!" said Amy, smiling.

"Is he married ?" asked Hope.

There was the least little blush upon Amy's cheek as she heard this question; but so slight, that if any body had thought he observed it, he would have looked again and said, "No, I was mistaken." Perhaps, too, there was the least little fluttering of a heart otherwise unconscious. But words are like breezes that blow hither and thither, and the leaves upon the most secluded trees in the very inmost covert of the wood may sometimes feel a breath, and stir with responsive music before they are aware.

Amy Waring replied, pleasantly, that he was not married. Hope Wayne said, "What a pity!" Amy smiled, and asked, "Why a pity?"

"Because such a man would be so happy if he were married, and would make others so happy! He has been in love, you may be sure."

"Yes," replied Amy; "I have no doubt of that. We don't see men of forty, or so, who have not been touched—"

"By what?" asked Lawrence Newt, who had come up silently, and now stood beside her.

"Yes, by what?" interposed Miss Fanny, who had been very busy during the whole evening, trying to get into her hands the threads of the various interests that she saw flying and streaming all around her. She had seen Mr. Alfred Dinks devoted to Miss Wayne, and was therefore confirmed in her belief that they were engaged. She had seen Abel flirting with Grace, and was therefore satisfied that he cared nothing about her. She had done the best she could with Alfred Dinks, but was extremely dissatisfied with her best; and, seeing Hope and Amy together, she had been hovering about them for a long time, anxious to overhear or to join in.

"Really," said Amy, looking up with a smile, "I was making a very innocent remark."

"Perfectly innocent, I'm sure!" replied Fanny, in her sweetest manner. It was such a different sweetness from Amy Waring's, that Hope turned and looked very curiously at Miss Fanny.

"There are few men of forty who have not been in love," said Amy, calmly. "That is what I was saying."

As there was only one man of forty, or near that age, in the little group, the appeal was evidently to him. Lawrence Newt looked at the three girls, with the swimming light in his eyes, half crushing them and smiling, so that every one of them felt, each in her own way, that they were as completely blinded by that smile as by a glare of sunlight—which also, like that smile, is warm, and not treacherous.

They could not see beyond the words, nor hope to.

"Miss Amy is right, as usual," said he.

"Why, Uncle Lawrence, tell us all about it!" said Fanny, with a hard, black smile in her eyes.

Uncle Lawrence was not in the slightest degree abashed.

"Fanny," said he, "I will speak to you in a parable. Remember, to *you*. There was a farmer whose neighbor built a curious tower upon his land. It was upon a hill, in a grove. The structure rose slowly, but public curiosity rose with fearful rapidity. The gossips gossiped about it in the public houses. Rumors of it stole up to the city, and down came reporters and special correspondents to describe it with an unctuous eloquence and picturesque splendor of style known only to them. The builder held his tongue, dear Fanny. The workmen speculated upon the subject, but their speculations were no more valuable than those of other people. They received private bribes to tell; and all the great newspapers announced that, at an enormous expense, they had secured the exclusive intelligence, and the exclusive intelligence was always wrong. The country was in commotion, dear Fanny, about a simple tower that a man was building upon his land. But the wonder of wonders, and the exasperation of exasperations, was, that the farmer whose estate adjoined never so much as spoke of the tower—was never known to have asked about it—and, indeed, it was not clear that he knew of the building of any tower within a hundred miles of him. Of course, my dearest Fanny, a self-respecting Public Sentiment could not stand that. It was insulting to the public, which manifested so profound an interest in the tower, that the immediate neighbor should preserve so strict a silence, and such a perfectly tranquil mind. There are but two theories possible in regard to that man, said the self-respecting Public Sentiment: he is either a fool or a knave—probably a little of each. In any case he must be dealt with. So Public Sentiment accosted the farmer, and asked him if he were not aware that a mysterious tower was going up close to him, and that the public curiosity was sadly exercised about it? He replied that he was blessed with tolerable eyesight, and had seen the tower from the very first stone upward. Tell us, then, all about it! shrieked Public Sentiment. Ask the builder, if you want to know, said the farmer. But he won't tell us, and we want you to tell us, because we know that you must have asked him. Now what, in the name of pity!—what is that tower for? I have never asked, replies the farmer. Never asked? shrieked Public Sentiment. Never, retorted Rusticus. And why, in the name of Heaven, have you never asked? cried the crowd. Because, said the farmer—"

Lawrence Newt looked at his auditors. "Are you listening, dear Fanny?"

"Yes, Uncle Lawrence."

"—because it's none of my business."

Lawrence Newt smiled; so did all the rest, including Fanny, who remarked that he might have told her in fewer words that she was impertinent.

"Yes, Fanny; but sometimes words help us to remember things. It is a great point gained when we have learned to hoe the potatoes in our own fields, and not vex our souls about our neighbor's towers."

Hope Wayne was not in the least abstracted. She was nervously alive to every thing that was said and done; and listened with a smile to Lawrence Newt's parable, liking him more and more.

The general restless distraction that precedes the breaking

up of a party had now set in. People were moving, and rus-
tling, and breaking off the ends of conversation. They began
to go. A few said good-evening, and had had such a charming time! The rest gradually followed, until there was a universal departure. Grace Plumer was leaning upon Sligo Moultrie's arm. But where was Abel?

Hope Wayne's eyes looked every where. But her only
glimpse of him during the evening had been that glimmering,
dreadful moment in the conservatory. There he had remained
ever since. There he still stood gazing through the door into
the drawing-room, seeing but not seen—his mind a wild whirl
of thoughts.

"What a fool I am!" thought Abel, bitterly. He was
steadily asking himself, "Have—I—lost—Hope Wayne—before—I—had—won—her?"

CHAPTER XIX.

DOG-DAYS.

THE great city roared, and steamed, and smoked. Along
the hot, glaring streets by the river a few panting people hurried, clinging to the house wall for a thin strip of shade, too
narrow even to cover their feet. All the windows of the
stores were open, and within the offices, with a little thinking,
a little turn of the pen, and a little tracing in ink, men were
magically warding off impending disaster, or adding thousands
to the thousands accumulated already—men, too, were writing without thinking, mechanically copying or posting, scribbling letters of form, with heads clear or heads aching, with
hearts burning or cold; full of ambition and hope, or vaguely
remembering country hill-sides and summer rambles—a day's
fishing—a night's frolic—Sunday-school—singing-school, and
the girl with the chip hat garlanded with sweet-brier; hearts
longing and loving, regretting, hoping, and remembering, and

all the while the faces above them calm and smooth, and the hands below them busily doing their part of the great work of the world.

In Wall Street there was restless running about. Men in white clothes and straw-hats darted in at doors, darted out of doors—carrying little books, and boxes, and bundles in their hands, nodding to each other as they passed, but all infected with the same fever; with brows half-wrinkled or tied up in hopeless seams of perplexity; with muttering pale lips, or lips round and red, and clearly the lips of clerks who had no great stakes at issue—a general rushing and hurrying as if every body were haunted by the fear of arriving too late every where, and losing all possible chances in every direction.

Within doors there were cool bank parlors and insurance offices, with long rows of comely clerks writing in those Russia red books which Thomas Tray loved—or wetting their fingers on little sponges in little glass dishes and counting whole fortunes in bank-notes—or perched high on office-stools eating apples — while Presidents and Directors, with shiny bald pates and bewigged heads, some heroically with permanent spectacles and others coyly and weakly with eye-glasses held in the hand, sat perusing the papers, telling the news, and gossiping about engagements, and marriages, and family rumors, and secrets with the air of practical men of the world, with no nonsense, no fanaticism, no fol-de-rol of any kind about them, but who profoundly believed the Burt theory that wives and daughters were a more sacred kind of property than sheep-pastures, or even than the most satisfactory bond and mortgage.

They talked politics, these banking and insurance, gentlemen, with vigor and warmth. "What on earth does this General Jackson mean, Sir? Is he going to lay the axe at the very roots of our national prosperity? What the deuce does a frontier soldier know about banking?"

They talked about Morgan who had been found in Lake Ontario; and the younger clerks took their turn at it, and furiously denied among themselves that Washington was a Mason. The younger clerks held every Mason responsible for the reported murder. Then they turned pale lest their neighbors were Masons, and might cause them to be found drowned off the Battery. The older men shook their heads.

Murders—did you speak of murders, Mr. Van Boozenberg? Why, this is a dreadful business in Salem! Old Mr. White murdered in his bed! The most awful thing on record. Terrible stories are told, Sir, about respectable people! It's getting to be dangerous to be rich. What are we coming to? What can you expect, Sir, with Fanny Wright disseminating her infidel sentiments, and the work-people buying *The Friend of Equal Human Rights?* Equal human fiddle-sticks, Mr. Van Boozenberg!

To which remarks from the mouths of many Directors that eminent officer nodded his head, and looked so wise that it was very remarkable so many foolish transactions took place under his administration.

And in all the streets of the great city, in all the lofty workshops and yards and factories, huge hammers smote and clashed, and men, naked to the waist, reeking in dingy interiors, bent like gnomes at their tasks, while saws creaked, wheels turned, planes and mallets, and chisels shoved and cut and struck; and down in damp cellars sallow ghastly men and women wove rag-carpets, and twisted baskets in the midst of litters of puny, pale children, with bleared eyes, and sore heads, and dirty faces, tumbling, playing, shouting, whimpering— scampering after the pigs that came rooting and nosing in the liquid filth that simmered and stank to heaven in the gutters at the top of the stairs; and the houses above the heads of the ghastly men and women were swarming rookeries, hot and close and bare, with window-panes broken, and hats, and coats, and rags stuffed in, and men with bloodshot eyes and desperate faces sitting dogged with their hats on, staring at nothing, or leaning on their ragged elbows on broken tables, scowling from between their dirty hands at the world and the

future; while in higher rooms sat solitary girls in hard wood-
en chairs, a pile of straw covered with a rug in the corner, and
a box to put a change of linen in, driving the needle silently
and ceaselessly through shirts or coats or trowsers, stooping
over in the foul air during the heat of the day, straining their
eyes when the day darkened to save a candle, hearing the
roar and the rush and the murmur far away, mingled in the
distance, as if they were dead and buried in their graves, and
dreaming a horrid dream until the resurrection.

Only sometimes an acute withering pain, as if something or
somebody were sewing the sewer and pierced her with a
needle sharp and burning, made the room swim and the straw
in the corner glimmer; and the girl dropped the work and
closed her eyes—the cheeks were black and hollow beneath
them—and she gasped and panted, and leaned back, while the
roar went on, and the hot sun glared, and the neighboring
church clock, striking the hour, seemed to beat on her heart
as it smote relentlessly the girl's returning consciousness.
Then she took up the work again, and the needle, with whose
little point in pain and sickness and consuming solitude, in
darkness, desolation, and flickering, fainting faith, she pricked
back death and dishonor.

At neighboring corners were the reefs upon which human
health, hope, and happiness lay stranded, broken up and gone
to pieces. Bloated faces glowered through the open doors—
their humanity sunk away into mere bestiality. Human forms
—men no longer—lay on benches, hung over chairs, babbled,
maundered, shrieked or wept aloud; while women came in
and took black bottles from under tattered shawls, and said
nothing, but put down a piece of money; and the man behind the counter said nothing, but took the money and filled
the bottles, which were hidden under the tattered shawl again,
and the speechless phantoms glided out, guarding that little
travesty of modesty even in that wild ruin.

In shops beyond, yards of tape, and papers of pins, and boots
and shoes and bread, and all the multitudinous things that are

bought and sold every minute, were being done up in papers
by complaisant, or surly, or conceited, or well-behaved clerks;
and in all the large and little houses of the city, in all the spacious and narrow streets, there were women cooking, washing,
sweeping, scouring, rubbing, lifting, carrying, sewing, reading,
sleeping—tens and twenties and fifties and hundreds and thousands of men, women, and children. More than two hundred
thousand of them were toiling, suffering, struggling, enjoying,
dreaming, despairing on a summer day, doing their share of
the world's work. The eye was full of the city's activity; the
ear was tired with its noise; the heart was sick with the
thought of it; the streets and houses swarmed with people,
but the world was out of town. There was nobody at home.

In the mighty stream, of which men and women are the
waves, that poured ceaselessly along its channels, friends met
surprised—touched each other's hands.

"Came in this morning—off to-night—droll it looks—nobody in town—"

And the tumultuous throng bore them apart.

In the evening the Park Theatre is jammed to hear Mr.
Forrest, who made his first appearance in Philadelphia nine
or ten years ago, and is already a New York favorite. Con-
toit's garden flutters with the cool dresses of the promenaders,
who move about between the arbors looking for friends and
awaiting ices. The click of billiard balls is heard in the glittering café at the corner of Reade Street, and a gay company
smokes and sips at the Washington Hotel. Life bursts from
every door, from every window, but there is nobody in town.

More than two hundred thousand men, women, and children
go to their beds and wake up to the morrow, but there is nobody in town. Nobody in town, because Mrs. Boniface Newt
& Co. have gone to Saratoga—no cathedral left, because some
plastering has tumbled off an upper stone—no forest left, because a few leaves have whirled away. Nobody in town, because Mrs. Boniface Newt & Co. have gone to Saratoga, and
are doing their part of the world's work there.

Mr. Alfred Dinks, Mr. Zephyr Wetherley, and Mr. Bowdoin Beacon, were slowly sauntering down Broadway, when they were overtaken and passed by a young woman walking rapidly for so warm a morning.

There was an immense explosion of adjectives expressing surprise when the three young gentlemen discovered that the young lady who was passing them was Miss Amy Waring.

"Why, Miss Waring!" cried they, simultaneously.

She bowed and smiled. They lifted their hats.

"You in town!" said Mr. Beacon.

"In town?" echoed Mr. Dinks.

"Town?" murmured Mr. Wetherley.

"Town," said Miss Waring, with her eyes sparkling.

"Where did you come from? I thought you were all at Saratoga," she continued.

"It's stupid there," said Mr. Beacon.

"Quite stupid," echoed Mr. Dinks.

"Stupid," murmured Mr. Wetherley.

"Stupid?" asked the lady, this time making the interrogation in the antistrophe of the chant.

"We wanted a little fun."

"A little fun."

"Fun," replied the gentlemen.

"Well, I'm going about my business," said she. "Good-morning."

"About your business?"

"Your business?"

"Business?" murmured the youths, in order. Zephyr concluding.

"Business!" said Miss Amy, bursting into a little laugh, in which the listless, perfectly good-humored youths cheerfully joined.

"It's dreadful hot," said Mr. Beacon.

"Oh! horrid!" said Mr. Dinks.

"Very," said Zephyr. And the gentlemen wiped their foreheads.

"Coming to Saratoga, Miss Waring?" they asked.

"Hardly, I think, but possibly," said she, and moved away, with her little basket; while the gentlemen, swearing at the heat, the dust, and the smells, sauntered on, asseverated that Amy Waring was an odd sort of girl; and finally went in to the Washington Hotel, where each lolled back in an arm-chair, with the white duck legs reposing in another—excepting Mr. Dinks, who poised his boots upon the window-sill that commanded Broadway; and so, comforted with a cigar in the mouth, and a glass of iced port-wine sangaree in the hand, the three young gentlemen labored through the hot hours until dinner.

Amy Waring walked quite as rapidly as the heat would permit. She crossed the Park, and, striking into Fulton Street, continued toward the river, but turned into Water Street. The old peach-women at the corners, sitting under huge cotton umbrellas, and parching in the heat, saw the lovely face going by, and marked the peculiarly earnest step, which the sitters in the streets, and consequent sharp students of faces and feet, easily enough recognized as the step of one who was bound upon some especial errand. Clerks looked idly at her from open shop doors, and from windows above; and when she entered the marine region of Water Street, the heavy stores and large houses, which here and there were covered with a dull grime, as if the squalor within had exuded through the dingy red bricks, seemed to glare at her unkindly, and sullenly ask why youth, and beauty, and cleanly modesty should insult with sweet contrast that sordid gloom.

The heat only made it worse. Half-naked children played in the foul gutters with the pigs, which roamed freely at large, and comfortably at home in the purlieus of the docks and the quarter of poverty. Carts jostled by with hogsheads, and boxes, and bales; the red-faced carmen, furious with their horses, or smoking pipes whose odor did not sweeten the air, staring, with rude, curious eyes, at the lady making her way among the casks and bales upon the sidewalks. There was

nothing that could possibly cheer the eye or ear, or heart or
imagination, in any part of the street—not even the haggard
faces, thin with want, rusty with exposure, and dull with
drink, that listlessly looked down upon her from the windows
of lodging-houses.

The door of one of these was open, and Amy Waring went
in. She passed rapidly through the desolate entry and up the
dirty stairs with the broken railing—stairs that creaked under
her light step. At a room upon the back of the house, in the
third story, she stopped and tapped at the door. A voice
cried, "Who's there?" The girl answered, "Amy," and the
door was immediately unlocked.

CHAPTER XX.

AUNT MARTHA.

THE room was clean. There was a rag carpet on the floor;
a pine bureau neatly varnished; a half dozen plain but whole
chairs; a bedstead, upon which the bedding was scrupulously
neat; a pine table, upon which lay a much-thumbed leather-
bound family Bible and a few religious books; and between
the windows, over the bureau, hung a common engraving of
Christ upon the Cross. The windows themselves looked upon
the back of the stores on South Street. Upon the floor was a
large basket full of work, with which the occupant of the room
was evidently engaged. The whole room had an air of severity and cheerlessness, yet it was clear that every thing was
most carefully arranged, and continually swept and washed
and dusted.

The person who had opened the door was a woman of nearly forty. She was dressed entirely in black. She had not so
much as a single spot of white any where about her. She
had even a black silk handkerchief twisted about her head in
the way that negro women twine gay cloths; and such was

her expression that it seemed as if her face, and her heart, and her soul, and all that she felt, or hoped, or remembered, or imagined, were clad and steeped in the same mourning garments and utter gloom.

AUNT MARTHA.

"Good - morning, Amy," said she, in a hard and dry, but not unkind voice. In fact, the rigidity of her aspect, the hardness of her voice, and the singular blackness of her costume, seemed to be too monotonously uniform and resolute not to indicate something willful or unhealthy in the woman's condition, as if the whole had been rather superinduced than naturally developed.

"Aunt Martha, I have brought you some things that I hope you will find comforting and agreeable."

The young woman glanced around the desolately regular and forbidding room, and sighed. The other took the basket and stepped to a closet, but paused as she opened it, and turning to Amy, said, in the same dry, hopeless manner,

"This bounty is too good for a sinner; and yet it would be the unpardonable sin for so great a sinner to end her own life willfully."

The solemn woman put the contents of the basket into the

closet; but it seemed as if, in that gloom, the sugar must have already lost its sweetness and the tea its flavor.

Amy still glanced round the room, and her eyes filled with tears.

"Dear Aunt Martha, when may I tell?" she asked, with piteous earnestness.

"Amy, would you thwart God? He is too merciful already. I almost fear that to tolerate your sympathy and kindness is a sore offense in me. Think what a worm I am! How utterly foul and rank with sin!"

She spoke with clasped hands lying before her in her lap, in the same hard tone as if the words were cut in ebony; with the same fixed lips—the same pale, unsmiling severity of face; above which the abundant hair, streaked with early gray, was almost entirely lost in the black handkerchief.

"But surely God is good!" said Amy, tenderly and sadly. "If we sin, He only asks us to repent and be forgiven."

"But we must pay the penalty, Amy," said the other. "There is a price set upon every sin; and mine is so vast, so enormous—"

She paused a moment, as if overwhelmed by the contemplation of it; then, in the same tone, she continued: "You, Amy, can not even conceive how dreadful it is. You know what it is, but not how bad it is."

She was silent again, and her soul appeared to wrap itself in denser gloom. The air of the room seemed to Amy stifling. The next moment she felt as if she were pierced with sharp spears of ice. She sprang up:

"I shall smother!" said she; and opened the window.

"Aunt Martha, I begin to feel that this is really wicked! If you only knew Lawrence Newt—"

The older woman raised one thin finger, without lifting the hand from her lap. Implacable darkness seemed to Amy to be settling upon her too.

"At least, aunt, let me have you moved to some less horrid place."

"Foulness and filth are too sweet and fair for me," said the dark woman; "and I have been too long idle already."

She lifted the work and began to sew. Amy's heart ached as she looked at her, with sympathy for her suffering and a sense of inability to help her.

There came a violent knock at the door.

"Who's there?" asked Aunt Martha, calmly.

"Come, come; open this door, and let's see what's going on!" cried a loud, coarse voice.

"Who is it?"

"Who is it? Why, it's me—Joseph!" replied the voice.

Aunt Martha rose and unlocked the door. A man whose face was like his voice bustled noisily into the room, with a cigar in his mouth and his hat on.

"Come, come; where's that work? Time's up! Quick, quick! No time, no pay!"

"It is not quite done, Mr. Joseph."

The man stared at Aunt Martha for a moment; then laughed in a jeering way.

"Old lady Black, when you undertake to do a piece of work what d'ye mean by not having it done? Damn it, there's a little too much of the lady about you! Show me that work!" and he seated himself.

The woman brought the basket to him, in the bottom of which were several pieces completed and carefully folded. The man turned them over rapidly.

"And why, in the devil's name, haven't you done the rest? Give 'em here!"

He took the whole, finished and unfinished, and, bundling them up, made for the door. "No time, no pay, old lady; that's the rule. That's the only way to work such infernally jimmy old bodies as you!"

The sewing woman remained perfectly passive as Mr. Joseph was passing out; but Amy sprang forward from the window:

"Stop, Sir!" said she, firmly. The man involuntarily turn-

"STOP, SIR!"

ed, and such was his overwhelming surprise at seeing a lady
suddenly standing before him, and a lady who spoke with perfect authority, that, with the instinct of obsequiousness instinctive in every man who depends upon the favor of customers, he took off his hat.

"If you take that work without paying for it you shall be

made to pay," said Amy, quietly, her eyes flashing, and her figure firm and erect.

The man hesitated for a moment.

" Oh yes, ma'am, oh certainly, ma'am ! Pay for it, of course, ma'am ! 'Twas only to frighten the woman, ma'am ; oh certainly, certainly—oh ! yes, ma'am, pay for it, of course."

" At once," said Amy, without moving.

" Certainly, ma'am ; here's the money," and Mr. Joseph counted it out upon the pine table.

" And you'd better leave the rest to be done at once."

" I'll do so, ma'am," said the man, putting down the bundle.

" And remember that if you ever harm this woman by a word or look, even," added Amy, bending her head toward her aunt, " you will repent it bitterly."

The man stared at her and fumbled with his hat. The cigar had dropped upon the floor. Amy pointed to it, and said, " Now go."

Mr. Joseph stooped, picked up the stump, and departed. Amy felt weak. Her aunt stood by her, and said, calmly,

" It was only part of my punishment."

Amy's eyes flashed.

" Yes, aunt ; and if any body should break into your room and steal every thing you have and throw you out of the window, or break your bones and leave you here to die of starvation, I suppose you would think it all part of your punishment."

" It would be no more than I deserve, Amy."

" Aunt Martha," replied Amy, " if you don't take care you will force me to break my promise to you."

" Amy, to do that would be to bring needless disgrace upon your mother and all her family and friends. They have considered me dead for nearly sixteen years. They have long ago shed the last tear of regret for one whom they believed to be as pure as you are now. Why should you take her to them from the tomb, living still, but a loathsome mass of sin ? I am equal to my destiny. The curse is great, but I will bear

it alone; and the curse of God will fall upon you if you betray me."

Amy was startled by the intensity with which these words
were uttered. There was no movement of the hands or head
upon the part of the older woman. She stood erect by the
table, and, as her words grew stronger, the gloom of her appearance appeared to intensify itself, as a thunder-cloud grows
imperceptibly blacker and blacker.

When she stopped, Amy made no reply; but, troubled and
uneasy, she drew a chair to the window and sat down. The
older woman took up her work again. Amy was lost in
thought, wondering what she could do. She saw nothing as
she looked down into the dirty yards of the houses; but after
some time, forgetting, in the abstraction of her meditation,
where she was, she was suddenly aware of the movement of
some white object; and looking curiously to see what it was,
discovered Lawrence Newt gazing up at her from the back
window of his store, and waving his handkerchief to attract
her attention.

As she saw the kindly face she smiled and shook her hand.
There was a motion of inquiry: "Shall I come round?" And
a very resolute telegraphing by the head back again: "No,
no!" There was another question, in the language of shoulders, and handkerchief, and hands: "What on earth are you
doing up there?" The answer was prompt and intelligible:
"Nothing that I am ashamed of." Still there came another
message of motion from below, which Amy, knowing Lawrence
Newt, unconsciously interpreted to herself thus: "I know you,
angel of mercy! You have brought some angelic soup to
some poor woman." The only reply was a smile that shone
down from the window into the heart of the merchant who
stood below. The smile was followed by a wave of the hand
from above that said farewell. Lawrence Newt looked up
and kissed his own, but the smiling face was gone.

CHAPTER XXI.

THE CAMPAIGN.

MISS FANNY NEWT went to Saratoga with a perfectly clear idea of what she intended to do. She intended to be engaged to Mr. Alfred Dinks.

That young gentleman was a second cousin of Hope Wayne's, and his mother had never objected to his little visits at Pinewood, when both he and Hope were young, and when the unsophisticated human heart is flexible as melted wax, and receives impressions which only harden with time.

" Let the children play together, my dear," she said, in conjugal seclusion to her husband, the Hon. Budlong Dinks, who needed only sufficient capacity and a proper opportunity to have been one of the most distinguished of American diplomatists. He thought he was such already. There was, indeed, plenty of diplomacy in the family, and that most skillful of all diplomatic talents, the management of distinguished diplomatists, was not unknown there.

Fanny Newt had made the proper inquiries. The result was that there were rumors—" How *do* such stories start?" asked Mrs. Budlong Dinks of all her friends who were likely to repeat the rumor—that it was a family understanding that Mr. Alfred Dinks and his cousin Hope were to make a match. " And they *do* say," said Mrs. Dinks, " what ridiculous things people are ! and they *do* say that, for family reasons, we are going to keep it all quiet ! What a world it is !"

The next day Mrs. Cod told Mrs. Dod, in a morning call, that Mrs. Budlong Dinks said that the engagement between her son Alfred and his cousin Hope Wayne was kept quiet for family reasons. Before sunset of that day society was keeping it quiet with the utmost diligence.

These little stories were brought by little birds to New

York, so that when Mrs. Dinks arrived the air was full of hints and suggestions, and the name of Hope Wayne was not unknown. Farther acquaintance with Mr. Alfred Dinks had revealed to Miss Fanny that there was a certain wealthy ancestor still living, in whom the Dinkses had an interest, and that the only participant with them in that interest was Miss Hope Wayne. That was enough for Miss Fanny, whose instinct at once assured her that Mrs. Dinks designed Hope Wayne for her son Alfred, in order that the fortune should be retained in the family.

Miss Fanny having settled this, and upon farther acquaintance with Mr. Dinks having discovered that she might as well undertake the matrimonial management of him as of any other man, and that the Burt fortune would probably descend, in part at least, to the youth Alfred, she decided that the youth Alfred must marry her.

But how should Hope Wayne be disposed of? Fanny reflected.

She lived in Delafield. Brother Abel, now nearly nineteen —not a childish youth—not unhandsome—not too modest— lived also in Delafield. Had he ever met Hope Wayne?

By skillful correspondence, alluding to the solitude of the country, et cetera, and his natural wish for society, and what pleasant people were there in Delafield, Fanny had drawn her lines around Abel to carry the fact of his acquaintance, if possible, by pure strategy.

In reply, Abel wrote about many things—about Mrs. Kingo and Miss Broadbraid—the Sutlers and Grabeaus—he praised the peaceful tone of rural society, and begged Fanny to beware of city dissipation; but not a word of old Burt and Hope Wayne.

Sister Fanny wrote again in the most confiding manner. Brother Abel replied in a letter of beautiful sentiments and a quotation from Dr. Peewee.

He overdid it a little, as we sometimes do in this world. We appear so intensely unconscious that it is perfectly evident we know that somebody is looking at us. So Fanny, knowing that Christopher Burt was the richest man in the village, and lived in a beautiful place, and that his lovely grand-daughter lived with him constantly, with which information in detail Alfred Dinks supplied her, and perceiving from Abel's letter that he was not a recluse, but knew the society of the village, arrived very naturally and easily at the conclusion that brother Abel did know Hope Wayne, and was in love with her. She inferred the latter from the fact that she had long ago decided that brother Abel would not fall in love with any poor girl, and therefore she was sure that if he were in the immediate neighborhood of a lady at once young, beautiful, of good family and very rich, he would be immediately in love—very much in love.

To make every thing sure, Abel had not been at home half an hour before Fanny's well-directed allusion to Hope as the future Mrs. Dinks had caused her brother to indicate an interest which revealed every thing.

"If now," pondered Miss Fanny, "somebody who shall be nameless becomes Mrs. Alfred Dinks, and the nameless somebody's brother marries Miss Hope Wayne, what becomes of the Burt property?"

She went, therefore, to Saratoga in great spirits, and with an unusual wardrobe. The opposing general, Field-marshal Mrs. Budlong Dinks, had certainly the advantage of position, for Hope Wayne was of her immediate party, and she could devise as many opportunities as she chose for bringing Mr. Alfred and his cousin together. She did not lose her chances. There were little parties for bowling in the morning, and early walking, and Fanny was invited very often, but sometimes omitted, as if to indicate that she was not an essential part of the composition. There was music in the parlor before dinner, and working of purses and bags before the dressing-bell. There was the dinner itself, and the promenade, with music, afterward. Drives, then, and riding; the glowing return at sunset—the cheerful cup of tea—the reappearance, in delight-

ful toilet, for the evening dance—windows—balconies—piazzas
—moonlight!

Every time that Fanny, warm with the dance, declared that
she must have fresh air, and that was every time she danced
with Alfred, she withdrew, attended by him, to the cool, dim
piazza, and every time Mrs. Dinks beheld the departure. On
the cool, dim piazza the music sounded more faintly, the quiet
moonlight filled the air, and life seemed all romance and festival.

"How beautiful after the hot room!" Fanny said, one evening as they sat there.

"Yes, how beautiful!" replied Alfred.

"How happy I feel!" sighed Fanny. "Ever since I have
been here I have been so happy!"

"Have you been happy? So I have been happy too. How
very funny!" replied Alfred.

"Yes; but pleasant too. Sympathy is always pleasant."
And Fanny turned her large black eyes upon him, while the
young Dinks was perplexed by a singular feeling of happiness.

They were content to moralize upon sympathy for some
time. Alfred was fascinated, and a little afraid. Fanny moved
her Junonine shoulders, bent her swan-like neck, drew off one
glove and played with her rings, fanned herself gently at intervals, and, with just enough embarrassment not to frighten her
companion, opened and closed her fan.

"What a fine fellow Bowdoin Beacon is!" said Miss Fanny,
a little suddenly, and in a tone of suppressed admiration, as
she drew on her glove and laid her fan in her lap, as if on the
point of departure.

"Yes, he's a very good sort of fellow."

"How cold you men always are in speaking of each other!
I think him a splendid fellow. He's so handsome. He has
such glorious dark hair—almost as dark as yours, Mr. Dinks."

Alfred half raged, half smiled.

"Do you know," continued Fanny, looking down a little,
and speaking a little lower—"do you know if he has any particular favorites among the girls here?"

Alfred was dreadfully alarmed.

"If he has, how happy they must be! I think him a magnificent sort of man; but not precisely the kind I should think a girl would fall in love with. Should you?"

"No," replied Alfred, mollified and bewildered. He rallied in a moment. "What sort of man do girls fall in love with, Miss Fanny?"

Fanny Newt was perfectly silent. She looked down upon the floor of the piazza, fixing her eyes upon a pine-knot, patiently waiting, and wondering which way the grain of the wood ran.

The silence continued. Every moment Alfred was conscious of an increasing nervousness. There were the Junonine shoulders—the neck—the downcast eyes—moonlight—the softened music.

"Why don't you answer?" asked he, at length.

Fanny bent her head nearer to him, and dropped these words into his waistcoat:

"How good you are! I am so happy!"

"What on earth have I done?" was the perplexed, and pleased, and ridiculous reply.

"Mr. Dinks, how could I answer the question you asked without betraying—?"

"What?" inquired Alfred, earnestly.

"Without betraying what sort of man _I_ love," breathed Fanny, in the lowest possible tone, which could be also perfectly distinct, and with her head apparently upon the point of dropping after her words into his waistcoat.

"Well?" said Dinks.

"Well, I can not do that, but I will make a bargain with you. If you will say what sort of girl you would love, I will answer your question."

Fanny dreaded to hear a description of Hope Wayne. But Alfred's mind was resolved. The foolish youth answered with his heart in his mouth, and barely whispering,

"If you will look in your glass to-night, you will see."

AT SARATOGA.

The next moment Fanny's head had fallen into the waistcoat—Alfred Dinks's arms were embracing her. He perceived the perfume from her abundant hair. He was frightened, and excited, and pleased.

"Dear Alfred!"

"Dear Fanny!"

"Come Hope, dear, it is very late," said Mrs. Dinks in the

ball-room, alarmed at the long absence of Fanny and Alfred, and resolved to investigate the reason of it.

The lovers heard the voice, and were sitting quietly just a little apart, as Mrs. Dinks and her retinue came out.

"Aren't you afraid of taking cold, Miss Newt?" inquired Alfred's mother.

"Oh not at all, thank you, I am very warm. But you are very wise to go in, and I shall join you. Good-night, Mr. Dinks." As she rose, she whispered—"After breakfast."

The ladies rustled along the piazza in the moonlight. Alfred, flushed and nervous and happy, sauntered into the barroom, lit a cigar, and drank some brandy and water.

Meanwhile the Honorable Budlong Dinks sat in an armchair at the other end of the piazza with several other honorable gentlemen—Major Scuppernong from Carolina, Colonel le. Fay from Louisiana, Captain Lamb from Pennsylvania, General Arcularius Belch of New York, besides Captain Jones, General Smith, Major Brown, Colonel Johnson, from other States, and several honorable members of Congress, including, and chief of all, the Honorable B. J. Ele, a leading statesman from New York, with whom Mr. Dinks passed as much time as possible, and who was the chief oracle of the wise men in armchairs who came to the springs to drink the waters, to humor their wives and daughters in their foolish freaks for fashion and frivolity, and who smiled loftily upon the gay young people who amused themselves with setting up ten-pins and knocking them down, while the wise men devoted themselves to talking politics and showing each other, from day to day, the only way in which the country could be made great and glorious, and fulfill its destiny.

"I am not so clear about General Jackson's policy," said the Honorable Budlong Dinks, with the cautious wisdom of a statesman.

"Well, Sir, I am clear enough about it," replied Major Scuppernong. "It will ruin this country just as sure as that," and the Major with great dexterity directed a stream of saliva which fell with unerring precision upon the small stone in the gravel walk at which it was evidently aimed.

The Honorable Budlong Dinks watched the result of the illustration with deep interest, and shook his head gravely when he saw that the stone was thoroughly drenched by the salivary cascade. He seemed to feel the force of the argument. But he was not in a position to commit himself.

"Now, *I* think," said the Honorable B. J. Ele, "that it is the only thing that can save the country."

"Ah! you do," said the Honorable B. Dinks.

And so they kept it up, day after day, pausing in the intervals to smile at the ardor with which the women played their foolish game of gossip and match-making.

When Mrs. Dinks withdrew from her idle employments to the invigorating air of the Honorable B.'s society, he tapped her cheek sometimes with his finger—as he had read great men occasionally did when they were with their wives in moments of relaxation from intellectual toil—asked her what would become of the world if it were given up to women, and by his manner refreshed her consciousness of the honor under which she labored in being Mrs. Budlong Dinks.

The weaker vessel smiled consciously, as if he very well knew that was the one particular thing which under no conceivable circumstances could she forget.

"Budlong, I really think Alfred ought to keep a horse."

"My dear!" replied the Honorable B., in a tone of mingled reproach, amusement, contempt, and surprise.

"Oh! I know we can't afford it. But it would be so pleasant if he could drive out his cousin Hope, as so many of the other young men do. People get so well acquainted in that way. Have you observed that Bowdoin Beacon is a great deal with her? How glad Mrs. Beacon would be!" Mrs. Dinks took off her cap, and was unpinning her collar, without in the least pressing her request. Not at all. His word was enough. She had evidently yielded the point. The horse was out of the question.

Now the state of the country did not so entirely engross
her husband's mind, that he had not seen all the advantage of
Hope's marrying Alfred.

"It *is* a pleasant thing for a young man to have his own
horse. My dear, I will see what can be done," said he.

Then the diplomatist untied his cravat as if he had been un-
doing the parchment of a great treaty. He fell asleep in the
midst of rehearsing the speech which he meant to make upon
occasion of his presentation as foreign minister somewhere;
while his beloved partner lay by his side, and resolved that
Alfred Dinks must immediately secure Hope Wayne before
Fanny Newt secured Alfred Dinks.

CHAPTER XXII.

THE FINE ARTS.

THE whole world of Saratoga congratulated Mrs. Dinks
upon her beautiful niece, Miss Wayne. Even old Mrs. Dagon
said to every body:

"How lovely she is! And to think she comes from Boston! Where did she get her style? Fanny dear, I saw you
hugging — I beg your pardon, I mean waltzing with Mr.
Dinks."

But when Hope Wayne danced there seemed to be nobody
else moving. She filled the hall with grace, and the heart of
the spectator with an indefinable longing. She carried strings
of bouquets. She made men happy by asking them to hold
some of her flowers while she danced; and then, when she returned to take them, the gentlemen were steeped in such a
gush of sunny smiling that they stood bowing and grinning—
even the wisest—but felt as if the soft gush pushed them back
a little; for the beauty which allured them defended her like
a fiery halo.

It was understood that she was engaged to Mr. Alfred

Dinks, her cousin, who was already, or was to be, very rich. But there was apparently nothing very marked in his devotion.

"It is so much better taste for young people who are engaged not to make love in public," said Mrs. Dinks, as she sat in grand conclave of mammas and elderly ladies, who all understood her to mean her son and niece, and entirely agreed with her.

Meanwhile all the gentlemen who could find one of her moments disengaged were walking, bowling, driving, riding, chatting, sitting, with Miss Wayne. She smiled upon all, and sat apart in her smiling. Some foolish young fellows tried to flirt with her. When they had fully developed their intentions she smiled full in their faces, not insultingly nor familiarly, but with a soft superiority. The foolish young fellows went down to light their cigars and drink their brandy and water, feeling as if their faces had been rubbed upon an iceberg, for not less lofty and pure were their thoughts of her, and not less burning was their sense of her superb scorn.

But Arthur Merlin, the painter, who had come to pass a few days at Saratoga on his way to Lake George, and whose few days had expanded into the few weeks that Miss Wayne had been there—Arthur Merlin, the painter, whose eyes were accustomed not only to look, but to see, observed that Miss Wayne was constantly doing something. It was dance, drive, bowl, ride, walk incessantly. From the earliest hour to the latest she was in the midst of people and excitement. She gave herself scarcely time to sleep.

The painter was introduced to her, and became one of her habitual attendants. Every morning after breakfast Hope Wayne held a kind of court upon the piazza. All the young men surrounded her and worshipped.

Arthur Merlin was intelligent and ingenuous. His imagination gave a kind of airy grace to his conversation and manner. Passionately interested in his art, he deserted its pursuit a little only when the observation of life around him seemed to him a study as interesting. He and Miss Wayne were sometimes alone together; but although she was conscious of a peculiar sympathy with his tastes and character, she avoided him more than any of the other young men. Mrs. Dagon said it was a pity Miss Wayne was so cold and haughty to the poor painter. She thought that people might be taught their places without cruelty.

Arthur Merlin constantly said to himself in a friendly way that if he had been less in love with his art, or had not perceived that Miss Wayne had a continual reserved thought, he might have fallen in love with her. As it was, he liked her so much that he cared for the society of no other lady. He read Byron with her sometimes when they went in little parties to the lake, and somehow he and Hope found themselves alone under the trees in a secluded spot, and the book open in his hand.

He also read to her one day a poem upon a cloud, so beautiful that Hope Wayne's cheek flushed, and she asked, eagerly,

"Whose is that?"

"It is one of Shelley's, a friend of Byron's."

"But how different!"

"Yes, they were different men. Listen to this."

And the young man read the ode to a Sky-lark.

"How joyous it is!" said Hope; "but I feel the sadness."

"Yes, I often feel that in people as well as in poems," replied Arthur, looking at her closely.

She colored a little—said that it was warm—and rose to go.

The cold black eyes of Miss Fanny Newt suddenly glittered upon them.

"Will you go home with us, Miss Wayne?"

"Thank you, I am just coming;" and Hope passed into the wood.

When Arthur Merlin was left alone he quietly lighted a cigar, opened his port-folio and spread it before him, then sharpened a pencil and began to sketch. But while he looked at the

THE ARTIST IN A REVERIE.

tree before him, and mechanically transferred it to the paper,
he puffed and meditated.

He saw that Hope Wayne was constantly with other people, and yet he felt that she was a woman who would naturally like her own society. He also saw that there was no person then at Saratoga in whom she had such an interest that
she would prefer him to her own society.

And yet she was always seeking the distraction of other
people.

Puff—puff—puff.

Then there was something that made the society of her own
thoughts unpleasant—almost intolerable.

Mr. Arthur Merlin vigorously rubbed out with a piece of
stale bread a false line he had drawn.

What is that something—or some-bod-y?

He stopped sketching, and puffed for a long time.

As he returned at sunset Hope Wayne was standing upon
the piazza of the hotel.

"Have you been successful?" asked she, dawning upon him.

"You shall judge."

He showed her his sketch of a tree-stump.

"Good; but a little careless," she said.

"Do you draw, Miss Wayne?"

A curious light glimmered across her face, for she remembered where she had last heard those words. She shrank a
little, almost imperceptibly, as if her eyes had been suddenly
dazzled. Then a little more distantly—not much more, but
Arthur had remarked every thing—she said:

"Yes, I draw a little. Good-evening."

"Stop, please, Miss Wayne!" exclaimed Arthur, as ne saw
that she was going. She turned and smiled—a smile that
seemed to him like starlight, it was so clear and cool and
dim.

"I have drawn this for you, Miss Wayne."

She bent and took the sketch which he drew from his port-
folio.

"It is Manfred in the Coliseum," said he.

She glanced at it; but the smile faded entirely. Arthur
stared at her in astonishment as the blood slowly ebbed from
her cheeks, then streamed back again. The head of Manfred
was the head of Abel Newt. Hope Wayne looked from the
sketch to the artist, searching him with her eye to discover if
he knew what he was doing. Arthur was sincerely unconscious.

Hope Wayne dropped the paper almost involuntarily. It floated into the road.

"I beg your pardon, Mr. Merlin," said she, making a step to recover it.

He was before her, and handed it to her again.

"Thank you," said she, quietly, and went in.

It was still twilight, and Arthur lighted a cigar and sat down to a meditation. The result of it was clear enough.

"That head looks like somebody, and that somebody is Hope Wayne's secret." Puff—puff—puff.

"Where did I get that head?" He could not remember. "Tut!" cried he, suddenly bringing his chair down upon its legs with a force that knocked his cigar out of his mouth, "I copied it from a head which Jim Greenidge has, and which he says was one of his school-fellows."

Meanwhile Hope Wayne had carefully locked the door of her room. Then she hurriedly tore the sketch into the smallest possible pieces, laid them in her hand, opened the window, and whiffed them away into the dark.

CHAPTER XXIII.

BONIFACE NEWT, SON, AND CO., DRY GOODS ON COMMISSION.

ABEL NEWT smoked a great many cigars to enable him to see his position clearly.

When he told his mother that he could not accompany her to the Springs because he was about entering his father's counting-room, it was not so much because he was enamored of business as that his future relations with Hope were entirely doubtful, and he did not wish to complicate them by exposing himself to the chances of Saratoga.

"Business, of course, is the only career in this country, my son," said Boniface Newt. "What men want, and women too, is money. What is this city of New York? A combination of men and machines for making money. Every body respects a rich man. They may laugh at him behind his back. They may sneer at his ignorance and awkwardness, and all that sort of thing, but they respect his money. Now there's old Jacob Van Boozenberg. I say to you in strict confidence, my son, that there was never a greater fool than that man. He absolutely knows nothing at all. When he dies he will be no more missed in this world than an old dead stage-horse who is made into a manure heap. He is coarse, and vulgar, and mean. His daughter Kate married his clerk, young Tom Witchet—not a cent, you know, but five hundred dollars salary. 'Twas against the old man's will, and he shut his door, and his purse, and his heart. He turned Witchet away; told his daughter that she might lie in the bed she had made for herself; told Witchet that he was a rotten young swindler, and that, as he had married his daughter for her money, he'd be d—d if he wouldn't be up with him, and deuce of a cent should they get from him. They live I don't know where, nor how. Some of her old friends send her money—actually give five-dollar bills to old Jacob Van Boozenberg's daughter, somewhere over by the North River. Every body knows it, you know; but, for all that, we have to make bows to old Van B. Don't we want accommodations? Look here, Abel; if Jacob were not worth a million of dollars, he would be of less consequence than the old fellow who sells apples at the corner of his bank. But as it is, we all agree that he is a shrewd, sensible old fellow; rough in some of his ways—full of little prejudices—rather sharp; and as for Mrs. Tom Witchet, why, if girls will run away, and all that sort of thing, they must take the consequences, you know. Of course they must. Where should we be if every rich merchant's daughters were at the mercy of his clerks? I'm sorry for all this. It's sad, you know. It's positively melancholy. It troubles me. Ah, yes! where was I? Oh, I was saying that money is the respectable thing. And mark, Abel, if this were the Millennium, things would be very different. But it isn't the Millennium. It's give one and take two, if you can get it. That's what it is here; and let him who wants to, kick against the pricks."

Abel hung his legs over the arms of the office-chairs in the counting-room, and listened gravely.

"I don't suppose, Sir, that 'tis money *as* money that is worth having. It is only money as the representative of intelligence and refinement, of books, pictures, society—as a vast influence and means of charity; is it not, Sir?"

Upon which Mr. Abel Newt blew a prodigious cloud of smoke.

Mr. Boniface Newt responded, "Oh fiddle! that's all very fine. But my answer to that is Jacob Van Boozenberg."

"Bless my soul! here he comes. Abel, put your legs down! throw that cigar away!"

The great man came in. His clothes were snuffy and baggy —so was his face.

"Good-mornin', Mr. Newt. Beautiful mornin'. I sez to ma this mornin', ma, sez I, I should like to go to the country to-day, sez I. Go 'long, pa! sez she. Werry well, sez I, I'll go 'long if you'll go too. Ma she laughed; she know'd I wasn't in earnest. She know'd 'twasn't only a joke."

Mr. Van Boozenberg drew out a large red bandana hand-kerchief, and blew his nose as if it had been a trumpet sounding a charge.

Messrs. Newt & Son smiled sympathetically. The junior partner observed, cheerfully,

"Yes, Sir."

The millionaire stared at the young man.

"Ma's going to Saratogy," remarked Mr. Van Boozenberg. "She said she wanted to go. Werry well, sez I, ma, go."

Messrs. Newt & Son smiled deferentially, and hoped Mrs. Van B. would enjoy herself.

"No, I ain't no fear of that," replied the millionaire.

"Mr. Van Boozenberg," said Boniface Newt, half-hesitating-ly, "you were very kind to undertake that little favor—I— I—"

OUR NEW PARTNER.

"Oh! yes, I come in to say I done that as you wanted.   It's all right."

"And, Mr. Van Boozenberg, I am pleased to introduce to you my son Abel, who has just entered the house."

Abel rose and bowed.

"Have you been in the store?" asked the old gentleman.

"No, Sir, I've been at school."

"What! to school till now? Why, you must be twenty years old!" exclaimed Mr. Van Boozenberg, in great surprise.

"Yes, Sir, in my twentieth year."

"Why, Mr. Newt," said Mr. Van B., with the air of a man who is in entire perplexity, "what on earth has your boy been doing at school until now?"

"It was his grandfather's will, Sir," replied Boniface Newt.

"Well, well, a great pity! a werry great pity! Ma wanted one of our boys to go to college. Ma, sez I, what on earth should Corlaer go to college for? To get learnin', pa, sez ma. To get learnin'! sez I. I'll get him learnin', sez I, down to the store. Werry well, sez ma. Werry well, sez I, and so 'twas; and I think I done a good thing by him."

Mr. Van Boozenberg talked at much greater length of his general intercourse with ma. Mr. Boniface Newt regarded him more and more contemptuously.

But the familiar style of the old gentleman's conversation begot a corresponding familiarity upon the part of Mr. Newt. Mr. Van Boozenberg learned incidentally that Abel had never been in business before. He observed the fresh odor of cigars in the counting-room—he remarked the extreme elegance of Abel's attire, and the inferential tailor's bills. He learned that Mrs. Newt and the family were enjoying themselves at Saratoga. He derived from the conversation and his observation that there were very large family expenses to be met by Boniface Newt.

Meanwhile that gentleman had continually no other idea of his visitor than that he was insufferable. He had confessed to Abel that the old man was shrewd. His shrewdness was a proverb. But he is a dull, ignorant, ungrammatical, and ridiculous old ass for all that, thought Boniface Newt; and the said ass sitting in Boniface Newt's counting-room, and amusing and fatiguing Messrs. Newt & Son with his sez I's, and sez shes, and his mas, and his done its, was quietly making up his mind that the house of Newt & Son had received no accession of capital or strength by the entrance of the elegant Abel into a share of its active management, and that some slight whispers which he had heard remotely affecting the standing of the house must be remembered.

"A werry pretty store you have here, Mr. Newt. Find Pearl Street as good as Beaver?"

"Oh yes, Sir," replied Boniface Newt, bowing and rubbing his hands. "Call again, Sir; it's a rare pleasure to see you here, Mr. Van Boozenberg."

"Well, you know, ma, sez she, now pa you mustn't sit in draughts. It's so sort of draughty down town in your horrid offices, pa, sez she—sez ma, you know—that I'm awful 'fraid you'll catch your death, sez she, and I must mind ma, you know. Good-mornin', Mr. Newt, a werry good-mornin', Sir," said the old gentleman, as he stepped out.

"Do you have much of that sort of thing to undergo in business, father?" asked Abel, when Jacob Van Boozenberg had gone.

"My dear son," replied the older Mr. Newt, "the world is made up of fools, bores, and knaves. Some of them speak good grammar and use white cambric pocket-handkerchiefs, some do not. It's dreadful, I know, and I am rather tired of a world where you are busy driving donkeys with a chance of their presently driving you."

Mr. Boniface Newt shook his foot pettishly.

"Father," said Abel.

"Well."

"Which is Uncle Lawrence—a fool, a bore, or a knave?"

Mr. Boniface Newt's foot stopped, and, after looking at his son for a few moments, he answered:

"Abel, your Uncle Lawrence is a singular man. He's a sort of exception to general rules. I don't understand him, and he doesn't help me to. When he was a boy he went to India and lived there several years. He came home once and staid a little while, and then went back again, although I believe he was rich. It was mysterious, I never could quite understand it—though, of course, I believe there was some woman in it. Neither your mother nor I could ever find out much about it. By-and-by he came home again, and has been in business here ever since. He's a bachelor, you know, and his business is different from mine, and he has queer friends and tastes, so that I don't often see him except when he comes to the house, and that isn't very often."

"He's rich, isn't he?" asked Abel.

"Yes, he's very rich, and that's the curious part of it," answered his father, "and he gives away a great deal of money in what seems to me a very foolish way. He's a kind of dreamer—an impracticable man. He pays lots of poor people's rents, and I try to show him that he is merely encouraging idleness and crime. But I can't make him see it. He declares that, if a sewing-girl makes but two dollars a week and has a helpless mother and three small sisters to support besides rent and fuel, and so on, it's not encouraging idleness to help her with the rent. Well, I suppose it *is* hard sometimes with some of those people. But you've no right to go by particular cases in these matters. You ought to go by the general rule, as I constantly tell him. ' Yes,' says he, in that smiling way of his which does put me almost beside myself, 'yes, you shall go by the general rule, and let people starve; and I'll go by particular cases, and feed 'em.' Then he is just as rich as if he were an old flint like Van Boozenberg. Well, it is the funniest, foggiest sort of world. I swear I don't see into it at all—I give it all up. I only know one thing; that it's first in first win. And that's extremely sad, too, you know. Yes, very sad! Where was I? Ah yes! that we are all dirty scoundrels."

Abel had relighted his cigar, after Mr. Van Boozenberg's departure, and filled the office with smoke until the atmosphere resembled the fog in which his father seemed to be floundering.

"Abel, merchants ought not to smoke cigars in their counting-rooms," said his father, in a half-pettish way.

"No, I suppose not," replied Abel, lightly; "they ought to

smoke other people. But tell me, father, do you know nothing about the woman that you say was mixed up with Uncle Lawrence's affairs?"

"Nothing at all."

"Not even her name?"

"Not a syllable."

"Pathetic and mysterious," rejoined Abel; "a case of unhappy love, I suppose."

"If it is so," said Mr. Newt, "your Uncle Lawrence is the happiest miserable man I ever knew."

"Well, there's a difference among men, you know, father. Some wear their miseries like an order in their button-holes. Some do as the Spartan boy did when the wolf bit him."

"How'd the Spartan boy do?" asked Mr. Newt.

"He covered it up, laughed, and dropped dead."

"Gracious!" said Mr. Boniface Newt.

"Or like Boccaccio's basil-pot," continued Abel, calmly; pouring forth smoke, while his befogged papa inquired,

"What on earth do you mean by Boccaccio's basil-pot?"

"Why, a girl's lover had his head cut off, and she put it in a flower-pot, and covered it up that way, and instead of laughing herself, set flowers to blooming over it."

"Goodness me, Abel, what are you talking about?"

"Of Love, the canker-worm, Sir," replied Abel, imperturbable, and emitting smoke.

It was evidently not the busy season in the Dry-goods Commission House of Boniface Newt & Son.

When Mr. Van Boozenberg went home to dinner, he said:

"Ma, you'd better improve this werry pleasant weather and start for Saratogy as soon as you can. Mr. Boniface Newt tells me his wife and family is there, and you'll find them werry pleasant folks. I jes' want you to write me all about 'em. You see, ma, one of our directors to-day sez to me, after board, sez he, 'The Boniface Newts is a going it slap-dash up to Saratogy.' I laughed, and sez I, 'Why shouldn't they? but I don't believe they be,' sez I. Sez he, 'I'll bet you a new

THE SWEET RESTORER.

shawl for your wife they be,' sez he. Sez I, 'Done.' So you
see ma, if so be they be, werry well. A new shawl for some
folks, you know; only jes' write me all about it."

Ma was not reluctant to depart at the earliest possible moment. Her son Corlaer, whose education had been intercepted
by his father, was of opinion, when he heard that the Newts
were at Saratoga, that his health imperatively required Congress water. But papa had other views.

"Corlaer, I wish you would make the acquaintance of young
Mr. Newt. I done it to-day. He is a well-edicated young

man; I shall ask him to dinner next Sunday. Don't be out of the way."

Jacob Van Boozenberg having dined, arose from the table, seated himself in a spacious easy-chair, and drawing forth the enormous red bandana, spread it over his head and face, and after a few muscular twitches, and a violent nodding of the head, which caused the drapery to fall off several times, finally propped the refractory head against the back of the chair, and bobbing and twitching no longer, dropped off into temporary oblivion.

CHAPTER XXIV.

"QUEEN AND HUNTRESS."

HOPE WAYNE leaned out of the window from which she had just scattered the fragments of the drawing Arthur Merlin had given her. The night was soft and calm, and trees, not far away, entirely vailed her from observation.

She thought how different this window was from that other one at home, also shaded by the trees; and what a different girl it was who looked from it. She recalled that romantic, musing, solitary girl of Pinewood, who lived alone with a silent, grave old nurse, and the quiet years that passed there like the shadows and sunlight over the lawn. She remembered the dark, handsome face that seemed to belong to the passionate poems that girl had read, and the wild dreams she had dreamed in the still, old garden. In the hush of the summer twilight she heard again the rich voice that seemed to that other girl of Pinewood sweeter than the music of the verses, and felt the penetrating glance that had thrilled the heart of that girl until her red cheek was pale.

How well for that girl that the lips which made the music had never whispered love! Because—because—

Hope raised herself from lightly leaning on the window-sill

as the thought flashed in her mind, and she stood erect, as if
straightened by a sudden, sharp, almost insupportable pain—
"because," she went on saying in her mind, "had they done
so, that other romantic, solitary girl at Pinewood"—dear child!
Hope's heart trembled for her—"might have confessed that
she loved!"

Hope Wayne clenched her hands, and, all alone in her dim
room, flushed, and then turned pale, and a kind of cold splendor settled on her face, so that if Arthur Merlin could have
seen her he would have called her Diana.

During the moment in which she thought these things—for
it was scarcely more—the little white bits of paper floated and
fell beneath her. She watched them as they disappeared, conscious of them, but not thinking of them. They looked like
rose-leaves, they were so pure; and how silently they sank
into the darkness below!

And if she had confessed she loved, thought Hope, how
would it be with that girl now? Might she not be standing
in the twilight, watching her young hopes scattered like rose-
leaves and disappearing in the dark?

She clasped her hands before her, and walked gently up and
down the room. The full moon was rising, and the tender,
tranquil light streamed through the trees into her chamber.

But, she thought, since she did not—since the young girl
dreamed, perhaps only for a moment, perhaps so very vaguely,
of what might have been—she has given nothing, she has lost
nothing. There was a pleasant day which she remembers, far
back in her childhood—oh! so pleasant! oh! so sunny, and
flowery, and serene! A pleasant day, when something came
that never comes—that never can come—but once.

She stopped by the window, and looked out to see if she
could yet discover any signs of the scattered paper. She
strained her eyes down toward the ground. But it was entirely dark there. All the light was above—all the light was
peaceful and melancholy, from the moon.

She laid her face in that moonlight upon the window-sill,

and covered it with her hands. The low wind shook the leaves, and the trees rustled softly as if they whispered to her. She heard them in her heart. She knew what they were saying. They sang to her of that other girl and her wishes, and struggles and prayers.

Then came the fierce, passionate, profuse weeping — the spring freshet of a woman's soul.

—She heard a low knock at the door. She remained perfectly silent. Another knock. Still she did not move.

The door was tried.

Hope Wayne raised her head, but said nothing.

There was a louder knock, and the voice of Fanny Newt:

"Miss Wayne, are you asleep? Please let me in."

It was useless to resist longer. Hope Wayne opened the door, and Fanny Newt entered. Hope sat down with her back to the window.

"I heard you come in," said Fanny, "and I did not hear you go out; so I knew you were still here. But I was afraid you would oversleep yourself, and miss the ball."

Hope replied that she had not been sleeping.

"Not sleeping, but sitting in the moonlight, all alone?" said Fanny. "How romantic!"

"Is it?"

"Yes, of course it is! Why, Mr. Dinks and I are romantic every evening. He *will* come and sit in the moonlight, and listen to the music. What an agreeable fellow he is!" And Fanny tried to see Hope's face, which was entirely hidden.

"He is my cousin, you know," replied Hope.

"Oh yes, we all know that; and a dangerous relationship it is too," said Fanny.

"How dangerous?"

"Why, cousins are such privileged people. They have all the intimacy of brothers, without the brotherly right of abusing us. In fact, a cousin is naturally half-way between a brother and a lover."

"Having neither brother nor lover," said Hope, quietly, "I stop half-way with the cousin."

Fanny laughed her cold little laugh. "And you mean to go on the other half, I suppose?" said she.

"Why do you suppose so?" asked Hope.

"It is generally understood, I believe," said Fanny, "that Mr. Alfred Dinks will soon lead to the hymeneal altar his beautiful and accomplished cousin, Miss Hope Wayne. At least, for further information inquire of Mrs. Budlong Dinks." And Fanny laughed again.

"I was not aware of the honor that awaited me," replied Hope.

"Oh no! of course not. The family reasons, I suppose—"

"My mind is as much in the dark as my body," said Hope. "I really do not see the point of the joke."

"Still you don't seem very much surprised at it."

"Why should I be? Every girl is at the mercy of tattlers."

"Exactly," said Fanny. "They've had me engaged to I don't know how many people. I suppose they'll doom Alfred Dinks to me next. You won't be jealous, will you?"

"No," said Hope, "I'll congratulate him."

Fanny Newt could not see Hope Wayne's face, and her voice betrayed nothing. She, in fact, knew no more than when she came in.

"Good-by, dear, *à ce soir!*" said she, as she sailed out of the room.

Hope lingered for some time at the window. Then she rang for candles, and sat down to write a letter.

CHAPTER XXV.

A STATESMAN—AND STATESWOMAN.

In the same twilight Mrs. Dinks and Alfred sat together in her room.

"Alfred, my dear, I see that Bowdoin Beacon drives out your Cousin Hope a good deal."

Mrs. Dinks arranged her cap-ribbon as if she were at present mainly interested in that portion of her dress.

"Yes, a good deal," replied Mr. Alfred, in an uncertain tone, for he always felt uncomfortably at the prospect of a conversation with his mother.

"I am surprised he should do so," continued Mrs. Dinks, with extraordinary languor, as if she should undoubtedly fall fast asleep before the present interview terminated. And yet she was fully awake.

"Why shouldn't he drive her out if he wants to?" inquired Alfred.

"Now, Alfred, be careful. Don't expose yourself even to me. It is too hot to be so absurd. I suppose there is some sort of honor left among young men still, isn't there?"

And the languid mamma performed a very well-executed yawn.

"Honor? I suppose there is. What do you mean?" replied Alfred.

Mamma yawned again.

"How drowsy one does feel here! I am so sleepy! What was I saying? Oh I remember. Perhaps, however, Mr. Beacon doesn't know. That is probably the reason. He doesn't know. Well, in that case it is not so extraordinary. But I should think he must have seen, or inferred, or heard. A man may be very stupid; but he has no right to be so stupid as that. How many glasses do you drink at the spring in the morning, Alfred? Not more than six at the outside, I hope. Well, I believe I'll take a little nap."

She played with her cap string, somehow as if she were an angler playing a fish. There is capital trouting at Saratoga—or was, thirty years ago. You may see to this day a good many fish that were caught there, and with every kind of line and bait.

Alfred bit again.

"I wish you wouldn't talk in such a puzzling kind of way, mother. What do you mean about his knowing, and hearing, and inferring?"

"Come, come, Alfred, you are getting too cunning. Why, you sly dog, do you think you can impose upon me with an air of ignorance because I am so sleepy. Heigh-ho."

Another successful yawn. Sportsmen are surely the best sport in the world.

"Now, Alfred," continued his mother, "are you so silly as to suppose for one moment that Bowdoin Beacon has not seen the whole thing and known it from the beginning?"

"Why," exclaimed Alfred, in alarm, "do you?"

"Of course. He has eyes and ears, I suppose, and every body understood it."

"Did they?" asked Alfred, bewildered and wretched; "I didn't know it."

"Of course. Every body knew it must be so, and agreed that it was highly proper—in fact the only thing."

"Oh, certainly. Clearly the only thing," replied Alfred, wondering whether his mother and he meant the same thing.

"And therefore I say it is not quite honorable in Beacon to drive her out in such a marked manner. And I may as well say at once that I think you had better settle the thing immediately. The world understands it already, so it will be a mere private understanding among ourselves, much more agreeable for all parties. Perhaps this evening even—hey, Alfred?"

Mrs. Dinks adjusted herself upon the sofa in a sort of final manner, as if the affair were now satisfactorily arranged.

"It's no use talking that way, mother; it's all done."

Mrs. Dinks appeared sleepy no longer. She bounced like an India-rubber ball. Even the cap-ribbons were left to shift for themselves. She turned and clasped Alfred in her arms.

"My blessed son!"

Then followed a moment of silent rapture, during which she moistened his shirt-collar with maternal tears.

"Alfred," whispered she, "are you really engaged?"

"Yes'm."

She squeezed him as if he were a bag of the million dollars of which she felt herself to be henceforth mistress.

"You dear, good boy! Then you *are* sly after all!"

"Yes'm, I'm afraid I am," rejoined Alfred very uncomfortably, and with an extremely ridiculous and nervous impression that his mother was congratulating him upon something she knew nothing about.

"Dear, *dear*, DEAR boy!" said Mrs. Dinks, with a crescendo affection and triumph. While she was yet embracing him, his father, the unemployed statesman, the Honorable Budlong Dinks, entered.

To the infinite surprise of that gentleman, his wife rose, came to him, put her arm affectionately in his, and leaning her head upon his shoulder, whispered exultingly, and not very softly,

"It's done without the wagon. Our dear boy has justified our fondest hopes, Budlong."

The statesman slipped his shoulder from under her head. If there were one thing of which he was profoundly persuaded it was that a really great man—a man to whom important public functions may be properly intrusted—must, under no circumstances, be wheedled by his wife. He must gently, but firmly, teach her her proper sphere. She must *not* attempt to bribe that judgment to which the country naturally looks in moments of difficulty.

Having restored his wife to an upright position, the honorable gentleman looked upon her with distinguished consideration; and, playing with the seals that hung at the end of his

IO TRIUMPHE.

watch-ribbon, asked her, with the most protective kindness in the world, what she was talking about.

She laid her cap-ribbons properly upon her shoulder, smooth-ed her dress, and began to fan herself in a kind of complacent triumph, as she answered,

"Alfred is engaged as we wished."

The honorable gentleman beamed approval with as much

G

cordiality as statesmen who are also fathers of private families, as well as of the public, ought to indulge toward their children. Shaking the hand of his son as if his shoulder wanted oiling, he said,

"Marriage is a most important relation. Young men can not be too cautious in regard to it. It is not an affair of the feelings merely; but common sense dictates that when new relations are likely to arise, suitable provision should be made. Hence every well-regulated person considers the matter from a pecuniary point of view. The pecuniary point of view is indispensable. We can do without sentiment in this world, for sentiment is a luxury. We can not dispense with money, because money is a necessity. It gives me, therefore, great pleasure to hear that the choice of my son has evinced the good sense which, I may say without affectation, I hope he has inherited, and has justified the pains and expense which I have been at in his education. My son, I congratulate you. Mrs. Dinks, I congratulate you."

The honorable gentleman thereupon shook hands with his wife and son, as if he were congratulating them upon having such an eloquent and dignified husband and father, and then blew his nose gravely and loudly. Having restored his handkerchief, he smiled in general, as it were—as if he hung out signals of amity with all mankind upon condition of good behavior on their part.

Poor Alfred was more speechless than ever. He felt very warm and red, and began to surmise that to be engaged was not necessarily to be free from carking care. He was sorely puzzled to know how to break the real news to his parents:

"Oh! dear me," thought Alfred; "oh! dear me, I wonder if Fanny wouldn't do it. I guess I'd better ask her. I wonder if Hope would have had me! Oh! dear me. I wonder if old Newt is rich. How'd I happen to do it? Oh! dear me."

He felt very much depressed indeed.

"Well, mother, I'm going down," said he.

" My dear, dear son ! Kiss me, Alfred," replied his mother.
He stooped and kissed her cheek.

" How happy we shall all be !" murmured she.

" Oh, very, very happy !" answered Alfred, as he opened
the door.

But as he closed it behind him, the best billiard-player at
the Trimountain billiard-rooms said, ruefully, in his heart,
while he went to his beloved,

" Oh! dear me ! Oh!—dear—me ! How'd I happen to do
it ?"

Fanny Newt, of course, had heard from Alfred of the interview with his mother on the same evening, as they sat in Mrs.
Newt's parlor before going into the ball. Fanny was arrayed
in a charming evening costume. It was low about the neck,
which, except that it was very white, descended like a hard,
round beach from the low shrubbery of her back hair to the
shore of the dress. It was very low tide; but there was a
gentle ripple of laces and ribbons that marked the line of divi-
sion. Mr. Alfred Dinks had taken a little refreshment since
the conversation with his mother, and felt at the moment quite
equal to any emergency.

" The fact is, Fanny dear," said he, " that mother has al-
ways insisted that I should marry Hope Wayne. Now Hope
Wayne is a very pretty girl, a deuced pretty girl; but, by
George! she's not the only girl in the world—hey, Fanny ?"

At this point Mr. Dinks made free with the lips of Miss
Newt.

" Pah! Alfred, my dear, you have been drinking wine," said
she, moving gently away from him.

" Of course I have, darling; haven't I dined ?" replied Alfred, renewing the endearment.

Now Fanny's costume was too careful, her hair too elabo-
rately arranged, to withstand successfully these osculatory on-
sets.

" Alfred, dear, we may as well understand these little matters at once," said she.

"What little matters, darling?" inquired Mr. Dinks, with interest. He was unwontedly animated, but, as he explained —he had dined.

"Why, this kissing business."

"You dear!" cried Alfred, impetuously committing a fresh breach of the peace.

"Stop, Alfred," said Fanny, imperiously. "I won't have this. I mean," said she, in a mollified tone, remembering that she was only engaged, not married—"I mean that you tumble me dreadfully. Now, dear, I'll make a little rule. You know you don't want your Fanny to look mussed up, do you, dear?" and she touched his cheek with the tip of one finger. Dinks shook his head negatively. "Well, then, you shall only kiss me when I am in my morning-dress, and one kiss, with hands off, when we say good-night."

She smiled a little cold, hard, black smile, smoothing her rumpled feathers, and darting glances at herself in the large mirror opposite, as if she considered her terms the most reasonable in the world.

"It seems to me very little," said Alfred Dinks, discontentedly; "besides, you always look best when you are dressed."

"Thank you, love," returned Fanny; "just remember the morning-dress, please, for I shall; and now tell me all about your conversation with your mother."

Alfred told the story. Fanny listened with alarm. She had watched Mrs. Dinks closely during the whole summer, and she was sure—for Fanny knew herself thoroughly, and reasoned accordingly—that the lady would stop at nothing in the pursuit of her object.

"What a selfish woman it is!" thought Fanny. "Not content with Alfred's share of the inheritance, she wants to bring the whole Burt fortune into her family. How insatiable some people are!"

"Alfred, has your mother seen Hope since she talked with you?"

"I'm sure I don't know."

" Why didn't you warn her not to ?"

" I didn't think of it."

" But why didn't you think of it ? If you'd only have put
her off, we could have got time," said Fanny, a little pettishly.

" Got time for what ?" asked Alfred, blankly.

" Alfred," said Fanny, coaxing herself to speak gently,
" I'm afraid you will be trying, dear. I am very much afraid
of it."

The lover looked doubtful and alarmed.

" Don't look like a fool, Alfred, for Heaven's sake!" cried
Fanny ; but she immediately recovered herself, and said, with
a smile, " You see, dear, how I can scold if I want to. But
you'll never let me, I know."

Mr. Dinks hoped certainly that he never should. " But I
sha'n't be a very hard husband, Fanny. I shall let you do
pretty much as you want to."

" Dearest, I know you will," rejoined his charmer. " But
the thing is now to know whether your mother has seen
Hope Wayne."

" I'll go and ask her," said Alfred, rising.

" My dear fellow," replied Fanny, with her mouth screwed
into a semblance of smiling, " you'll drive me distracted. I
must insist on common sense. It is too delicate a question
for you to ask."

Mr. Dinks grinned and look bewildered. Then he assumed
a very serious expression.

" It doesn't seem to me to be hard to ask my mother if she
has seen my cousin."

" Pooh! you silly—I mean, my precious darling, your mother's too smart for you. She'd have every thing out of you in
a twinkling."

" I suppose she would," said Alfred, meekly.

Fanny Newt wagged her foot very rapidly, and looked fixedly upon the floor. Alfred gazed at her admiringly—thought
what a splendid Mrs. Alfred Dinks he had secured, and smacked his lips as if he were tasting her. He kissed his hand to her

as he sat. He kissed the air toward her. He might as well have blown kisses to the brown spire of Trinity Church.

"Alfred, you must solemnly promise me one thing," she said, at length.

"Sweet," said Alfred, who began to feel that he had dined very much, indeed—"sweet, come here!"

Fanny flushed and wrinkled her brow. Mr. Dinks was frightened.

"Oh no, dear—no, not at all," said he.

"My love," said she, in a voice as calm but as black as her eyes, "do you promise or not? That's all."

Poor Dinks! He said Yes, in a feeble way, and hoped she wouldn't be angry. Indeed—indeed, he didn't know how much he had been drinking. But the fellers kept ordering wine, and he had to drink on; and, oh! dear, he wouldn't do so again if Fanny would only forgive him. Dear, dear Fanny, please to forgive a miserable feller! And Miss Newt's betrothed sobbed, and wept, and half writhed on the sofa in maudlin woe.

Fanny stood erect, patting the floor with her foot and looking at this spectacle. She thought she had counted the cost. But the price seemed at this instant a little high. Twenty-two years old now, and if she lived to be only seventy, then forty-eight years of Alfred Dinks! It was a very large sum, indeed. But Fanny bethought her of the balm in Gilead. Forty-eight years of married life was very different from an engagement of that period. *Courage, ma chère!*

"Alfred," said she, at length, "listen to me. Go to your mother before she goes to bed to-night, and say to her that there are reasons why she must not speak of your engagement to any body, not even to Hope Wayne. And if she begins to pump you, tell her that it is the especial request of the lady— whom you may call 'she,' you needn't say Hope—that no question of any kind shall be asked, or the engagement may be broken. Do you understand, dear?"

Fanny leaned toward him coaxingly as she asked the question.

"Oh yes, I understand," replied Alfred.

" And you'll do just as Fanny says, won't you, dear ?" said she, even more caressingly.

" Yes, I will, I promise," answered Alfred.

" You may kiss me, dear," said Fanny, leaning toward him, so that the operation need not disarrange her toilet.

Alfred Dinks kept his word ; and his mother was perfectly willing to do as she was asked. She smiled with intelligence whenever she saw her son and his cousin together, and remarked that Hope Wayne's demeanor did not in the least betray the engagement. And she smiled with the same intelligence when she remarked how devoted Alfred was to Fanny Newt.

" Can it possibly be that Alfred knows so much ?" she asked herself, wondering at the long time during which her son's cunning had lain dormant.

CHAPTER XXVI.

THE PORTRAIT AND THE MINIATURE.

THE golden days of September glimmered through the dark sighing trees, and relieved the white brightness that had burned upon the hills during the dog-days. Mr. Burt drove into town and drove out. Dr. Peewee called at short intervals, played backgammon with his parishioner, listened to his stories, told stories of his own, and joined him in his little excursions to the West Indies. Mrs. Simcoe was entirely alone.

One day Hiram brought her a letter, which she took to her own room and sat down by the window to read.

" SARATOGA.

" DEAR AUNTY,—We're about going away, and we have been so gay that you would suppose I had had ' society' enough. Do you remember our talk ? There have been a great many people here from every part of the country ; and it has been nothing but bowling, walking, riding, dancing, dining at the lake, and listening to music in the moonlight, all the time. Aunt Dinks has been very kind, but although I have met a great many people I have not made many friends. I have seen nobody whom I like as much as Amy Waring or Mr. Lawrence Newt, of whom I wrote you from New York, and they have neither of them been here. I think of Pinewood a great deal, but it seems to me long and long ago that I used to live there. It is strange how much older and different I feel. But I never forget you, dearest Aunty, and I should like this very moment to stand by your side at your window as I used to, and look out at the hills, or, better still, to lie in your lap or on my bed, and hear you sing one of the dear old hymns. I thought I had forgotten them until lately. But I remember them very often now. I think of Pinewood a great deal, and I love you dearly; and yet somehow I do not feel as if I cared to go back there to live. Isn't that strange? Give my love to Grandpa, and tell him I am neither engaged to a foreign minister, nor a New York merchant, nor a Southern planter—nor to any body else. But he must keep up heart, for there's plenty of time yet. Good-by, dear Aunty. I seem to hear you singing,

'Oh that I now the rest might know!'

Do you know how often you used to sing that? Good-by.

"Your affectionate   HOPE."

Mrs. Simcoe held the letter in her hand for a long time, looking, as usual, out of the window.

Presently she rose and went to a bureau, and unlocked a drawer with a key that she carried in her pocket. Taking out an ebony box like a casket, she unlocked that in turn, and then lifted from it a morocco case, evidently a miniature. She returned to her chair and seated herself again, swaying her body gently to and fro as if confirming some difficult resolution, but with the same inscrutable expression upon her face. Still ho'ling the case in her hands unopened, she murmured:

"I want a sober mind,
    A self-renouncing will,
That tramples down and casts behind
    The baits of pleasing ill."

She repeated the whole hymn several times, as if it were a kind of spell or incantation, and while she was yet saying it she opened the miniature.

The western light streamed over the likeness of a man of a gallant, graceful air, in whom the fires of youth were not yet burned out, and in whose presence there might be some peculiar fascination. The hair was rather long and fair—the features were handsomely moulded, but wore a slightly jaded expression, which often seems to a woman an air of melancholy, but which a man would have recognized at once as the result of dissipation. There was a singular cast in the eye, and a kind of lofty, irresistible command in the whole aspect, which appeared to be quite as much an assumption of manner as a real superiority. In fact it was the likeness of what is technically called a man of the world, whose frank insolence and symmetry of feature pass for manly beauty and composure.

The miniature was in the face of a gold locket, on the back of which there was a curl of the same fair hair. It was so fresh and glossy that it might have been cut off the day before. But the quaintness of the setting and the costume of the portrait showed that it had been taken many years previous, and that in the order of nature the original was probably dead.

As Mrs. Simcoe held the miniature in both hands and looked at it, her body still rocked over it, and her lips still murmured.

Then rocking and murmuring stopped together, and she seemed like one listening to music or the ringing of distant bells.

And as she sat perfectly still in the golden September sunshine, it was as if it had shone into her soul; so that a softer light streamed into her eyes, and the hard inscrutability of her face melted as by some internal warmth, and a tender rejuvenescence somehow blossomed out upon her cheeks until all the sweetness became sadness, and heavy tears dropped from her eyes upon the picture.

Then, with the old harshness stealing into her face again, she rose calmly, carrying the miniature in her hand, and went out of the room, and down the stairs into the library, which was opposite the parlor in which Abel Newt had seen the picture of old Grandpa Burt at the age of ten, holding a hoop and book.

There were book-shelves upon every side but one—stately ranges of well-ordered books in substantial old calf and gilt English bindings, and so carefully placed upon the shelves, in such methodical distribution of shapes and sizes, that the whole room had an air of preternatural propriety utterly foreign to a library. It seemed the most select and aristocratic society of books—much too fine to permit the excitement of interest in any thing they contained—much too high-bred to be of the slightest use in imparting information. Glass doors were carefully closed over them and locked, as if the books were beatified and laid away in shrines. And the same solemn order extended to the library table, which was precisely in the middle of the room, with a large, solemn family Bible precisely in the middle of the table, and smaller books, like satellites, precisely upon the corners, and precisely on one side an empty glass inkstand, innocent of ink spot or stain of any kind, with a pen carefully mended and evidently carefully never used, and an exemplary pen-wiper, which was as unsullied as might be expected of a wiper which had only wiped that pen which was never dipped into that inkstand which had been always empty. The inkstand was supported on the other side of the Bible by an equally immaculate ivory paper-knife.

The large leather library chairs were arranged in precisely the proper angle at the corners of the table, and the smaller chairs stood under the windows two by two. All was cold and clean, and locked up—all—except a portrait that hung against the wall, and below which Mrs. Simcoe stopped, still holding the miniature in her hand.

It was the likeness of a lovely girl, whose rich, delicate loveliness, full of tender but tremulous character, seemed to be a kind of foreshadowing of Hope Wayne. The eyes were of a deep, soft darkness, that held the spectator with a dreamy fascination. The other features were exquisitely moulded, and suffused with an airy, girlish grace, so innocent that the look became almost a pathetic appeal against the inevitable griefs of life.

As Mrs. Simcoe stood looking at it and at the miniature she held, the sadness which had followed the sweetness died away, and her face resumed the old rigid inscrutability. She held the miniature straight before her, and directly under the portrait; and, as she looked, the apparent pride of the one and the tremulous earnestness of the other indescribably blended into an expression which had been long familiar to her, for it was the look of Hope Wayne.

While she thus stood, unconscious of the time that passed, the sun had set and the room was darkening. Suddenly she heard a sound close at her side, and started. Her hand instinctively closed over the miniature and concealed it.

There stood a man kindly regarding her. He was not an old man, but there was a touch of quaintness in his appearance. He did not speak when she saw him, and for several minutes they stood silent together. Then their eyes rose simultaneously to the picture, met again, and Mrs. Simcoe, putting out her hand, said, in a low voice,

"Lawrence Newt!"

He shook her hand warmly, and made little remarks, while she seemed to be studying into his face, as if she were looking for something she did not find there. Every body did it. Every body looked into Lawrence Newt's face to discover what he was thinking of, and nobody ever saw. Mrs. Simcoe remembered a time when she had seen.

"It is more than twenty years since I saw you. Have I grown very old?" asked he.

"No, not old. I see the boy I remember; but your face is not so clear as it used to be."

Lawrence Newt laughed.

"You compliment me without knowing it. My face is the lid of a chest full of the most precious secrets; would you have the lid transparent? I am a merchant. Suppose every body could look in through my face and see what I really think of the merchandise I am selling! What profit do you think I should make? No, no, we want no tell-tale faces in South Street."

He said this in a tone that corresponded with the expression which baffled Mrs. Simcoe, and perplexed her only the more. But it did not repel her nor beget distrust. A porcupine hides his flesh in bristling quills; but a magnolia, when its time has not yet come, folds its heart in and in with over-lacing tissues of creamy richness and fragrance. The flower is not sullen, it is only secret.

"I suppose you are twenty years wiser than you were," said Mrs. Simcoe.

"What is wisdom?" asked Lawrence Newt.

"To give the heart to God," replied she.

"That I have discovered," he said.

"And have you given it?"

"I hope so."

"Yes, but haven't you the assurance?" asked she, earnestly.

"I hope so," responded Lawrence Newt, in the same kindly tone.

"But assurance is a gift," continued she.

"A gift of what?"

"Of Peace," replied Mrs. Simcoe.

"Ah! well, I have that," said the other, quietly, as his eyes rested upon the portrait.

There was moisture in the eyes.

"Her daughter is very like her," he said, musingly; and the two stood together silently for some time looking at the picture.

"Not entirely like her mother," replied Mrs. Simcoe, as if to assert some other resemblance.

"Perhaps not; but I never saw her father."

As Lawrence Newt said this, Mrs. Simcoe raised her hand, opened it, and held the miniature before his eyes. He took it and gazed closely at it.

"And this is Colonel Wayne," said he, slowly. "This is the man who broke another man's heart and murdered a woman."

A mingled expression of pain, indignation, passionate regret, and resignation suddenly glittered on the face of Mrs. Simcoe.

"Mr. Newt, Mr. Newt," said she, hurriedly, in a thick voice, "let us at least respect the dead!"

Lawrence Newt, still holding the miniature in his hand, looked surprised and searchingly at his companion. A lofty pity shot into his eyes.

"Could I speak of her otherwise?"

The sudden change in Mrs. Simcoe's expression conveyed her thought to him before her words:

"No, no! not of *her*, but—"

She stopped, as if wrestling with a fierce inward agony. The veins on her forehead were swollen, and her eyes flashed with singular light. It was not clear whether she were trying to say something to conceal something, or simply to recover her self-command. It was a terrible spectacle, and Lawrence Newt felt as if he must veil his eyes, as if he had no right to look upon this great agony of another.

"But—" said he, mechanically, as if by repeating her last word to help her in her struggle.

The sad, severe woman stood before him in the darkening twilight, erect, and more than erect, drawn back from him, and quivering and defiant. She was silent for an instant; then, leaning forward and reaching toward him, she took the miniature from Lawrence Newt, closed her hand over it convulsively, and gasped in a tone that sounded like a low, wailing cry:

"But of *him*."

Lawrence Newt raised his eyes from the vehement woman to the portrait that hung above her.

"I LOVED HIM."

In the twilight that lost loveliness glimmered down into his
very heart with appealing pathos. Perhaps those parted lips
in their red bloom had spoken to him—lips so long ago dust!
Perhaps those eyes, in the days forever gone — gone with
hopes and dreams, and the soft lustre of youth—had looked
into his own, had answered his fond yearning with equal fondness. By all that passionate remembrance, by a lost love, by

the early dead, he felt himself conjured to speak, nor suffer his silence even to seem to shield a crime.

"And why not of him?" he began, calmly, and with profound melancholy rather than anger. "Why not of him, who did not hesitate to marry the woman whom he knew loved another, and whom the difference of years should rather have made his daughter than his wife? Why not of him, who brutally confessed, when she was his wife, an earlier and truer love of his own, and so murdered her slowly, slowly—not with blows of the hand, oh no!—not with poison in her food, oh no!" cried Lawrence Newt, warming into bitter vehemence, clenching his hand and shaking it in the air, "but who struck her blows on the heart—who stabbed her with sharp icicles of indifference—who poisoned her soul with the tauntings of his mean suspicions—mean and false—and the meaner because he knew them to be false? Why not of him, who—"

"Stop! in the name of God!" she cried, fiercely, raising her hand as if she appealed to Heaven.

It fell again. The hard voice sank to a tremulous, pitiful tone:

"Oh! stop, if you are a man!"

They stood opposite each other in utter silence. The light had almost faded. The face in the picture was no longer visible.

Bewildered and awed by the passionate grief of his companion, Lawrence Newt said, gently,

"Why should I stop?"

The form before him had sunk into a chair. Both its hands were clasped over the miniature. He heard the same strange voice like the wailing cry of a child:

"Because I am the woman he loved—because I loved him."

CHAPTER XXVII.

GABRIEL AT HOME.

DURING all this time Gabriel Bennet is becoming a merchant. Every morning he arrives at the store with the porter or before him. He helps him sweep and dust; and it is Gabriel who puts Lawrence Newt's room in order, laying the papers in place, and taking care of the thousand nameless details that make up comfort. He reads the newspapers before the other clerks arrive, and sits upon chests of tea or bales of matting in the loft, that fill the air with strange, spicy, Oriental odors, and talks with the porter. In the long, warm afternoons, too, when there is no pressure of business, and the heat is overpowering, he sits also alone among those odors, and his mind is busy with all kinds of speculations, and dreams, and hopes.

As he walks up Broadway toward evening, his clear, sweet eyes see every thing that floats by. He does not know the other side of the fine dresses he meets any more than of the fine houses, with the smiling, glittering windows. The sun shines bright in his eyes—the street is gay—he nods to his friends—he admires the pretty faces—he wonders at the fast men driving fast horses—he sees the flowers in the windows, the smiling faces between the muslin curtains—he gazes with a kind of awe at the funerals going by, and marks the white bands of the clergymen and the physicians—the elm-trees in the hospital yard remind him of the woods at Delafield; and here comes Abel Newt, laughing, chatting, smoking, with an arm in the arms of two other young men, who are also smoking. As Gabriel passes Abel their eyes meet. Abel nods airily, and Gabriel quietly; the next moment they are back to back again—one is going up street, the other down.

It is not one of the splendid houses before which Gabriel

stops when he has reached the upper part of the city. It is
not a palace, nor is it near Broadway. Nor are there curtains
at the window, but a pair of smiling faces, of friendly women's
faces. One is mild and maternal, with that kind of tender
anxiety which softens beauty instead of hardening it. It has
that look which, after she is dead, every affectionate son thinks
he remembers to have seen in his mother's face; and the other is younger, brighter—a face of rosy cheeks, and clustering
hair, and blue eyes—a beaming, loyal, loving, girlish face.

They both smile welcome to Gabriel, and the younger face,
disappearing from the window, reappears at the door. Gabriel naturally kisses those blooming lips, and then goes into
the parlor and kisses his mother. Those sympathetic friends
ask him what has happened during the day. They see if he
looks unusually fatigued; and if so, why so? they ask. Gabriel must tell the story of the unlading the ship *Mary B.*,
which has just come in—which is Lawrence Newt's favorite
ship; but why called *Mary B.* not even Thomas Tray knows,
who knows every thing else in the business. Then sitting on
each side of him on the sofa, those women wonder and guess
why the ship should be called *Mary B.* What Mary B.?
Oh! dear, there might be a thousand women with those ini-
tials. And what has ever happened to Mr. Newt that he
should wish to perpetuate a woman's name? Stop! remembers mamma, his mother's name was Mary. Mary what? asks
the daughter. Mamma, *you* remember, of course.

Mamma merely replies that his mother's name was Bunley
—Mary Bunley—a famous belle of the close of the last century, when she was the most beautiful woman at President
Washington's levees—Mary Bunley, to whom Aaron Burr paid
his addresses in vain.

"Yes, mamma; but who was Aaron Burr?" ask those
blooming lips, as the bright young eyes glance from under
the clustering curls at her mother.

"Ellen, do you remember this spring, as we were coming
up Broadway, we passed an old man with a keen black eye,

who was rather carelessly dressed, and who wore a cue, with thick hair of his own, white as snow, whom a good many people looked at and pointed out to each other, but nobody spoke to?—who gazed at you as we passed so peculiarly that you pressed nearer to me, and asked who it was, and why such an old man seemed to be so lonely, and in all that great throng, which evidently knew him, was as solitary as if he had been in a desert?"

"Perfectly—I remember it," replies Ellen.

"That friendless old man, my dear, whom at this moment perhaps scarcely a single human being in the world loves, was the most brilliant beau and squire of dames that has ever lived in this country; handsome, accomplished, and graceful, he has stepped many a stately dance with the queenly Mary Bunley, mother of Lawrence Newt. But that was half a century ago."

"Mamma," asks Ellen, full of interest in her mother's words, "but why does nobody speak to him? Why is he so alone? Had he not better have died half a century ago?"

"My dear, you have seen Mrs. Beriah Dagon, an aunt of Mr. Lawrence Newt's? She was Cecilia Bunley, sister of Mary. When she was younger she used to go to the theatre with a little green snake coiled around her arm like a bracelet. It was the most lovely green—the softest color you ever saw; it had the brightest eyes, the most sinuous grace; it had a sort of fascination, but it filled you with fear; fortunately, it was harmless. But, Ellen, if it could have stung, how dreadful it would have been! Aaron Burr was graceful, and accomplished, and brilliant; he coiled about many a woman, fascinating her with his bright eyes and his sinuous manner; but if he had stung, dear?"

Ellen shakes her head as her mother speaks, and Gabriel involuntarily thinks of Abel Newt.

When Mrs. Bennet goes out of the room to attend to the tea, Gabriel says that for his part he doesn't believe in the least that the ship was named for old Mrs. Newt; people are not romantic about their mothers; and Miss Ellen agrees with him.

The room in which they sit is small, and very plain. There are only a sofa, and table, and some chairs, with shelves of books, and a coarse carpet. Upon the wall hangs a portrait representing a young and beautiful woman, not unlike Mrs. Bennet; but the beauty of the face is flashing and passionate, not thoughtful and mild like that of Gabriel's mother. But although every thing is very plain, it is perfectly cheerful. There is nothing forlorn in the aspect of the room. Roses in a glass upon the table, and the voice and manner of the mother and daughter, tell every thing.

Presently they go in to tea, and Mr. Bennet joins them. His face is pale, and of gentle expression, and he stoops a little in his walk. He wears slippers and an old coat, and has the air of a clergyman who has made up his mind to be disappointed. But he is not a clergyman, although his white cravat, somewhat negligently tied, and his rusty black dress-coat, favor that theory. There is a little weariness in his expression, and an involuntary, half-deferential smile, as if he fully assented to every thing that might be presented—not because he is especially interested in it or believes it, but because it is the shortest way of avoiding discussion and getting back to his own thoughts.

"Gabriel, my son, I am glad to see you!" his father says, as he seats himself, not opposite his wife, but at one side of the table. He inquires if Mr. Newt has returned, and learns that he has been at home for several days. He hopes that he has enjoyed his little journey; then sips his tea, and looks to see if the windows are closed; shakes himself gently, and says he feels chilly; that the September evenings are already autumnal, and that the time is coming when we must begin to read aloud again after tea. And what book shall we read? Perhaps the best of all we can select is Irving's Life of Columbus; Mr. Bennet himself has read it in the previous year, but he is sure his children will be interested and delighted by it;

and, for himself, he likes nothing better than to read over and over a book he knows and loves. He puts down his knife as he speaks, and plays with his tea-spoon on the edge of the cup.

"I find myself enchanted with the description of the islands in the Gulf, and the life of those soft-souled natives. As I read on, I smell the sweet warm odors from the land; I pick up the branches of green trees floating far out upon the water; I see the drifting sea-weed, and the lights at night upon the shore; then I land, and lie under the palm-trees, and hear the mellow tongue of the tropics; I taste the luscious fruits; I bask in that rich, eternal sun—" His eyes swim with tropical languor as he speaks. He still mechanically balances the spoon upon the cup, while his mind is deep sunk in reverie. As his wife glances at him, both the look of tenderness and of anxiety in her face deepen. But the moment of silence rouses him, and with the nervous smile upon his face, he says, " Oh —ah!—I—yes—let it be Irving's Columbus!"

Toward his wife Mr. Bennet's manner is almost painfully thoughtful. His eye constantly seeks hers; and when he speaks to her, the mechanical smile which greets every body else is replaced by a kind of indescribable, touching appeal for forgiveness. It is conveyed in no particular thing that he says or does, but it pervades his whole intercourse with her. As Gabriel and Ellen grow up toward maturity, Mrs. Bennet observes that the same peculiarity is stealing into his manner toward them. It is as if he were involuntarily asking pardon for some great wrong that he has unconsciously done them. And yet his mildness, and sweetness, and simplicity of nature are such, that this singular manner does not disturb the universal cheerfulness.

"You look a little tired to-night, father," says Gabriel, when they are all seated in the front room again, by the table, with the lamp lighted.

"Yes," replies the father, who sits upon the sofa, with his wife by his side— "yes; Mr. Van Boozenberg was very an-

"HOW CAN YE BLOOM SAE FRESH AND FAIR?"

gry to-day about some error he thought he had discovered, and he was quite short with us book-keepers, and spoke rather sharply."

A slight flush passes over Mr. Bennet's face, as if he recalled something extremely disagreeable. His eyes become dreamy again; but after a moment the old smile returns, and, as if begging pardon, in a half-bewildered way, he resumes:

"However, his position is trying. Fortunately there wasn't any mistake except of his own."

He is silent again. After a little while he asks, "Couldn't we have some music? Ellen, can't you sing something?"

Ellen thinks she can, if Gabriel will sing second; Gabriel says he will try, with pleasure; but really—he is so overwhelmed—the state of his voice—he feigns a little cough—if the crowded and fashionable audience will excuse—he really —in fact, he will—but he is sure—

During this little banter Nellie cries, "Pooh, pooh!" mamma looks pleased, and papa smiles gently. Then the fresh young voices of the brother and sister mingle in "Bonnie Doon."

The room is not very light, for there is but one lamp upon the table by which the singers sit. The parents sit together upon the sofa; and as the song proceeds the hand of the mother steals into that of the father, which holds it closely, while his arm creeps noiselessly around her waist. Their hearts float far away upon that music. His eyes droop as when he was speaking of the tropic islands—as if he were hearing the soft language of those shores. As his wife looks at him she sees on his face, beneath the weariness of its expression, the light which shone there in the days when they sang "Bonnie Doon" together. He draws her closer to him, and his head bows as if by long habit of humility. Her eyes gradually fill with tears; and when the song is over her head is lying on his breast.

While they are still sitting in silence there is a ring at the door, and Lawrence Newt and Amy Waring enter the room.

CHAPTER XXVIII.

BORN TO BE A BACHELOR.

"THE truth is, Madame," began Lawrence Newt, addressing Mrs. Bennet, "that I am ashamed of myself—I ought to
have called a hundred times. I ask your pardon, Sir," he
continued, turning to Mr. Bennet, who was standing irreso-
lutely by the sofa, half-leaning upon the arm.

"Oh!—ah! I am sure," replied Mr. Bennet, with the nervous smile flitting across his face and apparently breaking out
all over him; and there he remained speechless and bowing,
while Mr. Newt hastened to seat himself, that every body else
might sit down also.

Mrs. Bennet said that she was really glad to see the face of
an old friend again whom she had not seen for so long.

"But I see you every day in Gabriel, my dear Madame,"
replied Lawrence Newt, with quaint dignity. Mother and son
both smiled, and the father bowed as if the remark had been
addressed to him.

Amy seated herself by Gabriel and Ellen, and talked very
animatedly with them, while the parents and Mr. Newt sat together. She praised the roses, and smelled them very often;
and whenever she did so, her eyes, having nothing in particular to do at the moment, escaped, as it were, under her brows
through the petals of the roses as she bent over them, and
wandered away to Lawrence Newt, whose kind, inscrutable
eyes, by the most extraordinary chance in the world, seemed
to be expecting hers, and were ready to receive them with
the warmest welcome, and a half-twinkle—or was it no twinkle
at all? which seemed to say, "Oh! you came—did you?"
And every time his eyes seemed to say this Amy burst out
into fresh praises of those beautiful roses to her younger cousins, and pressed them close to her cheek, as if she found their

moist, creamy coolness peculiarly delicious and refreshing—
pressed them so close, indeed, that she seemed to squeeze
some of their color into her cheeks, which Gabriel and Ellen
both thought, and afterward declared to their mother, to be
quite as beautiful as roses.

Amy's conversation with her young cousins was very lively
indeed, but it had not a continuous interest. There were incessant little pauses, during which the eyes slipped away again
across the room, and fell as softly as before, plump into the
same welcome and the same little interrogation in those other
eyes, twinkling with that annoying " did you?"

Amy Waring was certainly twenty-five, although Gabriel
laughed and jeered at any such statement. But mamma and
the Family Bible were too much for him. Lawrence Newt
was certainly more than forty. But the Newt Family Bible
was under a lock of which the key lay in Mrs. Boniface
Newt's bureau, who, in a question of age, preferred tradition,
which she could judiciously guide, to Scripture. When Boniface Newt led Nancy Magot to the altar, he recorded, in a
large business hand, both the date of his marriage and his
wife's birth. She protested it was vulgar. And when the
bridegroom inquired whether the vulgarity were in the fact
of being born or in recording it, she said: " Mr. Newt, I am
ashamed of you," and locked up the evidence.

There was a vague impression in the Newt family—Boniface had already mentioned it to his son Abel—that there was
something that Uncle Lawrence never talked about — many
things indeed, of course, but still something in particular.
Outside the family nothing was suspected. Lawrence Newt
was simply one of those incomprehensibly pleasant, eccentric,
benevolent men, whose mercantile credit was as good as Jacob
Van Boozenberg's, but who perversely went his own way.
One of these ways led to all kinds of poor people's houses;
and it was upon a visit to the widow of the clergyman to
whom Boniface Newt had given eight dollars for writing a
tract entitled "Indiscriminate Almsgiving a Crime," that Law-

rence Newt had first met Amy Waring. As he was leaving
money with the poor woman to pay her rent, Amy came in
with a basket of comfortable sugars and teas. She carried the
flowers in her face. Lawrence Newt was almost blushing at
being caught in the act of charity; and as he was sliding past
her to get out, he happened to look at her face, and stopped.

"Bless my soul! my dear young lady, surely your name is
Darro!"

The dear young lady smiled and colored, and replied,

"No, mine is not, but my mother's was."

"Of course it was. Those eyes of yours are the Darro
eyes. Do you think I do not know the Darro eyes when I
see them?"

And he took Amy's hand, and said, "Whose daughter are
you?"

"My name is Amy Waring."

"Oh! then you are Corinna's daughter. Your aunt Lucia
married Mr. Bennet, and—and—" Lawrence Newt's voice
paused and hesitated for a moment, "and—there was another."

There was something so tenderly respectful in the tone
that Amy, with only a graver face, replied,

"Yes, there was my Aunt Martha."

"I remember all. She is gone; my dear young lady, you
will forgive me, but your face recalls other years." Then
turning to the widow, he said, "Mrs. Simmer, I am sure that
you could have no kinder, no better friend than this young
lady."

The young lady looked at him with a gentle inquiry in her
eyes as who should say, "What do you know about it?"

Lawrence Newt's eyes understood in a moment, and he
answered:

"Oh, I know it as I know that a rose smells sweet."

He bowed as he said it, and took her hand.

"Will you remember to ask your mother if she remembers
Lawrence Newt, and if he may come and see her?"

Amy Waring said Yes, and the gentleman, bending and

H

touching the tips of her fingers with his lips, said, "Good-by, Mrs. Simmer," and departed.

He called at Mrs. Waring's within a few days afterward. He had known her as a child, but his incessant absence from home when he was younger had prevented any great intimacy with old acquaintances. But the Darros were dancing-school friends and partners. Since those days they had become women and mothers. He had parted with Corinna Darro, a black-eyed little girl in short white frock and short curling hair and red ribbons. He met her as Mrs. Delmer Waring, a large, maternal, good-hearted woman.

This had happened two years before, and during all the time since then Lawrence Newt had often called—had met Amy in the street on many errands—had met her at balls whenever he found she was going. He did not ask her to drive with him. He did not send her costly gifts. He did nothing that could exclude the attentions of younger men. But sometimes a basket of flowers came for Miss Waring— without a card, without any clue. The good-hearted mother thought of various young men, candidates for degrees in Amy's favor, who had undoubtedly sent the flowers. The good-hearted mother, who knew that Amy was in love with none of them, pitied them—thought it was a great shame they should lose their time in such an utterly profitless business as being in love with Amy; and when any of them called said, with a good-humored sigh, that she believed her daughter would never be any thing but a Sister of Charity.

Sometimes also a new book came, and on the fly-leaf was written, "To Miss Amy Waring, from her friend Lawrence Newt." Then the good-hearted mother remarked that some men were delightfully faithful to old associations, and that it was really beautiful to see Mr. Newt keeping up the acquaintance so cordially, and complimenting his old friend so delicately by thinking of pleasing her daughter. What a pity he had never married, to have had daughters of his own! "But I suppose, Amy, some men are born to be bachelors."

"I suppose they are, mother," Amy replied, and found immediately after that she had left her scissors, she couldn't possibly remember where; perhaps in your room, mamma, perhaps in mine.

They must be looked for, however, and, O how curious! there they lay in her own room upon the table. In her own room, where she opened the new book and read in it for half an hour at a time, but always poring on the same page. It was such a profound work. It was so full of weighty matter. When would she ever read it through at this rate, for the page over which she pored had less on it than any other page in the book. In fact it had nothing on it but that very commonplace and familiar form of words, "To Miss Amy Waring, from her friend Lawrence Newt."

Amy was entirely of her mother's opinion. Some men are undoubtedly born to be bachelors. Some men are born to be as noble as the heroes of romances—simple, steadfast, true; to be gentle, intelligent, sagacious, with an experience that has mellowed by constant and various intercourse with men, but with a heart that that intercourse has never chilled, and a faith which that experience has only confirmed. Some men are born to possess every quality of heart, and mind, and person that can awaken and satisfy the love of a woman. Yes, unquestionably, said Amy Waring in her mind, which was so cool, so impartial, so merely contemplating the subject as an abstract question, some men—let me see, shall I say like Lawrence Newt, simply as an illustration?—well, yes—some men like Lawrence Newt, for instance, are born to be all that some women dream of in their souls, and they are the very ones who are born to be bachelors.

It might be very sad not to be aware of it, thought Amy. What a profound pity it would be if any young woman should not see it, for instance, in the case of Lawrence Newt. But when a young woman is in no doubt at all, when she knows perfectly well that such a man is not intended by nature to be a marrying man, and therefore never thinks of such a

thing, but only with a grace, and generosity, and delicacy beyond expression offers his general homage to the sex by giving
little gifts to her, " why, then—then," thought Amy, and she
was thinking so at the very moment when she sat with Gabriel and Ellen, talking in a half wild, lively, incoherent way,
" why, then—then," and her eyes leaped across the room and
fell, as it were, into the arms of Lawrence Newt's, which caressed them with soft light, and half-laughed " You came again,
did you?"—" why, then—then," and Amy buried her face in
the cool, damp roses, and did not dare to look again, " then she
had better go and be a Sister of Charity."

CHAPTER XXIX.

MR. ABEL NEWT, GRAND STREET.

As the world returned to town and the late autumnal fes-
tivities began, the handsome person and self-possessed style
of Mr. Abel Newt became the fashion. Invitations showered
upon him. Mrs. Dagon proclaimed every where that there
had been nobody so fascinating since the days of the brilliant
youth of Aaron Burr, whom she declared that she well remembered, and added, that if she could say it without blushing,
or if any reputable woman ought to admit such things, she
should confess that in her younger days she had received
flowers and even notes from that fascinating man.

"I don't deny, my dears, that he was a naughty man. But
I can tell you one thing, all the naughty men are not in disgrace yet, though he is. And, if you please, Miss Fanny, with
all your virtuous sniffs, dear, and all your hugging of men in
waltzing, darling, Colonel Burr was not sent to Coventry because he was naughty. He might have been naughty all the
days of his life, and Mrs. Jacob Van Boozenberg and the rest
of 'em would have been quite as glad to have him at their
houses. No, no, dears, society doesn't punish men for being

naughty—only women. I am older than you, and I have observed that society likes spice in character. It doesn't harm
a man to have stories told about him."

No ball was complete without Abel Newt. Ladies, meditating parties, engaged him before they issued a single invitation. At dinners he was sparkling and agreeable, with tact
enough not to extinguish the other men, who yet felt his superiority and did not half like it. They imitated his manner;
but what was ease or gilded assurance in him was open insolence, or assurance with the gilt rubbed off, in them. The
charm and secret of his manner lay in an utter devotion, which
said to every woman, " There's not a woman in the world who
can resist me, except you. Have you the heart to do it?"
Of course this manner was assisted by personal magnetism and
beauty. Wilkes said he was only half an hour behind the
handsomest man in the world. But he would never have
overtaken him if the handsome man had been Wilkes.

In his dress Abel was costly and elegant. With the other
men of his day, he read " Pelham" with an admiration of which
his life was the witness. Pelham was the Byronic hero made
practicable, purged of romance, and adapted to society. Mr.
Newt, Jun., was one of a small but influential set of young
men about town who did all they could to repair the misfortune of being born Americans, by imitating the habits of foreign life.

It was presently clear to him that residence under the pa-
rental roof was incompatible with the habits of a strictly fashionable man.

"There are hours, you know, mother, and habits, which
make a separate lodging much more agreeable to all parties.
I have friends to smoke, or to drink a glass of punch, or to
play a game of whist; and we must sing, and laugh, and make
a noise, as young men will, which is not seemly for the paternal
mansion, mother mine." With which he took his admiring
mother airily under the chin and kissed her—not having mentioned every reason which made a separate residence desirable.

So Abel Newt hired a pleasant set of rooms in Grand Street, near Broadway, in the neighborhood of other youth of the right set. He furnished them sumptuously, with the softest carpets, the most luxurious easy-chairs, the most costly curtains, and pretty, bizarre little tables, and bureaus, and shelves. Various engravings hung upon the walls ; a profile-head of Bulwer, with a large Roman nose and bushy whiskers, and one of his Majesty George IV., in that famous cloak which Lord Chesterfield bought at the sale of his Majesty's wardrobe for eleven hundred dollars, and of which the sable lining alone originally cost four thousand dollars. Then there were little vases, and boxes, and caskets standing upon all possible places, with a rare flower in some one of them often, sent by some kind dowager who wished to make sure of Abel at a dinner or a select soirée. Pipes, of course, and boxes of choice cigars, were at hand, and in a convenient closet such a beautiful set of English cut glass for the use of a gentleman!

It was no wonder that the rooms of Abel Newt became a kind of club-room and elegant lounge for the gay gentlemen about town. He even gave little dinners there to quiet parties, sometimes including two or three extremely vivacious and pretty, as well as fashionably dressed, young women, whom he was not in the habit of meeting in society, but who were known quite familiarly to Abel and his friends.

Upon other occasions these little dinners took place out of town, whither the gentlemen drove alone in their buggies by daylight, and, meeting the ladies there, had the pleasure of driving them back to the city in the evening. The "buggy" of Abel's day was an open gig without a top, very easy upon its springs, but dangerous with stumbling horses. The drive was along the old Boston road, and the rendezvous, Cato's— Cato Alexander's—near the present shot-tower. If the gentlemen returned alone, they finished the evening at Benton's, in Ann Street, where they played a game of billiards; or at Thiel's retired rooms over the celebrated Stewart's, opposite the Park, where they indulged in faro. Abel Newt lost and

won his money with careless grace—always a little glad when
he won, for somebody had to pay for all this luxurious life.

Boniface Newt remonstrated. His son was late at the office in the morning. He drew large sums to meet his large
expenses. Several times, instead of instantly filling out the
checks as Abel directed, the book-keeper had delayed, and
said casually to Mr. Newt during Abel's absence at lunch,
which was usually prolonged, that he supposed it was all right
to fill up a check of that amount to Mr. Abel's order? Mr.
Boniface Newt replied, in a dogged way, that he supposed it
was.

But one day when the sum had been large, and the paternal
temper more than usually ruffled, he addressed the junior partner upon his return from lunch and his noontide glass with his
friends at the Washington Hotel, to the effect that matters
were going on much too rapidly.

"To what matters do you allude, father?" inquired Mr.
Abel, with composure, as he picked his teeth with one hand,
and surveyed a cigar which he held in the other.

"I mean, Sir, that you are spending a great deal too much
money."

"Why, how is that, Sir?" asked his son, as he called to the
boy in the outer office to bring him a light.

"By Heavens! Abel, you're enough to make a man crazy!
Here I have put you into my business, over the heads of the
clerks who are a hundred-fold better fitted for it than you;
and you not only come down late and go away early, and destroy all kind of discipline by smoking and lounging, but you
don't manifest the slightest interest in the business; and, above
all, you are living at a frightfully ruinous rate! Yes, Sir, ruinous! How do you suppose I can pay, or that the business
can pay, for such extravagance?"

Abel smoked calmly during this energetic discourse, and
blew little rings from his mouth, which he watched with interest as they melted in the air.

"Certain things are inevitable, father."

His parent, frowning and angry, growled at him as he made this remark, and muttered,

"Well, suppose they are."

"Now, father," replied his son, with great composure, "let us proceed calmly. Why should we pretend not to see what is perfectly plain? Business nowadays proceeds by credit. Credit is based upon something, or the show of something. It is represented by a bank-bill. Here now—" And he opened his purse leisurely and drew out a five-dollar note of the Bank of New York, "here is a promise to pay five dollars—in gold or silver, of course. Do you suppose that the Bank of New York has gold and silver enough to pay all those promises it has issued? Of course not."

Abel knocked off the ash from his cigar, and took a long contemplative whiff, as if he were about making a plunge into views even more profound. Mr. Newt, half pleased with the show of philosophy, listened with less frowning brows.

"Well, now, if by some hocus-pocus the Bank of New York hadn't a cent in coin at this moment, it could redeem the few claims that might be made upon it by borrowing, could it not?"

Mr. Newt shook his head affirmatively.

"And, in fine, if it were entirely bankrupt, it could still do a tremendous business for a very considerable time, could it not?"

Mr. Newt assented.

"And the managers, who knew it to be so, would have plenty of time to get off before an explosion, if they wanted to?"

"Abel, what do you mean?" inquired his father.

The young man was still placidly blowing rings of smoke from his mouth, and answered:

"Nothing terrible. Don't be alarmed. It is only an illustration of the practical value of credit, showing how it covers a retreat, so to speak. Do you see the moral, father?"

"No; certainly not. I see no moral at all."

"Why, suppose that nobody wanted to retreat, but that

the Bank was only to be carried over a dangerous place, then credit is a bridge, isn't it? If it were out of money, it could live upon its credit until it got the money back again."

"Clearly," answered Mr. Newt.

"And if it extended its operations, it would acquire even more credit?"

"Yes."

"Because people, believing in the solvency of the Bank, would suppose that it extended itself because it had more means?"

"Yes."

"And would not feel any dust in their eyes?"

"No," said Mr. Newt, following his son closely.

"Well, then; don't you see?"

"No, I don't see," replied the father; "that is, I don't see what you mean."

"Why, father, look here! I come into your business. The fact is known. People look. There's no whisper against the house. We extend ourselves; we live liberally, but we pay the bills. Every body says, 'Newt & Son are doing a thumping business.' Perhaps we are—perhaps we are not. We are crossing the bridge of credit. Before people know that we have been living up to our incomes—quite up, father dear"—Mr. Newt frowned an entire assent—"we have plenty of money!"

"How, in Heaven's name!" cried Boniface Newt, springing up, and in so loud a tone that the clerks looked in from the outer office.

"By my marriage," returned Abel, quietly.

"With whom?" asked Mr. Newt, earnestly.

"With an heiress."

"What's her name?"

"Just what I am trying to find out," replied Abel, lightly, as he threw his cigar away. "And now I put it to you, father, as a man of the world and a sensible, sagacious, successful merchant, am I not more likely to meet and marry such a girl, if I live generously in society, than if I shut myself up to be a mere dig?"

Mr. Newt was not sure. Perhaps it was so. Upon the whole, it probably was so.

Mr. Abel did not happen to suggest to his father that, for the purpose of marrying an heiress, if he should ever chance to be so fortunate as to meet one, and, having met her, to become enamored so that he might be justified in wooing her for his wife—that for all these contingencies it was a good thing for a young man to have a regular business connection and apparent employment—and very advantageous, indeed, that that connection should be with a man so well known in commercial and fashionable circles as his father. That of itself was one of the great advantages of credit. It was a frequent joke of Abel's with his father, after the recent conversation, that credit was the most creditable thing going.

CHAPTER XXX.

CHECK.

DURING these brilliant days of young bachelorhood Abel, by some curious chance, had not met Hope Wayne, who was passing the winter in New York with her Aunt Dinks, and who had hitherto declined all society. It was well known that she was in town. The beautiful Boston heiress was often enough the theme of discourse among the youth at Abel's rooms.

"Is she really going to marry that Dinks? Why, the man's a donkey!" said Corlaer Van Boozenberg.

"And are there no donkeys among your married friends?" inquired Abel, with the air of a naturalist pursuing his researches.

One day, indeed, as he was passing Stewart's, he saw Hope alighting from a carriage. He was not alone; and as he passed their eyes met. He bowed profoundly. She bent her

SHOPPING, *ET CÆTERA.*

head without speaking, as one acknowledges a slight acquaintance. It was not a "cut," as Abel said to himself; "not at
all. It was simply ranking me with the herd."

"Who's that stopping to speak with her?" asked Corlaer,
as he turned back to see her.

"That's Arthur Merlin. Don't you know? He's a painter. I wonder how the deuce he came to know her!"

In fact, it was the painter. It was the first time he had
met her since the summer days of Saratoga; and as he stood
talking with her upon the sidewalk, and observed that her
cheeks had an unusual flush, and her manner a slight excitement, he could not help feeling a secret pleasure—feeling, in
truth, so deep a delight, as he looked into that lovely face,
that he found himself reflecting, as he walked away, how very
fortunate it was that he was so entirely devoted to his art. It
is very fortunate indeed, thought he. And yet it might be a
pity, too, if I should chance to meet some beautiful and sympathetic woman; because, being so utterly in love with my art,
it would be impossible for me to fall in love with her! Quite
impossible! Quite out of the question!

Just as he thought this he bumped against some one, and
looked up suddenly. A calm, half-amused face met his glance,
as Arthur said, hastily, "I beg your pardon."

"My pardon is granted," returned the gentleman; "but
still you had better look out for yourself."

"Oh! I shall not hit any body else," said Arthur, as he
bowed and was passing on.

"I am not speaking of other people," replied the other, with
a look which was very friendly, but very puzzling.

"Whom do you mean, then?" asked Arthur Merlin.

"Yourself, of course," said the gentleman with the half-
amused face.

"How?" inquired Arthur.

"To guard against Venus rising from the fickle sea, or Hope
descending from a carriage," rejoined his companion, putting
out his hand.

Arthur looked surprised, and, could he have resisted the
face of his new acquaintance, he would have added indignation
to his expression. But it was impossible.

"To whom do I owe such excellent advice?"

"To Lawrence Newt," answered that gentleman, putting
out his hand. "I am glad to make your acquaintance, Mr.
Arthur Merlin."

The painter shook the merchant's hand cordially. They had some further conversation, and finally Mr. Merlin turned, and the two men strolled together down town. While they yet talked, Lawrence Newt observed that the eyes of his companion studied every carriage that passed. He did it in a very natural, artless way; but Lawrence Newt smiled with his eyes, and at length said, as if Arthur had asked him the question, "There she comes!"

Arthur was a little bit annoyed, and said, suddenly, and with a fine air of surprise, "Who?"

Lawrence turned and looked him full in the face; upon which the painter, who was so fanatically devoted to his art that it was clearly impossible he should fall in love, said, "Oh!" as if somebody had answered his question.

The next moment both gentlemen bowed to Hope Wayne, who passed with Mrs. Dinks in her carriage.

"Who are those gentlemen to whom you are bowing, Hope?" Mrs. Dinks asked, as she saw her niece lean forward and blush as she bowed.

"Mr. Merlin and Mr. Lawrence Newt," replied Hope.

"Oh, I did not observe."

After a while she said, "Don't you think, Hope, you could make up your mind to go to Mrs. Kingfisher's ball next week? You know you haven't been out at all."

"Perhaps," replied Hope, doubtfully.

"Just as you please, dear. I think it is quite as well to stay away if you want to. Your retirement is very natural, and proper, and beautiful, under the circumstances, although it is unusual. Of course I don't fully understand. But I have perfect confidence in the justice of your reasons."

Mrs. Dinks looked at Hope tenderly and sagaciously as she said this, and smiled meaningly.

Hope was entirely bewildered. Then a sudden apprehension shot through her mind as she thought of what her aunt had said. She asked suddenly and a little proudly,

"What do you mean by 'circumstances,' aunt?"

Mrs. Dinks was uneasy in her turn.   But she pushed bravely on, and said kindly,

"Why on earth shouldn't I know why you are unwilling to
have it known, Hope?   You know I am as still as the grave."

"Have what known, aunt?" asked Hope.

"Why, dear," replied Mrs. Dinks, confused by Hope's air
of innocence, "your engagement, of course."

"My engagement?" said Hope, with a look of utter amazement; "to whom, I should like to know?"

Mrs. Dinks looked at her for an instant, and asked, in a
clear, dry tone:

"Are you not engaged to Alfred?"

Hope Wayne's look of anxious surprise melted into an expression of intense amusement.

"To Alfred Dinks!" said she, in a slow, incredulous tone, and
with her eyes sparkling with laughter.   "Why, my dear aunt?"

Mrs. Dinks was overwhelmed by a sudden consciousness of
bitter disappointment, mingled with an exasperating conviction that she had been somehow duped.   The tone was thick
in which she answered.

"What is the meaning of this?   Hope, are you deceiving
me?"

She knew Hope was not deceiving her as well as she knew
that they were sitting together in the carriage.

Hope's reply was a clear, ringing, irresistible laugh.   Then
she said,

"It's high time I went to balls, I see.   I will go to Mrs.
Kingfisher's.   But, dear aunt, have you seriously believed such
a story?"

"Do I think my son is a liar?" replied Mrs. Dinks, sardon-
ically.

The laugh faded from Hope's face.

"Did he say so?" asked she.

"Certainly he did."

"Alfred Dinks told you I was engaged to him?"

"Alfred Dinks told me you were engaged to him."

They drove on for some time without speaking.

"What does he mean by using my name in that way?" said Hope, with the Diana look in her eyes.

"Oh! that you must settle with him," replied the other. "I'm sure I don't know."

And Field-marshal Mrs. Dinks settled herself back upon the seat and said no more. Hope Wayne sat silent and erect by her side.

CHAPTER XXXI.

AT DELMONICO'S.

LAWRENCE NEWT had watched with the warmest sympathy the rapid development of the friendship between Amy Waring and Hope Wayne. He aided it in every way. He called in the assistance of Arthur Merlin, who was in some doubt whether his devotion to his art would allow him to desert it for a moment. But as the doubt only lasted while Lawrence Newt was unfolding a plan he had of reading books aloud with the ladies—and—in fact, a great many other praiseworthy plans which all implied a constant meeting with Miss Waring and Miss Wayne, Mr. Merlin did not delay his co-operation in all Mr. Newt's efforts.

And so they met at Amy Waring's house very often and pretended to read, and really did read, several books together aloud. Ostensibly poetry was pursued at the meetings of what Lawrence Newt called the Round Table.

"Why not? We have our King Arthur, and our Merlin the Enchanter," he said.

"A speech from Mr. Merlin," cried Amy, gayly, while Hope looked up from her work with encouraging, queenly eyes. Arthur looked at them eagerly.

"Oh, Diana! Diana!" he thought, but did not say. That was the only speech he made, and nobody heard it.

The meetings of the Round Table were devoted to poetry, but of a very practical kind. It was pure romance, but without any thing technically romantic. Mrs. Waring often sat with the little party, and, as she worked, talked with Lawrence Newt of earlier days—"days when you were not born, dears," she said, cheerfully, as if to appropriate Mr. Newt. And whenever she made this kind of allusion Amy's work became very intricate indeed, demanding her closest attention. But Hope Wayne, remembering her first evening in his society, raised her eyes again with curiosity, and as she did so Lawrence smiled kindly and gravely, and his eyes hung upon hers as if he saw again what he had thought never to see; while Hope resolved that she would ask him under what circumstances he had known Pinewood. But the opportunity had not yet arrived. She did not wish to ask before the others. There are some secrets that we involuntarily respect, while we only know that they are secrets.

The more Arthur Merlin saw of Hope Wayne the more delighted he was to think how impossible it was for him, in view of his profound devotion to his art, to think of beautiful wo men in any other light than that of picturesque subjects.

"Really, Mr. Newt," Arthur said to him one evening as they were dining together at Delmonico's—which was then in William Street—"if I were to paint a picture of Diana when she loved Endymion—a picture, by-the-by, which I intend to paint—I should want to ask Miss Wayne to sit to me for the principal figure. It is really remarkable what a subdued splendor there is about her—Diana blushing, you know, as it were—the moon delicately veiled in cloud. It would be superb, I assure you."

Lawrence Newt smiled—he often smiled—as he wiped his mouth, and asked,

"Who would you ask to sit for Endymion?"

"Well, let me see," replied Arthur, cheerfully, and pondering as if to determine who was exactly the man. It was really beautiful to see his exclusive enthusiasm for his art. "Let me see. How would it do to paint an ideal figure for Endymion?"

"No, no," said Lawrence Newt, laughing; "art must get its ideal out of the real. I demand a good, solid, flesh-and-blood Endymion."

"I can't just think of any body," replied Arthur Merlin, musingly, looking upon the floor, and thinking so intently of Hope, in order to image to himself a proper Endymion, that he quite forgot to think of the candidates for that figure.

"How would my young friend Hal Battlebury answer?" asked Lawrence Newt.

"Oh, not at all," replied Arthur, promptly; "he's too light, you know."

"Well, let me see," continued the other, "what do you think of that young Southerner, Sligo Moultrie, who was at Saratoga? I used to think he had some of the feeling for Hope Wayne that Diana wanted in Endymion, and he has the face for a picture."

"Oh, he's not at all the person. He's much too dark, you see," answered Arthur, at once, with remarkable readiness.

"There's Alfred Dinks," said Lawrence Newt, smiling.

"Pish!" said Arthur, conclusively.

"Really, I can not think of any body," returned his companion, with a mock gravity that Arthur probably did not perceive. The young artist was evidently very closely occupied with the composition of his picture. He half-closed his eyes, as if he saw the canvas distinctly, and said,

"I should represent her just lighting upon the hill, you see, with a rich, moist flush upon her face, a cold splendor just melting into passion, half floating, as she comes, so softly superior, so queenly scornful of all the world but him. Jove! it would make a splendid picture!"

Lawrence Newt looked at his friend as he imagined the condescending Diana. The artist's face was a little raised as he spoke, as if he saw a stately vision. It was rapt in the intensity of fancy, and Lawrence knew perfectly well that he saw Hope Wayne's Endymion before him. But at the same moment his eye fell upon his nephew Abel sitting with a choice company of gay youths at another table. There was instantly a mischievous twinkle in Lawrence Newt's eye.

"Eureka! I have Endymion."

Arthur started and felt a half pang, as if Lawrence Newt had suddenly told him of Miss Wayne's engagement. He came instantly out of the clouds on Latmos, where he was dreaming.

"What did you say?" asked he.

"Why, of course, how dull I am! Abel will be your Endymion, if you can get him."

"Who is Abel?" inquired Arthur.

"Why, my nephew, Abel Don Juan Pelham Newt, of Grand Street, and Boniface Newt, Son, & Company, Dry Goods on Commission, Esquire," replied Lawrence Newt, with perfect gravity.

Arthur looked at him bewildered.

"Don't you know my nephew, Abel Newt?"

"No, not personally. I've heard of him, of course."

"Well, he's a very handsome young man; and though he be dark, he may also be Endymion. Why not? Look at him; there he sits. 'Tis the one just raising the glass to his lips."

Lawrence Newt bent his head as he spoke toward the gay revelers, who sat, half a dozen in number, and the oldest not more than twenty-five, all dandies, all men of pleasure, at a neighboring table spread with a profuse and costly feast. Abel was the leader, and at the moment Arthur Merlin and Lawrence Newt turned to look he was telling some anecdote to which they all listened eagerly, while they sipped the red wine of France, poured carefully from a bottle reclining in a basket, and delicately coated with dust. Abel, with his glass in his hand and the glittering smile in his eye, told the story with careless grace, as if he were more amused with the listeners' eagerness than with the anecdote itself. The extreme gayety of his life was already rubbing the boyish bloom from his face,

A SEARCH FOR ENDYMION.

but it developed his peculiar beauty more strikingly by removing that incongruous innocence which belongs to every boyish countenance.

As he looked at him, Arthur Merlin was exceedingly impressed by the air of reckless grace in his whole appearance, which harmonized so entirely with his face. Lawrence Newt watched his friend as the latter gazed at Abel. Lawrence al-

ways saw a great deal whenever he looked any where. Perhaps he perceived the secret dissatisfaction and feeling of sudden alarm which, without any apparent reason, Arthur felt as
he looked at Abel.

But the longer Arthur Merlin looked at Abel the more curiously perplexed he was. The feeling which, if he had not
been a painter so utterly devoted to his profession that all dis-
tractions were impossible, might have been called a nascent
jealousy, was gradually merged in a half-consciousness that he
had somewhere seen Abel Newt before, but where, and under what circumstances, he could not possibly remember. He
watched him steadily, puzzling himself to recall that face.

Suddenly he clapped his hand upon the table. Lawrence
Newt, who was looking at him, saw the perplexity of his expression smooth itself away; while Arthur Merlin, with an
" oh !" of surprise, satisfaction, and alarm, exclaimed—and his
color changed—

" Why, it's Manfred in the Coliseum !"

Lawrence Newt was confounded. Was Arthur, then, not
deceiving himself, after all ? Did he really take an interest
in all these people only as a painter, and think of them merely
as subjects for pictures ?

Lawrence Newt was troubled. He had seen in Arthur with
delight what he supposed the unconscious beginnings of affection for Hope Wayne. He had pleased himself in bringing
them together—of course Amy Waring must be present too
when he himself was, that any *tête-à-tête* which arose might
not be interrupted—and he had dreamed the most agreeable
dreams. He knew Hope—he knew Arthur—it was evidently
the hand of Heaven. He had even mentioned it confidentially to Amy Waring, who was profoundly interested, and who
charitably did the same offices for Arthur with Hope Wayne
that Lawrence Newt did for the young candidates with her.
The conversation about the picture of Diana had only confirmed Lawrence Newt in his conviction that Arthur Merlin
really loved Hope Wayne, whether he himself knew it or not.

And now was he all wrong, after all? Ridiculous! How could he be?

He tried to persuade himself that he was not. But he could not forget how persistently Arthur had spoken of Hope only as a fine Diana; and how, after evidently being struck with Abel Newt, he had merely exclaimed, with a kind of suppressed excitement, as if he saw what a striking picture he would make, "Manfred in the Coliseum!"

Lawrence Newt drank a glass of wine, thoughtfully. Then he smiled inwardly.

"It is not the first time I have been mistaken," thought he. "I shall have to take Amy Waring's advice about it."

As he and his friend passed the other table, on their way out, Abel nodded to his uncle; and as Arthur Merlin looked at him carefully, he was very sure that he saw the person whose face so singularly resembled that of Manfred's in the picture he had given Hope Wayne.

"I am all wrong," thought Lawrence Newt, ruefully, as they passed out into the street.

"Abel Newt, then, is Hope Wayne's somebody," thought Arthur Merlin, as he took his friend's arm.

CHAPTER XXXII.

MRS. THEODORE KINGFISHER AT HOME. *On dansera.*

SOCIETY stared when it beheld Miss Hope Wayne entering the drawing-room of Mrs. Theodore Kingfisher.

"Really, Miss Wayne, I am delighted," said Mrs. Kingfisher, with a smile that might have been made at the same shop with the flowers that nodded over it.

Mrs. Kingfisher's friendship for Miss Wayne and her charming aunt consisted in two pieces of pasteboard, on which was printed, in German text, "Mrs. Theodore Kingfisher, St. John's Square," which she had left during the winter; and her pleas-

ure at seeing her was genuine—not that she expected they
would solace each other's souls with friendly intercourse, but
that she knew Hope to be a famous beauty who had held herself retired until now at the very end of the season, when she
appeared for the first time at her ball.

This reflection secured an unusually ardent reception for
Mrs. Dagon, who followed Mrs. Dinks's party, and who, hav-
ing made her salutation to the hostess, said to Mr. Boniface
Newt, her nephew, who accompanied her,

"Now I'll go and stand by the pier-glass, so that I can rake
the rooms.   And, Boniface, mind, I depend upon your getting
me some lobster salad at supper, with plenty of dressing—
mind, now, plenty of dressing."

Perched like a contemplative vulture by the pier, Mrs. Dagon declined chairs and sofas, but put her eye-glass to her
eyes to spy out the land.   She had arrived upon the scene of
action early.   She always did.

"I want to see every body come in.   There's a great deal
in watching how people speak to each other.   I've found out
a great many things in that way, my dear, which were not
suspected."

Presently a glass at the other end of the room that was bobbing up and down and about at every body and thing—at the ceiling, and the wall, and the carpet—discovering the rouge upon
cheeks whose ruddy freshness charmed less perceptive eyes—re-
ducing the prettiest lace to the smallest terms in substance and
price—detecting base cotton with one fell glance, and the part
of the old dress ingeniously furbished to do duty as new—this
philosophic and critical glass presently encountered Mrs. Dagon's in mid-career.   The two ladies behind the glasses glared
at each other for a moment, then bowed and nodded, like two
Chinese idols set up on end at each extremity of the room.

"Good-evening, dear, good Mrs. Winslow Orry," said the
smiling eyes of Mrs. Dagon to that lady.   "How doubly
scraggy you look in that worn-out old sea-green satin!" said
the smiling old lady to herself.

AUNT DAGON RAKING THE ROOM.

"How do, darling Mrs. Dagon?" said the responsive glance of Mrs. Orry, with the most gracious effulgence of aspect, as she glared across the room—inwardly thinking, "What a silly old hag to lug that cotton lace cape all over town!"

People poured in. The rooms began to swarm. There was a warm odor of kid gloves, scent-bags, and heliotrope. There was an incessant fluttering of fans and bobbing of heads.

One hundred gentlemen said, "How warm it is!" One hun‑ dred ladies of the highest fashion answered, "Very." Fifty young men, who all wore coats, collars, and waistcoats that seemed to have been made in the lump, and all after the same pattern, stood speechless about the rooms, wondering what under heaven to do with their hands. Fifty older married men, who had solved that problem, folded their hands behind their backs, and beamed vaguely about, nodding their heads whenever they recognized any other head, and saying, " Good‑ evening," and then, after a little more beaming, "How are yer?" Waiters pushed about with trays covered with little glasses of lemonade and port-sangaree, which offered favora‑ ble openings to the unemployed young men and the married gentlemen, who crowded along with a glass in each hand, frightening all the ladies and begging every body's pardon.

All the Knickerbocker jewels glittered about the rooms. Mrs. Bleecker Van Kraut carried not less than thirty thou‑ sand dollars' worth of diamonds upon her person—at least that was Mrs. Orry's deliberate conclusion after a careful estimate. Mrs. Dagon, when she heard what Mrs. Orry said, merely ex‑ claimed, "Fiddle! Anastatia Orry can tell the price of lute‑ string a yard because Winslow Orry failed in that business, but she knows as much of diamonds as an elephant of good manners."

The Van Kraut property had been bowing about the draw‑ ing-rooms of New York for a year or two, watched with pal‑ pitating hearts and longing eyes. Until that was disposed of, nothing else could win a glance. There were several single hundreds of thousands openly walking about the same rooms, but while they were received very politely, they were made to feel that two millions were in presence and unappropriated, and they fell humbly back.

Fanny Newt, upon her début in society, had contemplated the capture of the Van Kraut property; but the very vigor with which she conducted the campaign had frightened the poor gentleman who was the present member for that proper‑

"SOCIETY."

ty, in society, so that he shivered and withdrew on the dizzy
verge of a declaration; and when he subsequently encountered
Lucy Slumb, she was immediately invested with the family
jewels.

"Heaven save me from a smart woman!" prayed Bleecker
Van Kraut; and Heaven heard and kindly granted his prayer.

Presently, while the hot hum went on, and laces, silks,

satins, brocades, muslins, and broadcloth intermingled and changed places, so that Arthur Merlin, whom Lawrence Newt had brought, declared the ball looked like a shot silk or a salmon's belly—upon overhearing which, Mrs. Bleecker Van Kraut, who was passing with Mr. Moultrie, looked unspeakable things—the quick eyes of Fanny Newt encountered the restless orbs of Mrs. Dinks.

Alfred had left town for Boston on the very day on which Hope Wayne had learned the story of her engagement. Neither his mother nor Hope, therefore, had had an opportunity of asking an explanation.

"I am glad to see Miss Wayne with you to-night," said Fanny.

"My niece is her own mistress," replied Mrs. Dinks, in a sub-acid tone.

Fanny's eyes grew blacker and sharper in a moment. An Indian whose life depends upon concealment from his pursuer is not more sensitive to the softest dropping of the lightest leaf than was Fanny Newt's sagacity to the slightest indication of discovery of her secret. There is trouble, she said to herself, as she heard Mrs. Dinks's reply.

"Miss Wayne has been a recluse this winter," remarked Fanny, with infinite blandness.

"Yes, she has had some kind of whim," replied Mrs. Dinks, shaking her shoulders as if to settle her dress.

"We girls have all suspected, you know, of course, Mrs. Dinks," said Miss Newt, with a very successful imitation of archness and a little bend of the neck.

"Have you, indeed !" retorted Mrs. Dinks, in almost a belli-cose manner.

"Why, yes, dear Mrs. Dinks; don't you remember at Saratoga—you know ?" continued Fanny, with imperturbable composure.

"What happened at Saratoga?" asked Mrs. Dinks, with smooth defiance on her face, and conscious that she had never actually mentioned any engagement between Alfred and Hope.

"Dear me! So many things happen at Saratoga," answered Fanny, bridling like a pert miss of seventeen. "And when a girl has a handsome cousin, it's very dangerous." Fanny Newt was determined to know where she was.

"Some girls are very silly and willful," tartly remarked Mrs. Dinks.

"I suppose," said Fanny, with extraordinary coolness, continuing the *rôle* of the arch maid of seventeen—"I suppose, if every thing one hears is true, we may congratulate you, dear Mrs. Dinks, upon an interesting event?" And Fanny raised her bouquet and smelled at it vigorously—at least, she seemed to be doing so, because the flowers almost covered her face, but really they made an ambush from which she spied the enemy, unseen.

The remark she had made had been made a hundred times before to Mrs. Dinks. In fact, Fanny herself had used it, under various forms, to assure herself, by the pleased reserve of the reply which Mrs. Dinks always returned, that the lady had no suspicion that she was mistaken. But this time Mrs. Dinks, whose equanimity had been entirely disturbed by her discovery that Hope was not engaged to Alfred, asked formally, and not without a slight sneer which arose from an impatient suspicion that Fanny knew more than she chose to disclose—

"And pray, Miss Newt, what do people hear? Really, if other people are as unfortunate as I am, they hear a great deal of nonsense."

Upon which Mrs. Budlong Dinks sniffed the air like a charger.

"I know it—it is really dreadful," returned Fanny Newt. "People do say the most annoying and horrid things. But this time, I am sure, there can be nothing very vexatious." And Miss Newt fanned herself with persistent complacency, as if she were resolved to prolong the pleasure which Mrs. Dinks must undoubtedly have in the conversation.

Hitherto it had been the policy of that lady to demur and insinuate, and declare how strange it was, and how gossipy

people were, and finally to retreat from a direct reply under
cover of a pretty shower of ohs! and ahs! and indeeds! and
that policy had been uniformly successful. Everybody said,
" Of course Alfred Dinks and his cousin are engaged, and Mrs.
Dinks likes to have it alluded to—although there are reasons
why it must be not openly acknowledged." So Field-marshal Mrs. Dinks outgeneraled Everybody. But the gallant
young private, Miss Fanny Newt, was resolved to win her
epaulets.

As Mrs. Dinks made no reply, and assumed the appearance
of a lady who, for her own private and inscrutable reasons,
had concluded to forego the prerogative of speech for ever-
more, while she fanned herself calmly, and regarded Fanny
with a kind of truculent calmness that seemed to say, "What
are you going to do about that last triumphant move of
mine?" Fanny proceeded in a strain of continuous sweetness
that fairly rivaled the smoothness of the neck, and the eyes,
and the arms of Mrs. Bleecker Van Kraut:

" I suppose there can be nothing very disagreeable to Miss
Wayne's friends in knowing that she is engaged to Mr. Alfred
Dinks?"

Alas! Mrs. Dinks, who knew Hope, knew that the time for
dexterous subterfuges and misleadings had passed. She resolved that people, when they discovered what they inevitably
soon must discover, should not suppose that she had been deceived. So, looking straight into Fanny Newt's eyes without
flinching—and somehow it was not a look of profound affection—she said,

" I was not aware of any such engagement."

" Indeed!" replied the undaunted Fanny, " I have heard that
love is blind, but I did not know that it was true of maternal
love. Mr. Dinks's mother is not his confidante, then, I presume?"

The bad passions of Mr. Dinks's mother's heart were like
the heathen, and furiously raged together at this remark. She
continued the fanning, and said, with a sickly smile,

"Miss Newt, you can contradict from me the report of any such engagement."

That was enough. Fanny was mistress of the position. If Mrs. Dinks were willing to say that, it was because she was persuaded that it never would be true. She had evidently discovered something. How much had she discovered? That was the next step.

As these reflections flashed through the mind of Miss Fanny Newt, and her cold black eye shone with a stony glitter, she was conscious that the time for some decisive action upon her part had arrived. To be or not to be Mrs. Alfred Dinks was now the question; and even as she thought of it she felt what must be done. She did not depreciate the ability of Mrs. Dinks, and she feared her influence upon Alfred. Poor Mr. Dinks! he was at that moment smoking a cigar upon the forward deck of the *Chancellor Livingston* steamer, that plied between New York and Providence. Mr. Bowdoin Beacon sat by his side.

"She's a real good girl, and pretty, and rich, though she is my cousin, Bowdoin. So why don't you?"

Mr. Beacon, a member of the upper sex, replied, gravely, "Well, perhaps!"

They were speaking of Hope Wayne.

At the same instant also, in Mrs. Kingfisher's swarming drawing-rooms, looking on at the dancers and listening to the music, stood Hope Wayne, Lawrence Newt, Amy Waring, and Arthur Merlin. They were chatting together pleasantly, Lawrence Newt usually leading, and Hope Wayne bending her beautiful head, and listening and looking at him in a way to make any man eloquent. The painter had been watching for Mr. Abel Newt's entrance, and, after he saw him, turned to study the effect produced upon Miss Wayne by seeing him.

But Abel, who saw as much in his way as Mrs. Dagon in hers, although without the glasses, had carefully kept in the other part of the rooms. He had planted his batteries before Mrs. Bleecker Van Kraut, having resolved to taste her, as

Herbert Octoyne had advised, notwithstanding that she had no flavor, as Abel himself had averred.

But who eats merely for the flavor of the food?

That lady clicked smoothly as Abel, metaphorically speaking, touched her. Louis Wilkottle, her cavalier, slipped away from her he could not tell how: he merely knew that Abel Newt was in attendance, vice Wilkottle, disappeared. So Wilkottle floated about the rooms upon limp pinions for some time, wondering where to settle, and brushed Fanny Newt in flying.

"Oh! Mr. Wilkottle, you are just the man. Mr. Whitloe, Laura Magot, and I were just talking about Batrachian reptiles. Which are the best toads, the fattest?"

"Or does it depend upon the dressing?" asked Mr. Whitloe.

"Or the quantity of jewelry in the head?" said Laura Magot.

Mr. Wilkottle smiled, bowed, and passed on.

If they had called him an ass—as they were ladies of the best position—he would have bowed, smiled, and passed on.

"An amiable fellow," said Fanny, as he disappeared; "but quite a remarkable fool."

Mr. Zephyr Wetherley, still struggling with the hand problem, approached Miss Fanny, and remarked that it was very warm.

"You're cool enough in all conscience, Mr. Wetherley," said she.

"My dear Miss Newt, 'pon honor," replied Zephyr, beginning to be very red, and wiping his moist brow.

"I call any man cool who would have told St. Lawrence upon the gridiron that he was frying," interrupted Fanny.

"Oh!—ah!—yes!—on the gridiron! Yes, very good! Ha! ha! Quite on the gridiron—very much so! 'Tis very hot here. Don't you think so? It's quite confusing, like—sort of bewildering. Don't you think so, Miss Newt?"

Fanny was leveling her black eyes at him for a reply, but Mr. Wetherley, trying to regulate his hands, said, hastily,

"Yes, quite on the gridiron—very!" and rapidly moved off it by moving on.

"Good evenin', Mrs. Newt," said a voice in another part of the room. "Good-evenin', marm. I sez to ma, Now ma, sez I, you'd better go to Mrs. Kingfisher's ball. Law, pa, sez she, I reckon 'twill be so werry hot to Mrs. Kingfisher's that I'd better stay to home, sez she. So she staid. Well, 'tis dreadful hot, Mrs. Newt. I'm all in a muck. As I was a-puttin' on my coat, I sez, Now, ma, sez I, I hate to wear that coat, sez I. A man does git so nasty sweaty in a great, thick coat, sez I. Whew! I'm all sticky."

And Mr. Van Boozenberg worked himself in his garments and stretched his arms to refresh himself.

Mrs. Boniface Newt, to whom he made this oration, had been taught by her husband that Mr. Van Boozenberg was an oaf, but an oaf whose noise was to be listened to with the utmost patience and respect. "He's a brute, my dear; but what can we do? When I am rich we can get rid of such people."

On the other hand, Jacob Van Boozenberg had his little theory of Boniface Newt, which, unlike that worthy commission merchant, he did not impart to his ma and the partner of his bosom, but locked up in the vault of his own breast. Mr. Van B. gloried in being what he called a self-made man. He was proud of his nasal twang and his want of grammar, and all amenities and decencies of speech. He regarded them as inseparable from his success. He even affected them in the company of those who were peculiarly elegant, and was secretly suspicious of the mercantile paper of all men who were unusually neat in their appearance, and who spoke their native language correctly. The partner of his bosom was the constant audience of his self-glorification.

A little while before, her lord had returned one day to dinner, and said, with a tone of triumph,

"Well, ma, Gerald Bennet & Co. have busted up—smashed all to pieces. Always knew they would. I sez to you, ma, a hundred times—don't you remember?—Now, ma, sez I, 'tain't no use. He's been to college, and he talks grammar, and all that; but what's the use? What's the use of talkin' grammar? Don't help nothin'. A man feels kind o' stuck up when he's been to college. But, ma, sez I, gi' me a self-made man—a man what knows werry well that twice two's four. A self-made man ain't no time for grammar, sez I. If a man expects to get on in this world he mustn't be too fine. This is the second time Bennet's busted. Better have no grammar and more goods, sez I. You remember—hey, ma?"

When, a little while afterward, Mr. Bennet applied for a situation as book-keeper in the bank of which Mr. Van Boozenberg was president, that officer hung, drew, and quartered the English language, before the very eyes of Mr. Bennet, to show him how he despised it, and to impress him with the great truth that he, Jacob Van Boozenberg, a self-made man, who had no time to speak correctly, nor to be comely or clean, was yet a millionaire before whom Wall Street trembled—while he, Gerald Bennet, with all his education, and polish, and care, and scrupulous neatness and politeness, was a poverty-stricken, shiftless vagabond; and what good had grammar done him? The ruined gentleman stood before the president—who was seated in his large arm-chair at the bank—holding his hat uncertainly, the nervous smile glimmering like heat lightning upon his pale, anxious face, in which his eyes shone with that singular, soft light of dreams.

"Now, Mr. Bennet, I sez to ma this very mornin'—sez I, 'Ma, I s'pose Mr. Bennet 'll be wantin' a place in our bank. If he hadn't been so werry fine,' sez I, 'he might have got on. He talks be-youtiful grammar, ma,'" said the worthy President, screwing in the taunt, as it were; "'but grammar ain't good to eat,' sez I. 'He ain't a self-made man, as some folks is,' sez I; 'but I suppose I'll have to stick him in somewheres,' sez I —that's all of it."

Gerald Bennet winced. Beggars mustn't be choosers, said he, feebly, in his sad heart, and he thankfully took the broken

victuals Jacob Van Boozenberg threw him. But he advised
Gabriel, as we saw, to try Lawrence Newt.

Mrs. Newt agreed with Mr. Van Boozenberg that it was
very warm.

"I heerd about you to Saratogy last summer, Mrs. Newt;
but you ain't been to see ma since you come home. 'Ma,' sez
I, 'why don't Mrs. Newt call and see us?' 'Law, pa,' sez
she, 'Mrs. Newt can't call and see such folks as we be!' sez
she. 'We ain't fine enough for Mrs. Newt,'" said the great
man of Wall Street, and he laughed aloud at the excellent joke.

"Mrs. Van Boozenberg is very much mistaken," replied
Mrs. Newt, anxiously. "I am afraid she did not get my card.
I am very sorry. But I hope you will tell her."

The great Jacob knew perfectly well that Mrs. Newt had
called, but he liked to show himself how vast his power was.
He liked to see fine ladies in splendid drawing-rooms bowing
down before his ungrammatical throne, and metaphorically
kissing his knobby red hand.

"Your son, Abel, seems to enjoy himself werry well, Mrs.
Newt," said Mr. Van Boozenberg, as he observed that youth,
in sumptuous array, dancing devotedly with Mrs. Bleecker Van
Kraut.

"Oh dear, yes," replied Mrs. Newt. "But you know what
young sons are, Mr. Van Boozenberg."

The conversation was setting precisely as that gentleman
wished, and as he had intended to direct it.

"Mercy, yes, Mrs. Newt! Ma sez to me, 'Pa, what a boy
Corlear is! how he does spend money!' And I sez to ma,
'Ma, he do.' Tut, tut! The bills I have to pay for that
boy—! I s'pose, now, your Abel don't lay up no money—ha!
ha!"

Mr. Van Boozenberg laughed again, and Mrs. Newt joined,
but in a low and rather distressed way, as if it were necessary to laugh, although nothing funny had been said.

"It's positively dreadful the way he spends money," replied
she. "I don't know where it will end."

I 2

" Oh ho! it's the way with all young men, marm. I always sez to ma she needn't fret her gizzard. Young men will sow their wild oats. Oh, 'tain't nothin'. Mr. Newt knows that werry well. Every man do."

He watched Mrs. Newt's expression as he spoke. She answered,

" I don't know about that; but Mr. Newt shakes his head dismally nowadays about something or other, and he's really grown old."

In uttering these words Mrs. Newt had sealed the fate of a large offering for discount made that very day by Boniface Newt, Son, & Co.

CHAPTER XXXIII.

ANOTHER TURN IN THE WALTZ.

THE music streamed through the rooms in the soft, yearning, lingering, passionate, persuasive measures of a waltz. Arthur Merlin had been very intently watching Hope Wayne, because he saw Abel Newt approaching with Mrs. Van Kraut, and he wished to catch the first look of Hope upon seeing him.

Mrs. Bleecker Van Kraut, when she waltzed, was simply a circular advertisement of the Van Kraut property. Her slow rising and falling motion displayed the family jewels to the utmost advantage. The same insolent smoothness and finish prevailed in the whole performance. It was almost as perfect as the Paris toys which you wind up, and which spin smoothly round upon the table. Abel Newt, conscious master of the dance and chief of brilliant youth, waltzed with an air of delicate deference toward his partner, and gay defiance toward the rest of the world.

The performance was so novel and so well executed that the ball instantly became a spectacle of which Abel and Mrs.

ABEL AND MRS. VAN KRAUT.

Van Kraut were the central figures. The crowd pressed around them, and Abel gently pushed them back in his fluctuating circles. Short ladies in the back-ground stood upon chairs for a moment to get a better view; while Mrs. Dagon and Mrs. Orry, whom no dexterous waltzer would ever clasp in the dizzy whirl, spattered their neighborhood with epithets of contempt and indignation, thanking Heaven that in their day things had not quite come to such a pass as that. Colonel Burr himself, my dears, never dared to touch more than the tips of his partner's fingers in the contra-dance.

Hope Wayne had not met Abel Newt since they had parted after the runaway at Delafield, except in his mother's conservatory, and when she was stepping from the carriage. In the mean while she had been learning every thing at once.

As her eyes fell upon him now she remembered that day upon the lawn at Pinewood, when he stood suddenly beside her, casting a shadow upon the page she was reading. The handsome boy had grown into this proud, gallant, gay young man, surrounded by that social prestige which gives graceful confidence to the bearing of any man. He knew that Hope had heard of his social success; but he could not justly estimate its effect upon her.

Of all those who stood by her Arthur Merlin was the only one who knew that she had ever known Abel, and Arthur only inferred it from Abel's resemblance to the sketch of Manfred, which had evidently deeply affected Hope. Lawrence Newt, who knew Delafield, had wondered if Abel and Hope had ever met. Perhaps he had a little fear of their meeting, knowing Abel to be audacious and brilliant, and Hope to be romantic. Perhaps the anxiety with which he now looked upon the waltz arose from the apprehension that Hope could not help, at least, fancying such a handsome fellow. And then—what?

Amy Waring certainly did not know, although Lawrence Newt's eyes seemed to ask hers the question.

Hope heard the music, and her heart beat time. As she saw Abel and remembered the days that were no more, for a moment her cheek flushed—not tumultuously, but gently— and Lawrence Newt and the painter remarked it. The emotion passed, almost imperceptibly, and her eyes followed the dancers calmly, with only a little ache in the heart—with only a vague feeling that she had lived a long, long time.

Abel Newt had not lost Hope Wayne from his attention for

ABEL AND HOPE.

a single moment during the evening; and before the interest
in the dance was palled, before people had begun to buzz again
and turn away, while Mrs. Van Kraut and he were still the
spectacle upon which all eyes were directed, he suddenly
whirled his partner toward the spot where Hope Wayne and
her friends were standing, and stopped.

It was no more necessary for Mrs. Van Kraut to fan herself
than if she had been a marble statue. But it is proper to fan
one's self when one has done dancing—so she waved the fan.
Besides, it was a Van Kraut heir-loom. It came from Amsterdam. It was studded with jewels. It was part of the property.

As for Abel, he turned and bowed profoundly to Miss
Wayne. Of course she knew that people were looking. She
bowed as if to a mere acquaintance. Abel said a few words,
signifying nothing, to his partner, then he remarked to Miss
Wayne that he was very glad indeed to meet her again; that he
had not called because he knew she had been making a convent
of her aunt's house—making herself a nun—a Sister of Charity,
he did not doubt, doing good as she always did—making every body in the world happy, as she could not help doing,
and so forth.

Abel rattled on, he did not know why; but he did know
that his Uncle Lawrence, and Amy Waring, and Mr. Merlin
heard every thing he said. Hope looked at him calmly, and
listened to the gay cascade of talk.

The music was still playing; Mr. Van Boozenberg spoke to
Lawrence Newt; Amy Waring said that she saw her Aunt
Bennet. Would Mr. Merlin take her to her aunt?—he should
return to his worship in one moment. Mr. Merlin was very
gallant, and replied with spirit that when her worship returned
—here he made a low bow—his would. As they moved away
Amy Waring laughed at him, and said that men would compliment as long as—as women are lovely, interpolated Mr.
Merlin. Arthur also wished to know what speech was good
for, if not to say the sweetest things; and so they were lost
to view, still gayly chatting with the pleasant freedom of a
young man and woman who know that they are not in love
with each other, and are perfectly content not to be so, because—whether they know it or not—they are each in love
with somebody else.

This movement had taken place as Abel was finishing his
scattering volley of talk.

"Yes," said he, as he saw that he was not overheard, and sinking his voice into that tone of tender music which Hope so well remembered—"yes, making every body in the world happy but one person."

His airy persiflage had not pleased Hope Wayne. The sudden modulation into sentiment offended her. Before she replied—indeed she had no intention of replying—the round eyes of Mrs. Van Kraut informed her partner that she was ready for another turn, and forth they whirled upon the floor.

"I jes' sez to Mrs. Dagon, you know, ma'am, sez I, I don't like to see a young man like Mr. Abel Newt, sez I, wasting himself upon married women. No, sez I, ma'am, when you women have made your market, sez I, you oughter stan' one side and give the t'others a chance, sez I."

Mr. Van Boozenberg addressed this remark to Lawrence Newt. In the eyes of the old gentleman it was another instance of imprudence on Abel's part not to be already engaged to some rich girl.

Lawrence Newt replied by looking round the room as if searching for some one, and then saying:

"I don't see your daughter, Mrs. Witchet, here to-night, Mr. Van Boozenberg."

"No," growled the papa, and moved on to talk with Mrs. Dagon.

"My dear Sir," said the Honorable Budlong Dinks, approaching just as Lawrence Newt finished his remark, and Van Boozenberg, growling, departed:

"That was an unfortunate observation. You are, perhaps, not aware—"

"Oh! thank you, yes, I am fully aware," replied Lawrence Newt. "But one thing I do not know."

The Honorable Budlong Dinks bowed with dignity as if he understood Mr. Newt to compliment him by insinuating that he was the man who knew all about it, and would immediately enlighten him.

"I do not know why, if a man does a mean and unfeeling,

yes, an inhuman act, it is bad manners to speak of it. Old Van Boozenberg ought to be sent to the penitentiary for his treatment of his daughter, and we all know it."

"Yes; but really," replied the Honorable Budlong Dinks, "really—you know—it would be impossible. Mr. Van Boozenberg is a highly respectable man—really—we should lapse into chaos," and the honorable gentleman rubbed his hands with perfect suavity.

"When did we emerge?" asked Lawrence Newt, with such a kindly glimmer in his eyes, that Mr. Dinks said merely, "really," and moved on, remarking to General Arcularius Belch, with a diplomatic shrug, that Lawrence Newt was a very odd man.

"Odd, but not without the coin. He can afford to be odd," replied that gentleman.

While these little things were said and done, Lawrence moved through the crowd and somehow found himself at the side of Amy Waring, who was talking with Fanny Newt.

"You young Napoleon," said Lawrence to his niece as he joined them.

"What do you mean, you droll Uncle Lawrence?" demanded Fanny, her eyes glittering with inquiry.

"Where's Mrs. Wurmser—I mean Mrs. Dinks?" continued Lawrence. "Why, when I saw you talking together a little while ago, I could think of nothing but the young Bonaparte and the old Wurmser."

"You droll Uncle Lawrence, aren't you ashamed of yourself?"

It was an astuter young Napoleon than Uncle Lawrence knew. Even then and there, in Mrs. Kingfisher's ball-room, had Fanny Newt resolved how to carry her Mantua by a sudden coup.

CHAPTER XXXIV.

HEAVEN'S LAST BEST GIFT.

"My dear Alfred, I am glad to see you. You may kiss me—carefully, carefully!"

Mr. Alfred Dinks therewith kissed lips upon his return from Boston.

"Sit down, Alfred, my dear, I wish to speak to you," said Fanny Newt, with even more than her usual decision. The eyes were extremely round and black. Alfred seated himself with vague trepidation.

"My dear, we must be married immediately," remarked Fanny, quietly.

The eyes of the lover shone with pleasure.

"Dear Fanny!" said he, "have you told mother?"

"No," answered she, calmly.

"Well, but then you know—" rejoined Alfred. He would have said more, but he was afraid. He wanted to inquire whether Fanny thought that her father would supply the sinews of matrimony. Alfred's theory was that he undoubtedly would. He was sure that a young woman of Fanny's calmness, intrepidity, and profound knowledge of the world would not propose immediate matrimony without seeing how the commissariat was to be supplied. She has all her plans laid, of course, thought he—she is so talented and cool that 'tis all right, I dare say. Of course she knows that I have nothing, and hope for nothing except from old Burt, and he's not sure for me, by any means. But Boniface Newt is rich enough.

And Alfred consoled himself by thinking of the style in which that worthy commission merchant lived, and especially of his son Abel's expense and splendor.

"Alfred, dear—just try not to be trying, you know, but think what you are about. Your mother has found out that something has gone wrong—that you are not engaged to Hope Wayne."

"Yes—yes, I know," burst in Alfred; "she treated me like a porcupine this morning—or ant-eater, which is it, Fanny—the thing with quills, you know?"

Miss Fanny Newt patted the floor with her foot. Alfred continued:

"Yes, and Hope sent down, and she wanted to see me alone some time to-day."

Fanny's foot stopped.

"Alfred, dear," said she, "you are a good fellow, but you are too amiable. You must do just as I want you to, dearest, or something awful will happen."

"Pooh! Fanny; nothing shall happen. I love you like any thing."

Smack! smack!

"Well, then, listen, Alfred! Your mother doesn't like me. She would do any thing to prevent your marrying me. The reasons I will tell you at another time. If you go home and talk with her and Hope Wayne, you can not help betraying that you are engaged to me; and—you know your mother, Alfred—she would openly oppose the marriage, and I don't know what she might not say to my father."

Fanny spoke clearly and rapidly, but calmly. Alfred looked utterly bewildered.

"It's a great pity, isn't it?" said he, feebly. "What do you think we had better do?"

"We must be married, Alfred, dear!"

"Yes; but when, Fanny?"

"To-day," said Fanny, firmly, and putting out her hand to her beloved.

He seized it mechanically.

"To-day, Fanny?" asked he, after a pause of amazement.

"Certainly, dear—to-day. I am as ready now as I shall be a year hence."

"But what will my mother say?" inquired Alfred, in alarm.

"It will be too late for her to say any thing. Don't you see, Alfred, dear!" continued Fanny, in a most assuring tone, "that if we go to your mother and say, 'Here we are, married!' she has sense enough to perceive that nothing can be done; and after a little while all will be smooth again?"

Her lover was comforted by this view. He was even pleased by the audacity of the project.

"I swear, Fanny," said he, at length, in a more cheerful and composed voice, "I think it's rather a good idea!"

"Of course it is, dear. Are you ready?"

Alfred gasped a little at the prompt question, despite his confidence.

"Why, Fanny, you don't mean actually now—this very day? Gracious!"

"Why not now? Since we think best to be married immediately and in private, why should we put it off until to-night, or next week, when we are both as ready now as we can be then?" asked Fanny, quietly; "especially as something may happen to make it impossible then."

Alfred Dinks shut his eyes.

"What will your father say?" he inquired, at length, without raising his eyelids.

"Do you not see he will have to make up his mind to it, just as your mother will?" replied Fanny.

"And my father!" said Alfred, in a state of temporary blindness continued.

"Yes, and your father too," answered Fanny, both she and Alfred treating the Honorable Budlong Dinks as a mere tender to that woman-of-war his wife, in a way that would have been incredible to a statesman who considered his wife a mere domestic luxury.

There was a silence of several minutes. Then Mr. Dinks opened his eyes, and said,

"Well, Fanny, dear!"

"Well, Alfred, dear!" and Fanny leaned toward him, with her head poised like that of a black snake. Alfred was fas-

cinated. Perhaps he was sorry he was so; perhaps he wanted to struggle. But he did not. He was under the spell.

There was still a lingering silence. Fanny waited patiently.
At length she asked again, putting her hand in her lover's:

" Are you ready?"

" Yes!" said Alfred, in a crisp, resolute tone.

Fanny raised her hand and rang the bell. The waiter appeared.

" John, I want a carriage immediately."

" Yes, Miss."

" And, John, tell Mary to bring me my things. I am going out."

" Yes, Miss." And hearing nothing farther, John disappeared.

It was perhaps a judicious instinct which taught Fanny not
to leave Alfred alone by going up to array herself in her own
chamber. The intervals of delay between the coming of the
maid and the coming of the carriage the young woman em-
ployed in conversing dexterously about Boston, and the friends
he had seen there, and in describing to him the great Kingfisher ball.

Presently she was bonneted and cloaked, and the carriage
was at the door.

Her home had not been a Paradise to Fanny Newt—nor
were Aunt Dagon, Papa and Mamma Newt, and brother Abel
altogether angels. She had no superfluous emotions of any
kind at any time; but as she passed through the hall she saw
her sister May—the youngest child—a girl of sixteen—Uncle
Lawrence's favorite—standing upon the stairs.

She said nothing; the hall was quite dim, and as the girl
stood in the half light her childlike, delicate beauty seemed to
Fanny more striking than ever. If Uncle Lawrence had seen
her at the moment he would have thought of Jacob's ladder
and the angels ascending and descending.

" Good-by, May!" said Fanny, going up to her sister, taking
her face between her hands and kissing her lips.

The sisters looked at each other, each inexplicably conscious that it was not an ordinary farewell.

"Good-by, darling!" said Fanny, kissing her again, and still holding her young, lovely face.

Touched and surprised by the unwonted tenderness of her sister's manner, May threw her arms around her neck and burst into tears.

"Oh! Fanny."

Fanny did not disengage the arms that clung about her, nor raise the young head that rested upon her shoulder. Perhaps she felt that somehow it was a benediction.

May raised her head at length, kissed Fanny gently upon the lips, smoothed her black hair for a moment with her delicate hand, half smiled through her tears as she thought that after this indication of affection she should have such a pleasant intercourse with her sister, and then pushed her softly away, saying,

"Mr. Dinks is waiting for you, Fanny."

Fanny said nothing, but drew her veil over her face, and Mr. Dinks handed her into the carriage.

CHAPTER XXXV.

MOTHER-IN-LAW AND DAUGHTER-IN-LAW.

MRS. DINKS and Hope Wayne sat together in their lodgings, waiting impatiently for Alfred's return. They were both working busily, and said little to each other. Mrs. Dinks had resolved to leave New York at the earliest possible moment. She waited only to have a clear explanation with her son. Hope Wayne was also waiting for an explanation. She was painfully curious to know why Alfred Dinks had told his mother that they were engaged. As her Aunt Dinks looked at her, and saw how noble and lofty her beauty was, yet how simple and candid, she was more than ever angry with her, because she felt that it was impossible she should ever have loved Alfred.

They heard a carriage in the street. It stopped at the door. In a moment the sound of a footstep was audible.

"My dear, I wish to speak to Alfred alone. I hear his step," said Mrs. Dinks.

"Yes, aunt," answered Hope Wayne, rising, and taking her little basket she moved toward the door. Just as she reached it, it opened, and Alfred Dinks and Fanny Newt entered. Hope bowed, and was passing on.

"Stop, Hope!" whispered Alfred, excitedly.

She turned at the door and looked at her cousin, who, with uncertain bravado, advanced with Fanny to his mother, who was gazing at them in amazement, and said, in a thick, hurried voice,

"Mother, this is your daughter Fanny—my wife—Mrs. Alfred Dinks."

As she heard these words Hope Wayne went out, closing the door behind her, leaving the mother alone with her children.

Mrs. Dinks sat speechless in her chair for a few moments, staring at Alfred, who looked as if his legs would not long support him, and at Fanny, who stood calmly beside him. At length she said to Alfred,

"Is that woman really your wife?"

"Yes, 'm," replied the new husband.

"What are you going to support her with?"

"I have my allowance," said Alfred, in a very small voice.

"Mrs. Alfred Dinks, your husband's allowance is six hundred dollars a year from his father. I wish you joy."

There was a sarcastic sparkle in her eyes. Mrs. Dinks had long felt that she and Fanny were contesting a prize. At this moment, while she knew that she had not won, she was sure that Fanny had lost.

Fanny was prepared for such a reception. She did not shrink. She remembered the great Burt fortune. But before

MRS. DINKS. *MERE ET FILLE.*

she could speak Mrs. Dinks rose, and, with an air of contemptuous defiance, inquired,

"Where are you living, Mrs. Dinks?"

Mr. Alfred looked at his wife in profound perplexity. He
thought, for his part, that he was living in that very house.
But his wife answered, quietly,

"We are at Bunker's, where we shall be delighted to see
you. Good-morning, Mrs. Dinks"

And Fanny took her husband by the arm and went out, having entirely confounded her mother-in-law, who meant to have wished her children good-morning, and then have left them to their embarrassment. But victory seemed to perch upon Fanny's standards along the whole line.

CHAPTER XXXVI.

THE BACK WINDOW.

LAWRENCE NEWT was not unmindful of the difference of age between Amy Waring and himself; and instinctively he did nothing which could show to others that he felt more for her than for a friend. Younger men, who could not help yielding to the charm of her presence, never complained of him. He was never " that infernal old bore, Lawrence Newt," to them. More than one of them, in the ardor of young feeling, had confided his passion to Lawrence, who said to him, bravely, "My dear fellow, I do not wonder you feel so. God speed you—and so will I, all I can."

And he did so. He mentioned the candidate kindly to Miss Waring. He repeated little anecdotes that he had heard to his advantage. Lawrence regarded the poor suitor as a painter does a picture. He took him up in the arms of his charity and moved him round and round. He put him upon his sympathy as upon an easel, and turned on the kindly lights and judiciously darkened the apartment.

His generosity was chivalric, but it was unavailing. Beautiful flowers arrived from the aspiring youths. They were so lovely, so fragrant! What taste that young Hal Battlebury has! remarks Lawrence Newt, admiringly, as he smells the flowers that stand in a pretty vase upon the centre-table. Amy Waring smiles, and says that it is Thorburn's taste, of whom Mr. Battlebury buys the flowers. Mr. Newt replies that it is at least very thoughtful in him. A young lady can not but feel kindly, surely, toward young men who express their good feeling in the form of flowers. Then he dexterously leads the conversation into some other channel. He will not harm the cause of poor Mr. Battlebury by persisting in speaking of him and his bouquets, when that persistence will evidently render the subject a little tedious.

Poor Mr. Hal Battlebury, who, could he only survey the Waring mansion from the lower floor to the roof, would behold his handsome flowers that came on Wednesday withering in cold ceremony upon the parlor-table—and in Amy Waring's bureau-drawer would see the little book she received from " her friend Lawrence Newt" treasured like a priceless pearl, with a pressed rose laid upon the leaf where her name and his are written—a rose which Lawrence Newt playfully stole one evening from one of the ceremonious bouquets pining under its polite reception, and said gayly, as he took leave, " Let this keep my memory fragrant till I return."

But it was a singular fact that when one of those baskets without a card arrived at the house, it was not left in superb solitary state upon the centre-table in the parlor, but bloomed as long as care could coax it in the strict seclusion of Miss Waring's own chamber, and then some choicest flower was selected to be pressed and preserved somewhere in the depths of the bureau.

Could the bureau drawers give up their treasures, would any human being longer seem to be cold? would any maiden young or old appear a voluntary spinster, or any unmarried octogenarian at heart a bachelor?

For many a long hour Lawrence Newt stood at the window of the loft in the rear of his office, and looked up at the window where he had seen Amy Waring that summer morning. He was certainly quite as curious about that room as Hope about his early knowledge of her home.

"I'll just run round and settle this matter," said the merchant to himself.

But he did not stir. His hands were in his pockets. He was standing as firmly in one spot as if he had taken root.

"Yes—upon the whole, I'll just run round," thought Law-rence, without the remotest approach to motion of any kind. But his fancy was running round all the time, and the fancies of men who watch windows, as Lawrence Newt watched this window, are strangely fantastic. He imagined every thing in that room. It was a woman with innumerable children, of course—some old nurse of Amy's—who had a kind of respect-ability to preserve, which intrusion would injure. No, no, by Heaven! it was Mrs. Tom Witchet, old Van Boozenberg's daughter! Of course it was. An old friend of Amy's, half-starving in that miserable lodging, and Amy her guardian an-gel. Lawrence Newt mentally vowed that Mrs. Tom Witchet should never want any thing. He would speak to Amy at the next meeting of the Round Table.

Or there were other strange fancies. What will not an India merchant dream as he gazes from his window? It was some old teacher of Amy's—some music-master, some French teacher—dying alone and in poverty, or with a large family. No, upon the whole, thought Lawrence Newt, he's not old enough to have a large family—he is not married—he has too delicate a nature to struggle with the world—he was a gentle-man in his own country; and he has, of course, it's only natu-ral—how could he possibly help it?—he has fallen in love with Miss Waring. These music-masters and Italian teachers are such silly fellows. I know all about it, thought Mr. Newt; and now he lies there forlorn, but picturesque and very hand-some, singing sweetly to his guitar, and reciting Petrarch's sonnets with large, melancholy eyes. His manners refined and fascinating. His age? About thirty. Poor Amy! Of course common humanity requires her to come and see that he does not suffer. Of course he is desperately in love, and she can only pity. Pity? pity? Who says something about the kinship of pity? I really think, says Lawrence Newt to himself, that I ought to go over and help that unfortunate young man. Perhaps he wishes to return to his native country. I am sure he ought to. His native air will be

LAWRENCE NEWT SEES THE REASON WHY.

balm to him. Yes, I'll ask Miss Waring about it this very
evening.

He did not. He never alluded to the subject. They had
never mentioned that summer noontide exchange of glance
and gesture which had so curious an effect on Lawrence Newt
that he now stood quite as often at his back window, looking
up at the old brick house, as at his front window, looking out

over the river and the ships, and counting the spires—at least it seemed so—in Brooklyn.

For how could Lawrence know of the book that was kept in the bureau drawer—of the rose whose benediction lay forever fragrant upon those united names?

"I am really sorry for Hal Battlebury," said the merchant to himself. "He is such a good, noble fellow! I should have supposed that Miss Waring would have been so very happy with him. He is so suitable in every way; in age, in figure, in tastes—in sympathy altogether. Then he is so manly and modest, so simple and true. It is really very—very—"

And so he mused, and asked and answered, and thought of Hal Battlebury and Amy Waring together.

It seemed to him that if he were a younger man—about the age of Battlebury, say—full of hope, and faith, and earnest endeavor—a glowing and generous youth—it would be the very thing he should do—to fall in love with Amy Waring. How could any man see her and not love her? His reflections grew dreamy at this point.

"If so lovely a girl did not return the affection of such a young man, it would be—of course, what else could it be?—it would be because she had deliberately made up her mind that, under no conceivable circumstances whatsoever, would she ever marry."

As he reached this satisfactory conclusion Lawrence Newt paced up and down before the window, with his hands still buried in his pockets, thinking of Hal Battlebury—thinking of the foreign youth with the large, melancholy eyes pining upon a bed of pain, and reciting Petrarch's sonnets, in the miserable room opposite—thinking also of that strange coldness of virgin hearts which not the ardors of youth and love could melt.

And, stopping before the window, he thought of his own boyhood—of the first wild passion of his young heart—of the little hand he held—of the soft darkness of eyes whose light mingled with his own—again the palm-trees—the rushing river—when, at the very window upon which he was unconsciously gazing, one afternoon a face appeared, with a black silk handkerchief twisted about the head, and looking down into the court between the houses.

Lawrence Newt stared at it without moving. Both windows were closed, nor was the woman at the other looking toward him. He had, indeed, scarcely seen her fully before she turned away. But he had recognized that face. He had seen a woman he had so long thought dead. In a moment Amy Waring's visit was explained, and a more heavenly light shone upon her character as he thought of her.

"God bless you, Amy dear!" were the words that unconsciously stole to his lips; and going into the office, Lawrence Newt told Thomas Tray that he should not return that afternoon, wished his clerks good-day, and hurried around the corner into Front Street.

CHAPTER XXXVII.

ABEL NEWT, *vice* SLIGO MOULTRIE REMOVED.

THE Plumers were at Bunker's. The gay, good-hearted Grace, full of fun and flirtation, vowed that New York was life, and all the rest of the world death.

"You do not compliment the South very much," said Sligo Moultrie, smiling.

"Oh no! The South is home, and we don't compliment relations, you know," returned Miss Grace.

"Yes, thank Heaven! the South *is* home, Miss Grace. New York is like a foreign city. The tumult is fearful; yet it is only a sea-port after all. It has no metropolitan repose. It never can have. It is a trading town."

"Then I like trading towns, if that is it," returned Miss Grace, looking out into the bustling street.

Mr. Moultrie smiled—a quiet, refined, intelligent, and accomplished smile.

He smiled confidently. Not offensively, but with that half-shy sense of superiority which gave the high grace of self-possession to his manner—a languid repose which pervaded his whole character. The symmetry of his person, the careless ease of his carriage, a sweet voice, a handsome face, were valuable allies of his intellectual accomplishments; and when all the forces were deployed they made Sligo Moultrie very fascinating. He was not audacious nor brilliant. It was a passive, not an active nature. He was not rich, although Mrs. Boniface Newt had a vague idea that every Southern youth was *ex-officio* a Crœsus. Scion of a fine old family, like the Newts, and Whitloes, and Octoynes of New York, Mr. Sligo Moultrie, born to be a gentleman, but born poor, was resolved to maintain his state.

Miss Grace Plumer, as we saw at Mrs. Boniface Newt's, had bright black eyes, profusely curling black hair, olive skin, pouting mouth, and pearly teeth. Very rich, very pretty, and very merry was Miss Grace Plumer, who believed with enthusiastic faith that life was a ball, but who was very shrewd and very kindly also.

Sligo Moultrie understood distinctly why he was sitting at the window with Grace Plumer.

"The roses are in bloom at your home, I suppose, Miss Grace?" said he.

"Yes, I suppose they are, and a dreadfully lonely time they're having of it. Southern life, of course, is a hundred times better than life here; but it is a little lonely, isn't it, Mr. Moultrie?"

Grace said this turning her neck slightly, and looking an arch interrogatory at her companion.

"Yes, it is lonely in some ways. But then there is so much. going up to town and travelling that, after all, it is only a few months that we are at home; and a man ought to be at home a good deal—he ought not to be a vagabond."

"Thank you," said Grace, bowing mockingly.

"I said 'a man,' you observe, Miss Grace."

"Man includes woman, I believe, Mr. Moultrie."

"In two cases—yes."

"What are they?"

"When he holds her in his arms or in his heart."

Here was a sudden volley masked in music. Grace Plumer was charmed. She looked at her companion. He had been "a vagabond" all winter in New York; but there were few more presentable men. Moreover, she felt at home with him as a *compatriot*. Yes, this would do very well.

Miss Grace Plumer had scarcely mentally installed Mr. Sligo Moultrie as first flirter in her corps, when a face she remembered looked up at the window from the street, more dangerous even than when she had seen it in the spring. It was the face of Abel Newt, who raised his hat and bowed to her with an admiration which he concealed that he took care to show.

The next moment he was in the room, perfectly *comme il faut*, sparkling, resistless.

"My dear Miss Plumer, I knew spring was coming. I felt it as I approached Bunker's. I said to Herbert Octoyne (he's off with the Shrimp; Papa Shrimp was too much, he was so old that he was rank)—I said, either I smell the grass sprouting in the Battery or I have a sensation of spring. I raise my eyes—I see that it is not grass, but flowers. I recognize the dear, delicious spring. I bow to Miss Plumer."

He tossed it airily off. It was audacious. It would have been outrageous, except that the manner made it seem persiflage, and therefore allowable. Grace Plumer blushed, bowed, smiled, and met his offered hand half-way. Abel Newt knew perfectly what he was doing, and raised it respectfully, bowed over it, kissed it.

"Moultrie, glad to see you. Miss Plumer, 'tis astonishing how this man always knows the pleasant places. If I want to know where the best fruits and the earliest flowers are, I ask Sligo Moultrie."

Mr. Moultrie bowed.

"The first rose of the year blooms in Mr. Moultrie's button-hole," continued Abel, who galloped on, laughing, and seating himself upon an ottoman, so that his eyes were lower than the level of Grace Plumer's.

She smiled, and joined the hunt.

"He talks nothing but 'ladies' delights,'" said she.

"Yes—two other things, please, Miss Grace," said Moultrie.

"What, Mr. Moultrie, two other cases? You always have two more."

"Better two more than too much," struck in Abel, who saw that Miss Plumer had put out her darling little foot from beneath her dress, and therefore had fixed his eyes upon it, with an admiration which was not lost upon the lady.

"Heavens!" cried Moultrie, laughing and looking at them. "You are both two more and too much for me."

"Good, good, good for Moultrie!" applauded Abel; "and now, Miss Plumer, I submit that he has the floor."

"Very well, Mr. Moultrie. What are the two other things that you talk?"

"Pansies and rosemary," said the young man, rising and bowing himself out.

"Miss Plumer, you have been the inspiration of my friend Sligo, who was never so brilliant in his life before. How generous in you to rise and shine on this wretched town! It is Sahara. Miss Plumer descends upon it like dew. Where have you been?"

"At home, in Louisiana."

"Ah! yes. Know ye the land where the cypress and myrtle— I have never been there; but it comes to me here when you come, Miss Plumer."

Still the slight persiflage to cover the audacity.

"And so, Mr. Newt, I have the honor of seeing the gentleman of whom I have heard most this winter."

"What will not our enemies say of us, Miss Plumer?"

"You have no enemies," replied she, "except, perhaps—no, I'll not mention them."

"Who? who? I insist," said Abel, looking at Grace Plumer earnestly for a moment, then dropping his eyes upon her very pretty and very be-ringed white hands, where the eyes lingered a little and worshipped in the most evident manner.

"Except, then, your own sex," said the little Louisianian, half blushing.

"I do them no harm," replied Abel.

"No; but you make them jealous."

"Jealous of what?" returned the young man, in a lower tone, and more seriously.

"Oh! it's only of—of—of—of what I hear from the girls," said Grace, fluttering a little, as she remembered the conservatory at Mrs. Boniface Newt's, which also Abel had not forgotten.

"And what do you hear, Miss Grace?" he asked, in pure music.

Grace blushed, and laughed.

"Oh! only of your success with poor, feeble women," said she.

"I have no success with women," returned Abel Newt, in a half-serious way, and in his most melodious voice. "Women are naturally generous. They appreciate and acknowledge an honest admiration, even when it is only honest."

"Only honest! What more could it be, Mr. Newt?"

"It might be eloquent. It might be fascinating and irresistible. Even when a man does not really admire, his eloquence makes him dangerous. If, when he truly admires, he were also eloquent, he would be irresistible. There is no victory like that. I should envy Alexander nothing and Napoleon nothing if I thought I could really conquer one woman's heart. My very consciousness of the worth of the prize paralyzes my efforts. It is musty, but it is true, that fools rush in where angels fear to tread."

He sat silent, gazing abstractedly at the two lovely feet of

Miss Grace Plumer, with an air that implied how far his mind had wandered in their conversation from any merely personal considerations. Miss Grace Plumer had not made as much progress as Mr. Newt since their last meeting. Abel Newt seemed to her the handsomest fellow she had ever seen. What he had said both piqued and pleased her. It pleased her because it piqued her.

" Women are naturally noble," he continued, in a low, rippling voice. " If they see that a man sincerely admires them they forgive him, although he can not say so. Yes, and a woman who really loves a man forgives him every thing."

He was looking at her hands, which lay white, and warm, and glittering in her lap. She was silent.

"What a superb ruby, Miss Grace! It might be a dewdrop from a pomegranate in Paradise."

She smiled at the extravagant conceit, while he took her hand as he spoke, and admired the ring. The white, warm hand remained passive in his.

" Let me come nearer to Paradise," he said, half-abstractedly, as if he were following his own thoughts, and he pressed his lips to the fingers upon which the ruby gleamed.

Miss Grace Plumer was almost frightened. This was a very different performance from Mr. Sligo Moultrie's—very different from any she had known. She felt as if she suggested, in some indescribable way, strange and beautiful thoughts to Abel Newt. He looked and spoke as if he addressed himself to the thoughts she had evoked rather than to herself. Yet she felt herself to be both the cause and the substance. It was very sweet. She did not know what she felt; she did not know how much she dared. But when he went away she knew that Abel Newt was appointed first flirter, *vice* Sligo Moultrie removed.

CHAPTER XXXVIII.

THE DAY AFTER THE WEDDING.

"On the 23d instant, Alfred Dinks, Esq., of Boston, to Fanny, oldest daughter of Boniface Newt, Esq., of this city."

Fanny wrote the notice with her own hands, and made Alfred take it to the papers. In this manner she was before her mother-in-law in spreading the news. In this manner, also, as Boniface Newt, Esq., sat at breakfast, he learned of his daughter's marriage. His face grew purple. He looked apoplectic as he said to his wife,

"Nancy, what in God's name does this mean?"

His frightened wife asked what, and he read the announcement aloud.

He rose from table, and walked up and down the room.

"Did you know any thing of this?" inquired he. "What does it mean?"

"Dear me! I thought he was engaged to Hope Wayne," replied Mrs. Newt, crying.

There was a moment's silence. Then Mr. Newt said, with a sneer,

"It seems to me that a mother whose daughter gets married without her knowledge is a very curious kind of mother—an extremely competent kind of mother."

He resumed his walking. Mrs. Newt went on with her weeping. But Boniface Newt was aware of the possibilities in the case of Alfred, and therefore tried to recover himself and consider the chances.

"What do you know about this fellow?" said he, petulantly, to his wife.

"I don't know any thing in particular," she sobbed.

"Do you know whether he has money, or whether his father has?"

"SHE SHALL LIE IN THE BED SHE HAS MADE."

"No; but old Mr. Burt is his grandfather."

"What! his mother's father?"

"I believe so. I know Fanny always said he was Hope Wayne's cousin."

Mr. Newt pondered for a little while. His brow contracted.

"Why on earth have they run away? Did Mr. Burt's

grandson suppose he would be unwelcome to me? Has he been in the habit of coming here, Nancy?"

"No, not much."

"Have you seen them since this thing?"

"No, indeed," replied the mother, bursting into tears afresh.

Her husband looked at her darkly.

"Don't blubber. What good does crying do? G——! if any thing happens in this world, a woman falls to crying her eyes out, as if that would help it."

Boniface Newt was not usually affectionate. But there was almost a ferocity in his address at this moment which startled his wife into silence. His daughter May turned pale as she saw and heard her father.

"I thought Abel was trial enough!" said he, bitterly; "and now the girl must fall to cutting up shines. I tell you plainly, Nancy, if Fanny has married a beggar, a beggar she shall be. There is some reason for a private marriage that we don't understand. It can't be any good reason; and, daughter or no daughter, she shall lie in the bed she has made."

He scowled and set his teeth as he said it. His wife did not dare to cry any more. May went to her mother and took her hand, while the father of the family walked rapidly up and down.

"Every thing comes at once," said he. "Just as I am most bothered and driven down town, this infernal business of Fanny's must needs happen. One thing I'm sure of—if it was all right it would not be a private wedding. What fools women are! And Fanny, whom I always thought so entirely able to take care of herself, turns out to be the greatest fool of all! This fellow's a booby, I believe, Mrs. Newt. I think I have heard even you make fun of him. But to be poor, too! To run away with a pauper-booby, by Heavens, it's too absurd!"

Mr. Newt laughed mockingly, while the tears flowed fast from the eyes of his wife, who said at intervals, "I vow," and "I declare," with such utter weakness of tone and move-

ment that her husband suddenly exclaimed, in an exasperated
tone,

"Nancy, if you don't stop rocking your body in that inane
way, and shaking your hand and your handkerchief, and saying those imbecile things, I shall go mad. I suppose this is
the kind of sympathy a man gets from a woman in his misfortunes!"

May Newt looked shocked and indignant. "Mother, I am
sorry for poor Fanny," said she.

She said it quietly and tenderly, and without the remotest
reference in look, or tone, or gesture to her father.

He turned toward her suddenly.

"Hold your tongue, Miss!"

"Mamma, I shall go and see Fanny to-day," May continued,
as if her father had not spoken. Her mother looked frightened,
and turned to her deprecatingly with a look that said, "For
Heaven's sake, don't!" Her father regarded her for a moment in amazement.

"What do you mean, you little vixen? Let me catch you
disobeying me and going to see that ungrateful wicked girl,
if you think fit!"

There was a moment in which May Newt turned pale, but
she said, in a very low voice,

"I must go."

"May, I forbid your going," said Mr. Newt, severely and
loudly.

"Father, you have no right to forbid me."

"I forbid your going," roared her father, planting himself
in front of her, and quite white with wrath.

May said no more.

"A pretty family you have brought up, Mrs. Nancy Newt,"
said he, at length, looking at his wife with all the contempt
which his voice expressed. "A son who ruins me by his extravagance, a daughter who runs away with—with"—he hesitated to remember the exact expression—"with a pauper-booby, and another daughter who defies and disobeys her father.

I congratulate you upon your charming family, upon your distinguished success, Mrs. Newt. Is there no younger brother
of your son-in-law whom you might introduce to Miss May
Newt? I beg your pardon, she is Miss Newt, now that her
sister is so happily married," said Boniface Newt, bowing cer-
emoniously to his daughter.

Mrs. Newt clasped her hands in an utterly helpless despair,
and unconsciously raised them in a beseeching attitude before
her.

"The husband's duty takes him away from home," continued Mr. Newt. "While he is struggling for the maintenance
of his family he supposes that his wife is caring for his children, and that she has, at least, the smallest speck of an idea
of what is necessary to be done to make them tolerably well
behaved. Some husbands are doomed to be mistaken."

Boniface Newt bowed, and smiled sarcastically.

"Yes, and as if it were not enough to have my wife such a
model trainer—and my son so careful—and my daughter so
obedient—and my younger daughter so affectionate—I must
also have trials in my business. I expected a great loan from
Van Boozenberg's bank, and I haven't got it. He's an old
driveling fool. Mrs. Newt, you must curtail expenses. There's
one mouth less, and one Stewart's bill less, at any rate."

"Father," said May, as if she could not bear the cool cutting adrift of her sister from the family, "Fanny is not dead."

"No," replied her father, sullenly. "No, the more's the—"

He stopped, for he caught May's eye, and he could not finish the sentence.

"Mr. Newt," said his wife, at length, "perhaps Alfred
Dinks is not poor."

That was the chance, but Mr. Newt was skeptical. He had
an instinctive suspicion that no rich young man, however
much a booby, would have married Fanny clandestinely. Men
are forced to know something of their reputations, and Boniface Newt was perfectly aware that it was generally understood he had no aversion to money. He knew also that he

was reputed rich, that his family were known to live expens.
ively, and he was quite shrewd enough to believe that any
youth in her own set who ran off with his daughter did so because he depended upon her father's money. He was satisfied that the Newt family was not to be a gainer by the new
alliance. The more he thought of it the more he was convinced, and the more angry he became. He was still storm-
ing, when the door was thrown open and Mrs. Dagon rushed in.

"What does it all mean?" asked she.

Mr. Newt stopped in his walk, smiled contemptuously, and
pointed to his wife, who sat with her handkerchief over her
eyes.

"Pooh!" said Mrs. Dagon, "I knew 'twould come to this.
I've seen her hugging him the whole winter, and so has every
body else who has eyes."

And she shook her plumage as she settled into a seat.

"Mrs. Boniface Newt is unfortunately blind; that is to say,
she sees every body's affairs but her own," said Mr. Newt,
tauntingly.

Mrs. Dagon, without heeding him, talked on.

"But why did they run away to be married? What does
it mean? Fanny's not romantic, and Dinks is a fool. He's
rich, and a proper match enough, for a woman can't expect
to have every thing. I can't see why he didn't propose regularly, and behave like other people. Do you suppose he was
actually engaged to his cousin Hope Wayne, and that our darling Fanny has outwitted the Boston beauty, and the Boston
beau too, for that matter? It looks like it, really. I think
that must be it. It's a pity a Newt should marry a fool—"

"It is not the first time," interrupted her nephew, making
a low bow to his wife.

Mrs. Dagon looked a little surprised. She had seen little
jars and rubs before in the family, but this morning she
seemed to have happened in upon an earthquake. She continued:

"But we must make the best of it. Are they in the house?"

"No, Aunt Dagon," said Mr. Newt. "I knew nothing of it until, half an hour ago, I read it in the paper with all the rest of the world. It seems it was a family secret." And he bowed again to his wife.

"Don't, don't," sobbed she. "You know I didn't know any thing about it. Oh! Aunt Dagon, I never knew him so unjust and wicked as he is to-day. He treats me cruelly." And the poor woman covered her red eyes again with her handkerchief, and rocked herself feebly. Mr. Newt went out, and slammed the door behind him.

CHAPTER XXXIX.

A FIELD-DAY.

"Now, Nancy, tell me about this thing," said Mrs. Dagon, when the husband was gone.

But Nancy had nothing to tell.

"I don't like his running away with her—that looks bad," continued Mrs. Dagon. She pondered a few moments, and then said:

"I can tell you one thing, Nancy, which it wasn't worth while to mention to Boniface, who seems to be nervous this morning—but I am sure Fanny proposed the running off. Alfred Dinks is too great a fool. He never would have thought of it, and he would never have dared to do it if he had."

"Oh dear me!" responded Mrs. Newt.

"Pooh! it isn't such a dreadful thing, if he is only rich enough," said Aunt Dagon, in a consoling voice. "Every thing depends on that; and I haven't much doubt of it. Alfred Dinks is a fool, my dear, but Fanny Newt is not; and Fanny Newt is not the girl to marry a fool, except for reasons. You may trust Fanny, Nancy. You may depend there was some foolish something with Hope Wayne, on the part of Al-

fred, and Fanny has cut the knot she was not sure of untying.
Pooh! pooh! When you are as old as I am you won't be
distressed over these things. Fanny Newt is fully weaned.
She wants an establishment, and she has got it. There are
plenty of people who would have been glad to marry their
daughters to Alfred Dinks. I can tell you there are some
great advantages in having a fool for your husband. Don't
you see Fanny never would have been happy with a man she
couldn't manage. It's quite right, my dear."

At this moment the bell rang, and Mrs. Newt, not wishing
to be caught with red eyes, called May, who had looked on at
this debate, and left the room.

While Mrs. Dagon had been so volubly talking she had also
been busily thinking. She knew that if Alfred were a fool
his mother was not—at least, not in the way she meant.
There had been no love lost between the ladies, so that Mrs.
Dagon was disposed to criticise the other's conduct very closely. She saw, therefore, that if Alfred Dinks were not rich—
and it certainly was a question whether he were so really, or
only in expectation from Mr. Burt—then also he might not
be engaged to Hope Wayne. But the story of his wealth and
his engagement might very easily have been the *ruse* by which
the skillful Mrs. Dinks meant to conduct her campaign in New
York. In that case, what was more likely than that she
should have improved Fanny's evident delusion in regard to
her son, and, by suggesting to him an elopement, have secured
for him the daughter of a merchant so universally reputed
wealthy as Boniface Newt?

Mrs. Dagon was clever—so was Mrs. Dinks; and it is the
homage that one clever person always pays to another to believe the other capable of every thing that occurs to himself.

In the matter of the marriage Mrs. Budlong Dinks had been
defeated, but she was not dismayed. She had lost Hope
Wayne, indeed, and she could no longer hope, by the marriage of Alfred with his cousin, to consolidate the Burt property in her family. She had been very indignant—very deep-

ly disappointed. But she still loved her son, and the medita-
tion of a night refreshed her.

Upon a survey of the field, Mrs. Dinks felt that under no
circumstances would Hope have married Alfred; and he had
now actually married Fanny. So much was done. It was
useless to wish impossible wishes. She did not desire her son
to starve or come to social shame, although he had married
Fanny; and Fanny, after all, was rather a belle, and the daughter of a rich merchant, who would have to support them. She
knew, of course, that Fanny supposed her husband would
share in the great Burt property. But as Mrs. Dinks herself
believed the same thing, that did not surprise her. In fact,
they would all be gainers by it; and nothing now remained
but to devote herself to securing that result.

The first step under the circumstances was clearly a visit to
the Newts, and the ring which had sent Mrs. Newt from the
room was Mrs. Dinks's.

Mrs. Dagon was alone when Mrs. Dinks entered, and Mrs.
Dagon was by no means sure, whatever she said to Nancy, that
Mrs. Dinks had not outwitted them all. As she entered Mrs.
Dagon put up her glasses and gazed at her; and when Mrs.
Dinks saluted her, Mrs. Dagon bowed behind the glasses, as if
she were bowing through a telescope at the planet Jupiter.

"Good-morning, Mrs. Dagon!"

"Good-morning, Mrs. Dinks!" replied that lady, still contemplating the other as if she were a surprising and incomprehensible phenomenon.

Profound silence followed. Mrs. Dinks was annoyed by
the insult which Mrs. Dagon was tacitly putting upon her,
and resolving upon revenge. Meanwhile she turned over
some illustrated books upon the table, as if engravings were
of all things those that afforded her the profoundest satisfaction.

But she was conscious that she could not deceive Mrs. Dagon by an appearance of interest; so, after a few moments,
Mrs. Dinks seated herself in a large easy-chair opposite that

AUNT DAGON AND MRS. DINKS.

lady, who was still looking at her, shook her dress, glanced into the mirror with the utmost nonchalance, and finally, slowly drawing out her own glasses, raised them to her eyes, and with perfect indifference surveyed the enemy.

The ladies gazed at each other for a few moments in silence.

"How's your daughter, Mrs. Alfred Dinks?" asked Mrs. Dagon, abruptly.

Mrs. Dinks continued to gaze without answering. She was resolved to put down this dragon that laid waste society. The dragon was instantly conscious that she had made a mistake in speaking, and was angry accordingly. She said nothing more; she only glared.

"Good-morning, my dear Mrs. Dinks," said Mrs. Newt, in a troubled voice, as she entered the room. "Oh my! isn't it —isn't it—singular?"

For Mrs. Newt was bewildered. Between her husband and Mrs. Dagon she had been so depressed and comforted that she did not know what to think. She was sure it was Fanny who had married Alfred, and she supposed, with all the world, that he had, or was to have, a pretty fortune. Yet she felt, with her husband, that the private marriage was suspicious. It seemed, at least, to prove the indisposition of Mrs. Dinks to the match. But, as they were married, she did not wish to alienate the mother of the rich bridegroom.

"Singular, indeed, Mrs. Newt!" rejoined Mrs. Dinks; "I call it extraordinary!"

"I call it outrageous," interpolated Mrs. Dagon. "Poor girl! to be run away with and married! What a blow for our family!"

Mrs. Dinks resumed her glasses, and looked unutterably at Mrs. Dagon. But Mrs. Dinks, on her side, knowing the limitations of Alfred's income, and believing in the Newt resources, did not wish to divert from him any kindness of the Newts. So she outgeneraled Mrs. Dagon again.

"Yes, indeed, it is an outrage upon all our feelings. We must, of course, be mutually shocked at the indiscretion of these members of both our families."

"Yes, oh yes!" answered Mrs. Newt. "I do declare! what do people do so for?"

Neither cared to take the next step, and make the obvious and necessary inquiries as to the future, for neither wished to betray the thought that was uppermost. At length Mrs. Dinks ventured to say,

"One thing, at least, is fortunate."

"Indeed!" ejaculated Mrs. Dagon behind the glasses, as if she scoffed at the bare suggestion of any thing but utter misfortune being associated with such an affair.

"I say one thing is fortunate," continued Mrs. Dinks, in a more decided tone, and without the slightest attention to Mrs. Dagon's remark.

"Dear me! I declare I don't see just what you mean, Mrs. Dinks," said Mrs. Newt.

"I mean that they **are** neither of them children," answered the other.

"They may not be children," commenced Mrs. Dagon, in the most implacable tone, "but they are both fools.   I shouldn't wonder, Nancy, if they'd both outwitted each other, after all; for whenever two people, without the slightest apparent reason, run away to be married, it is because one of them is poor."

This was a truth of which the two mothers were both vaguely conscious, and which by no means increased the comfort of the situation.   It led to a long pause in the conversation. Mrs. Dinks wished Aunt Dagon on the top of Mont Blanc, and while she was meditating the best thing to say, Mrs. Dagon, who had rallied, returned to the charge.

"Of course," said she, "that is something that would hardly be said of the daughter of Boniface Newt."

And Mrs. Dagon resumed the study of Mrs. Dinks.

"Or of the grand-nephew of Christopher Burt," said the latter, putting up her own glasses and returning the stare.

"Grand-nephew!   Is Alfred Dinks not the grandson of Mr. Burt?" asked Mrs. Newt, earnestly.

"No, he is his grand-nephew.   I am the niece of Mr. Burt —daughter of his brother Jonathan, deceased," replied Mrs. Dinks.

"Oh!" said Mrs. Newt, dolefully.

"Not a very near relation," added Mrs. Dagon.   "Grand-nephews don't count."

That might be true, but it was thin consolation for Mrs. Newt, who began to take fire.

"But, Mrs. Dinks, how did this affair come about?" asked she.

"Exactly," chimed in Aunt Dagon; "how did it come about?"

"My dear Mrs. Newt," replied Mrs. Dinks, entirely overlooking the existence of Mrs. Dagon, "you know my son Alfred and your daughter Fanny. So do I. Do you believe that Alfred ran away with Fanny, or Fanny with Alfred. Theoretically, of course, the man does it. Do you believe Alfred did it?"

Mrs. Dinks's tone was resolute. Mrs. Newt was on the verge of hysterics.

"Do you mean to insult my daughter to her mother's face?" exclaimed she. "Do you mean to insinuate that—"

"I mean to insinuate nothing, my dear Mrs. Newt. I say plainly what I mean to say, so let us keep as cool as we can for the sake of all parties. They are married—that's settled. How are they going to live?"

Mrs. Newt opened her mouth with amazement.

"I believe the husband usually supports the wife," ejaculated the dragon behind the glasses.

"I understand you to say, then, my dear Mrs. Newt," continued Mrs. Dinks, with a superb disregard of the older lady, who had made the remark, "that the husband usually supports the family. Now in this matter, you know, we are going to be perfectly cool and sensible. You know as well as I that Alfred has no profession, but that he will by-and-by inherit a fortune from his grand-uncle—"

At this point Mrs. Dagon coughed in an incredulous and contemptuous manner. Mrs. Dinks put her handkerchief to her nose, which she patted gently, and waited for Mrs. Dagon to stop.

"As I was saying—a fortune from his grand-uncle. Now until then provision must be made—"

"Really," said Mrs. Dagon, for Mrs. Newt was bewildered into silence by the rapid conversation of Mrs. Dinks—"really, these are matters of business which, I believe, are usually left to gentlemen."

"I know, of course, Mrs. Newt," continued the intrepid Mrs. Dinks, utterly regardless of Mrs. Dagon, for she had fully considered her part, and knew her own intentions, "that such things are generally arranged by the gentlemen. But I think sensible women like you and I, mothers, too, are quite as much interested in the matter as fathers can be. Our honor is as much involved in the happiness of our children as their fathers' is. So I have come to ask you, in a purely friendly and private manner, what the chances for our dear children are?"

"I am sure I know nothing," answered Mrs. Newt; "I only know that Mr. Newt is furious."

"Perfectly lunatic," added Aunt Dagon, in full view of Mrs. Dinks.

"Pity, pity!" returned Mrs. Dinks, with an air of compassionate unconcern; "because these things can always be so easily settled. I hope Mr. Newt won't suffer himself to be disturbed. Every thing will come right."

"What does Mr. Dinks say?" feebly inquired Mrs. Newt.

"I really don't know," replied Mrs. Dinks, with a cool air of surprise that any body should care what he thought—which made Mrs. Dagon almost envious of her enemy, and which so impressed Mrs. Newt, who considered the opinion of her husband as the only point of importance in the whole affair, that she turned pale.

"I mean that his mind is so engrossed with other matters that he rarely attends to the domestic details," added Mrs. Dinks, who had no desire of frightening any of her new relatives. "Have you been to see Fanny yet?"

"No," returned Mrs. Newt, half-sobbing again, "I have only just heard of it; and—and—I don't think Mr. Newt would wish me to go."

Mrs. Dinks raised her eyebrows, and again touched her face gently with the handkerchief. Mrs. Dagon rubbed her glasses and waited, for she knew very well that Mrs. Dinks had not yet discovered what she had come to learn. The old General was not deceived by the light skirmishing.

"I am sorry not to have seen Mr. Newt before he went down town," began Mrs. Dinks, after a pause. "But since we must all know these matters sooner or later—that is to say, those of us whose business it is"—here she glanced at Mrs. Dagon—"you and I, my dear Mrs. Newt, may talk confidentially. How much will your husband probably allow Fanny until Alfred comes into his property?"

Mrs. Dinks leaned back and folded her shawl closely around her, and Mrs. Dagon hemmed and smiled a smile of perfect incredulity.

"Gracious, gracious! Mrs. Dinks, Mr. Newt won't give her a cent!" answered Mrs. Newt. As she uttered the words Mrs. Dagon held the enemy in full survey.

Mrs. Dinks was confounded. That there would be some trouble in arranging the matter she had expected. But the extreme dolefulness of Mrs. Newt had already perplexed her; and the prompt, simple way in which she answered this question precluded the suspicion of artifice. Something was clearly, radically wrong. She knew that Alfred had six hundred a year from his father. She had no profound respect for that gentleman; but men are willful. Suppose he should take a whim to stop it? On the other side, she knew that Boniface Newt was an obstinate man, and that fathers were sometimes implacable. Sometimes, even, they did not relent in making their wills. She knew all about Miss Van Boozenberg's marriage with Tom Witchet, for it was no secret in society. Was it possible her darling Alfred might be in actual danger of such penury—at least until he came into his property? And what property was it, and what were the chances that old Burt would leave him a cent?

These considerations instantly occupied her mind as Mrs.

L

Newt spoke; and she saw more clearly than ever the necessity of propitiating old Burt.

At length she asked, with an undismayed countenance, and with even a show of smiling:

"But, Mrs. Newt, why do you take so cheerless a view of your husband's intentions in this matter?"

The words that her husband had spoken in his wrath had rung in Mrs. Newt's mind ever since, and they now fell, echolike, from her tongue.

"Because he said that, daughter or no daughter, she shall lie in the bed she has made."

Mrs. Dinks could not help showing a little chagrin. It was the sign for Mrs. Newt to burst into fresh sorrow. Mrs Dagon was as rigid as a bronze statue.

"Very well, then, Mrs. Newt," said her visitor, rising, "Mr. Newt will have the satisfaction of seeing his daughter starve."

"Oh, her husband will take care of that," said the bronze statue, blandly.

"My son Alfred," continued Mrs. Dinks, "has an allowance of six hundred dollars a year, no profession, and expectations from his grand-uncle. These are his resources. If his father chooses, he can cut off his allowance. Perhaps he will. You can mention these facts to Mr. Newt."

"Oh! mercy! mercy!" exclaimed Mrs. Newt. "What shall we do? What will people say?"

"Good-morning, ladies!" said Mrs. Dinks, with a comprehensive bow. She was troubled, but not overwhelmed; for she believed that the rich Mr. Newt would not, of course, allow his daughter to suffer. Mrs. Dagon was more profoundly persuaded than ever that Mrs. Dinks had managed the whole matter.

"Nancy," said she, as the door closed upon Mrs. Dinks, "it is a scheming, artful woman. Her son has no money, and I doubt if he ever will have any. Boniface will be implacable. I know him. He is capable of seeing his daughter suffer. Fanny has made a frightful mistake. Poor Fanny! she was

not so clever as she thought herself. There is only one hope
—that is in old Burt. I think we had better present that
view chiefly to Boniface. We must concede the poverty, but
insist and enlarge upon the prospect. No Newt ought to be
allowed to suffer if we can help it. Poor Fanny! She was
always pert, but not quite so smart as she thought herself!"

Mrs. Dagon indulged in a low chuckle of triumph, while
Mrs. Newt was overwhelmed with a vague apprehension that
all her husband's wrath at his daughter's marriage would be
visited upon her.

CHAPTER XL.

AT THE ROUND TABLE.

MRS. DINKS had informed Hope that she was going home.
That lady was satisfied, by her conversation with Mrs. Newt,
that it would be useless for her to see Mr. Newt—that it was
one of the cases in which facts and events plead much more
persuasively than words. She was sure the rich merchant
would not allow his daughter to suffer. Fathers do so in
novels, thought she. Of course they do, for it is necessary to
the interest of the story. And old Van Boozenberg does in
life, thought she. Of course he does. But he is an illiterate,
vulgar, hard old brute. Mr. Newt is of another kind. She
had herself read his name as director of at least seven different associations for doing good to men and women.

But Mrs. Dinks still delayed her departure. She knew that
there was no reason for her staying, but she staid. She loved
her son dearly. She was unwilling to leave him while his
future was so dismally uncertain; and every week she informed Hope that she was on the point of going.

Hope Wayne was not sorry to remain. Perhaps she also
had her purposes. At Saratoga, in the previous summer,
Arthur Merlin had remarked her incessant restlessness, and

had connected it with the picture and the likeness of some. body. But when afterward, in New York, he cleared up the mystery and resolved who the somebody was, to his great surprise he observed, at the same time, that the restlessness of Hope Wayne was gone. From the months of seclusion which she had imposed upon herself he saw that she emerged older, calmer, and lovelier than he had ever seen her. The calmness was, indeed, a little unnatural. To his sensitive eye—for, as he said to Lawrence Newt, in explanation of his close observation, it is wonderful how sensitive an exclusive devotion to art will make the eye—to his eye the calmness was still too calm, as the gayety had been too gay.

In the solitude of his studio, as he drew many pictures upon the canvas, and sang, and smoked, and scuffled across the floor to survey his work from a little distance—and studied its progress through his open fist—or as he lay sprawling upon his lounge in a cotton velvet Italian coat, illimitably befogged and bebuttoned — and puffed profusely, following the intervolving smoke with his eye—his meditations were always the same. He was always thinking of Hope Wayne, and befooling himself with the mask of art, actually hiding himself from himself: and not perceiving that when a man's sole thought by day and night is a certain woman, and an endless speculation about the quality of her feeling for another man, he is simply a lover thinking of his mistress and a rival.

The infatuated painter suddenly became a great favorite in society. He could not tell why. Indeed there was no other secret than that he was a very pleasant young gentleman who made himself agreeable to young women, because he wished to know them and to paint them—not, as he wickedly told Lawrence Newt, who winked and did not believe a word of it, because the human being is the noblest subject of art—but only because he wished to show himself by actual experience how much more charming in character, and sprightly in intelligence, and beautiful in person and manner, Hope Wayne was than all other young women.

He proved that important point to his perfect satisfactión. He punctually attended every meeting of the Round Table, as Lawrence called the meetings at which he and Arthur read and talked with Hope Wayne and Amy Waring, that he might lose no opportunity of pursuing the study. He found Hope Wayne always friendly and generous. She frankly owned that he had shown her many charming things in poetry that she had not known, and had helped her to form juster opinions. It was natural she should think it was Arthur who had helped her. She did not know that it was a very different person who had done the work—a person whose name was Abel Newt. For it was her changing character—changing in consequence of her acquaintance with Abel—which modified her opinions; and Arthur arrived upon her horizon at the moment of the change.

She was always friendly and generous with him. But somehow he could not divest himself of the idea that she must be the Diana of his great picture. There was an indescribable coolness and remoteness about her. Has it any thing to do with that confounded sketch at Saratoga, and that—equally confounded Abel Newt? thought he.

For the conversation at the Round Table sometimes fell upon Abel.

"He is certainly a handsome fellow," said Amy Waring. "I don't wonder at his success."

"It's beauty that does it, then, Miss Waring?" asked Arthur.

"Does what?" said she.

"Why, that gives what you call social success."

"Oh! I mean that I don't wonder such a handsome, bright, graceful, accomplished young man, who lives in fine style, drives pretty horses, and knows every body, should be a great favorite with the girls and their mothers. Don't you see, Abel Newt is a sort of Alcibiades?"

Lawrence Newt laughed.

"You don't mean Pelham?" said he.

"No, for he has sense enough to conceal the coxcomb. But

yöu ought to know your own nephew, Mr. Newt," answered Amy.

"Perhaps; but I have a very slight acquaintance with him," said Mr. Newt.

"I don't exactly like him," said Arthur Merlin, with perfect candor.

"I didn't know you knew him," replied Amy, looking up.

Arthur blushed, for he did not personally know him; but he felt as if he did, so that he unwittingly spoke so.

"No, no," said he, hastily; "I don't know him, I believe; but I know about him."

As he said this he looked at Hope Wayne, who had been sitting, working, in perfect silence. At the same moment she raised her eyes to his inquiringly.

"I mean," said Arthur, quite confused, "that I don't—somehow—that is to say, you know, there's a sort of impression you get about people—"

Lawrence Newt interposed—

"I suppose that Arthur doesn't like Abel for the same reason that oil doesn't like water; for the same reason that you, Miss Amy, and Miss Wayne, would probably not like such a man."

Arthur Merlin looked fixedly at Hope Wayne.

"What kind of man is Mr. Newt?" asked Hope, faintly coloring. She was trying herself.

"Don't you know him?" asked Arthur, abruptly and keenly.

"Yes," replied Hope, as she worked on, only a little more rapidly.

"Well, what kind of man do you think him to be?" continued Arthur, nervously.

"That is not the question," answered Hope, calmly.

Lawrence Newt and Amy Waring looked on during this little conversation. They both wanted Hope to like Arthur. They both doubted how Abel might have impressed her. Lawrence Newt had not carelessly said that neither Amy nor Hope would probably like Abel.

"Miss Hope is right, Arthur," said he. "She asks what kind of man my nephew is. He is a brilliant man—a fascinating man."

"So was Colonel Burr," said Hope Wayne, without looking up.

"Exactly, Miss Hope. You have mentioned the reason why neither you nor Amy would like my nephew."

Hope and Amy understood. Arthur Merlin was bewildered.

"I don't quite understand," said he; "I am such a great fool."

Nobody spoke.

"I am sorry for that poor little Grace Plumer," Lawrence Newt gravely said.

"Don't you be troubled about little Grace Plumer. She can take proper care of herself," answered Arthur, merrily.

Hope Wayne's busy fingers did not stop. She remembered Miss Grace Plumer, and she did not agree with Arthur Merlin. Hope did not know Grace; but she knew the voice, the manner, the magnetism to which the gay girl was exposed.

"If Mr. Godefroi Plumer is really as rich as I hear," said Lawrence, "I think we shall have a Mrs. Abel Newt in the autumn. Poor Mrs. Abel Newt!"

He shook his head with that look, mingled of feeling and irony, which was very perplexing. The tone in which he spoke was really so full of tenderness for the girl, that Hope, who heard every word and felt every tone, was sure that Lawrence Newt pitied the prospective bride sincerely.

"I beg pardon, Mr. Newt, and Miss Wayne," said Arthur Merlin; "but how can a man have a high respect for women when he sees his sister do what Fanny Newt has done?"

"Why should a man complain that his sister does precisely what he is trying to do himself?" asked Lawrence.

CHAPTER XLI.

A LITTLE DINNER.

WHEN Mrs. Dinks told her husband of Alfred's marriage, the Honorable Budlong said it was a great pity, but that it all came of the foolish fondness of the boy's mother; that nothing was more absurd than for mothers to be eternally coddling their children. Although who would have attended to Mr. Alfred if his mother had not, the unemployed statesman forgot to state, notwithstanding that he had just written a letter upon public affairs, in which he eloquently remarked that he had no aspirations for public life; but that, afar from the turmoils of political strife, his modest ambition was satisfied in the performance of the sweet duties which the wise Creator, who has set the children of men in families, has imposed upon all parents.

"However," said he, "Mr. Newt is a wealthy merchant. It's all right, my dear! Women, and especially mothers, are peculiarly silly at such times. Endeavor, Mrs. Dinks, to keep the absurdity—which, of course, you will not be able to suppress altogether—within bounds. Try to control your nerves, and rely upon Providence."

Therewith the statesman stroked his wife's chin. He controlled his own nerves perfectly, and went to dress for dinner with a select party at General Belch's, in honor of the Honorable B. J. Ele, who, in his capacity as representative in Washington, had ground an axe for his friend the General. Therefore, when the cloth was removed, the General rose and said: "I know that we are only a party of friends, but I can not help indulging my feelings, and gratifying yours, by proposing the health of our distinguished, able, and high-minded representative, whose Congressional career proves that there is no office in the gift of a free and happy people to which he may not legitimately aspire. I have the honor and pleasure to propose, with three times three, the Honorable B. Jawley Ele."

The Honorable Budlong Dinks led off in gravely pounding the table with his fork; and when the rattle of knives, and forks, and spoons, and glasses had subsided, and when Major Scuppernong, of North Carolina—who had dined very freely, and was not strictly following the order of events, but cried out in a loud voice in the midst of the applause, " Encore, encore! good for Belch!"—had been reduced to silence, then the honorable gentleman who had been toasted rose, and expressed his opinion of the state of the country, to the general effect that General Jackson—Sir, and fellow-citizens—I mean my friends, and you, Mr. Speaker—I beg pardon, General Belch, that General Jackson, gentlemen and ladies, that is to say, the relatives here present—I mean—yes—is one of the very greatest—I venture to say, and thrust it in the teeth and down the throat of calumny—*the* greatest human being that now lives, or ever did live, or ever can live.

Mr. Ele sat down amidst a fury of applause. Major Scuppernong, of North Carolina, and Captain Lamb, of Pennsylvania, turned simultaneously to the young gentleman who sat between them, and who had been introduced to them by General Belch as Mr. Newt, son of our old Tammany friend Boniface Newt, and said to him, with hysterical fervor,

" By G—, Sir! that is one of the greatest men in this country. He does honor, Sir, to the American name!"

The gentlemen, without waiting for a reply, each seized a decanter and filled their glasses. Abel smiled and bowed on each side of him, filled his own glass and lighted a cigar.

Of course, after General Belch had spoken and Mr. Ele had responded, it was necessary that every body else should be brought to a speech. General Belch mentioned the key-stone of the arch of States; and Captain Lamb, in reply, enlarged upon the swarthy sons of Pennsylvania. General Smith, of Vermont, when green mountains were gracefully alluded to by General Belch, was proud to say that he came—or, rather, he

might say—yes, he *would* say, *hailed* from the hills of Ethan
Allen; and, in closing, treated the company to the tale of
Ticonderoga. The glittering mouth of the Father of Waters
was a beautiful metaphor which brought Colonol le Fay, of
Louisiana, to his feet; and the Colonel said that really he did
not know what to say. "Say that the Mississippi has more
water in its mouth than ever you had!" roared Major Scuppernong, with great hilarity. The company laughed, and the
Colonel sat down. When General Belch mentioned Plymouth
Rock, the Honorable Budlong Dinks sprang upon it, and congratulated himself and the festive circle he saw around him
upon the inestimable boon of religious liberty which, he might
say, was planted upon the rock of Plymouth, and blazed until
it had marched all over the land, dispensing from its vivifying
wings the healing dew of charity, like the briny tears that lave
its base.

"Beautiful! beautiful! My God, Sir, what a poetic idea!"
murmured, or rather gurgled, Major Scuppernong to Abel at
his side.

But when General Belch rose and said that eloquence was
unnecessary when he mentioned one name, and that he therefore merely requested his friends to fill and pledge, without
further introduction, "The old North State," there was a prolonged burst of enthusiasm, during which Major Scuppernong
tottered on to his feet and wavered there, blubbering in maudlin woe, and wiping his eyes with a napkin; while the company,
who perceived his condition, rattled the table, and shouted,
and laughed, until Sligo Moultrie, who sat opposite Abel, declared to him across the table that it was an abominable shame,
that the whole South was insulted, and that he should say
something.

"Fiddle-de-dee, Moultrie," said Abel to him, laughing; "the
South is no more insulted because Major Scuppernong, of
North Carolina, gets drunk and makes a fool of himself than
the North is insulted because General Smith, of Vermont, and
the Honorable Dinks, of Boston, make fools of themselves with-

A LITTLE SPEECH,

out getting drunk. Do you suppose that, at this time of
night, any of these people have the remotest idea of the points
of the compass? Their sole interest at the present moment is
to know whether the gallant Major will tumble under the
table before he gets through his speech."

But the gallant Major did not get through his speech at all,
because he never began it. The longer he stood the unstead-
ier he grew, and the more profusely he wept. Once or twice

he made a motion, as if straightening himself to begin. The noise at table then subsided a little. The guests cried "H'st." There was a moment of silence, during which the eloquent and gallant Major mopped the lingering tears with his napkin, then his mouth opened in a maudlin smile; the roar began again, until at last the smile changed into a burst of sobbing, and to Abel Newt's extreme discomfiture, and Sligo Moultrie's secret amusement, Major Scuppernong suddenly turned and fell upon Abel's neck, and tenderly embraced him, whispering with tipsy tenderness, "My dearest Belch, I love you! Yes, by Heaven! I swear I love you!"

Abel called the waiters, and had the gallant and eloquent Major removed to a sofa.

"He enjoys life, the Major, Sir," said Captain Lamb, of Pennsylvania, at Abel's left hand; "a generous, large-hearted man. So is our host, Sir. General Belch is a man who knows enough to go in when it rains."

Captain Lamb, of Pennsylvania, cocked one eye at his glass, and then opening his mouth, and throwing his head a little back, tipped the entire contents down at one swallow. He filled the glass again, took a puff at his cigar, scratched his head a moment with the handle of a spoon, then opening his pocket-knife, proceeded to excavate some recesses in his teeth with the blade.

"Is Dinks a rising man in Massachusetts, do you know, Sir?" asked Captain Lamb of Abel, while the knife waited and rested a moment on the outside of the mouth.

"I believe he is, Sir," said Abel, at a venture.

"Wasn't there some talk of his going on a foreign mission? Seems to me I heard something."

"Oh! yes," replied Abel. "I've heard a good deal about it. But I am not sure that he has received his commission yet."

Captain Lamb cocked his eye at Abel as if he had been a glass of wine.

Abel rose, and, seating himself by Sligo Moultrie, entered into conversation.

But his object in moving was not talk. It was to give the cue to the company of changing their places, so that he might sit where he would. He drifted and tacked about the table for some time, and finally sailed into the port toward which he had been steering—an empty chair by Mr. Dinks. They said, good - evening. Mr. Dinks added, with a patronizing air,

"I presume you are not often at dinners of this kind, Mr. Newt?"

"No," replied Abel; "I usually dine on veal and spring chickens."

"Oh!" said Mr. Dinks, who thought Abel meant that he generally ate that food.

"I mean that men of my years usually feed with younger and softer people than I see around me here," explained the young man.

"Yes, of course, I understand," replied Mr. Dinks, loftily, who had not the least idea what Abel meant; "young men must expect to begin at women's dinners."

"They must, indeed," replied Abel. "Now, Mr. Dinks, one of the pleasantest I remember was this last winter, under the auspices of your wife. Let me see, there were Mr. Moultrie there, Mr. Whitloe and Miss Magot, Mr. Bowdoin Beacon and Miss Amy Waring—and who else? Oh! I beg pardon, your son Alfred and my sister Fanny."

As he spoke the young gentleman filled a glass of wine, and looked over the rim at Mr. Dinks as he drained it.

"Yes," returned the Honorable Mr. Dinks, "I don't go to women's dinners."

He seemed entirely unconscious that he was conversing with the brother of the young lady with whom his son had eloped. Abel smiled to himself.

"I suppose," said he, "we ought to congratulate each other, Mr. Dinks."

The honorable gentleman looked at Abel, paused a moment, then said:

"My son marries at his own risk, Sir. He is of years of dis-cretion, I believe, and having an income of only six hundred dollars a year, which I allow him, I presume he would not marry without some security upon the other side. However, Sir, as that is his affair, and as I do not find it very interesting —no offense, Sir, for I shall always be happy to see my daugh-ter-in-law—we had better, perhaps, find some other topic. The art of life, my young friend, is to avoid what is disagree-able. Don't you think Mr. Ele quite a remarkable man? I regard him as an honor to your State, Sir."

"A very great honor, Sir, and all the gentlemen at this charming dinner are honors to the States from which they come, and to our common country, Mr. Dinks. We younger men are content to dine upon veal and spring chickens so long as we know that such intellects have the guidance of public affairs."

Mr. Abel Newt bowed to Mr. Dinks as he spoke, while that gentleman listened with the stately gravity with which a Presi-dent of the United States hears the Latin oration in which he is made a Doctor of Laws. He bowed in reply to the little speech of Abel's, as if he desired to return thanks for the com-bined intellects that had been complimented.

"And yet, Sir," continued Abel, "if my father should un-happily conceive a prejudice in regard to this elopement, and decline to know any thing of the happy pair, six hundred dol-lars, in the present liberal style of life incumbent upon a man who has moved in the circles to which your son has been ac-customed, would be a very limited income for your son and daughter-in-law—very limited."

Abel lighted another cigar. Mr. Dinks was a little con-founded by the sudden lurch of the conversation.

"Very, very," he replied, as if he were entirely loth to lin-ger upon the subject.

"The father of the lady in these cases is very apt to be ob-durate," said Abel.

"I think very likely," replied Mr. Dinks, with the polite air

of a man assenting to an axiom in a science of which, unfortunately, he has not the slightest knowledge.

"Now, Sir," persisted Abel, "I will not conceal from you
—for I know a father's heart will wish to know to what his
son is exposed—that my father is in quite a frenzy about this
affair."

"Oh! he'll get over it," interrupted Mr. Dinks, complacent-
ly. "They always do; and now, don't you think that we had
better—"

"Exactly," struck in the other. "But I, who know my father well, know that he will not relent. Oh, Sir, it is dreadful to think of a family divided!" Abel puffed for a moment
in silence. "But I think my dearest father loves me enough
to allow me to mould him a little. If, for instance, I could say
to him that Mr. Dinks would contribute say fifteen hundred
dollars a year, until Mr. Alfred comes into his fortune, I think
in that case I might persuade him to advance as much; and
so, Sir, your son and my dear sister might live somewhat as
they have been accustomed, and their mutual affection would
sustain them, I doubt not, until the grandfather died. Then
all would be right."

Abel blew his nose as if to command his emotion, and looked
at Mr. Dinks.

"Mr. Newt, I should prefer to drop the subject. I can not
afford to give my son a larger allowance. I doubt if he ever
gets a cent from Mr. Burt, who is not his grandfather, but
only the uncle of my wife. Possibly Mrs. Dinks may receive
something. I repeat that I presume my son understands what
he is about. If he has done a foolish thing, I am sorry. I
hope he has not. Let us drink to the prosperity of the romantic young pair, Sir."

"With all my heart," said Abel.

He was satisfied. He had come to the dinner that he might
discover, in the freedom of soul which follows a feast, what
Alfred Dinks's prospects really were, and what his father
would do for him. Boniface Newt, upon coming to the store

after the *tête-à-tête* with his wife, had told Abel of his sister's marriage. Abel had comforted his parent by the representation of the probable Burt inheritance. But the father was skeptical. Therefore, when General Arcularius Belch requested the pleasure of Mr. Abel Newt's company at dinner, to meet the Honorable B. Jawley Ele—an invitation which was dictated by General Belch's desire to stand well with Boniface Newt, who contributed generously to the expenses of the party—the father and son both perceived the opportunity of discovering what they wished.

"Mr. and Mrs. Alfred Dinks will have six hundred a year, as long as papa Dinks chooses to pay it," said Abel to his father the day after the dinner.

Mr. Newt clenched his teeth and struck his fist upon the table.

"Not a cent shall they have from me!" cried he. "What the devil does a girl mean by this kind of thing?"

Abel was not discomposed. He did not clench his teeth or strike his fist.

"I tell you what they can do, father," said he.

His father looked at him inquiringly.

"They can take Mr. and Mrs. Tom Witchet to board."

Mr. Newt remembered every thing he had said of Mr. Van Boozenberg. But of late his hair was growing very gray, his brow very wrinkled, his expression very anxious and weary. When he remembered the old banker, it was with no self-reproach that he himself was now doing what, in the banker's case, he had held up to Abel's scorn. It was only to remember that the wary old man had shut down the portcullis of the bank vaults, and that loans were getting to be almost impossible. His face darkened. He swore a sharp oath. "That —— —— old villain!"

CHAPTER XLII.

CLEARING AND CLOUDY.

It was summer again, and Aunt Martha sat sewing in the hardest of wooden chairs, erect, motionless. Yet all the bleakness of the room was conquered by the victorious bloom of Amy's cheeks, and the tender maidenliness of Amy's manner, and the winning, human, sympathetic sweetness which was revealed in every word and look of Amy, who sat beside her aunt, talking.

"Amy, Lawrence Newt has been here."

The young woman looked almost troubled.

"No, Amy, I know you did not tell him," said Aunt Martha. "I was all alone here, as usual, and heard a knock. I cried, 'Who's there?' for I was afraid to open the door, lest I should see some old friend. 'A friend,' was the reply. My knees trembled, Amy. I thought the time had come for me to be exposed to the world, that the divine wrath might be fulfilled in my perfect shame. I had no right to resist, and said, 'Come in!' The door opened, and a man entered whom I did not at first recognize. He looked at me for a moment kindly—so kindly, that it seemed to me as if a gentle hand were laid upon my head. Then he said, 'Martha Darro.' 'I am ready,' I answered. But he came to me and took my hand, and said, 'Why, Martha, have you forgotten Lawrence Newt?'"

She stopped in her story, and leaned back in her chair. The work fell from her thin fingers, and she wept—soft tears, like a spring rain.

"Well?" said Amy, after a few moments, and her hand had taken Aunt Martha's, but she let it go again when she saw that it helped her to tell the story if she worked.

"He said he had seen you at the window one day, and he was resolved to find out what brought you into Front Street.

But before he could make up his mind to come, he chanced to
see me at the same window, and then he waited no longer."

The tone was more natural than Amy had ever heard from
Aunt Martha's lips. She remarked that the severity of her
costume was unchanged, except that a little strip of white collar around the throat somewhat alleviated its dense gloom.
Was it Amy's fancy merely that the little line of white was
symbolical, and that she saw a more human light in her aunt's
eyes and upon her face?

"Well?" said Amy again, after another pause.

The solemn woman did not immediately answer, but went
on sewing, and rocking her body as she did so. Amy waited
patiently until her aunt should choose to answer. She waited
the more patiently because she was telling herself who it was
that had brought that softer light into the face, if, indeed, it
were really there. She was thinking why he had been curious
to know the reason that she had come into that room. She
was remembering a hundred little incidents which had revealed his constant interest in all her comings, and goings, and do-
ings; and therefore she started when Aunt Martha, still rocking and sewing, said, quietly,

"Why did Lawrence Newt care what brought you here?"

"I'm sure I don't know, Aunt Martha."

Miss Amy looked as indifferent as she could, knowing that
her companion was studying her face. And it was a study
that companion relentlessly pursued, until Amy remarked that
Lawrence Newt was such a generous gentleman that he could
get wind of no distress but he instantly looked to see if he
could relieve it.

Finding the theme fertile, Amy Waring, looking with tender eyes at her relative, continued.

And yet with all the freedom with which she told the story
of Lawrence Newt's large heart, there was an unusual softness
and shyness in her appearance. The blithe glance was more
drooping. The clear, ringing voice was lower. The words
that generally fell with such a neat, crisp articulation from her

lips now lingered upon them as if they were somehow honeyed, and so flowed more smoothly and more slowly. She told of her first encounter with Mr. Newt at the Widow Simmers's— she told of all that she had heard from her cousin, Gabriel Bennet.

"Indeed, Aunt Martha, I should like to have every body think of me as kindly as he thinks of every body."

She had been speaking for some time. When she stopped, Aunt Martha said, quietly,

"But, Amy, although you have told me how charitable he is, you have not told me why he wanted to come here because he saw you at the window."

"I suppose," replied Amy, "it was because he thought there must be somebody to relieve here."

"Don't you suppose he thinks there is somebody to relieve in the next house, and the next, and has been ever since he has had an office in South Street?"

Amy felt very warm, and replied, carelessly, that she thought it was quite likely.

"I have plenty of time to think up here, my child," continued Aunt Martha. "God is so good that He has spared my reason, and I have satisfied myself why Lawrence Newt wanted to come here."

Amy sat without replying, as if she were listening to distant music. Her head drooped slightly forward; her hands were clasped in her lap; the delicate color glimmered upon her cheek, now deepening, now paling. The silence was exquisite, but she must break it.

"Why?" said she, in a low voice.

"Because he loves you, Amy," said the dark woman, as her busy fingers stitched without pausing.

Amy Waring was perfectly calm. The words seemed to give her soul delicious peace, and she waited to hear what her aunt would say next.

"I know that he loves you, from the way in which he spoke of you. I know that you love him for the same reason."

Aunt Martha went on working and rocking. Amy turned pale. She had not dared to say to herself what another had now said to her. But suddenly she started as if stung. "If Aunt Martha has seen this so plainly, why may not Lawrence Newt have seen it?" The apprehension frightened her.

A long silence followed the last words of Aunt Martha. She did not look at Amy, for she had no external curiosity to satisfy, and she understood well enough what Amy was thinking.

They were still silent, when there was a knock at the door.

"Come in," said the clear, hard voice of Aunt Martha.

The door opened—the two women looked—and Lawrence Newt walked into the room. He shook hands with Aunt Martha, and then turned to Amy.

"This time, Miss Amy, I have caught you. Have I not kept your secret well?"

Amy was thinking of another secret than Aunt Martha's living in Front Street, and she merely blushed, without speaking.

"I tried very hard to persuade myself to come up here after I saw you at the window. But I did not until the secret looked out of the window and revealed itself. I came to-day to say that I am going out of town in a day or two, and that I should like, before I go, to know that I may do what I can to take Aunt Martha out of this place."

Aunt Martha shook her head slowly. "Why should it be?" said she. "Great sin must be greatly punished. To die, while I live; to be buried alive close to my nearest and dearest; to know that my sister thinks of me as dead, and is glad that I am so—"

"Stop, Aunt Martha, stop!" cried Amy, with the same firm tone in which, upon a previous visit, in this room, she had dismissed the insolent shopman, "how can you say such things?" and she stood radiant before her aunt, while Lawrence Newt looked on.

"Amy, dear, you can not understand. Sons and daughters

of evil, when we see that we have sinned, we must be brave enough to assist in our own punishment. God's mercy en ables me tranquilly to suffer the penalty which his justice awards me. My path is very plain. Please God, I shall walk in it."

She said it very slowly, and solemnly, and sadly. Whatever her offense was, she had invested her situation with the dignity of a religious duty. It was clear that her idea of obedience to God was to do precisely what she was doing. And this was so deeply impressed upon Amy Waring's mind that she was perplexed how to act. She knew that if her aunt suspected in her any intention of revealing the secret of her abode, she would disappear at once, and elude all search. And to betray it while it was unreservedly confided to her was impossible for Amy, even if she had not solemnly promised not to do so.

Observing that Amy meant to say nothing, Lawrence Newt turned to Aunt Martha.

"I will not quarrel with what you say, but I want you to grant me a request."

Aunt Martha bowed, as if waiting to see if she could grant it.

"If it is not unreasonable, will you grant it?"

"I will," said she.

"Well, now please, I want you to go next Sunday and hear a man preach whom I am very fond of hearing, and who has been of the greatest service to me."

"Who is it?"

"First, do you ever go to church?"

"Always."

"Where?"

Aunt Martha did not directly reply. She was lost in reverie.

"It is a youth like an angel," said she at length, with an air of curious excitement, as if talking to herself. "His voice is music, but it strikes my soul through and through, and I am frightened and in agony, as if I had been pierced with the flaming sword that waves over the gate of Paradise. The light of his words makes my sin blacker and more loathsome. Oh! what crowds there are! How he walks upon a sea of sinners, with their uplifted faces, like waves white with terror! How fierce his denunciation! How sweet the words of promise he speaks! 'The sacrifices of God are a broken spirit; a broken and a contrite heart, O God, thou wilt not despise.'"

She had risen from her chair, and stood with her eyes lifted in a singular condition of mental exaltation, which gave a lyrical tone and flow to her words.

"That is Summerfield," said Lawrence Newt. "Yes, he is a wonderful youth. I have heard him myself, and thought that I saw the fire of Whitfield, and heard the sweetness of Charles Wesley. I have been into the old John Street meeting-house, where the crowds hung out at the windows and doors like swarming bees clustered upon a hive. He swayed them as a wind bends a grain-field, Miss Amy. He swept them away like a mountain stream. He is an Irishman, with all the fervor of Irish genius. But," continued Lawrence Newt, turning again to Aunt Martha, "it is a very different man I want you to hear."

She looked at him inquiringly.

"His name is Channing. He comes from Boston."

"Does he preach the truth?" she asked.

"I think he does," answered Lawrence, gravely.

"Does he drive home the wrath of God upon the sinful, rebellious soul?" exclaimed she, raising both hands with the energy of her words.

"He preaches the Gospel of Christ," said Lawrence Newt, quietly; "and I think you will like him, and that he will do you good. He is called—"

"I don't care what he is called," interrupted Aunt Martha, "if he makes me feel my sin."

"That you will discover for yourself," replied Lawrence, smiling. "He makes me feel mine."

Aunt Martha, whose ecstasy had passed, seated herself, and

said she would go, as Mr. Newt requested, on the condition that neither he nor Amy, if they were there, would betray that they knew her.

This was readily promised, and Amy and Lawrence Newt left the room together.

CHAPTER XLIII.

WALKING HOME.

"Miss Amy," said Lawrence Newt, as they walked slowly toward Fulton Street, "I hope that gradually we may overcome this morbid state of mind in your aunt, and restore her to her home."

Amy said she hoped so too, and walked quietly by his side. There was something almost humble in her manner. Her secret was her own no longer. Was it Lawrence Newt's? Had she indeed betrayed herself?

"I didn't say why I was going out of town. Yet I ought to tell you," said he.

"Why should you tell me?" she answered, quickly.

"Because it concerns our friend Hope Wayne," said Lawrence. "See, here is the note which I received this morning."

As he spoke he opened it, and read aloud:

"My dear Mr. Newt,—Mrs. Simcoe writes me that grandfather has had a stroke of paralysis, and lies very ill. Aunt Dinks has, therefore, resolved to leave on Monday, and I shall go with her. She seems very much affected, indeed, by the news. Mrs. Simcoe writes that the doctor says grandfather will hardly live more than a few days, and she wishes you could go on with us. I know that you have some kind of association with Pinewood—you have not told me what. In this summer weather you will find it very beautiful; and you know how glad I shall be to have you for my guest. My guest, I say; for while grandfather lies so dangerously ill I must be what my mother would have been—mistress of the house. I shall hardly feel more lonely than I always did when he was active, for we had but little intercourse. In case of his death, which I suppose to be very near, I shall not care to live at the old place. In fact, I do not very clearly see what I am to do. But there is One who does; and I remember my dear old nurse's hymn, 'On Thee I cast my care.' Come, if you can.

    "Your friend,   HOPE WAYNE."

Lawrence Newt and Amy walked on for some time in silence. At length Amy said,

"It is just one of the cases in which it is a pity she is not married or engaged."

"Isn't that always a pity for a young woman?" asked Lawrence, shooting entirely away from the subject.

"Theoretically, yes," replied Amy, firmly, "but not actually. It may be a pity that every woman is not married; but it might be a greater pity that she should marry any of the men who ask her."

"Of course," said Lawrence Newt, dryly, "if she didn't love him."

"Yes, and sometimes even if she did."

Amy Waring was conscious that her companion looked at her in surprise as she said this, but she fixed her eyes directly before her, and walked straight on.

"Oh yes," said Mr. Newt; "I see. You mean when he does not love her."

"No, I mean sometimes even when they do love each other," said the resolute Amy.

Lawrence Newt was alarmed. "Does she mean to convey to me delicately that there may be cases of true mutual love where it is better not to marry?" thought he. "Where, for instance, there is a difference of age perhaps, or where there has been some other and earlier attachment?"

"I mean," said Amy, as if answering his thoughts, "that

there may sometimes be reasons why even lovers should not marry—reasons which every noble man and woman understand; and therefore I do not agree with you that it is always a pity for a girl not to be married."

Lawrence Newt said nothing. Amy Waring's voice almost trembled with emotion, for she knew that her companion might easily misunderstand what she said; and yet there was no way to help it. At any rate, thought she, he will see that I do not mean to drop into his arms.

They walked silently on. The people in the street passed them like spectres. The great city hummed around them unheard. Lawrence Newt said to himself, half bitterly, "So you have waked up at last, have you? You have found that because a beautiful young woman is kind to you, it does not follow that she will one day be your wife."

Neither spoke. "She sees," thought Lawrence Newt, "that I love her, and she wishes to spare me the pain of hearing that it is in vain."

"At least," he thought, with tenderness and longing toward the beautiful girl that walked beside him—"at least, I was not mistaken. She was nobler and lovelier than I supposed."

At length he said,

"I have written to ask Hope Wayne to go and hear my preacher to-morrow. Miss Amy, will you go too?"

She looked at him and bowed. Her eyes were glistening with tears.

"My dearest Miss Amy," said Lawrence Newt, impetuously, seizing her hand, as her face turned toward him.

Oh! please, Mr. Newt—please—" she answered, hastily, in a tone of painful entreaty, withdrawing her hand from his grasp, confused and very pale.

The words died upon his lips.

"Forgive me—forgive me!" he said, with an air of surprise and sadness, and with a voice trembling with tenderness and respect. "She can not bear to give me the pain of plainly saying that she does not love me," thought Lawrence; and he

FAREWELL!

gently took her hand and laid her arm in his, as if to show that
now they understood each other perfectly, and all was well.

"At least, Miss Amy," he said, by-and-by, tranquilly, and
with the old cheerfulness, "at least we shall be friends."

Amy Waring bent her head and was silent. It seemed to
her that she was suffocating, for his words apprised her how
strangely he had mistaken her meaning.

They said nothing more. Arm in arm they passed up Broadway. Every moment Amy Waring supposed the merchant would take leave of her and return to his office. But every moment he was farther from doing it. Abel Newt and Grace Plumer passed them, and opened their eyes; and Grace said to Abel,

"How long has Amy Waring been engaged to your Uncle Lawrence?"

When they reached Amy's door Lawrence Newt raised her hand, bent over it with quaint, courtly respect, held it a moment, then pressed it to his lips. He looked up at her. She was standing on the step; her full, dark eyes, swimming with moisture, were fixed upon his; her luxuriant hair curled over her clear, rich cheeks—youth, love, and beauty, they were all there. Lawrence Newt could hardly believe they were not all his. It was so natural to think so. Somehow he and Amy had grown together. He understood her perfectly.

"Perfectly?" he said to himself. "Why you are holding her hand; you are kissing it with reverence; you are looking into the face which is dearer and lovelier to you than all other human faces; and you are as far off as if oceans rolled between."

CHAPTER XLIV.

CHURCH GOING.

The Sunday bells rang loud from river to river. Loud and sharp they rang in the clear, still air of the summer morning, as if the voice of Everardus Bogardus, the old Dominie of New Amsterdam, were calling the people in many tones to be up and stirring, and eat breakfast, and wash the breakfast things, and be in your places early, with bowed heads and reverend minds, and demurely hear me tell you what sinners you always have been and always will be, so help me God—I,

Everardus Bogardus, in the clear summer morning, ding, dong, bell, amen!

So mused Arthur Merlin, between sleeping and waking, as the bells rang out, loud and low—distant and near—flowing like a rushing, swelling tide of music along the dark inlets of narrow streets—touching arid hearts with hope, as the rising water touches dry spots with green. Come you, too, out of your filthy holes and hovels—come to church as in the days when you were young and had mothers, and you, grisly, drunken, blear-eyed thief, lisped in your little lessons—come, all of you, come! The day has dawned; the air is pure; the hammer rests—come and repent, and be renewed, and be young again. The old, weary, restless, debauched, defeated world—it shall sing and dance. You shall be lambs. I see the dawn of the millennium on the heights of Hoboken—yea, even out of the Jerseys shall a good thing come! It is I who tell you—it is I who order you—I, Everardus Bogardus, Dominie of New Amsterdam—ding, dong, bell, amen!

The streets were quiet and deserted. A single hack rattled under his window, and Arthur could hear its lessening sound until it was lost in the sweet clangor of the bells. He lay in bed, and did not see the people in the street; but he heard the shuffling and the slouching, the dragging step and the bright, quick footfall. There were gay bonnets and black hats already stirring—early worshippers at the mass at St. Peter's or St. Patrick's—but the great population of the city was at home.

Except, among the rest, a young man who comes hastily out of Thiel's, over Stewart's—a young man of flowing black hair and fiery black eyes, which look restlessly and furtively up and down Broadway, which seems to the young man odiously and unnaturally bright. He gains the street with a bound. He hurries along, restless, disordered, excited—the black eyes glancing anxiously about, as if he were jealous of any that should see his yesterday was not over, and that somehow his wild, headlong night had been swept into the serene, open bay of morning. He hurries up the street; tossing many thoughts together—calculating his losses, for the black-haired young man has lost heavily at Thiel's faro-table—wondering about payments—remembering that it is Sunday morning, and that he is to attend a young lady from the South to church—a young lady whose father has millions, if universal understanding be at all correct—thinking of revenge at the table, of certain books full of figures in a certain counting-room, and the story they tell—story known to not half a dozen people in the world; the black-eyed youth, in evening dress, alert, graceful, but now meandering and gliding swiftly like a snake, darts up Broadway, and does not seem to hear the bells, whose first stroke startled him as he sat at play, and which are now ringing strange changes in the peaceful air: Come, Newt! Come, Newt! Abel Newt! Come, Newt! It is I, Everardus, Dominie Bogardus—come, come, come! and be d—ing, dong, bell, amen-n-n-n!

Later in the morning the bells rang again. The house doors opened, and the sidewalk swarmed with well-dressed people. Boniface Newt and his wife sedately proceeded to church—not a new bonnet escaping Mrs. Nancy, while May walked tranquilly behind—like an angel going home, as Gabriel Bennet said in his heart when he passed her with his sister Ellen leaning on his arm. The Van Boozenberg carriage rolled along the street, conveying Mr. and Mrs. Jacob to meditate upon heavenly things. Mrs. Dagon and Mrs. Orry passed, and bowed sweetly, on their way to learn how to love their neighbors as themselves. And among the rest walked Lawrence Newt with Amy Waring, and Arthur Merlin with Hope Wayne.

The painter had heard the voice of the Dominie Bogardus, which his fancy had heard in the air; or was he obeying another Dominie, of a wider parish, whose voice he heard in his heart? It was not often that the painter went to church. More frequently, in his little studio at the top of a house in Fulton Street, he sat smoking meditative cigars during the

Sunday hours; or, if the day were auspicious, even touching his canvas!

In vain his sober friends remonstrated. Aunt Winnifred, with whom he lived, was never weary of laboring with him. She laid good books upon the table in his chamber. He returned late at night, often, and found little tracts upon his bureau, upon the chair in which he usually laid his clothes when he retired—yes, even upon his pillow. "Aunt Winnifred's piety leaves its tracts all over my room," he said, smilingly, to Lawrence Newt.

But when the good lady openly attacked him, and said,

"Arthur, how can you? What will people think? Why don't you go to church?"

Arthur replied, with entire coolness,

"Aunt Winnifred, what's the use of going to church when Van Boozenberg goes, and is not in the least discomposed? I'm afraid of the morality of such a place!"

Aunt Winnifred's eyes dilated with horror. She had no argument to throw at Arthur in return, and that reckless fellow always had to help her out.

"However, dear aunt, you go; and I suppose you ought to be quite as good a reason for going as Van Boozenberg for staying away."

After such a conversation it fairly rained tracts in Arthur's room. The shower was only the signal for fresh hostilities upon his part; but for all the hostility Aunt Winnifred was not able to believe her nephew to be a very bad young man.

As he and his friends passed up Broadway toward Chambers Street they met Abel Newt hastening down to Bunker's to accompany Miss Plumer to Grace Church. The young man had bathed and entirely refreshed himself during the hour or two since he had stepped out of Thiel's. There was not a better-dressed man upon Broadway; and many a hospitable feminine eye opened to entertain him as long and as much as possible as he passed by. He had an unusual flush in his cheek and spring in his step. Perhaps he was excited

by the novelty of mixing in a throng of church-goers. He
had not done such a thing since on summer Sunday mornings
he used to stroll with the other boys along the broad village
road, skirted with straggling houses, to Dr. Peewee's. Heavens! in what year was that? he thought, unconsciously. Am
I a hundred years old? On those mornings he used to see—
Precisely the person he saw at the moment the thought crossed
his mind—Hope Wayne—who bowed to him as he passed
her party. How much calmer, statelier, and more softly superior she was than in those old Delafield days!

She remembered, too; and as the lithe, graceful figure of
the handsome and fascinating Mr. Abel Newt bent in passing,
Arthur Merlin, who felt, at the instant Abel passed, as if his
own feet were very large, and his clothes ugly, and his movement stupidly awkward—felt, in fact, as if he looked like a
booby—Arthur Merlin observed that his companion went on
speaking, that she did not change color, and that her voice
was neither hurried nor confused.

Why did the young painter, as he observed these little
things, feel as if the sun shone with unusual splendor? Why
did he think he had never heard a bird sing so sweetly as one
that hung at an open window they passed? Nay, why in that
moment was he almost willing to paint Abel Newt as the Endymion of his great picture?

CHAPTER XLV.

IN CHURCH.

THEY turned into Chambers Street, in which was the little
church where Dr. Channing was to preach. Lawrence Newt
led the way up the aisle to his pew. The congregation, which
was usually rather small, to-day quite filled the church. There
was a general air of intelligence and shrewdness in the faces,
which were chiefly of the New England type. Amy Waring

saw no one she had ever seen before. In fact, there were but few present in whose veins New England blood did not run, except some curious hearers who had come from a natural desire to see and hear a celebrated man.

When our friends entered the church a slow, solemn voluntary was playing upon the organ. The congregation sat quietly in the pews. Chairs and benches were brought to accommodate the increasing throng. Presently the house was full. The bustle and distraction of entering were over—there was nothing heard but the organ.

In a few moments a slight man, wrapped in a black silk gown, slowly ascended the pulpit stairs, and, before seating himself, stood for a moment looking down at the congregation. His face was small, and thin, and pale; but there was a pure light, an earnest, spiritual sweetness in the eyes—the irradiation of an anxious soul—as they surveyed the people. After a few moments the music stopped. There was perfect silence in the crowded church. Then, moving like a shadow to the desk, the preacher, in a voice that was in singular harmony with the expression of his face, began to read a hymn. His voice had a remarkable cadence, rising and falling with yearning tenderness and sober pathos. It seemed to impart every feeling, every thought, every aspiration of the hymn. It was full of reverence, gratitude, longing, and resignation:

> "While Thee I seek, protecting Power,
>   Be my vain wishes stilled;
> And may this consecrated hour
>   With better hopes be filled."

When he had read it and sat down again, Hope Wayne felt as if a religious service had already been performed.

The simplicity, and fervor, and long-drawn melody with which he had read the hymn apparently inspired the choir with sympathy, and after a few notes from the organ they began to sing an old familiar tune. It was taken up by the congregation until the church trembled with the sound, and the saunterers in the street outside involuntarily ceased laughing and talking, and, touched by some indefinable association, raised their hats and stood bareheaded in the sunlight, while the solemn music filled the air.

The hymn was sung, the prayer was offered, the chapter was read; then, after a little silence, that calm, refined, anxious, pale, yearning face appeared again at the desk. The preacher balanced himself for a few moments alternately upon each foot—moved his tongue, as if tasting the words he was about to utter—and announced his text: "Peace I leave with you: my peace I give unto you."

He began in the same calm, simple way. A natural, manly candor certified the truth of every word he spoke. The voice —at first high in tone, and swinging, as it were, in long, wave-like inflections—grew gradually deeper, and more equally sustained. There was very little movement of the hands or arms; only now and then the finger was raised, or the hand gently spread and waved. As he warmed in his discourse a kind of celestial grace glimmered about his person, and his pale, thoughtful face kindled and beamed with holy light. His sentences were entirely simple. There was no rhetoric, no declamation or display. Yet the soul of the hearer seemed to be fused in a spiritual eloquence which, like a white flame, burned all the personality of the speaker away. The people sat as if they were listening to a disembodied soul.

But the appeal and the argument were never to passion, or prejudice, or mere sensibility. Fear and horror, and every kind of physical emotion, so to say, were impossible in the calmness and sweetness of the assurance of the Divine presence. It was a Father whose message the preacher brought. Like as a father so the Lord pitieth His children, said he, in tones that trickled like tears over the hearts of his hearers, although his voice was equable and unbroken. He went on to show what the children of such a Father must needs be—to show that, however sinful, and erring, and lost, yet the Father had sent to tell them that the doctrine of wrath was of old time; that the eye for the eye, and the tooth for the tooth, was

M 2

the teaching of an imperfect knowledge; that a faith which was truly childlike knew the Creator only as a parent; and that out of such faith alone arose the life that was worthy of him.

Wandering princes are we! cried the preacher, with a profound ecstasy and exultation in his tone, while the very light of heaven shone in his aspect—wandering princes are we, sons of the Great King. In foreign lands outcast and forlorn, groveling with the very swine in the mire, and pining for the husks that the swine do eat; envying, defying, hating, forgetting—but never hated nor forgot; in the depths of our rage, and impotence, and sin—in the darkest moment of our moral death, when we would crucify the very image of that Parent who pities us—there is one voice deeper and sweeter than all music, the voice of our elder brother pleading with that common Father—"Forgive them, forgive them, for they know not what they do!"

He sat down, but the congregation did not move. Leaning forward, with upraised eyes glistening with tears and beaming with sympathy, with hope, with quickened affection, they sat motionless, seemingly unwilling to destroy the holy calm in which, with him, they had communed with their Father. There were those in the further part of the church who did not hear; but their mouths were open with earnest attention, their eyes glittered with moisture; for they saw afar off that slight, rapt figure; and so strong was the common sympathy of the audience that they seemed to feel what they could not hear.

Lawrence Newt did not look round for Aunt Martha. But he thought of her listening to the discourse, as one thinks of dry fields in a saturating summer rain. She sat through the whole—black, immovable, silent. The people near her looked at her compassionately. They thought she was an inconsolable widow, or a Rachel refusing comfort. Nor, had they watched her, could they have told if she had heard any thing to comfort or relieve her sorrow. From the first word to the last she gazed fixedly at the speaker. With the rest she rose and went out. But as she passed by the pulpit stairs she looked up for a moment at that pallid face, and a finer eye than any human saw that she longed, like another woman of old looking at another teacher, to kiss the hem of his garment. Oh! not by earthquake nor by lightning, but by the soft touch of angels at midnight, is the stone rolled away from the door of the sepulchre.

CHAPTER XLVI.

IN ANOTHER CHURCH.

WHILE thus one body of Christian believers worshipped, another was assembled in the Methodist chapel in John Street, where Aunt Martha usually went.

A vast congregation crowded every part of the church. They swarmed upon the pulpit stairs, upon the gallery railings, and wherever a foot could press itself to stand, or room be found to sit. As the young preacher, Summerfield, rose in the pulpit, every eye in the throng turned to him and watched his slight, short figure—his sweet blue eye, and his face of earnest expression and a kind of fiery sweetness. He closed his eyes and lifted his hands in prayer; and the great responsibility of speaking to that multitude of human beings of their most momentous interests evidently so filled and possessed him, that in the prayer he seemed to yearn for strength and the gifts of grace so earnestly—he cried, so as if his heart were bursting, "Help, Lord, or I perish!" that the great congregation, murmuring with sobs, with gasps and sighs, echoed solemnly, as if it had but one voice, and it were muffled in tears, "Help, Lord, or I perish!"

When the prayer was ended a hymn was sung by all the people, to a quick, martial melody, and seemed to leave them nervously awake to whatever should be said. The preacher,

with the sweet boyish face, began his sermon gently, and in a
winning voice. There was a kind of caressing persuasion in
his whole manner that magnetized the audience. He grew
more and more impassioned as he advanced, while the people
sat open-mouthed, and responding at intervals, "Amen!"

"Ah! sinner, sinner, it is he, our God, who shoots us
through and through with the sharp sweetness of his power.
It is our God who scatters the arrows of his wrath; but they
are winged with the plumes of the dove, the feathers of softness, and the Gospel. Oh! the promises! the promises!—
Come unto me, all ye that labor and are heavy laden, and I
will give you rest. Yes, patriarch of white hairs, of wasted
cheeks, and tottering step! the burden bears you down almost to the ground to-day—into the ground to-morrow.
Here stands the Judge to give you rest. Yes, mother of sad
eyes and broken spirit! whose long life is a sorrowful vigil,
waiting upon the coming of wicked sons, of deceitful daughters—weary, weary, and heavy laden with tribulation, here is
the Comforter who shall give you rest. And you, young man,
and you, young maiden, sitting here to-day in the plenitude
of youth, and hope, and love, Remember your Creator in the
days of your youth, for the dark day cometh—yea, it is at
hand!"

So fearfully did his voice, and look, and manner express
apprehension, as if something were about to fall upon the congregation, that there was a sudden startled cry of terror.
There were cries of "Lord! Lord! have mercy!" Smothered
shrieks and sobs filled the air; pale faces stared at each other
like spectres. People fell upon their knees, and cried out that
they felt the power of the Lord. "My soul sinks in deep waters, Selah;" cried the preacher, "but they are the waters of
grace and faith, and I am convicted of all my sins." Then
pausing a moment, while the vast crowd swayed and shook
with the tumult of emotion, with his arms outspread, the veins
on his forehead swollen, and the light flashing in his eyes, he
raised his arms and eyes to heaven, and said, with inexpressi-

ble sweetness, in tones which seemed to trickle with balm into
the very soul, as soft spring rains ooze into the ground, " Yea,
it is at hand, but so art thou!   Come, Lord Jesus, come quickly; and when youth, and hope, and love have become dead
weights and burdens in these young hearts, teach them how
to feel the peace that passeth understanding.   Draw them to
thee, for they wearily labor: they are heavily laden, gracious
Father!   Oh, give them rest!"

"Come!" he exclaimed, "freely come!   It is the eternal
spring of living water.   It is your life, and it flows for you.
Come! come! it is the good shepherd who calls his flock to
wander by the still waters and in the green pastures.   Will
you abide outside?   Then, woe! woe! when the night cometh,
and the shepherd folds his flock, and you are not there.   Will
you seek Philosophy, and confide in that?   It is a ravening
wolf, and ere morning you are consumed.   Will you lean on
human pride—on your own sufficiency?   It is a broken reed,
and your fall will be forever fatal.   Will you say there is no
God ?"—his voice sank into a low, menacing whisper—" will
you say there is no God?"   He raised his hands warningly,
and shook them over the congregation while he lowered his
voice.   "Hush! hush! lest he hear—lest he mark—lest the
great Jehovah"—his voice swelling suddenly into loud, piercing tones—"Maker of heaven and earth, Judge of the quick
and the dead, the Alpha and the Omega, the Beginning and
the End, the eternal Godhead from everlasting to everlasting,
should know that you, pitiable, crawling worm—that you, cor-
rupt in nature and conceived in sin! child of wrath and of the
devil! say that there is no God!   Woe, woe! for the Judge
cometh!   Woe, woe! for the gnashing of teeth and the outer
darkness!   Woe, woe! for those who crucified him, and buf-
feted him, and pierced him with thorns!   Woe, woe! for the
Lord our God is a just God, slow to anger, and plenteous in
mercy.   But oh! when the day of mercy is past!   Oh! for
the hour—sinner, sinner, beware! beware!—when that anger
rises like an ingulfing fiery sea, and sweeps thee away forever!"

It seemed as if the sea had burst into the building; for the congregation half rose, and a smothered cry swept over the people. Many rose upright with clasped hands and cried, "Hallelujah!" "Praise be to God!" Others lay cowering and struggling upon the seats; others sobbed and gazed with frantic earnestness at the face of the young apostle. Children with frightened eyes seized the cold hands of their mothers. Some fainted, but could not be borne out, so solid was the throng. Their neighbors loosened their garments and fanned them, repeating snatches of hymns, and waiting for the next word of the preacher. "The Lord is dealing with his people," they said; "convicting sinners, and calling the lost sheep home."

The preacher stood as if lifted by an inward power, beholding with joy the working of the Word, but with a total unconsciousness of himself. The young man seemed meek and lowly while he was about his Father's business. And after waiting for a few moments, the music of his voice poured out peace upon that awakened throng.

"'Come unto me, all ye that labor and are heavy laden, and I will give you rest.' Yes, fellow-sinners, rest. For all of us, rest. For the weariest, rest. For you who, just awakened, tremble in doubt, rest. For you, young woman, who despairest of heaven, rest. For you, young man, so long in the bondage of sin, rest. Oh! that I had the wings of a dove, for then would I fly away and be at rest. Brother, sister, it shall be so. To your weary soul those wings shall be fitted. Far from the world of grief and sin, of death and disappointment, you shall fly away. Deep in the bosom of your God, you shall be at rest. That dove is his holy grace. Those wings are his tender promises. That rest is the peace of heaven.

> "Come, O thou all-victorious Lord,
>   Thy power to us make known;
> Strike with the hammer of thy word,
>   And break these hearts of stone.

"Oh that we all might now begin
  Our foolishness to mourn;
And turn at once from every sin,
  And to the Saviour turn.

"Give us ourselves and thee to know,
  In this our gracious day:
Repentance unto life bestow,
  And take our sins away.

"Convince us first of unbelief,
  And freely then release;
Fill every soul with sacred grief,
  And then with sacred peace."

CHAPTER XLVII.

DEATH.

THE clover-blossom perfumed the summer air. The scythe and the sickle still hung in the barn. Grass and grain swayed and whispered and sparkled in the sun and wind. June loitered upon all the gentle hills, and peaceful meadows, and winding brook sides. June breathed in the sweet-brier that climbed the solid stone posts of the gate-way, and clustered along the homely country stone wall. June blossomed in the yellow barberry by the road-side, and in the bright rhodora and the pale orchis in the dark woods. June sang in the whistle of the robin swinging on the elm and the cherry, and the gushing warble of the bobolink tumbling, and darting, and fluttering in the warm meadow. June twinkled in the keen brightness of the fresh green of leaves, and swelled in the fruit buds. June clucked and crowed in the cocks and hens that stepped about the yard, followed by the multitudinous peep of little chickens. June lowed in the cattle in the pasture. June sprang, and sprouted, and sang, and grew in all the sprouting and blooming, in all the sunny new life of the world.

White among the dark pine-trees stood the old house of Pinewood—a temple of silence in the midst of the teeming, overpowering murmur of new life; of silence and darkness in the midst of jubilant sunshine and universal song, that seemed to press against the very windows over which the green blinds were drawn.

But that long wave of rich life, as it glided across the lawn and in among the solemn pine-trees, was a little hushed and subdued. The birds sang in the trees beyond—the bobolinks gushed in the meadows below. But there was a little space of silence about the house.

In the large drawing-room, draped in cool-colored chintz, where once Gabriel Bennet and Abel Newt had seen Hope Wayne, on the table where books had lain like porcelain ornaments, lay a strange piece of furniture, long, and spreading at one end, smelling of new varnish, studded with high silver-headed nails, and with a lid. It was lined with satin. Yes, it was a casket.

The room was more formal, and chilly, and dim than ever. Puffs of air crept through it as if frightened—frightened to death before they got out again. The smell of the varnish was stronger than that of the clover-blossoms, or the roses or honey-suckles outside in the fields and gardens, and about the piazzas.

Upon the wall hung the portrait of Christopher Burt at the age of ten, standing in clean clothes, holding a hoop in one hand and a book in the other. It was sixty-four years before that the portrait was painted, and if one had come searching for that boy he would have found him—by lifting that lid he would have seen him; but in those sunken features, that white hair, that startling stillness of repose, would he have recognized the boy of the soft eyes and the tender heart, whose June clover had not yet blossomed?

There was a creaking, crackling sound upon the gravel in the avenue, and then a carriage emerged from behind the hedge, and another, and another. They were family carriages, and stopped at the front door, which was swung wide open. There was no sound but the letting down of steps and slamming of doors, and the rolling away of wheels. People with grave faces, which they seemed to have put on for the occasion as they put on white gloves for weddings, stepped out and came up the steps. They were mostly clad in sober colors, and said nothing, or conversed in a low, murmuring tone, or in whispers. They entered the house and seated themselves in the library, with the large, solemn Family Bible, and the empty inkstand, and the clean pen-wiper, and the paper knife, and the melancholy recluses of books locked into their cells.

Presently some one would come to the door and beckon with his finger to some figure sitting in the silent library. The sitter arose and walked out quietly, and went with the beckoner and looked in at the lid, and saw what had once been a boy with soft eyes and tender heart. Coming back to the library the smell of varnish was for a moment blown out of the wide entry by the breath of the clover that wandered in, and reminded the silent company of the song and the sunshine and bloom that were outside.

At length every thing was waiting. No more carriages came—no more people. There was no more looking into the casket—no more whispering and moving. The rooms were full of a silent company, and they were all waiting. The clock ticked audibly. The wind rustled in the pine-trees. What next? Would not the master of the house appear to welcome his guests?

He did not come; but from the upper entry, at the head of the stairs, near a room in which sat Hope Wayne, and Lawrence Newt, and Mrs. Simcoe, and Fanny Dinks, and Alfred, and his parents, and a few others, was heard the voice of Dr. Peewee, saying, "Let us pray!"

And he prayed a long prayer. He spoke of the good works of this life, and the sweet promises of the next; of the Christian hero, who fights the good fight encompassed by a crowd

"DUST TO DUST."

of witnesses; of those who do justice and love mercy, and
walk in the way of the Lord. He referred to our dear departed brother, and eulogized Christian merchants, calling
those blessed who, being rich, are almoners of the Lord's
bounty. He prayed for those who remained, reminding them
that the Lord chastens whom he loves, and that they who die,
although full of years and honors, do yet go where the wicked

cease from troubling, and the weary are at rest, and at last pass beyond to enter into the joy of their Lord.

His voice ceased, and silence fell again upon the house. Every body sat quietly; the women fanned themselves, and the men looked about. Here was again the sense of waiting —of vague expectation. What next?

Three or four workmen went into the parlor. One of them put down the lid and screwed it tight. The casket was closed forever. They lifted it, and carried it out carefully down the steps. They rolled it into a hearse that stood upon the gravel, and the man who closed the lid buttoned a black curtain over the casket.

The same man went to the front door and read several names from a paper in a clear, dry voice. The people designated came down stairs, went out of the door, and stepped into carriages. The company rose in the library and drawing-room, and, moving toward the hall, looked at the mourners— at Hope Wayne and Mrs. Simcoe, at Mr. and Mrs. Budlong Dinks, Mr. and Mrs. Alfred Dinks, and others, as they passed out.

Presently the procession began to move slowly along the avenue. Those who remained stepped out upon the piazza and watched it; then began to bustle about for their own carriages. One after another they drove away. Mr. Kingo said to Mr. Sutler that he believed the will was in the hands of Mr. Budlong Dinks, and would be opened in the morning. They looked around the place, and remarked that Miss Wayne would probably become its mistress.

"Mrs. Alfred Dinks seems to be a very—a very—" said Mr. Kingo, gravely, pausing upon the last word.

"Very much so, indeed," replied Mr. Sutler, with equal gravity.

"And yet," said Mr. Grabeau, "if it had been so ordered that young Mr. Dinks should marry his cousin, Miss Wayne, he would—that is, I suppose he would—;" and he too hesi tated.

"Undoubtedly," replied both the other gentlemen, seriously, "without question it would have been a very good thing.
Mr. Burt must have left a very large property."

"He made every cent tell," said Mr. Sutler, taking the reins
and stepping into his carriage.

"Rather — rather — a screw, perhaps?" inquired Mr. Grabeau, gravely, as he took out his whip.

"Awful!" replied Mr. Kingo, as he drove away.

The last carriage went, and the stately old mansion stood
behind its trees deserted. The casket and its contents had
been borne away forever; but somebody had opened all the
windows of the house, and June, with its song, and perfume,
and sunshine, overflowed the silent chambers, and banished the
smell of the varnish and every thought of death.

CHAPTER XLVIII.

THE HEIRESS.

THE next morning it was hard to believe in the spectacle of
the preceding day. The house of Pinewood was pleasantly
open to the sun and air. Hope Wayne, in a black dress of the
lightest possible texture, so thin that her arms could be seen
through the sleeves, sat by a window. Lawrence Newt sat
beside her. Dr. Peewee was talking with Mrs. Dinks. Her
son Alfred was sitting alone in a chair, looking at his mother,
and Mrs. Fanny Newt Dinks was looking out at a window
upon the lawn. Mrs. Simcoe sat near Hope Wayne. There
was a table in the middle of the room, from which every thing
had been removed. The Honorable Budlong Dinks was walking slowly up and down the room; and several legal-looking
gentlemen, friends of his, were conversing and smiling among
themselves.

Mr. Dinks stopped in his walk, and, leaning upon the table
with the tips of two fingers and the thumb of his left hand,

he thrust the right hand into his waistcoat, by the side of the ruffle of his shirt, as if he were about to address the house upon a very weighty question.

"In accordance," said he, with an air of respect and resignation, "with the wishes of the late Christopher Burt, as expressed in a paper found in his secretary drawer after his decease, I am about to open his will."

The Honorable Mr. Dinks cleared his throat. Mrs. Fanny Newt Dinks turned back from the window, and conversation ceased. All eyes were fixed upon the speaker, who became more pigeon-breasted every moment. He took out his glasses and placed them upon his nose, and slowly surveyed the company. He then drew a sealed paper from his pocket, clearing his throat with great dignity as he did so:

"This is the document," said he, again glancing about the room. At this point Hiram stepped gently in, and stood by the door.

Mr. Dinks proceeded to break the seal as if it had been sacramental bread, and with occasional looks at the groups around him, opened the document—shook it—creased it back —smoothed it—and held it carefully in the attitude of reading.

When the audience had been sufficiently impressed with this ceremony, and with a proper conviction of the fact that he of all other men had been selected to reveal the contents of that important paper to mankind, he began, and read that, being of sound mind and body, etc., etc., Christopher Burt, etc., etc., as an humble Christian, and loving the old forms, gave his body to the ground, his soul to his God, in the hope of a happy resurrection, etc., etc.; and devised and bequeathed his property, etc., etc., in the manner following, to wit: that is to say:

At this point Mr. Dinks paused, and blew his nose with profound gravity. He proceeded:

"*First.* I give to my housekeeper, Jane Simcoe, the friend of my darling daughter Mary, and the life-long friend and guardian of my dear grand-daughter, Hope Wayne, one thousand dollars per annum, as hereinafter specified."

Mrs. Simcoe's face did not change; nobody moved except Alfred Dinks, who changed the position of his legs, and thought within himself—" By Jove!"

" *Second.* I give to Almira Dinks, the daughter of my brother Jonathan Burt, and the wife of Budlong Dinks, of Boston, the sum of five thousand dollars."

The voice of Mr. Dinks faltered. His wife half rose and sat down again—her face of a dark mahogany color. Fanny Newt sat perfectly still and looked narrowly at her father-in-law, with an expression which was very black and dangerous. Alfred had an air of troubled consternation, as if something fearful were about to happen. The whole company were disturbed. They seemed to be in an electrical condition of apprehension, like the air before a thunder-burst.

Mr. Dinks continued:

" *Third.* I give to Alfred Dinks, my grand-nephew, my silver shoe-buckles, which belonged to his great-grandfather Burt."

"*Fourth.* And all the other estate, real and personal, of which I may die seized, I give, devise, and bequeath to Budlong Dinks, Timothy Kingo, and Selah Sutler, in trust, nevertheless, and for the sole use, behoof, and benefit of my dearly-beloved grand-daughter, Hope Wayne."

Mr. Dinks stopped. There were some papers annexed, containing directions for collecting the annuity to be paid to Mrs. Simcoe, and a schedule of the property. The Honorable B. Dinks looked hastily at the schedule.

"Miss Wayne's property will be at least a million of dollars," said he, in a formal voice.

There were a few moments of utter silence. Even the legal gentlemen ceased buzzing; but presently the forefinger of one of them was laid in the palm of his other hand, and as he stated his proposition to his neighbor, a light conversation began again.

Mrs. Fanny Dinks Newt seemed to have been smitten. She sat crushed up, as it were, biting her nails nervously; her brow wrinkled incredulously, and glaring at her father-in-law, as he folded the paper. Her face grew altogether as black as her hair and her eyes; as if she might discharge a frightful flash and burst of tempest if she were touched or spoken to, or even looked at.

But Mrs. Dinks the elder did look at her, not at all with an air of sullen triumph, but, on the contrary, with a singularly inquisitive glance of apprehension and alarm, as if she felt that the petty trial of wits between them was insignificant compared with the chances of Alfred's happiness. In one moment it flashed upon her mind that the consequences of this will to her Alfred — to her son whom she loved — would be overwhelming. Good Heavens! she turned pale as she thought of him and Fanny together.

The young man had merely muttered "By Jove, that's too d—— bad!" and flung himself out of the room.

His wife did not observe that her mother-in-law was regarding her; she did not see that her husband had left the room; she thought of no contest of wits, of no game she had won or lost. She thought only of the tragical mistake she had made— the dull, blundering crime she had committed; and still bowed over, and gnawing her nails, she looked sideways with her hard, round, black eyes, at Hope Wayne.

The heiress sat quietly by the side of her friend Lawrence Newt. She was holding the hand of Mrs. Simcoe, who glanced sometimes at Lawrence, calmly, and with no sign of regretful or revengeful remembrance. The Honorable Budlong Dinks was walking up and down the room, stroking his chin with his hand, not without a curiously vague indignation with the late lamented proprietor of Pinewood.

It was a strange spectacle. A room full of living men and women who had just heard what some of them considered their doom pronounced by a dead man. They had carried him out of his house, cold, powerless, screwed into the casket.

They had laid him in the ground beneath the village spire, and yet it was his word that troubled, enraged, disappointed, surprised, and envenomed them. Beyond their gratitude, reproaches, taunts, or fury, he lay helpless and dumb—yet the most terrible and inaccessible of despots.

The conversation was cool and indifferent. The legal gentlemen moved about with a professional and indifferent air, as if they assisted at such an occasion as medical students at dissections. It was in the way of business. As Mr. Quiddy, the confidential counsel of the late lamented Mr. Burt, looked at Mrs. Alfred Dinks, he remarked to Mr. Baze, a younger member of the bar, anxious to appear well in the eyes of Quiddy, that it was a pity the friends of deceased parties permitted their disappointments to overpower them upon these occasions. Saying which, Mr. Quiddy waved his forefinger in the air, while Mr. Baze, in a deferential manner and tone, answered, Certainly, because they could not help themselves. There was no getting round a will drawn as that will was— here a slight bow to Mr. Quiddy, who had drawn the will, was interpolated—and if people didn't like what they got, they had better grin and bear it. Mr. Quiddy further remarked, with the forefinger still wandering in the air as if restlessly seeking for some argument to point, that the silver shoe-buckles which had so long been identified with the quaint costume of Mr. Burt, would be a very pretty and interesting heirloom in the family of young Mr. Dinks.

Upon which the eminent confidential counsel took snuff, and while he flirted the powder from his fingers looked at his young friend Baze.

Young Mr. Baze said, "Very interesting!" and continued the attitude of listening for further wisdom from his superior.

Lawrence Newt meanwhile had narrowly watched his niece Fanny. Nobody else cared to approach her; but he went over to her presently.

"Well, Fanny."

"Well, Uncle Lawrence."

"Beautiful place, Fanny."

"Is it?"

"So peaceful after the city."

"I prefer town."

"Fanny!"

"Uncle Lawrence."

"What are you going to do?"

She had not looked at him before, but now she raised her eyes to his. She might as well have closed them. Dropping them, she looked upon the floor and said nothing.

"I'm sorry for you, Fanny."

She looked fierce. There was a snake-like stealthiness in her appearance, which Alfred's mother saw across the room and trembled. Then she raised her eyes again to her uncle's, and said, with a kind of hissing sneer,

"Indeed, Uncle Lawrence, thank you for nothing. It's not very hard for you to be sorry."

Not dismayed, not even surprised by this speech, Lawrence was about to reply, but she struck in,

"No, no; I don't want to hear it. I've been cheated, and I'll have my revenge. As for you, my respected uncle, you have played your cards better."

He was surprised and perplexed.

"Why, Fanny, what cards? What do you mean?"

"I mean that an old fox is a sly fox," said she, with the hissing sneer.

Lawrence looked at her in amazement.

"I mean that sly old foxes who have lined their own nests can afford to pity a young one who gets a silver shoe-buckle," hissed Fanny, with bitter malignity. "If Alfred Dinks were not a hopeless fool, he'd break the will. Better wills than this have been broken by good lawyers before now. Probably," she added suddenly, with a sarcastic smile, "my dear uncle does not wish to have the will broken?"

Lawrence Newt was pondering what possible interest she thought he could have in the will.

"What difference could it make to me in any case, Fanny?"

"Only the difference of a million of dollars," said she, with her teeth set.

Gradually her meaning dawned upon Lawrence Newt. With a mingled pain, and contempt, and surprise, and a half-startled apprehension that others might have thought the same thing, and that all kinds of disagreeable consequences might flow from such misapprehension, he perceived what she was thinking of, and said, so suddenly and sharply that even Fanny started,

"You think I want to marry Hope Wayne?"

"Of course I do. So does every body else. Do you suppose we have not known of your intimacies? Do you think we have heard nothing of your meetings all winter with that artist and Amy Waring, and your reading poetry, and your talking poetry?" said Fanny, with infinite contempt.

There was a look of singular perplexity upon the face of Lawrence Newt. He was a man not often surprised, but he seemed to be surprised and even troubled now. He looked musingly across the room to Hope Wayne, who was sitting engaged in earnest conversation with Mrs. Simcoe. In her whole bearing and aspect there was that purity and kindliness which are always associated with blue eyes and golden hair, and which made the painters paint the angels as fair women. A lambent light played all over her form, and to Lawrence Newt's eyes she had never seemed so beautiful. The girlish quiet which he had first known in her had melted into a sweet composure —a dignified serenity which comes only with experience. The light wind that blew in at the window by which she sat raised her hair gently, as if invisible fingers were touching her with airy benedictions. Was it so strange that such a woman should be loved? Was it not strange that any man should see much of her, be a great deal with her, and not love her? Was Fanny's suspicion, was the world's gossip, unnatural?

He asked himself these questions as he looked at her, while a cloud of thoughts and memories floated through his mind.

Yet a close observer, who could read men's hearts in their faces—and that could be more easily done with every one else than with him—would have seen another expression gradually supplanting the first, or mingling with it rather: a look as of joy at some unexpected discovery—as if, for instance, he had said to himself, " She must be very dear whom I love so deeply that it has not occurred to me I could love this angel !"

Something of that kind, perhaps; at least, something that brought a transfigured cheerfulness into his face.

" Believe me, Fanny," he said, at length, " I am not anxious to marry Miss Wayne; nor would she marry me if I asked her."

Then he rose and passed across the room to her side.

" We were talking about the future life of the mistress of this mansion," said Hope Wayne to Lawrence as he joined them.

" What does she wish ?" asked he ; " that is always the first question."

" To go from here," said she, simply.

" Forever ?"

" Forever !"

Hope Wayne said it quietly. Mrs. Simcoe sat holding her hand. The three seemed to be all a little serious at the word.

" Aunty says she has no particular desire to remain here," said Hope.

" It is like living in a tomb," said Mrs. Simcoe, turning her calm face to Lawrence Newt.

" Would you sell it outright ?" asked he. Hope Wayne bent her head in assent.

" Why not ? My own remembrances here are only gloomy. I should rather find or make another home. We could do it, aunty and I."

She said it simply. Lawrence shook his head smilingly, and replied,

" I don't think it would be hard."

" I am going to see my trustees this morning, Uncle Dinks

says," continued Hope, "and I shall propose to them to sell immediately."

"Where will you go?" asked Lawrence.

"My best friends are in New York," replied she, with a tender color.

Lawrence Newt thought of Arthur Merlin.

"With my aunty," continued she, looking fondly at Mrs. Simcoe, "I think I need not be afraid."

Lunch was brought in; and meanwhile Mr. Kingo and Mr. Sutler had been sent for, and arrived. Mr. Burt had not apprised them of his intention of making them trustees.

They fell into conversation with Mr. Quiddy, and Mr. Baze, and Mr. Dinks. Dr. Peewee took his leave, "H'm ha! yes. My dear Miss Wayne, I congratulate you; congratulate you! h'm ha, yes, oh yes—congratulate you." The other legal gentlemen, friends of Mr. Dinks, drove off. Nobody was left behind but the trustees and the family and Lawrence Newt— the Dinks were of the family.

After business had been discussed, and the heiress—the owner of Pinewood—had announced her wishes in regard to that property, she also invited the company to remain to dinner, and to divert themselves as they chose meanwhile.

Mrs. Fanny Newt Dinks declined to stay. She asked her husband to call their carriage, and when it came to the door she made a formal courtesy, and did not observe—at least she did not take—the offered hand of Hope Wayne. But as she bowed and looked at Hope that young lady visibly changed color, for in the glance which Fanny gave her she seemed to see the face of her brother Abel; and she was not glad to see it.

Toward sunset of that soft June day, when Uncle and Aunt Dinks—the latter humiliated and alarmed—were gone, and the honest neighbors were gone, Hope Wayne was sitting upon the very bench where, as she once sat reading, Abel Newt had thrown a shadow upon her book. But not even the memory of that hour or that youth now threw a shadow upon her heart or life. The eyes with which she watched the setting sun were as free from sorrow as they were from guile.

Lawrence Newt was standing near the window in the library, looking up at the portrait that hung there, and deep into the soft, dark eyes. He had a trustful, candid air, as if he were seeking from it a benediction or consolation. As the long sunset light swept across the room, and touched tenderly the tender girl's face of the portrait, it seemed to him to smile tranquilly and trustingly, as if it understood and answered his confidence, and a deep peace fell upon his heart.

And high above, from her window that looked westward— with a clearer, softer gaze, as if Time had cleared and softened the doubts and obscurities of life—Mrs. Simcoe's face was turned to the setting sun.

Behind the distant dark-blue hills the June sun set—set upon three hearts, at least, that Time and Life had taught and tempered—upon three hearts that were brought together then and there, not altogether understanding each other, but ready and willing to understand. As it darkened within the library and the picture was hidden, Lawrence Newt stood at the window and looked upon the lawn where Hope was sitting. He heard a murmuring voice above him, and in the clear, silent air Hope heard it too. It was only a murmur mingling with the whisper of the pine-trees. But Hope knew what it was, though she could not hear the words. And yet the words were heard:

> "I hold Thee with a trembling hand,
>   And will not let Thee go;
> Till steadfastly by faith I stand,
>   And all Thy goodness know."

CHAPTER XLIX.

A SELECT PARTY.

On a pleasant evening in the same month of June Mr. Abel
Newt entertained a few friends at supper. The same June
air, with less fragrance, perhaps, blew in at the open windows,
which looked outside upon nothing but the street and the
house walls opposite, but inside upon luxury and ease.

It mattered little what was outside, for heavy muslin curtains hung over the windows; and the light, the beauty, the
revelry, were all within.

The boyish look was entirely gone now from the face of
the lord of the feast. It was even a little sallow in hue and
satiated in expression. There was occasionally that hard,
black look in his eyes which those who had seen his sister
Fanny intimately had often remarked in her—a look with
which Alfred Dinks, for instance, was familiar. But the companions of his revels were not shrewd of vision. It was not
Herbert Octoyne, nor Corlaer Van Boozenberg, nor Bowdoin
Beacon, nor Sligo Moultrie, nor any other of his set, who especially remarked his expression; it was, oddly enough, Miss
Grace Plumer, of New Orleans.

She sat there in the pretty, luxurious rooms, prettier and
more luxurious than they. For, at the special solicitation of
Mr. Abel Newt, Mrs. Plumer had consented to accept an invitation to a little supper at his rooms—very small and very
select; Mrs. Newt, of course, to be present.

The Plumers arrived, and Laura Magot; but a note from
mamma excused her absence—papa somewhat indisposed, and
so forth; and Mr. Abel himself so sorry—but Mrs. Plumer
knows what these husbands are! Meanwhile the ladies have
thrown off their shawls.

The dinner is exquisite, and exquisitely served. Prince

A BACHELOR'S SUPPER.

Abel, with royal grace, presides. By every lady's plate a pretty bouquet; the handsomest of all not by Miss, but by Mrs. Plumer. Flowers are every where. It is Grand Street, indeed, in the city; but the garden at Pinewood, perhaps, does not smell more sweetly.

"There is, indeed, no perfume of the clover, which is the very breath of our Northern June, Mrs. Plumer; but clover does not grow in the city, Miss Grace."

Prince Abel begins the little speech to the mother, but his voice and face turn toward the daughter as it ends.

Flowers are in glasses upon the mantle, and in vases of many-colored materials and of various shapes upon tables about the room. The last new books, in English editions often, and a few solid classics, are in sight. Pictures also.

"What a lovely Madonna!" says Miss Plumer, as she raises her eyes to a beautiful and costly engraving that hangs opposite upon the wall; which, indeed, was intended to be observed by her.

"Yes. It is the Sistine, you know," says the Prince, as he sees that the waiter pours wine for Mrs. Plumer.

The Prince forgets to mention that it is not the engraving which usually hangs there. Usually it is a pretty-colored French print representing "Lucille," a young woman who has apparently very recently issued from the bath. Indeed there is a very choice collection of French prints which the young men sometimes study over their cigars, but which are this evening in the port-folio, which is not in sight.

The waiters move very softly. The wants of the guests are revealed to them by being supplied. Quiet, elegance, luxury prevail.

"Really, Mr. Newt"—it is Mrs. Plumer, of New Orleans, who speaks—"you have created Paris in Grand Street!"

"Ah! madame, it is you who graciously bring Versailles and the Tuileries with you!"

He speaks to the mother; he looks, as he ends, again at the daughter.

The daughter for the first time is in the sanctuary of a bachelor—of a young man about town. It is a character which always interests her—which half fascinates her. Miss Plumer, of New Orleans, has read more French literature of the lighter sort—novels and romances, for instance—than most of the young women whom Abel Newt meets in society. Her eyes are very shrewd, and she is looking every where to see if she shall not light upon some token of bachelor habits—

something that shall reveal the man who occupies those pretty rooms.

Every where her bright eyes fall softly, but every where upon quiet, elegance, and luxury. There is the Madonna; but there are also the last winner at the Newmarket, the profile of Mr. Bulwer, and a French landscape. The books are good, but not too good. There is an air of candor and honesty in the room, united with the luxury and elegance, that greatly pleased Miss Grace Plumer. The apartment leads naturally up to that handsome, graceful, dark-haired, dark-eyed gentle-man whose eye is following hers, while she does not know it; but whose mind has preceded hers in the very journey around the room it has now taken.

Sligo Moultrie sits beyond Miss Plumer, who is at the left of Mr. Newt. Upon his right sits Mrs. Plumer. The friendly relations of Abel and Sligo have not been disturbed. They seem, indeed, of late to have become even strengthened. At least the young men meet oftener; not infrequently in Mrs. Plumer's parlor. Somehow they are aware of each other's movements; somehow, if one calls upon the Plumers, or drives with them, or walks with them alone, the other knows it. And they talk together freely of all people in the world, ex-cept the Plumers of New Orleans. In Abel's room of an even-ing, at a late hour, when a party of youth are smoking, there are many allusions to the pretty Plumer—to which it happens that Newt and Moultrie make only a general reply.

As the dinner proceeds from delicate course to course, and the wines of varying hue sparkle and flow, so the conversation purls along—a gentle, continuous stream. Good things are said, and there is that kind of happy appreciation which makes the generally silent speak and the clever more witty.

Mrs. Godefroi Plumer has traveled much, and enjoys the world. She is a Creole, with the Tropics in her hair and com-plexion, and Spain in her eyes. She wears a Parisian head-dress, a brocade upon her ample person, and diamonds around her complacent neck and arms. Diamonds also flash in the fan which she sways gently, admiring Prince Abel. Diamonds —huge solitaires—glitter likewise in the ears of Miss Grace. She wears also a remarkable bracelet of the same precious stones; for the rest, her dress is a cloud of Mechlin lace. She has quick, dark eyes, and an olive skin. Her hands and feet are small. She has filbert nails and an arched instep. Prince Abel, who hangs upon his wall the portrait of the last New-market victor, has not omitted to observe these details. He thinks how they would grace a larger house, a more splendid table.

Sligo Moultrie remembers a spacious country mansion, sur- rounded by a silent plantation, somewhat fallen from its state, whom such a mistress would superbly restore. He looks a man too refined to wed for money, perhaps too indolently lux- urious to love without it.

Half hidden under the muslin drapery by the window hangs a cage with a canary. The bird sits silent; but as the feast proceeds he pours a shrill strain into the murmur of the guests. For the noise of the golden-breasted bird Sligo Moultrie can not hear something that is said to him by the ripe mouth be- tween the solitaires. He asks pardon, and it is repeated.

Then, still smiling and looking toward the window, he says, and, as he says it, his eyes—at which he knows his companion is looking—wander over the room,

"A very pretty cage!"

The eyes drop upon hers as they finish the circuit of the room. They say no more than the lips have said. And Miss Grace Plumer answers,

"I thought you were going to say a very noisy bird."

"But the bird is not very noisy," says the young man, his dark eyes still holding hers.

There is a moment of silence, during which Miss Plumer may have her fancy of what he means. If so, she does not choose to betray it. If her eyes are clear and shrewd, the woman's wit is not less so. It is with an air of the utmost simplicity that she replies,

"It was certainly noisy enough to drown what I was saying."

There is a sound upon her other side as if a musical bell rang.

"Miss Plumer!"

Her head turns. This time Mr. Sligo Moultrie sees the massive dark braids of her hair behind. The ripe mouth half smiles upon Prince Abel.

He holds a porcelain plate with a peach upon it, and a silver fruit-knife in his hand. She smiles, as if the music had melted into a look. Then she hears it again:

"Here is the sunniest side of the sunniest peach for Miss Plumer."

Sligo Moultrie can not help hearing, for the tone is not low. But, while he is expecting to catch the reply, Miss Magot, who sits beyond him, speaks to him. The Prince Abel, who sees many things, sees this; and, in a tone which is very low, Miss Plumer hears, and nobody else in the room hears:

"May life always be that side of a sweet fruit to her!"

It is the tone and not the words which are eloquent.

The next instant Sligo Moultrie, who has answered Miss Magot's question, hears Miss Plumer say:

"Thank you, with all my heart."

It seems to him a warm acknowledgment for a piece of fruit.

"I did not speak of the bird; I spoke of the cage," are the words that Miss Plumer next hears, and from the other side.

She turns to Sligo Moultrie and says, with eyes that expect a reply,

"Yes, you are right; it is a very pretty cage."

"Even a cage may be a home, I suppose."

"Ask the canary."

"And so turned to the basest uses," says Mr. Moultrie, as if thinking aloud.

He is roused by a little ringing laugh:

"A pleasant idea of home you suggest, Mr. Moultrie."

He smiles also.

"I do not wonder you laugh at me; but I mean sense, for all that," he says.

"You usually do," she says, sincerely, and eyes and solitaires glitter together.

Sligo Moultrie is happy—for one moment. The next he hears the musical bell of that other voice again. Miss Plumer turns in the very middle of a word which she has begun to address to him.

"Miss Grace?"

"Well, Mr. Newt."

"You observe the engraving of the Madonna?"

"Yes."

"You see the two cherubs below looking up?"

"Yes."

"You see the serene sweetness of their faces?"

"Yes."

"Do you know what it is?"

Grace Plumer looks as if curiously speculating. Sligo Moultrie can not help hearing every word, although he pares a peach and offers it to Miss Magot.

"Miss Grace, do you remember what I said once of honest admiration—that if it were eloquent it would be irresistible?"

Grace Plumer bows an assent.

"But that its mere consciousness—a sort of silent eloquence —is pure happiness to him who feels it?"

She thinks she remembers that too, although the Prince apparently forgets that he never said it to her before.

"Well, Miss Plumer, it seems to me the serene sweetness of that picture is the expression of the perfect happiness of entire admiration—that is to say, of love; whoever loves is like those cherubs—perfectly happy."

He looks attentively at the picture, as if he had forgotten his own existence in the happiness of the cherubs. Grace Plumer glances at him for a few moments with a peculiar expression. It is full of admiration, but it is not the look with which she would say, as she just now said to Sligo Moultrie, "You always speak sincerely."

She is still looking at the Prince, when Mr. Moultrie begins again:

"I ought to be allowed to explain that I only meant that as a cage is a home, so it is often used as a snare. Do you know, Miss Grace, that the prettiest birds are often put into the prettiest cages to entice other birds? By-the-by, how lovely Laura Magot is this evening!"

He cuts a small piece of the peach with his silver knife and puts it into his mouth.

"Peaches are luxuries in June," he says, quietly.

This time it is at Sligo Moultrie that Miss Grace Plumer looks fixedly.

"What kind of birds, Mr. Moultrie?" she says, at length.

"Miss Grace, do you know the story of the old Prince of Este?" answers he, as he lays a bunch of grapes upon her plate. She pulls one carelessly and lets it drop again. He takes it and puts it in his mouth.

"No; what is the story?"

"There was an old Prince of Este who had a beautiful villa and a beautiful sister, and nothing else in the world but a fiery eye and an eloquent tongue."

Sligo Moultrie flushes a little, and drinks a glass of wine. Grace Plumer is a little paler, and more serious. Prince Abel plies Madame Plumer with fruit and compliments, and hears every word.

"Well."

"Well, Miss Grace, she was so beautiful that many a lady became her friend, and many of those friends sighed for the brother's fiery eyes and blushed as they heard his honeyed tongue. But he was looking for a queen. At length came the Princess of Sheba—"

"Are you talking of King Solomon?"

"No, Miss Plumer, only of Alcibiades. And when the Princess of Sheba came near the villa the Prince of Este entreated her to visit him, promising that the sister should be there. It was a pretty cage, I think; the sister was a lovely bird. And the Princess came."

He stops and drinks more wine.

"Very well! And then?"

"Why, then, she had a very pleasant visit," he says, gayly.

"Mr. Moultrie, is that the whole of the story?"

"No, indeed, Miss Plumer; but that is as far as we have got."

"I want to hear the rest."

"Don't be in such a hurry; you won't like the rest so well."

"Yes; but that is my risk."

"It *is* your risk," says Sligo Moultrie, looking at her; "will you take it?"

"Of course I will," is the clear-eyed answer.

"Very well. The Princess came; but she did not go away."

"How curious! Did she die of a peach-stone at the banquet?"

"Not at all. She became Princess of Este instead of Sheba."

"Oh-h-h," says Grace Plumer, in a long-drawn exclamation. "And then?"

"Why, Miss Grace, how insatiable you are!—then I came away."

"You did? I wouldn't have come away."

"No, Miss Grace, you didn't."

"How—I didn't? What does that mean, Mr. Moultrie?"

"I mean the Princess remained."

"So you said. Is that all?"

"No."

"Well."

"Oh! the rest is nothing. I mean nothing new."

"Let me hear the old story, then, Mr. Moultrie."

"The rest is merely that the Princess found that the fiery eyes burned her and the eloquent tongue stung her, and truly that is the whole. Isn't it a pretty story? The moral is that cages are sometimes traps."

Sligo Moultrie becomes suddenly extremely attentive to Miss Magot. Grace Plumer ponders many things, and among others wonders how, when, where, Sligo Moultrie learned to talk in parables. She does not ask herself *why* he does so. She is a woman, and she knows why.

CHAPTER L.

WINE AND TRUTH.

THE conversation takes a fresh turn. Corlaer Van Boozenberg is talking of the great heiress, Miss Wayne. He has drunk wine enough to be bold, and calls out aloud from his end of the table,

"Mr. Abel Newt!"

That gentleman turns his head toward his guest.

"We are wondering down here how it is that Miss Wayne went away from New York unengaged."

"I am not her confidant," Abel answers; and gallantly adds, "I am sure, like every other man, I should be glad to be so."

"But you had the advantage of every body else."

"How so?" asks Abel, conscious that Grace Plumer is watching him closely.

"Why, you were at school in Delafield until you were no chicken."

Abel bows smilingly.

"You must have known her."

"Yes, a little."

"Well, didn't you know what a stunning heiress she was, and so handsome! How'd you, of all men in the world, let her slip through your fingers?"

A curious silence follows this effusion. Corlaer Van Boozenberg is slightly flown with wine. Hal Battlebury, who sits near him, looks troubled. Herbert Octoyne and Mellish Whitloe exchange meaning glances. The young ladies—Mrs. Plumer is the only matron, except Mrs. Dagon, who sits below—smile pleasantly. Sligo Moultrie eats grapes. Grace Plumer waits to hear what Abel says, or to observe what he does. Mrs. Dagon regards the whole affair with an approving smile, nodding almost imperceptibly a kind of Freemason's sign to Mrs. Plumer, who thinks that the worthy young Van Boozenberg has probably taken too much wine.

Abel Newt quietly turns to Grace Plumer, saying,

"Poor Corlaer! There are disadvantages in being the son of a very rich man; one is so strongly inclined to measure every thing by money. As if money were all!"

He looks her straight in the eyes as he says it. Perhaps it is some effort he is making which throws into his look that cold, hard blackness which is not beautiful. Perhaps it is some kind of exasperation arising from what he has heard Moultrie say privately and Van Boozenberg publicly, as it were, that pushes him further than he means to go. There is a dangerous look of craft; an air of sarcastic cunning in his eyes and on his face. He turns the current of talk with his neighbors, without any other indication of disturbance than the unpleasant look. Van Boozenberg is silent again. The gentle, rippling murmur of talk fills the room, and at a moment when Moultrie is speaking with his neighbor, Abel says, looking at the engraving of the Madonna,

"Miss Grace, I feel like those cherubs."

"Why so, Mr. Newt?"

"Because I am perfectly happy."

"Indeed!"

"Yes, Miss Grace, and for the same reason that I entirely love and admire."

Her heart beats violently. Sligo Moultrie turns and sees her face. He divines every thing in a moment, for he loves Grace Plumer.

"Yes, Miss Grace," he says, in a quick, thick tone, as if he

were continuing a narration—"yes, she became Princess of
Este; but the fiery eyes burned her, and the sweet tongue
stung her forever and ever."

Mrs. Plumer and Mrs. Dagon are rising. There is a rust-
ling tumult of women's dresses, a shaking out of handker-
chiefs, light gusts of laughter, and fragments of conversation.
The handsome women move about like birds, with a plumy,
elastic motion, waving their fans, smelling their bouquets, and
listening through them to tones that are very low. The Prince
of the house is every where, smiling, sinuous, dark in the eyes
and hair.

It is already late, and there is no disposition to be seated.
Sligo Moultrie stands by Grace Plumer, and she is very glad
and even grateful to him. Abel, passing to and fro, looks at
her occasionally, and can not possibly tell if her confusion is
pain or pleasure. There is a reckless gayety in the tone with
which he speaks to the other ladies. "Surely Mr. Newt was
never so fascinating," they all think in their secret souls; and
they half envy Grace Plumer, for they know the little supper
is given for her, and they think it needs no sibyl to say why,
or to prophesy the future.

It is nearly midnight, and the moon is rising. Hark!

A band pours upon the silent night the mellow, passionate
wail of "Robin Adair." The bright company stands listening
and silent. The festive scene, the hour, the flowers, the luxury of the place, the beauty of the women, impress the imagination, and touch the music with a softer melancholy. Hal
Battlebury's eyes are clear, but his heart is full of tears as he
listens and thinks of Amy Waring. He knows that all is in
vain. She has told him, with a sweet dignity that made her
only lovelier and more inaccessible, that it can not be. He is
trying to believe it. He is hoping to show her one day that
she is wrong. Listening, he follows in his mind the song the
band is playing.

Sligo Moultrie feels and admires the audacious skill of Abel
in crowning the feast with music. Grace Plumer leans upon

his arm. Abel Newt's glittering eyes are upon them. It is the very moment he had intended to be standing by her side, to·hold her arm in his, and to make her feel that the music which pealed in long cadences through the midnight, and streamed through the draped windows into the room, was the passionate entreaty of his heart, the irresistible pathos of the love he bore her.

Somehow Grace Plumer is troubled. She fears the fascination she enjoys. She dreads the assumption of power over her which she has observed in Abel. She recoils from the cold blackness she has seen in his eyes. She sees it at this moment again, in that glittering glance which slips across the room and holds her as she stands. Involuntarily she leans upon Sligo Moultrie, as if clinging to him.

There is more music—a lighter, then a sadder and lingering strain. It recedes slowly, slowly up the street. The company stand in the pretty parlor, and not a word is spoken. It is past midnight; the music is over.

"What a charming party! Mr. Newt, how much we are obliged to you!" says Mrs. Godefroi Plumer, as Abel hands her into the carriage.

"The pleasure is all mine, Madame," replies Mr. Newt, as he sees with bitterness that Sligo Moultrie stands ready to offer his hand to assist Miss Plumer. The footman holds the carriage door open. Miss Plumer can accept the assistance of but one, and Mr. Abel is resolved to know which one.

"Permit me, Miss Plumer," says Sligo.

"Allow me, Miss Grace," says Abel.

The latter address sounds to her a little too free. She feels, perhaps, that he has no rights of intimacy—at least not yet —or what does she feel? But she gives her hand to Sligo Moultrie, and Abel bows.

"Thank you for a delightful evening, Mr. Newt. Good· night!"

The host bows again, bareheaded, in the moonlight.

"By-the-by, Mr. Moultrie," says the ringing voice of the

WHICH?

clear-eyed girl, who remembers that Abel is listening, but who is sure that only Sligo can understand, "I ought to have told you that the story ended differently. The Princess left the villa. Good-night! good-night!"

The carriage rattles down the street.

"Good-night, Newt; a very beautiful and pleasant party."

"Good-night, Moultrie—thank you; and pleasant dreams."

The young Georgian skips up the street, thinking only of Grace Plumer's last words. Abel Newt stands at his door for a moment, remembering them also, and perfectly understanding them. The next instant he is shawling and cloaking the other ladies, who follow the Plumers; among them Mrs. Dagon, who says, softly,

"Good-night, Abel. I like it all very well. A very proper girl! Such a complexion! and such teeth! Such lovely little hands, too! It's all very right. Go on, my dear. What a dreadful piece of work Fanny's made of it! I wonder you don't like Hope Wayne. Think of it, a million of dollars! However, it's all one, I suppose—Grace or Hope are equally pleasant. Good-night, naughty boy! Behave yourself. As for your father, I'm afraid to go to the house lest he should bite me. He's dangerous. Good-night, dear!"

Yes, Abel remembers with singular distinctness that it was a word, only one word, just a year ago to Grace Plumer—a word intended only to deceive that foolish Fanny—which had cost him—at least, he thinks so—Hope Wayne.

He bows his last guests out at the door with more sweetness in his face than in his soul. Returning to the room he looks round upon the ruins of the feast, and drinks copiously of the wine that still remains. Not at all inclined to sleep, he goes into his bedroom and finds a cigar. Returning, he makes a few turns in the room while he smokes, and stops constantly to drink another glass. He half mutters to himself, as he addresses the chair in which Grace Plumer has been sitting,

"Are you or I going to pay for this feast, Madame? Somebody has got to do it. Young woman, Moultrie was right, and you are wrong. She *did* become Princess of Este. I'll pay now, and you'll pay by-and-by. Yes, my dear Grace, you'll pay by-and-by."

He says these last words very slowly, with his teeth set, the head a little crouched between the shoulders, and a stealthy, sullen, ugly glare in the eyes.

"I've got to pay now, and you shall pay by-and-by. Yes,

Miss Grace Plumer; you shall pay for to-night and for the evening in my mother's conservatory."

He strides about the room a little longer. It is one o'clock, and he goes down stairs and out of the house. Still smoking, he passes along Broadway until he reaches Thiel's. He hurries up, and finds only a few desperate gamblers. Abel himself looks a little wild and flushed. He sits down defiantly and plays recklessly. The hours are clanged from the belfry of the City Hall. The lights burn brightly in Thiel's rooms. Nobody is sleeping there. One by one the players drop away—except those who remark Abel's game, for that is so careless and furious that it is threatening, threatening, whether he loses or wins.

He loses constantly, but still plays on. The lights are steady. His eyes are bright. The bank is quite ready to stay open for such a run of luck in its favor.

The bell of the City Hall clangs three in the morning as a young man emerges from Thiel's, and hurries, then saunters, up Broadway. His motions are fitful, his dress is deranged, and his hair matted. His face, in the full moonlight, is dogged and dangerous. It is the Prince of the feast, who had told Grace Plumer that he was perfectly happy.

CHAPTER LI.

A WARNING.

A few evenings afterward, when Abel called to know how the ladies had borne the fatigues of the feast, Mrs. Plumer said, with smiles, that it was a kind of fatigue ladies bore without flinching. Miss Grace, who was sitting upon a sofa by the side of Sligo Moultrie, said that it was one of the feasts at which young women especially are supposed to be perfectly happy. She emphasized the last words, and her bright black eyes opened wide upon Mr. Abel Newt, who could not tell if

THREE IN THE MORNING.

he saw mischievous malice or a secret triumph and sense of
release in them.

"Oh!" said he, gayly, "it would be too much for me to
hope to make any ladies, and especially young ladies, perfectly happy."

And he returned Miss Plumer's look with a keen glance
masked in merriment.

Sligo Moultrie wagged his foot.

"There now is conscious power!" said Abel, with a laugh, as he pointed at Miss Plumer's companion.

They all laughed, but not very heartily. There appeared to be some meaning lurking in whatever was said; and like all half-concealed meanings, it seemed, perhaps, even more signifi-cant than it really was.

Abel was very brilliant, and told more and better stories than usual. Mrs. Plumer listened and laughed, and declared that he was certainly the best company she had met for a long time. Nor were Miss Plumer and Mr. Moultrie reluctant to join the conversation. In fact, Abel was several times sur-prised by the uncommon spirit of Sligo's replies.

"What is it?" said Abel to himself, with a flash of the black eyes that was startling.

All the evening he felt particularly belligerent toward Sligo Moultrie; and yet a close observer would have discovered no occasion in the conduct of the young man for such a feeling upon Abel's part. Mr. Moultrie sat quietly by the side of Grace Plumer—"as if somehow he had a right to sit there," thought Abel Newt, who resolved to discover if indeed he had a right.

During that visit, however, he had no chance. Moultrie sat persistently, and so did Abel. The clock pointed to eleven, and still they did not move. It was fairly toward midnight when Abel rose to leave, and at the same moment Sligo Moul-trie rose also. Abel bade the ladies good-evening, and passed out as if Moultrie were close by him. But that young man remained standing by the sofa upon which Grace Plumer was seated, and said quietly to Abel,

"Good-evening, Newt!"

Grace Plumer looked at him also, with the bright black eyes, and blushed.

For a moment Abel Newt's heart seemed to stand still! An expression of some bitterness must have swept over his face, for Mrs. Plumer stepped toward him, as he stood with his hand upon the door, and said,

"Are you unwell?"

The cloud dissolved in a forced smile.

"No, thank you; not at all!" and he looked surprised, as if he could not imagine why any one should think so.

He did not wait longer, and the next moment was in the street.

Mrs. Plumer also left the room almost immediately after his departure. Sligo Moultrie seated himself by his companion.

"My dear Grace, did you see that look?"

"Yes."

"He suspects the truth," returned Sligo Moultrie; and he might have added more, but that his lips at that instant were otherwise engaged.

Abel more than suspected the truth. He was sure of it, and the certainty made him desperate. He had risked so much upon the game! He had been so confident! As he half ran along the street he passed many things rapidly in his mind. He was like a seaman in doubtful waters, and the breeze was swelling into a gale.

Turning out of Broadway he ran quickly to his door, opened it, and leaped up stairs.

To his great surprise his lamp was lighted and a man was sitting reading quietly at his table. As Abel entered his visitor closed his book and looked up.

"Why, Uncle Lawrence," said the young man, "you have a genius for surprises! What on earth are you doing in my room?"

His uncle said, only half smiling,

"Abel, we are both bachelors, and bachelors have no hours. I want to talk with you."

Abel looked at his guest uneasily; but he put down his hat and lighted a cigar; then seated himself, almost defiantly, opposite his uncle, with the table between them.

"Now, Sir; what is it?"

Lawrence Newt paused a moment, while the young man

still calmly puffed the smoke from his mouth, and calmly regarded his uncle.

"Abel, you are not a fool. You know the inevitable results of certain courses. I want to fortify your knowledge by my experience. I understand all the temptations and excitements that carry you along. But I don't like your looks, Abel; and I don't like the looks of other people when they speak of you and your father. Remember, we are of the same blood. Heaven knows its own mysteries! Your father and I were sons of one woman. That is a tie which we can neither of us escape, if we wanted to. Why should you ruin yourself?"

"Did you come to propose any thing for me to do, Sir, or only to inform me that you considered me a reprobate?" asked Abel, half-sneeringly, the smoke rising from his mouth.

Lawrence Newt did not answer.

"I am like other young men," continued Abel. "I am fond of living well, of a good horse, of a pretty woman. I drink my glass, and I am not afraid of a card. Really, Uncle Lawrence, I see no such profound sin or shame in it all, so long as I honestly pay the scot. Do I cheat at cards? Do I lie in the gutters?"

"No!" answered Lawrence.

"Do I steal?"

"Not that I know," said the other.

"Please, Uncle Lawrence, what do you mean, then?"

"I mean the way, the spirit in which you do things. If you are not conscious of it, how can I make you? I can not say more than I have. I came merely—"

"As a handwriting upon the wall, Uncle Lawrence?"

Lawrence Newt rose and stood a little back from the table.

"Yes, if you choose, as a handwriting on the wall. Abel, when the prodigal son *came to himself*, he rose and went to his father. I came to ask you to return to yourself."

"From these husks, Sir?" asked Abel, as he looked around

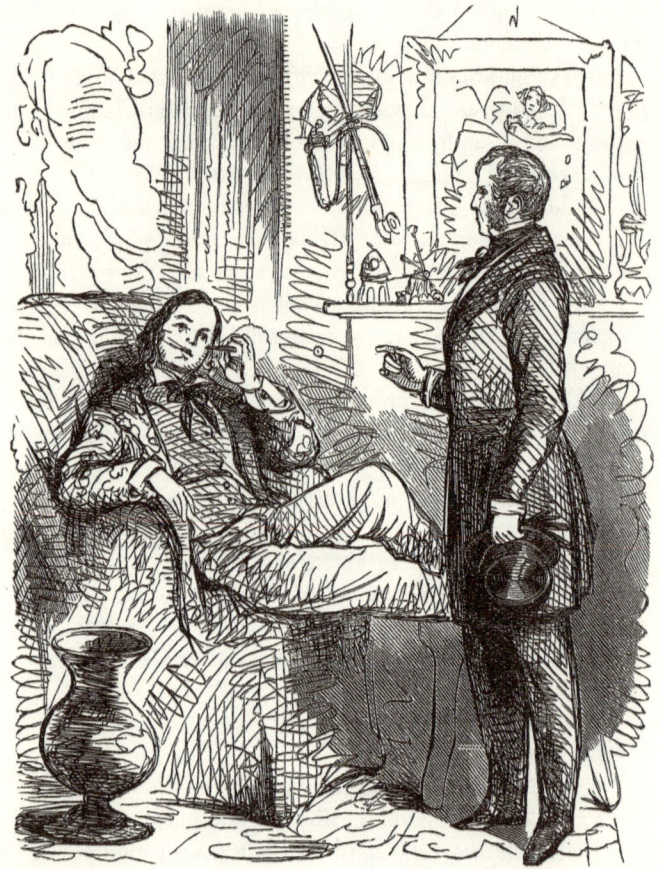

"THOU ART THE MAN!"

his luxurious rooms, his eye falling last upon the French print of Lucille, fresh from the bath.

Lawrence Newt looked at his nephew with profound gravity. The young man lay back in his chair, lightly holding his cigar, and carelessly following the smoke with his eye. The beauty and intelligence of his face, the indolent grace of his person, seen in the soft light of the lamp, and set like a picture in the voluptuous refinement of the room, touched the imagination and the heart of the older man. There was a look of earnest, yearning entreaty in his eyes as he said,

"Abel, you remember Milton's Comus?"

The young man bowed.

"Do you think the revelers were happy?"

Abel smiled, but did not answer. But after a few minutes he said, with a smile,

"I was not there."

"You *are* there," answered Lawrence Newt, with uplifted finger, and in a voice so sad and clear that Abel started.

The two men looked at each other silently for a few moments.

"Good-night, Abel."

"Good-night, Uncle Lawrence."

The door closed behind the older man. Abel sat in his chair, intently thinking. His uncle's words rang in his memory. But as he recalled the tone, the raised finger, the mien, with which they had been spoken, the young man looked around him, and seemed half startled and frightened by the stillness, and awe-struck by the midnight hour. He moved his head rapidly and arose, like a person trying to rouse himself from sleep or nightmare. Passing the mirror, he involuntarily started at the haggard paleness of his face under the clustering black hair. He was trying to shake something off. He went uneasily about the room until he had lighted a match, and a candle, with which he went into the next room, still half-looking over his shoulder, as if fearing that something dogged him. He opened the closet where he kept his wine. He restlessly filled a large glass and poured it down his throat—not as if he were drinking, but as if he were taking an antidote. He rubbed his forehead with his hand, and half-smiled a sickly smile.

But still his eyes wandered nervously to the spot in which his uncle had stood; still he seemed to fear that he should see a ghostly figure standing there and pointing at him; should see himself, in some phantom counterpart, sitting in the chair. His eyes opened as if he were listening intently. For in the midnight he thought he heard, in that dim light he thought he saw, the Prophet and the King. He did not remember more the words his uncle had spoken. But he heard only, "Thou art the man! Thou art the man!"

And all night long, as he dreamed or restlessly awoke, he heard the same words, spoken as if with finger pointed— "Thou art the man! Thou art the man!"

CHAPTER LII.

BREAKERS.

LAWRENCE NEWT had certainly told the truth of his brother's home. Mr. Boniface Newt had become so surly that it was not wise to speak to him. He came home late, and was angry if dinner were not ready, and cross if it were. He banged all the doors, and swore at all the chairs. After dinner he told May not to touch the piano, and begged his wife, for Heaven's sake, to take up some book, and not to sit with an air of imbecile vacancy that was enough to drive a man distracted. He snarled at the servants, so that they went about the house upon tip-toe and fled his presence, and were constantly going away, causing Mrs. Newt to pass many hours of the week in an Intelligence Office. Mr. Newt found holes in the carpets, stains upon the cloths, knocks upon the walls, nicks in the glasses and plates at table, scratches upon the furniture, and defects and misfortunes every where. He went to bed without saying good-night, and came down without a good-morning. He sat at breakfast morose and silent; or he sighed, and frowned, and muttered, and went out without a smile or a good-by. There was a profound gloom in the house, an unnatural order. Nobody dared to derange the papers or books upon the tables, to move the chairs, or to touch any thing. If May appeared in a new dress he frowned, and his wife trembled every time she put in a breast-pin.

Only in her own room was May mistress of every thing. If any body had looked into it he would have seen only the traces of a careful and elegant hand, and often enough he would have seen a delicate girl-face, almost too thoughtful for so young a face, resting upon the hand, as if May Newt were troubled and perplexed by the gloom of the house and the silence of the household. Her window opened over the street, and there were a few horse-chestnut trees before the house. She made friends with them, and they covered themselves with blossoms for her pleasure. She sat for hours at her window, looking into the trees, sewing, reading, musing—solitary as a fairy princess in a tower.

Sometimes flowers came, with Uncle Lawrence's love. Or fine fruit for Miss May Newt, with the same message. Several times from her window May had seen who the messenger was: a young man with candid eyes, with a quick step, and an open, almost boyish face. When the street was still she heard him half-singing as he bounded along—as nobody sings, she thought, whose home is not happy.

Solitary as a fairy princess in a tower, she looked down upon the figure as it rapidly disappeared. The sewing or the reading stopped entirely; nor were they resumed when he had passed out of sight. May Newt thought it strange that Uncle Lawrence should send such a messenger in the middle of the day. He did not look like a porter. He was not an office boy. He was evidently one of the upper-clerks. It was certainly very kind in Uncle Lawrence.

So thought the solitary Princess in the tower, her mind wandering from the romance she was reading to a busy speculation upon the reality in the street beneath her.

The blind was thrown partly back as she sat at the open window. A simple airy dress, made by her own hands, covered her flower-like figure. The brown hair was smoothed over the white temples, and the sweet girl eyes looked kindly into the street from which the figure of the young man had just passed. If by chance the eyes of that young man had been turned upward, would he not have thought—since one Sunday morning, when he passed her on the way to church, he was sure that she looked like an angel going home—would he not have thought that she looked like an angel bending down toward him out of heaven?

It was not strange that Uncle Lawrence had sent him. For somehow Uncle Lawrence had discovered that if there was any thing to go to May Newt, there was nothing in the world that Gabriel Bennet was so anxious to do as to carry it.

But while the young man was always so glad to go to Boniface Newt's gloomy house—for some reason which he did not explain, and which even his sister Ellen did not know—or, at least, which she pretended not to know, although one evening that wily young girl talked with brother Gabriel about May Newt, as if she had some particular purpose in the conversation, until she seemed to have convinced herself of some hitherto doubtful point—yet with all the willingness to go to the house, Gabriel Bennet never went to the office of Boniface Newt, Son, & Co.

If he had done so it would not have been pleasant to him, for it was perpetual field-day in the office. A few days after Uncle Lawrence's visit to his nephew, the senior partner sat bending his hard, anxious face over account-books and letters. The junior partner lounged in his chair as if the office had been a club-room. The "Company" never appeared.

"Father, I've just seen Sinker."

"D— Sinker!"

"Come, come, father, let's be reasonable! Sinker says that the Canal will be a clear case of twenty per cent. per annum for ten years at least, and that we could afford to lose a cent or two upon the Bilbo iron to make it up, over and over again."

Mr. Abel Newt threw his leg over the arm of the chair and looked at his boot. Mr. Boniface Newt threw his head around suddenly and fiercely.

"And what's Sinker's commission? How much money do you suppose he has to put in? How much stock will he take?"

"He has sold out in the Mallow Mines to put in," said Abel, a little doggedly.

"Are you sure?"

"He says so," returned Abel, shortly.

"Don't believe a word of it!" said his father, tartly, turning back again to his desk.

Abel put both hands in his pockets, and both feet upon the ground, side by side, and rocked them upon the heels backward and forward, looking all the time at his father. His face grew cloudy—more cloudy every moment. At length he said,

"I think we'd better do it."

His father did not speak or move. He seemed to have heard nothing, and to be only inwardly cursing the state of things revealed by the books and papers before him.

Abel looked at him for a moment, and then, raising his voice, continued:

"As one of the firm, I propose that we sell out the Bilbo and buy into the Canal."

Not a look or movement from his father.

Abel jumped up—his eyes black, his face red. He took his hat and went to the door, saying,

"I shall go and conclude the arrangement!"

As he reached the door his father raised his eyes and looked at him. The eyes were full of contempt and anger, and a sneering sound came from his lips.

"You'll do no such thing."

The young man glanced sideways at his parent.

"Who will prevent me?"

"I!" roared the elder.

"I believe I am one of the firm," said Abel, coldly.

"You'd better try it!" said the old man, disregarding Abel's remark.

Abel was conscious that his father had this game, at least,

in his hands. The word of the young man would hardly avail against a simultaneous veto from the parent. No transaction would stand a moment under such circumstances. The young man slowly turned from the door, and fixing his eyes upon his father, advanced toward him with a kind of imperious insolence.

"I should like to understand my position in this house," said he, with forced calmness.

"Good God! Sir, a bootblack, if I choose!" returned his father, fiercely. "The unluckiest day of my life was when you came in here, Sir. Ever since then the business has been getting more and more complicated, until it is only a question of days how long it can even look respectable. We shall all be beggars in a month. We are ruined. There is no chance," cried the old man, with a querulous wail through his set teeth. "And you know who has done it all. You know who has brought us all to shame and disgrace—to utter poverty;" and, rising from his chair, the father shook his clenched hands at Abel so furiously that the young man fell back abashed.

"Don't talk to me, Sir. Don't dare to say a word," cried Mr. Newt, in a voice shrill with anger. "All my life has come to nothing. All my sacrifices, my industry, my efforts, are of no use. I am a beggar, Sir; so are you!"

He sank back in his chair and covered his face with his hands. The noise made the old book-keeper outside look in. But it was no new thing. The hot debates of the private room were familiar to his ear. With the silent, sad fidelity of his profession he knew every thing, and was dumb. Not a turn of his face, not a light in his eye, told any tales to the most careful and sagacious inquirer. Within the last few months Mr. Van Boozenberg had grown quite friendly with him. When they met, the President had sought to establish the most familiar intercourse. But he discovered that for the slightest hint of the condition of the Newt business he might as well have asked Boniface himself. Like a mother, who knows the crime her son has committed, and perceives that he can only a little longer hide it, but who, with her heart break-ing, still smiles away suspicion, so the faithful accountant, who supposed that the crash was at hand, was as constant and calm as if the business were never before so prosperous.

CHAPTER LIII.

SLIGO MOULTRIE *vice* ABEL NEWT.

ABEL NEWT had now had two distinct warnings of some-thing which nobody knew must happen so well as he. He dined sumptuously that very day, and dressed very carefully that evening, and at eight o'clock was sitting alone with Grace Plumer. The superb ruby was on her finger. But on the third finger of her left hand he saw a large glowing opal. His eyes fastened upon it with a more brilliant glitter. They looked at her too so strangely that Grace Plumer felt troubled and half alarmed. "Am I too late?" he thought.

"Miss Grace," said Abel, in a low voice.

The tone was significant.

"Mr. Newt," said she, with a half smile, as if she accepted a contest of badinage.

"Do you remember I said I was perfectly happy?"

He moved his chair a little nearer to hers. She drew back almost imperceptibly.

"I remember you *said* so, and I was very glad to hear it."

"Do you remember my theory of perfect happiness?"

"Yes," said Miss Plumer, calmly, "I believe it was perfect love. But I think we had better talk of something else;" and she rose from her chair and stood by the table.

"Miss Plumer!"

"Mr. Newt."

"It was you who first emboldened me."

"I do not understand, Sir."

"It was a long time ago, in my mother's conservatory."

Grace Plumer remembered the evening, and she replied, more softly,

"I am very sorry, Mr. Newt, that I behaved so foolishly: I was young. But I think we did each other no harm."

"No harm, I trust, indeed, Miss Grace," said Abel. "It is surely no harm to love; at least, not as I love you."

He too had risen, and tried to take her hand. She stepped back. He pressed toward her.

"Grace; dear Grace!"

"Stop, Sir, stop!" said his companion, drawing herself up and waving him back; "I can not hear you talk so. I am engaged."

Abel turned pale. Grace Plumer was frightened. He sprang forward and seized her hand.

"Oh! Grace, hear me but one word! You knew that I loved you, and you allowed me to come. In honor, in truth, before God, you are mine!"

She struggled to release her hand. As she looked in his face she saw there an expression which assured her that he was capable of saying any thing, of doing any thing; and she trembled to think how much she might be—how much any woman is—in the power of a desperate man.

"Indeed, Mr. Newt, you must let me go!"

"Grace, Grace, say that you love me!"

The frightened girl broke away from him, and ran toward the door. Abel followed her, but the door opened, and Sligo Moultrie entered.

"Oh, Sligo!" cried Grace, as he put his arm around her.

Abel stopped and bowed.

"Pardon me, Miss Plumer. Certainly Mr. Moultrie will understand the ardor of a passion which in his case has been so fortunate. I am sorry, Sir," he said, turning to Sligo, "that my ignorance of your relation to Miss Plumer should have betrayed me. I congratulate you both from my soul!"

He bowed again, and before they could speak he was gone. The tone of his voice lingering upon their ears was like a hiss. It was a most sinister felicitation.

CHAPTER LIV.

CLOUDS AND DARKNESS.

" At least, Miss Amy—at least, we shall be friends."

Amy Waring sat in her chamber on the evening of the day that Lawrence Newt had said these words. Her long rich brown hair clustered upon her shoulders, and the womanly brown eyes were fixed upon a handful of withered flowers. They were the blossoms she had laid away at various times—gifts of Lawrence Newt, or consecrated by his touch.

She sat musing for a long time. The womanly brown eyes were soft with a look of aching regret rather than of sharp disappointment. Then she rose—still holding the withered remains—and paced thoughtfully up and down the room. The night hours passed, and still she softly paced, or tranquilly seated herself, without the falling of a tear, and only now and then a long deep breath rather than a sigh.

At last she took all the flowers—dry, yellow, lustreless—and opened a sheet of white paper. She laid them in it, and the brown womanly eyes looked at them with yearning fondness. She sat motionless, as if she could not prevail upon herself to fold the paper. But at length she sank gradually to her knees—a sinless Magdalen; her brown hair fell about her bending face, and she said, although her lips did not move, "To each, in his degree, the cup is given. Oh, Father! strengthen each to drain it and believe!"

She rose quietly and folded the paper, with the loving care and lingering delay with which a mother smooths the shroud that wraps her baby. She tied it with a pure white ribbon, so that it looked not unlike a bridal gift; and pressing her lips to it long and silently, she laid it in the old drawer. There it still remained. The paper was as white, the ribbon was as pure as ever. Only the flowers were withered. But her heart was not a flower.

"Well, Aunt Martha," said she, several months after the death of old Christopher Burt, "I really think you are coming back to this world again."

The young woman smiled, while the older one busily drove her needle.

"Why," continued Amy, "here is a white collar; and you have actually smiled at least six times in as many months!"

The older woman still said nóthing. The old sadness was in her eyes, but it certainly had become more natural—more human, as it were—and the melodramatic gloom in which she had hitherto appeared was certainly less obvious.

"Amy," she said at length, "God leads his erring children through the dark valley, but he does lead them—he does not leave them. I did not know how deeply I had sinned until I heard the young man Summerfield, who came to see me even in this room."

She looked up and about, as if to catch some lingering light upon the wall.

"And it was Lawrence Newt's preacher who made me feel that there was hope even for me."

She sewed on quietly.

"I thank God for those two men; and for one other," she added, after a little pause.

Amy only looked, she did not ask who.

"Lawrence Newt," said Aunt Martha, calmly looking at Amy—"Lawrence Newt, who came to me as a brother comes to a sister, and said, 'Be of good cheer!' Amy, what is the matter with you and Lawrence Newt?"

"How, aunty?"

"How many months since you met here?"

"It was several months ago, aunty."

Aunt Martha sat quietly sewing, and after some time said,

"He is no longer a young man."

"But, Aunt Martha, he is not old."

Still sewing, the grave woman looked at the burning cheeks of her younger companion. Amy did not speak.

The older woman continued: "When you and he went from this room months ago I supposed you would be his wife before now."

Still Amy did not speak. It was not because she was unwilling to confide entirely in Aunt Martha, but there was something she did not wish to say to herself. Yet suddenly, as if lifted upon a calm, irresistible purpose—as a leaf is lifted upon the long swell of the sea—she said, with her heart as quiet as her eyes,

"I do not think Lawrence Newt loves me."

The next moment the poor leaf is lost in the trough of the sea. The next moment Amy Waring's heart beat tumultuously; she felt as if she should fall from her seat. Her eyes were blind with hot tears. Aunt Martha did not look up— did not start or exclaim—but deliberately threaded her needle carefully, and creased her work with her thumb-nail. After a little while, during which the sea was calming itself, she said, slowly, repeating Amy's words syllable by syllable,

"You do not believe Lawrence Newt loves you?"

"No," was the low, firm whisper of reply.

"Whom do you think he loves?"

There was an instant of almost deathly stillness in that turbulent heart. For a moment the very sea of feeling seemed to be frozen.

Then, and very slowly, a terrible doubt arose in Amy Waring's mind. Before this conversation every perplexity had resolved itself in the consciousness that somehow it must all come right by-and-by. It had never occurred to her to ask, Does he love any one else? But she saw now at once that if he did, then the meaning of his words was plain enough; and so, of course, he did.

Who was it?

Amy knew there was but one person in the world whose name could possibly answer that question.

But had Lawrence not watched with her—and with delight
—the progress of Arthur Merlin's feeling for that other?

Yes; but if, as he watched so closely, he saw and felt how
lovely that other was, was it so wonderful that he should love
her?

These things flashed through her mind as she sat motionless
by Aunt Martha; and she said, with profound tranquillity,

"Very possibly, Hope Wayne."

Aunt Martha did not look up. She seemed to feel that she
should see something too sad if she did so; but she asked,

"Is she worthy of him?"

"Perfectly!" answered Amy, promptly.

At this word Aunt Martha did look up, and her eyes met
Amy's. Amy Waring burst into tears. Her aunt laid aside her
work, and gently put her arms about her niece. She waited until the first gush of feeling had passed, and then said, tenderly,

"Amy, it is by the heart that God leads us women to himself.
Through love I fell; but through love, in another way, I hope
to be restored. Do you really believe he loves Hope Wayne?"

"I don't know," was the low reply.

"I know, Amy."

The two women had risen, and were walking, with their
arms clasped around each other, up and down the room.
They stopped at the window and looked out. As they did
so, their eyes fell simultaneously upon the man of whom they
were speaking, who was standing at the back of his lofts,
looking up at the window, which was a shrine to him.

"There she stood and smiled at me," he said to himself
whenever he looked at it.

As their eyes met, he smiled and waved his hand. With
his eyes and head he asked, as when he had first seen her there,

"May I come up?" and he waved his handkerchief.

The two women looked at him. As Amy did so, she felt as
if there had been a long and gloomy war; and now, in his
eager eyes and waving hand, she saw the illumination and
waving flags of victory and peace.

She smiled as she looked, and nodded No to him with her head.

But Aunt Martha nodded Yes so vehemently that Lawrence Newt immediately disappeared from his window.

Alarmed at his coming, doubtful of Aunt Martha's intention, Amy Waring suddenly cried, "Oh! Aunt Martha!" and was gone in a moment. Lawrence Newt dashed round, and knocked at the door.

" Come in!"

He rushed into the room. Some sweet suspicion had winged his feet and lightened his heart; but he was not quick enough. He looked eagerly about him.

" She is gone!" said Aunt Martha.

His eager eyes drooped, as if light had gone out of his life also.

"Mr. Newt," said Aunt Martha, "sit down. You have been of the greatest service to me. How can I repay you?"

Lawrence Newt, who had felt during the moment in which he saw Amy at the window, and the other in which he had been hastening to her, that the cloud was about rolling from his life, was confounded by finding that it was an account between Aunt Martha, instead of Amy, and himself that was to be settled.

He bowed in some confusion, but recovering in a moment, he said, courteously,

" I am aware of nothing that you owe me in any way."

"Lawrence Newt," returned the other, solemnly, "you have known my story; you knew the man to whom I supposed myself married; you have known of my child; you have known how long I have been dead to the world and to all my family and friends, and when, by chance, you discovered me, you became as my brother. How many an hour we have sat talking in this room, and how constantly your sympathy has been my support and your wisdom my guide!"

Lawrence Newt, whose face had grown very grave, waved his hand deprecatingly.

"I know, I know," she continued. "Let that remain un-said. It can not be unforgotten. But I know your secrets too."

They looked at each other.

"You love Amy Waring."

His face became inscrutable, and his eyes were fixed quiet-ly upon hers. She betrayed no embarrassment, but continued,

"Amy Waring loves you."

A sudden light shot into that inscrutable face. The clear eyes were veiled for an instant by an exquisite emotion.

"What separates you?"

There was an authority in the tone of the question which Lawrence Newt found hard to resist. It was an authority natural to such intimate knowledge of the relation of the two persons. But he was so entirely unaccustomed to confide in any body, or to speak of his feelings, that he could not utter a word. He merely looked at Aunt Martha as if he expected her to answer all her own questions, and solve every difficulty and doubt.

Meanwhile she had resumed her sewing, and was rocking quietly in her chair. Lawrence Newt arose and found his tongue. He bowed in that quaint way which seemed to in-volve him more closely in himself, and to warn off every body else.

"I prefer to hear that a woman loves me from her own lips."

The tone was perfectly kind and respectful; but Aunt Mar-tha felt that she had been struck dumb.

"I thank you from my heart," Lawrence Newt said to her. And taking her hand, he bent over it and kissed it. She sat looking at him, and at length said,

"Mayn't I do any thing to show my gratitude?"

"You have already done more than I deserve," replied Lawrence Newt. "I must go now. Good-by! God bless you!"

She heard his quick footfalls as he descended the stairs. For a long time the sombre woman sat rocking idly to and fro, holding her work in her hand, and with her eyes fixed upon the floor. She did not seem to see clearly, whatever it might be she was looking at. She shook out her work and straightened it, and folded it regularly, and looked at it as if the secret would pop out of the proper angle if she could only find it. Then she creased it and crimped it—still she could not see. Then she took a few stitches slowly, regarding fixedly a corner of the room as if the thought she was in search of was a mouse, and might at any moment run out of his hole and over the floor.

And after all the looking, she shook her head intelligently and fell quietly to work, as if the mystery were plain enough, saying to herself,

"Why didn't I trust a girl's instinct who loves as Amy does? Of course she is right. Dear! dear! Of course he loves Hope Wayne."

CHAPTER LV.

ARTHUR MERLIN'S GREAT PICTURE.

ARTHUR MERLIN had sketched his great picture of Diana and Endymion a hundred times. He talked of it with his friends, and smoked scores of boxes of cigars during the conversations. He had completed what he called the study for the work, which represented, he said, the Goddess alighting upon Latmos while Endymion slept. He pointed out to his companions, especially to Lawrence Newt, the pure antique classical air of the composition.

"You know," he said, as he turned his head and moved his hands over the study as if drawing in the air, "you know it ought somehow to seem silent, and cool, and remote; for it is ancient Greece, Diana, and midnight. You see?"

Then came a vast cloud of smoke from his mouth, as if to assist the eyes of the spectator.

"Oh yes, I see," said every one of his companions—espe-

AUNT WINNIFRED IN ARTHUR'S STUDIO.

cially Lawrence Newt, who did see, indeed, but saw only a
head of Hope Wayne in a mist. The Endymion, the mountain, the Greece, the antiquity, were all vigorous assumptions
of the artist. The study for his great picture was simply an
unfinished portrait of Hope Wayne.

Aunt Winnifred, who sometimes came into her nephew's
studio, saw the study one day, and exclaimed, sorrowfully,

"Oh, Arthur! Arthur!"

The young man, who was busily mixing colors upon his pallet, and humming, as he smoked, "'Tis my delight of a shiny night," turned in dismay, thinking his aunt was suddenly ill.

"My dear aunt!" and he laid down his pallet and ran toward her.

She was sitting in an arm-chair holding the study. Arthur stopped.

"My dear Arthur, now I understand all."

Arthur Merlin was confused. He, perhaps, suspected that his picture of Diana resembled a certain young lady. But how should Aunt Winnifred know it, who, as he supposed, had never seen her? Besides, he felt it was a disagreeable thing, when he was and had been in love with a young lady for a long time, to have his aunt say that she understood all about it. How could she understand all about it? What right has any body to say that she understands all about it? He asked himself the petulant question because he was very sure that he himself did not by any means understand all about it.

"What do you understand, Aunt Winnifred?" demanded Arthur, in a resolute and defiant tone, as if he were fully prepared to deny every thing he was about to hear.

"Yes, yes," continued Aunt Winnifred, musingly, and in a tone of profound sadness, as she still held and contemplated the picture—"yes, yes! I see, I see!"

Arthur was quite vexed.

"Now really, my dear aunt," said he, remonstratingly, "you must be aware that it is not becoming in a woman like you to go on in this way. You ought to explain what you mean," he added, decidedly.

"Well, my poor boy, the hotter you get the surer I am. Don't you see?"

Mr. Merlin did not seem to be in the least pacified by this reply. It was, therefore, in an indignant tone that he answered:

"Aunt Winnifred, it is not kind in you to come up here and

make me lose my time and temper, while you sit there coolly and talk in infernal parables!"

"Infernal parables!" cried the lady, in a tone of surprise and horror.

"Oh, Arthur, Arthur! that comes of not going to church. Infernal parables! My soul and body, what an awful idea!"

The painter smiled. The contest was too utterly futile. He went slowly back to his easel, and, after a few soothing puffs, began again to rub his colors upon the pallet. He was humming carelessly once more, and putting his brush to the canvas before him, when his aunt remarked,

"There, Arthur! now that you are reasonable, I'll tell you what I meant."

The artist looked over his shoulder and laughed.

"Go on, dear aunt."

"I understand now why you don't go to our church."

It was a remark so totally unexpected that Arthur stopped short and turned quite round.

"What do you mean, Aunt Winnifred?"

"I mean," said she, holding up the study as if to overwhelm him with resistless proof, "I mean, Arthur—and I could cry as I say it—that you are a Roman Catholic!"

Aunt Winnifred, who was an exemplary member of the Dutch Reformed Church, or, as Arthur gayly called her to her face, a Dutch Deformed Woman, was too simple and sincere in her religious faith to tolerate with equanimity the thought that any one of the name of Merlin should be domiciled in the House of Sin, as she poetically described the Church of Rome.

"Arthur! Arthur! and your father a clergyman. It's too dreadful!"

And the tender-hearted woman burst into tears.

But still weeping, she waved the picture in melancholy confirmation of her assertion. Arthur was amused and perplexed.

"My dear aunt, what has put such a droll idea into your head?"

"Because—because," said Aunt Winnifred, sobbing and wiping her eyes, "because this picture, which you keep locked up so carefully, is a picture of the Holy Virgin. Oh dear! just to think of it!"

There was a fresh burst of feeling from the honest and affectionate woman, who felt that to be a Roman Catholic was to be visibly sealed and stamped for eternal woe. But there was an answering burst of laughter from Arthur, who staggered to a sofa, and lay upon his back shouting until the tears also rolled from his eyes.

His aunt stopped, appalled, and made up her mind that he was not only a Catholic but a madman. Then, as Arthur grew more composed, he and his aunt looked at each other for some moments in silence.

"Aunt, you are right. It is the Holy Virgin!"

"Oh! Arthur," she groaned.

"It is my Madonna!"

"Poor boy!" sighed she.

"It is the face I worship."

"Arthur! Arthur!" and his aunt despairingly patted her knees slowly with her hands.

"But her name is not Mary."

Aunt Winnifred looked surprised.

"Her name is Diana."

"Diana?" echoed his aunt, as if she were losing her mind. "Oh! I beg your pardon. Then it's only a portrait after all? Yes, yes. Diana who?"

Arthur Merlin curled one foot under him as he sat, and, lighting a fresh cigar, told Aunt Winnifred the lovely legend of Latmos—talking of Diana and Endymion, and thinking of Hope Wayne and Arthur Merlin.

Aunt Winnifred listened with the utmost interest and patience. Her nephew was eloquent. Well, well, thought the old lady, if interest in his pursuit makes a great painter, my dear nephew will be a great man. During the course of the story Arthur paused several times, evidently lost in reverie—perhaps tracing the analogy. When he ended there was a moment's silence. Then Aunt Winnifred looked kindly at him, and said :

"Well?"

"Well," said Arthur, as he uncurled his leg, and with a half sigh, as if it were pleasanter to tell old legends of love than to paint modern portraits.

"Is that the whole?"

"That is the whole."

"Well; but Arthur, did she marry him after all?"

Arthur looked wistfully a moment at his aunt.

"Marry him! Bless you, no, Aunt Winnifred. She was a goddess. Goddesses don't marry."

Aunt Winnifred did not answer. Her eyes softened like eyes that see days and things far away—like eyes in which shines the love of a heart that, under those conditions, would rather not be a goddess.

CHAPTER LVI.

REDIVIVUS.

ELLEN BENNET, like May Newt, was a child no longer— hardly yet a woman, or only a very young one. Rosy cheeks, and clustering hair and blue eyes, showed only that it was May—June almost, perhaps—instead of gusty March or gleaming April.

"Ellen," said Gabriel, in a low voice—while his mother, who was busily sewing, conversed in a murmuring undertone with her husband, who sat upon the sofa, slowly swinging his slippered foot—"Ellen, Lawrence Newt didn't say that he should ask Edward to his dinner on my birthday."

Ellen's cheeks answered—not her lips, nor her eyes, which were bent upon a purse she was netting.

"But I think he will," added Gabriel. "I think I have mistaken Lawrence Newt if he does not."

"He is usually very thoughtful," whispered Ellen, as she netted busily.

"Ellen, how handsome Edward is!" said Gabriel, with enthusiasm.

The young woman said nothing.

"And how good!" added Gabriel.

"He is," she answered, scarcely audibly. Then she said she had left something up stairs. How many things are discovered by young women, under certain circumstances, to have been left up stairs! Ellen rose and left the room.

"I was saying to your father, Gabriel," said his mother, raising her voice, and still sewing, "that Edward comes here a great deal."

"Yes, mother; and I am glad of it. He has very few friends in the city."

"He looks like a Spaniard," said Mr. Bennet, slowly, dwelling upon every word. "How rich that lustrous tropical complexion is! Its duskiness is mysterious. The young man's eyes are like summer moonlight."

Mr. Bennet's own eyes half closed as he spoke, as if he were dreaming of gorgeous summer nights and the murmur of distant music.

Gabriel and his mother were instinctively silent. The click of her needle was the only sound.

"Oh yes, yes—that is—I mean, my dear, he does come here very often. I do go off on such foolish fancies!" remarked Mr. Bennet, at length.

"He comes very often when you are not at home, Gabriel," said Mrs. Bennet, after a kind glance at her husband, and still sewing.

"Yes, mother."

"Then it isn't only to see you?"

"No, mother."

"And often when your father and I return from an evening stroll in the streets we find him here."

"Yes, mother."

"It isn't to see us altogether, then?"

"No, mother."

Mrs. Bennet turned her work, and in so doing glanced for a moment at her son. His eyes were upon her face, but he seemed to have said all he had to say.

"I always feel," said Mr. Bennet, in a tone and with an expression as if he were looking at something very far away, "as if King Arthur must have lived in the tropics. There is that sort of weird, warm atmosphere in the romance. Where is Ellen? Shall we read some more in this little edition of the old story?"

He laid his hand, as he spoke, upon a small copy of old Malory's Romance of Arthur. It was a kind of reading of which he was especially fond, and to which the rest were always willing and glad to listen.

"Call Ellen," said he to Gabriel; "and now then for King Arthur!"

As he spoke the door-bell rang. The next moment a young man, apparently of Gabriel's age, entered the room. His large melancholy black eyes, the massive black curls upon his head, the transparent olive complexion, a natural elegance of form and of movement—all corresponded with what Mr. Bennet had been saying. It was evidently Edward.

"Good-evening, Little Malacca!" cried Gabriel, gayly, as he rose and put out his hand.

"Good-evening, Gabriel!" he answered, in a soft, ringing voice; then bowed and spoke to Mr. and Mrs. Bennet.

"Gabriel doesn't forget old school-days," said the new-comer to Mrs. Bennet.

"No, he has often told us of his friendship with Little Malacca," returned the lady calmly, as she resumed her work.

"And how little I thought I was to see him when I came to Mr. Newt's store," said the young man.

"Where did you first know Mr. Lawrence Newt?" asked Mrs. Bennet.

UNDER THE PORTRAIT.

"I don't remember when I didn't know him, Madam," replied Edward.

"Happy fellow!" said Gabriel.

Meanwhile Miss Ellen had probably found the mysterious something which she had left up stairs; for she entered the room, and bowed very calmly upon seeing Edward, and, seating herself upon the side of the table farthest from him, was presently industriously netting. As for Edward, he had

P

snapped a sentence in the middle as he rose and bowed to her, and could not possibly fit the two ends together when he sat down again, and so lost it.

Gradually, as the evening wore on, the conversation threatened to divide itself into *têtes-à-tête ;* for Gabriel suddenly discovered that he had an article upon Hemp to read in the Encyclopædia which he had recently purchased, and was already profoundly immersed in it, while Mr. and Mrs. Bennet resumed their murmuring talk, and the chair of the youth with the large black eyes, somehow — nobody saw how or when — slipped round until it was upon the same side of the table with that of Ellen, who was busily netting.

Mrs. Bennet was conscious that the chair had gone round, and the swimming eyes of her husband lingered with pleasure upon the mass of black curls bent toward the golden hair which was bowed over that intricate purse. Ellen was sitting under that portrait of the lady, with the flashing, passionate eyes, who seemed to bear a family likeness to Mrs. Bennet.

. The more closely he looked at the handsome youth and the lovely girl the more curious Mr. Bennet's eyes became. He watched the two with such intentness that his wife several times looked up at him surprised when she received no answer to her remarks. Evidently something had impressed Mr. Bennet exceedingly.

His wife bent her head a little nearer to his.

" My dear, did you never see a pair of lovers before ?"

He turned his dreaming eyes at that, smiled, and pressed his lips silently to the face which was so near his own that if it had been there for the express purpose of being caressed it could hardly have been nearer.

Then slipping his arm around her waist, Mr. Bennet drew his wife toward him and pointed with his head, but so imperceptibly that only she perceived it, toward the young people, as if he saw something more than a pair of lovers. The fond woman's eyes followed her husband's. Gradually they became as intently fixed as his. They seemed to be curiously comparing the face of the young man who sat at their daughter's side with the face of the portrait that hung above her head. Mrs. Bennet grew perceptibly paler as she looked. The unconscious Edward and Ellen murmured softly together. She did not look at him, but she felt the light of his great eyes falling upon her, and she was not unhappy.

"My dear," began Mr. Bennet in a low tone, still studying the face and the portrait.

"Hush!" said his wife, softly, laying her head upon his shoulder; "I see it all, I am sure of it."

Gabriel turned at this moment from his Encyclopedia. He looked intently for some time at the group by the table, as if studying all their thoughts, and then said, gravely, in a loud, clear voice, so that Ellen dropped a stitch, Edward stopped whispering, and Mr. and Mrs. Bennet sat erect,

"Exactly. I knew how it was. It says distinctly, 'This plant is supposed to be a native of India; but it has long been naturalized and extensively cultivated elsewhere, particularly in Russia, where it forms an article of primary importance.'"

CHAPTER LVII.

DINING WITH LAWRENCE NEWT.

GABRIEL BENNET was not confident that Edward Wynne would be at the birthday dinner given in his honor by Lawrence Newt, but he was very sure that May Newt would be there, and so she was. It was at Delmonico's; and a carriage arrived at the Bennets' just in time to convey them. Another came to Mr. Boniface Newt's, to whom brother Lawrence explained that he had invited his daughter to dinner, and that he should send a young friend—in fact, his confidential clerk, to accompany Miss Newt. Brother Boniface, who looked as. if he were the eternally relentless enemy of all young friends, had nevertheless the profoundest confidence in brother Law-

rence, and made no objection. So the hero of the day conducted Miss May Newt to the banquet.

The hero of the day was so engaged in conversation with
Miss May Newt that he said very little to his neighbor upon
the other side, who was no other than Hope Wayne. She
had been watching very curiously a young man with black
curls and eyes, who seemed to have words only for his neighbor, Miss Ellen Bennet. She presently turned and asked Gabriel if she had never seen him before. "I have, surely, some
glimmering remembrance of that face," she said, studying it
closely.

Her question recalled a day which was strangely remote
and unreal in Gabriel's memory. He even half blushed, as
if Miss Wayne had reminded him of some early treason to a
homage which he felt in the very bottom of his heart for his
blue-eyed neighbor. But the calm, unsuspicious sweetness of
Hope Wayne's face consoled him. He looked at her for a
moment without speaking. It was really but a moment, yet,
as he looked, he lay in a heavily-testered bed—he heard the
beating of the sea upon the shore—he saw the sage Mentor,
the ghostly Calypso putting aside the curtain—for a moment
he was once more the little school-boy, bruised and ill at Pinewood; but this face—no longer a girl's face—no longer anxious, but sweet, serene, and tender—was this the half-haughty
face he had seen and worshipped in the old village church—
the face whose eyes of sympathy, but not of love, had filled his
heart with such exquisite pain?

"That young man, Miss Wayne, is Edward Wynne," he
said, in reply to the question.

It did not seem to resolve her perplexity.

"I don't recall the name," she answered. "I think he must
remind me of some one I have known."

"He is as black as Abel Newt," said Gabriel, looking with
his clear eyes at Hope Wayne.

"But much handsomer than Mr. Newt now is," she answered, with perfect unconcern. "His eyes are softer; and,

in fact," she said, smiling pleasantly, " I am not surprised to
see what a willing listener his neighbor is. I wish I could recall him. I don't think that he resembles Mr. Newt at all, except in complexion."

Arthur Merlin heard every word, and watched every movement, and marked every expression of Hope Wayne's, at
whose other hand he sat, during this little remark. Gabriel
said, in reply to it,

" The truth is, Miss Wayne, you have seen him before. The
first time you ever saw me he was with me."

The clear eyes of the young man were turned full upon her
again.

"Oh yes, I remember now!" she answered. "He was your
friend in that terrible battle with Abel Newt. It seems long
ago, does it not?"

However far away it may have seemed, it was apparently a
remembrance that roused no especial emotion in Miss Hope
Wayne's heart. Having satisfied herself, she released the attention of Gabriel, who had other subjects of conversation
with May Newt than his quarrel with her brother for the favor of Hope Wayne.

But Arthur Merlin observed that while Hope Wayne listened with her ears to him, with her eyes she listened to Lawrence Newt. His simple, unselfish, and therefore unconscious
urbanity—his genial, kindly humor—and the soft, manly earnestness of his face, were not unheeded—how could they be?—
by her. Since the day the will was read he had been a faithful friend and counselor. It was he who negotiated for her
house. It was he who daily called and gave her a thousand
counsels in the details of management, of which every woman
who comes into a large property has such constant need. And
in all the minor arrangements of business she found in him the
same skill and knowledge, combined with a womanly reserve
and softness, which had first so strongly attracted her.

Yet his visits as financial counsel, as he called himself, did
not destroy, they only heightened, the pleasure of the meet-

ings of the Round Table. For the group of friends still met. They talked of poetry still. They talked of many things, and perhaps thought of but a few. The pleasure to all of them was evident enough; but it seemed more perplexed than formerly. Hope Wayne felt it. Amy Waring felt it. Arthur Merlin felt it. But not one of them could tell whether Lawrence Newt felt it. There was a vague consciousness of something which nearly concerned them all, but not one of them could say precisely what it was—except, possibly, Amy Waring; and except, certainly, Lawrence Newt.

For Aunt Martha's question had drawn from Amy's lips what had lain literally an unformed suspicion in her mind, until it leaped to life and rushed armed from her mouth. Amy Waring saw how beautiful Hope Wayne was. She knew how lovely in character she was. And she was herself beautiful and lovely; so she said in her mind at once, "Why have I never seen this? Why did I not know that he must of course love her?"

Then, if she reminded herself of the conversation she had held with Lawrence Newt about Arthur Merlin and Hope Wayne, she was only perplexed for a moment. She knew that he could not but be honest; and she said quietly in her soul, "He did not know at that time how well worthy his love she was."

CHAPTER LVIII.

THE HEALTH OF THE JUNIOR PARTNER.

"I CALL for a bumper!" said Lawrence Newt, when the fruit was placed upon the table.

The glasses were filled, and the host glanced around his table. He did not rise, but he said:

"Ladies and gentlemen, commercial honesty is not impossible, but it is rare. I do not say that merchants are worse

THE JUNIOR PARTNER.

than other people; I only say that their temptations are as
great, and that an honest man—a man perfectly honest every
how and every where—is a wonder. Whatever an honest
man does is a benefit to all the rest of us. If he become a
lawyer, justice is more secure; if a doctor, quackery is in danger; if a clergyman, the devil trembles; if a shoemaker, we
don't wear rotten leather; if a merchant, we get thirty-six

inches to the yard. I have been long in business. I have met
many honest merchants. But I know that 'tis hard for a merchant to be honest in New York. Will you show me the
place where 'tis easy? When we are all honest because honesty is the best policy, then we are all ruined, because that is
no honesty at all. Why should a man make a million of dollars and lose his manhood? He dies when he has won them,
and what are the chances that he can win his manhood again
in the next world as easily as he has won the dollars in this?
For he can't carry his dollars with him. Any firm, therefore,
that gets an honest man into it gets an accession of the most
available capital in the world. This little feast is to celebrate
the fact that my firm has been so enriched. I invite you to
drink the health of Gabriel Bennet, junior partner of the firm
of Lawrence Newt & Co.!"

There was a moment of perfect silence. Then every body
looked at Gabriel except his mother, whose eyes were so full
of tears that she could see nothing. Gabriel himself was entirely surprised. He had had no hint from Lawrence Newt of
this good fortune. He had worked faithfully, constantly, and
intelligently—honestly, of course—that was all Gabriel knew
about his position. He had been for some time confidential
clerk, so that he was fully cognizant of the state of the business, and knew how prosperous it was. And yet, in this moment of delight and astonishment, he had but one feeling,
which seemed entirely alien and inadequate to the occasion,
for it was merely the hope that now he might be a regular
visitor at the house of Boniface Newt.

Hope Wayne's eye had hung upon Lawrence Newt, during
the little speech he had made, so intently, that Arthur Merlin's
merriment had been entirely checked. He found himself curiously out of spirits. Until that moment, and especially after
the little conversation between Hope and Gabriel, in which
Abel Newt's name had been mentioned, Arthur had thought
it, upon the whole, the pleasantest little dinner he had ever
known. He was not of the same opinion now.

Edward Wynne and Ellen Bennet showed entire satisfaction with the dinner, and especially with Lawrence Newt's toast. And when the first hum of applause and pleasure had ceased, Edward cried out lustily,

"A speech from the junior partner! A speech! a speech!"

There was a general call. Gabriel could not help rising, and blushing, and bowing, and stuttering, and sitting down again, amidst tempestuous applause, without the slightest coherent idea of what he had said, except that he was very happy, and very glad, and very sure, and very, etc., etc.

But he did not care a song for what he had said, nor for the applause that greeted it, when he saw certain blue eyes glistening, and a soft shyness upon certain cheeks and lips, as if they had themselves been speaking, and had been saying— what was palpably, undeniably, conspicuously true—that they were very happy, and very glad, and very sure, and very, etc., etc. Very, indeed!

CHAPTER LIX.

MRS. ALFRED DINKS.

It was but a few days after the dinner that the junior partner was taking the old path that led under the tower of the fairy princess, when lo! he met her in the way. In her eyes there was that sweet light of expectation and happiness which illuminated all Gabriel's thoughts of her, and persuaded him that he was the happiest and unworthiest of men.

"Where are you going, May?"

"I am going to Fanny's."

"May I go too?"

May Newt looked at him and said, gravely, "No, I am going to ask Little Malacca to go with me."

"Oh, very well," replied Mr. Gabriel Bennet, with equal gravity.

"What splendid, melancholy eyes he has!" said May, with unusual ardor.

"Ah! you think so?"

"Of course I do, and such hair! Why, Mr. Bennet, did you ever see such magnificent hair—"

"Oh, you like black hair?"

"And his voice—"

"Now, May—"

"Well, Sir."

"Please—"

What merry light in the fairy eyes! What dazzling splendor of love and happiness in the face that turned to his as he laid her arm in his own! One would have thought she, too, had been admitted a junior partner in some most prosperous firm.

They passed along the street, which was full of people, and Gabriel and May unconsciously looked at the crowd with new eyes and thoughts. Can it be possible that all these people are so secretly happy as two that we know? thought they. "All my life," said Gabriel to himself, without knowing it, "have I been going up and down, and never imagined how much honey there was hived away in all the hearts of which I saw only the rough outside?" "All my life," mused May, with sweet girl-eyes, "have I passed lovers as if they were mere men and women?" And under her veil, where no eye could see, her cheek was flushed, and her eyes were sweeter.

They passed up Broadway and turned across to the Bowery. Crossing the broad pavement of the busy thoroughfare, they went into a narrow street beyond, and so toward the East River. At length they stopped before a low, modest house near a quiet corner. A sloppy kitchen-maid stood upon the area steps abreast of the street. A few miserable trees, pining to death in the stone desert of the town, were boxed up along the edge of the sidewalk. A scavenger's cart was joggling along, and a little behind, a ragman's wagon with a string of jangling bells. The smell of the sewer was the chief odor, and the long lines of low, red brick houses, with wooden steps and balustrades, and the blinds closed, completed a permanent camp of dreariness.

"Does Fanny Newt live there?" asked Gabriel, in a tone which indicated that there might be hearts in which honey was not abundantly hived.

"Yes," said May, gravely. "You know they have very little to live upon, and—and—oh dear, I don't like to speak of it, Gabriel, but they are very miserable."

Gabriel said nothing, but rang the bell.

The sloppy servant having stared wildly for a moment at the apparition of blooming love that had so incomprehensibly alighted upon the steps, ducked under them, and in a moment reappeared at the door. She seemed to recognize May, and said "Yes'm" before any question had been asked.

Gabriel and May walked into the little parlor. It was dark and formal. There was a black haircloth sofa with wooden edges all over it, so that nobody could lean or lounge, or do any thing but sit uncomfortably upright. There were black haircloth chairs, a table with two or three books; two lamps with glass drops upon the mantle; a thin cheap carpet; gloom, silence, and a complicated smell of grease—as if the ghosts of all the wretched dinners that had ever been cooked in the house haunted it spitefully.

While May went up stairs to find Fanny, Gabriel Bennet looked and smelled around him. He had not believed that a human home could be so dismal, and he could not understand how haircloth furniture and dimness could make it so. His father's house was certainly not very large; and it was scantily and plainly furnished, but no Arabian palace had ever seemed so splendid to his imagination as that home was dear to his heart. No, it isn't the furniture nor the smell, thought he. I am quite sure it is something that I neither see nor smell that makes the difference.

As he sat on the uncomfortable sofa and heard the jangling bells of the ragman die away into the distance, and the loud,

long, mournful whoop of the chimney-sweep, his fancy was
busy with the figures of a thousand things that might be—of
a certain nameless somebody, mistress of that poor, sombre
house, but so lighting it up with grace and gay sweetness
that the hard sofa became the most luxurious lounge, and the
cheap table more gorgeous than ormolu; and of a certain
other nameless somebody coming home at evening—an opening door—a rustle in the hall as of women's robes—a singular
sound as of meeting lips—then a coming together arm in arm
into the dingy furnished little parlor, but with such a bright
fire blazing under the wooden mantle—and then—and then—
a pattering of little feet down the stairs—Hem! hem! said
Gabriel Bennet, clearing his throat, as if to arouse himself by
making a noise. For there was a sound of feet upon the
stairs, and the next moment May and her sister Fanny entered the room. Gabriel rose and bowed, and held out his
hand. Mrs. Alfred Dinks said, "How do you do?" and seated herself without taking the hand.

Time had not softened her face, but sharpened it, and her
eyes were of a fierce blackness. She looked forty years old;
and there was a permanent frown of her dark brows.

"So this silly May is going to marry you?" said she, addressing Gabriel.

Surprised by this kind of congratulation, but also much
amused by it, as if there could be nothing so ludicrous as the
idea of May not marrying a man who loved her as he loved,
Gabriel gravely responded,

"Yes, ma'am, she is set upon it."

Fanny Newt, who had seated herself with an air of utter
and chronic contempt and indifference, and who looked away
from Gabriel the moment she had spoken to him, now turned
toward him again suddenly with an expression like that of an
animal which pricks up his ears. The keen fire of the old
days shot for a moment into her eyes, for it was the first word
of badinage or humor that Fanny Newt had heard for a long,
long time.

"A woman who is such a fool as to marry ought to be unhappy," she replied, with her eyes fixed upon Gabriel.

"A man who persuades her to do it ought to be taken out and hung," answered he, with aphoristic gravity.

Fanny was perplexed.

"Better to be the slave of a parent than a husband," she continued.

"I'd lock him out," retorted Gabriel, with pure irrelevancy; "I'd scotch his sheets; I'd pour water in his boots; I'd sift sand in his hair-brush; I'd spatter vitriol on his shirts. A man who marries a woman deserves nothing better."

He wagged his foot carelessly, took up one of the books upon the table, and looked into it indifferently. Fanny Newt turned to her sister, who sat smiling by her side.

"What is the matter with this man?" asked Mrs. Alfred Dinks, audibly, of May.

"There is a pregnant text, my dear Mrs. Dinks, née Newt, a name which I delight to pronounce," said Gabriel, striking in before May could reply, with the lightest tone and the soberest face in the world, "which instructs us to answer a fool according to his folly."

Fanny was really confounded. She had heard Abel in old days speak of Gabriel Bennet as a spooney—a saint in the milk—a goodsey, boodsey, booby—a sort of youth who would turn pale and be snuffed out by one of her glances. She found him incomprehensible. She owed him the first positive emotion of human interest she had known for years.

May Newt looked and listened without speaking. The soft light glimmered in her eyes, for she knew what it all meant. It meant precisely what her praises of Little Malacca meant. It meant that she and Gabriel loved each other.

The junior partner was still holding the book when a heavy step was heard in the entry. Fanny's eyes grew darker and the frown deeper. There was a blundering movement outside—a hat fell—a cane struck something—and Gabriel knew as perfectly as if he could look through the wall what kind of man was coming. The door opened with a burst, and Mr. Alfred Dinks stopped as his eye fell upon the company. A heavy, coarse, red-faced, dull-eyed man, with an air of brutish obstinacy in every lineament and movement, he stared for a moment without a word or sign of welcome, and then looking at his wife, said, in a grunting, surly tone,

"Look here; don't be fooling round. The old man's bust up!"

He banged the door violently to, and they heard his clumsy footsteps creaking up the stairs.

CHAPTER LX.

POLITICS.

"In course; I sez to ma—why, Lord bless me, it must have been three or four years ago—that 'twould all turn out so. What's rotten will come to pieces, ma, sez I. Every year she sez to me, sez she, why ain't the Newts failed yet? as you said they was going to. Jest you be quiet, sez I, ma, it's comin'. So 'twas. I know'd all about it."

President Van Boozenberg thus unburdened his mind and justified his vaticinations to the knot of gentlemen who were perpetually at the bank. They listened, and said ah! and yes, and shook their heads; and the shaky ones wondered whether the astute financier had marked them and had said to ma, sez he, that for all they looked so bright and crowded canvas so smartly, they are shaky, ma—shaky.

General Belch heard the news at his office. He was sitting on the end of his back-bone, which was supported on the two hind legs of a wooden chair, while the two fore legs and his own were lifted in the air. His own, however, went up at a more precipitate angle and rested with the feet apart upon the mantle. By a skillful muscular process the General ejected tobacco juice from his mouth, between his legs, and usually

PATRIOTISM.

lodged it in the grate before him. It was evident, however, that many of his friends had not been so successful, for the grate, the hearth, and the neighboring floor were spotted with the fluid.

The Honorable Mr. Ele was engaged in conversation with his friend Belch, who was giving him instructions for the next Congressional session.

" You see, Ele, if we could only send something of the right
stamp—the right stamp, I say, in the place of Watkins Bodley
from the third district, we should be all right. Bodley is very
uncertain."

" I know," returned the Honorable Mr. Ele, " Bodley is not
sound. He has not the true party feeling. He is not willing
to make sacrifices. And yet I think that—that—perhaps—"

He looked at General Belch inquiringly. That gentleman
turned, beamed approval, and squirted a copious cascade.

" Exactly," said Mr. Ele, " I was saying that I think if Mr.
Bodkins, who is a perfectly honorable man—"

" Oh, perfectly ; nothing against his character. Besides,
it's a free country, and every body may have his opinions,"
said General Belch.

" Precisely," resumed Mr. Ele, " as I was saying ; being a
perfectly honorable man—in fact, unusually honorable, I happen to know that he is in trouble—ahem! ahem! pecuniary
trouble."

He paused a moment, while his friend of the military title
looked hard at the grate, as if selecting a fair mark, then made
a clucking noise, and drenched it completely. He then said,
musingly,

" Yes, yes—ah yes—I see. It is a great pity. The best
men get into such trouble. How much money did you say he
wanted ?"

" I said he was in pecuniary trouble," returned Mr. Ele,
with a slight tone of correction.

" I understand, Mr. Ele," answered the other, a little pompously, and with an air of saying, " Know your place, Sir."

" I understand, and I wish to know how large a sum would
relieve Mr. Bodley from his immediate pressure."

" I think about eight or nine thousand dollars. Perhaps a
thousand more."

" I suppose," said General Belch, slowly, still looking into
the blank, dismal grate, and rubbing his fat nose steadily with
his fat forefinger and thumb, " I suppose that a man situated as

Mr. Bodley is finds it very detrimental to his business to be engaged in public life, and might possibly feel it to be his duty to his family and creditors to resign his place, if he saw a promising way of righting his business, without depending upon the chances of a Congressional career."

As he drew to the end of this hypothetical harangue General Belch looked sideways at his companion to see if he probably understood him.

The Honorable Mr. Ele shook his head in turn, looked solemnly into the empty grate, and said, slowly and with gravity:

"The supposition might be entertained for the sake of the argument."

The General was apparently satisfied with this reply, for he continued:

"Let us, then, suppose that a sum of eight or nine thousand dollars having been raised—and Mr. Bodley having resigned —that a new candidate is to be selected who shall—who shall, in fact, serve his country from our point of view, who ought the man to be?"

"Precisely; who ought the man to be?" replied Mr. Ele.

The two gentlemen looked gravely into the grate. General Belch squirted reflectively. The Honorable Mr. Ele raised his hand and shaded his eyes, and gazed steadfastly, as if he expected to see the candidate emerge from the chimney. While they still sat thoughtfully a knock was heard at the door. The General started and brought down his chair with a crash. Mr. Ele turned sharply round, as if the candidate had taken him by surprise in coming in by the door.

A boy handed General Belch a note:

"My dear Belch,—B. Newt, Son, & Co. have stopped. We do not hear of an assignment, so desire you to take steps at once to secure judgment upon the inclosed account.

"Yours,   Periwing & Buddby."

"Hallo!" said General Belch, as the messenger retired,

" old Newt's smashed!   However, it's a great while since he
has done any thing for the party.—By Jove!"

The last exclamation was sudden, as if he had been struck
by a happy thought.   He took a fresh quid in his mouth, and,
putting his hands upon his knees, sat silently for five minutes,
and then said,

" I have the man!"

" You have the man?" said Ele, looking at him with interest.

" Certainly.   Look here!"

Mr. Ele did look, as earnestly as if he expected the General
to take the man out of his pocket.

" You know we want to get the grant, at any rate.   If
we only have men who see from our point of view, we are
sure of it.   I think I know a man who can be persuaded to
look at the matter from that point—a man who may be of
very great service to the party, if we can persuade him to see
from our point of view."

" Who is that?" asked Mr. Ele.

" Abel Newt," replied General Belch.

Mr. Ele seemed somewhat surprised.

" Oh—yes—ah—indeed.   I did not know he was in political life," said he.

" He isn't," returned General Belch.

Mr. Ele looked for further instructions.

" Every body must begin," said Belch.   " Look here.   If
we don't get this grant from Congress, what on earth is the
use of having worked so long in this devilish old harness of
politics?   Haven't we been to primary meetings, and conven-
tions, and elections, and all the other tomfoolery, speechifying
and plotting and setting things right, and being bled, by Jupiter!—bled to the tune of more hundreds than I mean to
lose; and now, just as we are where a bold push will save every thing, and make it worth while to have worked in the
nasty mill so long, we must have our wits about us.   Do you
know Abel Newt?"

"No."

"I do. He is a gentleman without the slightest squeamishness. He is perfectly able to see things from particular points of view. He has great knowledge of the world, and he is a friend of the people, Sir. His politics are of the right kind," said General Belch, in a tone which seemed to be setting the tune for any future remarks Mr. Ele might have to make about Mr. Newt — at public meetings, for instance, or elsewhere.

"I am glad to hear he is a friend of the people," returned Mr. Ele.

"Yes, Sir, he is the consistent enemy of a purse-proud aristocracy, Sir."

"Exactly; purse-proud aristocracy," repeated Mr. Ele, as if conning a lesson by rote.

"Dandled in the lap of luxury, he does not hesitate to descend from it to espouse the immortal cause of popular rights."

"Popular rights," returned the Honorable Mr. Ele, studying his lesson.

"Animated by a glowing patriotism, he stands upon the people, and waves above his head the glorious flag of our country."

"Glorious flag of our country," responded the other.

"The undaunted enemy of monopoly, he is equally the foe of class legislation and the friend of State rights."

"Friend of State rights."

"Ahem!" said General Belch, looking blankly at Mr. Ele, "where was I?"

"Friend of State rights," parroted Mr. Ele.

"Exactly; oh yes! And if ever the glorious fabric of our country's—our country's—our country's—d— it! our country's what, Mr. Ele?"

That honorable gentleman was engaged with his own thoughts while he followed with his tongue the words of his friend, so that, perhaps a little maliciously, perhaps a little unconsciously, he went on in the same wooden tone of repetition.

"D— it! Our country's what, Mr. Ele?"

General Belch looked at his companion. They both smiled.

"How the old phrases sort o' slip out, don't they?" asked the General, squirting.

"They do," said Mr. Ele, taking snuff.

"Well, now, don't you see what kind of man Abel Newt is?"

"I do, indeed," replied Ele.

"I tell you, if you fellows from the city don't look out for yourselves, you'll find him riding upon your shoulders. He is a smart fellow. I am very sorry for Watkins Bodley. Any family?"

"Yes—a good deal," replied Mr. Ele, vaguely.

"Ah indeed! Pity! pity! I suppose, then, that a proper sense of what he owes to his family—eh?"

"Without question. Oh! certainly."

General Belch rose.

"I do not see, then, that we have any thing else that ought to detain you. I will see Mr. Newt, and let you know. Good-morning, Mr. Ele—good-morning, my dear Sir."

And the General bowed out the representative so imperatively that the Honorable B. Jawley Ele felt very much as if he had been kicked down stairs.

CHAPTER LXI.

GONE TO PROTEST.

THERE was an unnatural silence and order in the store of Boniface Newt, Son, & Co. The long linen covers were left upon the goods. The cases were closed. The boys sat listlessly and wonderingly about. The porter lay upon a bale reading a newspaper. There was a sombre regularity and repose, like that of a house in which a corpse lies, upon the morning of the funeral.

Boniface Newt sat in his office haggard and gray. His face, like his daughter Fanny's, had grown sharp, and almost fierce. The blinds were closed, and the room was darkened. His port-folio lay before him upon the desk, open. The paper was smooth and white, and the newly-mended pens lay carefully by the inkstand. But the merchant did not write. He had not written that day. His white, bony hand rested upon the port-folio, and the long fingers drummed upon it at intervals, while his eyes half-vacantly wandered out into the store and saw the long shrouds drawn over the goods. Occasionally a slight sigh of weariness escaped him. But he did not seem to care to distract his mind from its gloomy intentness; for the morning paper lay beside him unopened, although it was afternoon.

In the outer office the book-keeper was still at work. He looked from book to book, holding the leaves and letting them fall carefully—comparing, computing, writing in the huge volumes, and filing various papers away. Sometimes, while he yet held the leaves in his hands and the pen in his mouth, with the appearance of the utmost abstraction in his task, his eyes wandered in to the inner office, and dimly saw his employer sitting silent and listless at his desk. For many years he had been Boniface Newt's clerk; for many years he had been a still, faithful, hard-worked servant. He had two holidays, besides the Sundays—New Year's Day and the Fourth of July. The rest of the year he was in the office by nine in the morning, and did not leave before six at night. During the time he had been quietly writing in those great red books he had married a wife and seen the roses fade in her cheeks—he had had children grow up around him—fill his evening home and his Sunday hours with light—marry, one after another, until his home had become as it was before a child was born to him, and then gradually grow bright and musical again with the eyes and voices of another generation. Glad to earn his little salary, which was only enough for decency of living, free from envy and ambition, he was bound by a kind of feudal tenure to his employer.

As he looked at the merchant and observed his hopeless listlessness, he thought of his age, his family, and of the frightful secrets hidden in the huge books that were every night locked carefully into the iron safe, as if they were written all over with beautiful romances instead of terrible truths—and the eyes of the patient plodder were so blurred that he could not see, and turning his head that no one might observe him, he winked until he could see again.

A young man entered the store hastily. The porter dropped the paper and sprang up; the boys came expectantly forward. Even the book-keeper stopped to watch the new-comer as he came rapidly toward the office. Only the head of the house sat unconcernedly at his desk—his long, pale, bony fingers drumming on the port-folio—his hard eyes looking out at the messenger.

"This way," said the book-keeper, suddenly, as he saw that he was going toward Mr. Newt's room.

"I want Mr. Newt."

"Which one?"

"The young one, Mr. Abel Newt."

"He is not here."

"Where is he?"

"I don't know."

Before the book-keeper was aware the young man had opened the door that communicated with Mr. Newt's room. The haggard face under the gray hair turned slowly toward the messenger. There was something in the sitting figure that made the youth lift his hand and remove his cap, and say, in a low, respectful voice,

"Can you tell me, Sir, where to find Mr. Abel Newt?"

The long, pale, bony fingers still listlessly drummed. The hard eyes rested upon the questioner for a few moments; then, without any evidence of interest, the old man answered simply, "No," and looked away as if he had forgotten the stranger's presence.

"Here's a note for him from General Belch."

The gray head beckoned mechanically toward the other room, as if all business were to be transacted there; and the young man bowing again, with a vague sense of awe, went in to the outer office and handed the note to the book-keeper.

It was very short and simple, as Abel found when he read it:

"My dear Sir,—I have just heard of your misfortunes. Don't be dismayed. In the shindy of life every body must have his head broken two or three times, and in our country 'tis a man's duty to fall on his feet. Such men as Abel Newt are not made to fail. I want to see you immediately.

"Yours very truly,

"Arcularius Belch."

CHAPTER LXII.

THE CRASH, UP TOWN.

The moment Mrs. Dagon heard the dismal news of Boniface Newt's failure she came running round to see his wife. The house was as solemnly still as the store and office down town. Mrs. Dagon looked in at the parlor, which was darkened by closed blinds and shades drawn over the windows, and in which all the furniture was set as for a funeral, except that the chilly chintz covers were not removed.

She found Mrs. Nancy Newt in her chamber with May.

"Well, well! What does this mean? It's all nothing. Don't you be alarmed. What's failing? It doesn't mean any thing; and I really hope, now that he has actually failed and done with it, Boniface will be a little more cheerful and liberal. Those parlor curtains are positively too bad! Boniface ought to have plenty of time to himself; and I hope he will give more of those little dinners, and cheer himself up! How is he?"

Mrs. Newt was dissolved in tears. She shook her head weakly, and rubbed her hands.

"Oh! Aunt Dagon, it's dreadful to see him. He don't seem himself. He does nothing but sit at the table and drum with his fingers; and in the night he lies awake, thinking. And, oh dear!" she said, giving way to a sudden burst of grief, "he doesn't scold at any thing."

Mrs. Dagon listened and reflected.

"My dear," she asked, "has he settled any thing upon you?"

"Nothing," replied Mrs. Newt.

"Aunt Dagon," said May, who sat by, looking at the old lady, "we are now poor people. We shall sell this house, and go and live in a small way out of sight."

"Fiddle, diddle! my dear," returned Mrs. Dagon, warmly; "you'll do no such thing. Poor people, indeed! Why, May, you know nothing about these things. Failing, failing; why, my dear, that's nothing. A New York merchant expects to fail, just as an English lord expects to have the gout. It isn't exactly a pleasant thing, but it's extremely respectable. Every body fails. It's understood."

"What's understood?" asked May.

"Why, that business is a kind of game, and that every body runs for luck. Oh, I know all about it, my dear! It's all a string of cards—as Colonel Burr used to say; and I think if any body knew the world he did—it's all a string of blocks. B trusts A, C trusts B, D trusts C, and so on. A tumbles over, and down go B, and C, and D. That's the whole of it, my dear. Colonel Burr used to say that his rule was to keep himself just out of reach of any other block. If they knock me over, my dear Miss Bunley, he once said to me—ah! May, what a voice he said it in, what an eye!—if they knock me over, I shall be so busy picking myself up that I shall be forced to be selfish, and can't help them, so I had better keep away, and then I can be of some service. That was Colonel Burr's principle. He declared it was the only way in which you could be sure of helping others. People talk about Colonel Burr. My dear, Colonel Burr was a man who minded his own business."

May Newt held her tongue. She felt instinctively that a woman of sixty-five, who had been trained by Colonel Burr, was not very likely to accept the opinions of a girl of her years. Mrs. Newt was feebly rocking herself during the conversation between her daughter and aunt; and when they had finished said, despairingly,

"Dear me! what will people say? Oh! I can't go and live poor. I'm not used to it. I don't know how."

"Live poor!" sniffed Mrs. Dagon; "of course you won't live poor. I've heard Boniface say often enough that it was too bad, but it was a world of good-for-nothing people; and you don't think he's going to let good-for-nothing people drive him from a becoming style of living? Fiddle! I'd like to see him undertake to live poor."

"Do you think people will come to see us?" gasped Mrs. Newt.

"Come? Of course they will. They'll all rush, the first thing, to see how you take it. Why, such a thing as this is a godsend to 'em. They'll have something to talk about for a week. And they'll all try to discover if you mean to sell out at auction. Oh, they will be *so* sorry!" said the old lady, imitating imaginary callers; "'and, my dear Mrs. Newt, what *are* you going to do? And to think of your being obliged to leave this lovely house!' Come?—did you ever know the vultures not to come to a carcass?"

Mrs. Nancy Newt looked appalled; and so energetic was Mrs. Dagon in her allusion to vultures and carcass, that her niece unconsciously put to her nose the smelling-bottle she held in her hand.

"Oh, it's dreadful!" she sighed, rocking and smelling, and with the tears oozing from her eyes.

"Fiddle! I won't hear of it. 'Tain't dreadful. It's no-

Q

thing at all. You must go out with me and make calls this
very morning. It's none of your business. If your husband
chooses to fail, let him fail. He can't expect you to take to
making shirts, and to give up society. I shall call at twelve
in the carriage; and, mind, don't you look red and mopy.
Remember. So, good-morning! And, May, I want to speak
to you."

They left Mrs. Newt rocking and weeping, with the smelling-bottle at her nose, and descended to the solemn parlor.

"What brought this about?" asked Mrs. Dagon, as she
closed the door. "Your mother is in such a state that it
does no good to talk to her. Where's Abel?"

"Aunt Dagon, I have my own opinion, but I know nothing.
I suppose Abel is down town."

"What's your opinion?"

May paused for a moment, and then said:

"From what I have heard drop from father during the last
few years since Abel has been in the business, I don't believe
that Abel has helped him—"

"Exactly," interrupted Mrs. Dagon, as if soliloquizing; "and
why on earth didn't the fellow marry Hope Wayne, or that
Southern girl, Grace Plumer?"

"Abel marry Hope Wayne?" asked May, with an air and
tone of such utter amazement and incredulity that Aunt Dagon
immediately recovered from her abstraction, and half smiled.

"Why, why not?" said she, with equal simplicity.

May Newt knew Hope Wayne personally, and she had also
heard of her from Gabriel Bennet. Indeed, Gabriel had no secrets from May. The whole school story of his love had been
told to her, and she shared the young man's feeling for the
woman who, as a girl, had so utterly enthralled his imagination. But Gabriel's story of school life also included her brother Abel, and what she heard of the boy agreed with what she
knew and felt of the man.

"I presume," said May Newt, loftily, "that Hope Wayne
would be as likely to marry Aaron Burr as Abel Newt."

Mrs. Dagon looked at her kindly, and with amused admiration.

"Well, May, at any rate I congratulate Gabriel Bennet."

May's lofty look drooped.

"And if"—continued Mrs. Dagon—"if it was so wonderfully impossible that Abel should marry Hope Wayne, why might he not have married Grace Plumer, or some other rich girl? I'm sure I don't care who. It was evidently the only thing for *him*, whatever it may be for other people. When you are of my age, May, you will rate things differently. Well-bred men and women in society ought to be able to marry any body. Society isn't heaven, and it's silly to behave as if it were. Your romance is very pretty, dear; we all have it when we are young, as we have the measles and the whooping-cough. But we get robust constitutions, my dear," said the old lady, smiling kindly, "when we have been through all that business. When you and Gabriel have half a dozen children, and your girls grow up to be married, you'll understand all about it. I suppose you know about Mellish Whitloe and Laura Magot, don't you, dear?"

May shook her head negatively.

"Well, they are people who were wise early. Just after they were married he said to her, 'Laura, I see that you are fond of this new dance which is coming in; you like to waltz.' 'Yes, I do,' said she. 'Well, I don't like it, and I don't want you to waltz.' She pouted and cried, and called him a tyrant. He hummed Yankee Doodle. 'I *will* waltz,' said she at length. 'Very well, my dear,' he answered. 'I'll make a bargain with you. If you waltz, I'll get drunk.' You see it works perfectly. They respect each other, and each does as the other wishes. I hope you'll be as wise with Gabriel, my dear."

"Aunt, I hope I shall never be as old as you are," said May, quietly. "I'd rather die."

Mrs. Dagon laughed her laugh. "That's right, dear, stand by your colors. You're all safe. Gabriel is Lawrence's partner. You can afford to be romantic, dear."

As she spoke the door opened, and Abel entered. His dress was disordered, his face was flushed, and his manner excited. He ran up to May and kissed her. She recoiled from the unaccustomed caress, and both she and Mrs. Dagon perceived in his appearance and manner, as well as in the odor which presently filled the room, that Abel was intoxicated.

"May, darling," he began in a maudlin tone, "how's our dear mother?"

"She's pretty well," replied May, "but you had better not go up and see her."

"No, darling, I won't go if you say not."

His eyes then fell uncertainly upon Mrs. Dagon, and he added, thickly,

"That's only Aunt Dagon. How do, Aunt Dagon?"

He smiled at her and at May, and continued,

"I don't mind Aunt Dagon. Do you mind her, May?"

"What do you want, Abel?" asked May, with the old expression sliding into her eyes that used to be there when she sat alone—a fairy princess in her tower, and thought of many things.

Abel had seated himself upon the sofa, with his hat still on his head. There was perhaps something in May's tone that alarmed him, for he began to shed tears.

"Oh! May, don't you love your poor Abel?"

She looked at him without speaking. At length she said, "Where have you been?"

"I've been to General Belch's," he sobbed, in reply; "and I don't mind Aunt Dagon, if you don't."

"What do you mean by that, you silly fool?" asked Mrs. Dagon, sharply.

Abel stopped and looked half angry, for a moment, but immediately fell into the old strain.

"I mean I'd just as lieve say it before her."

"Then say it," said May.

"Well, May, darling, couldn't you now just coax Gabriel— good fellow, Gabriel—used to know him and love him at

"REP—REP—SENTIVE OFS—OFS—DEAR PE—PE."

school—couldn't you coax him to get Uncle Lawrence to do
something?"

May shook her head. Abel began to snivel.

"I don't mean for the house. D—n it, that's gone to smash.
I mean for myself, May, for your poor brother Abel. You
might just try."

He lay back and looked at her ruefully.

"Aunt Dagon," she said, quietly, "we had better go out of the room. Abel, don't you come up stairs while you are in this state. I know all that Uncle Lawrence has done for father and you, and he will do nothing more. Do you expect him to pay your gambling debts?" she asked, indignantly.

Abel raised himself fiercely, while the bad blackness filled his eyes.

"D—d old hunks!" he shouted.

But nobody heard. Mrs. Dagon and May Newt had closed the door, and Abel was left alone.

"It's no use," he said, moodily and aloud, but still thickly. "I can't help it. I shall have to do just as Belch wishes. But he must help me. If he expects me to serve him, he must serve me. He says he can—buy off—Bodley—and then—why, then—devil take it!" he said, vacantly, with heavy eyes, "then —then—oh yes!" He smiled a maudlin smile. "Oh yes! I shall be a great—a great—great—man—I'll be—rep—rep— sentive—ofs—ofs—dear pe—pe."

His head fell like a lump upon the cushion of the sofa, and he breathed heavily, until the solemn, dark, formal parlor smelled like a bar-room.

CHAPTER LXIII.

ENDYMION.

LAWRENCE NEWT had told Aunt Martha that he preferred to hear from a young woman's own lips that she loved him. Was he suspicious of the truth of Aunt Martha's assertion?

When the Burt will was read, and Fanny Dinks had hissed her envy and chagrin, she had done more than she would willingly have done: she had said that all the world knew he was in love with Hope Wayne. If all the world knew it, then surely Amy Waring did; "and if she did, was it so strange," he thought, "that she should have said what she did to me?"

He thought often of these things. But one of the days when he sat in his office, and the junior partner was engaged in writing the letters which formerly Lawrence wrote, the question slid into his mind as brightly, but as softly and benignantly, as daylight into the sky.

"Does it follow that she does not love me? If she did love me, but thought that I loved Hope Wayne, would she not hide it from me in every way—not only to save her own pride, but in order not to give me pain?"

So secret and reticent was he, that as he thought this he was nervously anxious lest the junior partner should happen to look up and read it all in his eyes.

Lawrence Newt rose and stood at the window, with his back to Gabriel, for his thoughts grew many and strange.

As he came down that morning he had stopped at Hope Wayne's, and they had talked for a long time. Gabriel had told his partner of his visit to Mrs. Fanny Dinks, and Lawrence had mentioned it to Hope Wayne. The young woman listened intently.

"You don't think I ought to increase the allowance?" she asked.

"Why should you?" he replied. "Alfred's father still allows him the six hundred, and Alfred has promised solemnly that he will never mention to his wife the thousand you allow him. I don't think he will, because he is afraid she would stop it in some way. As it is, she knows nothing more than that six hundred dollars seems to go a very great way. Your income is large; but I think a thousand dollars for the support of two utterly useless people is quite as much as you are called upon to pay, although one of them is your cousin, and the other my niece."

They went on to talk of many things. In all she showed the same calm candor and tenderness. In all he showed the same humorous quaintness and good sense. Lawrence Newt observed that these interviews were becoming longer and longer, although the affairs to arrange really became fewer. He could not discover that there was any particular reason for it; and yet he became uncomfortable in the degree that he was conscious of it.

When the Round Table met, it was evident from the conversation between Hope Wayne and Lawrence Newt that he was very often at her house; and sometimes, whenever they all appeared to be conscious that each one was thinking of that fact, the cloud of constraint settled more heavily, but just as impalpably as before, over the little circle. It was not removed by the conviction which Amy Waring and Arthur Merlin entertained, that at all such times Hope Wayne was trying not to show that she was peculiarly excited by this consciousness.

And she was excited by it. She knew that the interviews were longer and longer, and that there was less reason than ever for any interviews whatsoever. But when Lawrence Newt was talking to her—when he was looking at her—when he was moving about the room—she was happier than she had ever been—happier than she had supposed she could ever be. When he went, that day was done. Nor did another dawn until he came again.

Perhaps Hope Wayne understood the meaning of that mysterious constraint which now so often enveloped the Round Table.

As for Arthur Merlin, the poor fellow did what all poor fellows do. So long as it was uncertain whether she loved him or not, he was willing to say nothing. But when he was perfectly sure that there was no hope for him, he resolved to speak.

In vain his Aunt Winnifred had tried to cheer him. Ever since the morning when he had told her in his studio the lovely legend of Latmos he could not persuade himself that he had not unwittingly told his own story. Aunt Winnifred showered the choicest tracts about his room. She said with a sigh that she was sure he had experienced no change of heart; and Arthur replied, with a melancholy smile, "Not the slightest."

The kind old lady was sorely puzzled. It did not occur to her that her Arthur could be the victim of an unfortunate attachment, like the love-lorn heroes of whom she had read in the evil days when she read novels. It did not occur to her, because she could as easily have supposed a rose-tree to resist June as any woman her splendid Arthur.

If some gossip to whom she sighed and shook her head, and wondered what could possibly ail Arthur—who still ate his dinner heartily, and had as many orders for portraits as he cared to fulfill—suggested that there was a woman in the case, good Aunt Winnifred smiled bland incredulity.

"Dear Mrs. Toxer, I should like to see that woman!"

Then she plied her knitting-needles nimbly, sighed, scratched her head with a needle, counted her stitches, and said,

"Sometimes I can't but hope that it is concern of mind, without his knowing it."

Mrs. Toxer also knitted, and scratched, and counted.

"No, ma'am; much more likely concern of heart with a full consciousness of it. One, two, three—bless my soul! I'm always dropping a stitch."

Aunt Winnifred, who never dropped stitches, smiled pleasantly, and answered,

"Yes, indeed, and this time you have dropped a very great one."

Meanwhile Arthur's great picture advanced rapidly. Diana, who had looked only like a portrait of Hope Wayne looking out of a cloud, was now more fully completed. She was still bending from the clouds indeed, but there was more and more human softness in the face every time he touched it. And lo! he had found at last Endymion. He lay upon a grassy knoll. Long whispering tufts sighed around his head, which rested upon the very summit of the mountain. There were no trees, no rocks. There was nothing but the sleeping figure with the shepherd's crook by his side upon the mountain top, all lying bare to the sky and to the eyes that looked from the cloud, and from which all the moonlight of the picture fell.

When Lawrence Newt came into the studio one morning, Arthur, who worked in secret upon his picture and never showed it, asked him if he would like to look at it. The merchant said yes, and seated himself comfortably in a large chair, while the artist brought the canvas from an inner room and placed it before him. As he did so, Arthur stepped a little aside, and watched him closely.

Lawrence Newt gazed for a long time and silently at the picture. As he did so, his face rapidly donned its armor of inscrutability, and Arthur's eyes attacked it in vain. Diana was clearly Hope Wayne. That he had seen from the beginning. But Endymion was as clearly Lawrence Newt! He looked steadily without turning his eyes, and after many minutes he said, quietly,

"It is beautiful. It is triumphant. Endymion is a trifle too old, perhaps. But Diana's face is so noble, and her glance so tenderly earnest, that it would surely rouse him if he were not dead."

"Dead!" returned Arthur; "why you know he is only sleeping."

"No, no," said Lawrence, gently, "dead; utterly dead—to her. If he were not, it would be simply impossible not to awake and love her. Who's that old gentleman on the wall over there?"

Lawrence Newt asked the same question of all the portraits so persistently that Arthur could not return to his Diana. When he had satisfied his curiosity—a curiosity which he had never shown before—the merchant rose and said good-by.

"Stop, stop!"

Lawrence Newt turned, with his hand upon the door.

"You like my picture—"

"Immensely. But if she looks forever she'll never waken nim. Poor Endymion! he's dead to all that heavenly splendor."

He was about closing the door.

"Hallo!" cried Arthur.

Lawrence Newt put his head into the room.

"It's fortunate that he's dead!" said the painter.

"Why so?"

"Because goddesses never marry."

Lawrence Newt's head disappeared.

CHAPTER LXIV.

DIANA.

"GOOD-MORNING, Miss Hope."

"Good-morning, Mr. Merlin."

He bowed and seated himself, and the conversation seemed to have terminated. Hope Wayne was embroidering. The moment she perceived that there was silence she found it very hard to break it.

"Are you busy now?" said she.

"Very busy."

"As long as men and women are vain, so long your profession will flourish, I suppose," she replied, lifting her eyes and smiling.

"I like it because it tells the truth," replied Arthur, crushing his hat.

"It omitted Alexander's wry neck," said Hope.

"It put in Cromwell's pimple," answered Arthur.

They both smiled.

"However, that is not the kind of truth I mean—I mean poetic truth. Michael Angelo's Last Judgment shows the whole Catholic Church."

Hope Wayne felt relieved, and looked interested. She did not feel so much afraid of the silence, now that Arthur seemed entering upon a disquisition. But he stopped and said,

"I've painted a picture."

"Full of poetic truth, I suppose," rejoined Hope, still smiling.

"I've come to ask you to go and see that for yourself."

"Now?"

"Now."

She laid aside her embroidery, and in a little while they had reached his studio. As Hope Wayne entered she was impressed by the spaciousness of the room, the chastened light, and the coruscations of rich color hanging upon the walls.

"It's like the garden of the Hesperides," she said, gayly— "such mellow shadows, and such gorgeous colors, like those of celestial fruits. I don't wonder you paint poetic truth."

Arthur Merlin smiled.

"Now you shall judge," said he.

Hope Wayne seated herself in the chair where Lawrence Newt had been sitting not two hours before, and settled herself to enjoy the spectacle she anticipated; for she had a secret faith in Arthur's genius, and she meant to purchase this great work of poetic truth at her own valuation. Arthur placed the picture upon the easel and drew the curtain from it, stepping aside as before to watch her face.

The airy smile upon Hope Wayne's face faded instantly. The blood rushed to her hair. But she did not turn her eyes, nor say a word. The moment she felt she could trust her voice, she asked, gravely, without looking at Arthur,

"What is it?"

"It is Diana and Endymion," replied the painter.

She looked at it for a long time, half-closing her eyes, which clung to the face of Endymion.

"I have not made Diana tender enough," thought Arthur, mournfully, as he watched her.

"How soundly he sleeps!" said Hope Wayne, at length, as if she had been really trying to wake him.

"You think he merely sleeps?" asked Arthur.

"Certainly; why not?"

"Oh! I thought so too. But Lawrence Newt, who sat two hours ago just where you are sitting, said, as he looked at the picture, that Endymion was dead."

Hope Wayne put her finger to her lip, and looked inquiringly at her companion.

"Dead! Did he say dead?" she asked.

"Dead," repeated Arthur Merlin.

"I thought Endymion only slept," continued Hope Wayne; "but Mr. Newt is a judge of pictures—he knows."

"He certainly spoke as if he knew," persisted the painter, recklessly, as he saw and felt the usual calmness return to his companion. "He said that if Endymion were not dead he couldn't resist such splendor of beauty."

As Arthur Merlin spoke he looked directly into Hope Wayne's face, as if he were speaking of her.

"Mr. Newt's judgment seems to be better than his memory," said she, pleasantly.

"How?"

"He forgets that Endymion *did* awake. He has not allowed time enough for the effect of Diana's eyes. Now I am sure," she said, shaking her finger at the picture, "I am sure that that silly shepherd will not sleep there forever. Never fear, he will wake up. Diana never looks or loves for nothing."

"It will do no good if he does," insisted Arthur, ruefully, as if he were sure that Hope Wayne understood that he was speaking in parables.

"Why?" she asked, as she rose, still looking at the picture.

"Because goddesses never marry."

He looked into her eyes with so much meaning, and the "do they?" which he did not utter, was so perfectly expressed by his tone, that Hope Wayne, as she moved slowly toward the door, looking at the pictures on the wall as she passed, said, with her eyes upon the pictures, and not upon the painter,

"Do you know the moral of that remark of yours?"

"Moral? Heaven forbid! I don't make moral remarks," replied Arthur.

"This time you have done it," she said, smiling; "you have

made a remark with a moral. I'm going, and I leave it with you as a legacy. The moral is, If goddesses never marry, don't fall in love with a goddess."

She put out her hand to him as she spoke. He involuntarily took it, and they shook hands warmly.

"Good-morning, Mr. Merlin," she said. "Remember the Round Table to-morrow evening."

She was gone, and Arthur Merlin sank into the chair she had just left.

"Oh Heavens!" said he, "did she understand or not?"

CHAPTER LXV.

THE WILL OF THE PEOPLE.

GENERAL BELCH's office was in the lower part of Nassau Street. At the outer door there was a modest slip of a tin sign, "Arcularius Belch, Attorney and Counselor." The room itself was dingy and forlorn. There was no carpet on the floor; the windows were very dirty, and slats were broken out of the blinds—the chairs did not match—there was a wooden book-case, with a few fat law-books lounging upon the shelves; the table was a chaos of pamphlets, printed forms, newspapers, and files of letters, with a huge inkstand, inky pens, and a great wooden sand-box. Upon each side of the chimney, the grate in which was piled with crushed pieces of waste paper, and the bars of which were discolored with tobacco juice, stood two large spittoons, the only unsoiled articles in the office.

This was the place in which General Belch did business. It had the atmosphere of Law. But, above all, it was the spot where, with one leg swinging over the edge of the table and one hand waving in earnest gesticulation, General Belch could say to every body who came, and especially to his poorer fellow-citizens, "I ask no office; I am content with my moderate practice. It is enough for me, in this glorious country, to be a friend of the people."

As he said this—or only implied it in saying something else —the broken slats, the dirty windows, the uncarpeted floor, the universal untidiness, whispered in the mind of the hearer, " Amen !"

His residence, however, somewhat atoned for the discomfort of his office. Not unfrequently he entertained his friends sumptuously ; and whenever any of the representatives of his party, who acted in Congress as his private agents, had succeeded—as on one occasion, already commemorated, the Hon Mr. Ele had—in putting a finer edge upon a favorite axe, General Belch entertained a select circle who agreed with him in his political philosophy, and were particular friends of the people and of the popular institutions of their country.

Abel Newt, in response to the General's note, had already called at that gentleman's office, and had received overtures from him, who offered him Mr. Bodley's seat in Congress, upon condition that he was able to see things from particular points of view.

" Mr. Watkins Bodley, it seems," said General Belch, " and I regret to say it, is in straitened pecuniary circumstances. I understand he will feel that he owes it to his family to resign before the next session. There will be a vacancy ; and I am glad to say that the party is just now in a happy state of harmony, and that my influence will secure your nomination. But come up to-night and talk it over. I have asked Ele and Slugby, and a few others—friends of course—and I hope Mr. Bat will drop in. You know Aquila Bat ?"

" By reputation," replied Abel.

" He is a very quiet man, but very shrewd. He gives great dignity and weight to the party. A tremendous lawyer Bat is. I suppose he is at the very head of the profession in this country. You'll come ?"

Abel was most happy to accept. He was happy to go any where for distraction. For the rooms in Grand Street had become inconceivably gloomy. There were no more little parties there: the last one was given in honor of Mrs. Sligo Moultrie—before her marriage. The elegant youth of the town gradually fell off from frequenting Abel's rooms, for he always proposed cards, and the stakes were enormous; which was a depressing circumstance to young gentlemen who mainly depended upon the paternal purse. Such young gentlemen as Zephyr Wetherley, who was for a long time devoted to young Mrs. Mellish Whitloe, and sent her the loveliest fans, and buttons, and little trinkets, which he selected at Marquand's. But when the year came round the bill was inclosed to Mr. Wetherley, senior, who, after a short and warm interview with his son Zephyr, inclosed it in turn to Whitloe himself; who smiled, and paid it, and advised his wife to buy her own jewelry in future.

It was not pleasant for young Wetherley, and his friends in a similar situation, to sit down to a night at cards with such a desperate player as Abel Newt. Besides, his rooms had lost that air of voluptuous elegance which was formerly so unique. The furniture was worn out, and not replaced. The decanters and bottles were no longer kept in a pretty side-board, but stood boldly out, ready for instant service; and whenever one of the old set of men happened in, he was very likely to find a gentleman — whose toilet was suspiciously fine, whose gold looked like gilt—who made himself entirely at home with Abel and his rooms, and whose conversation indicated that his familiar haunts were race-courses, bar-rooms, and gambling-houses.

It was unanimously decreed that Abel Newt had lost tone. His dress was gradually becoming flashy. Younger sisters, who had heard their elders—who were married now—speak of the fascinating Mr. Newt, perceived that the fascinating Mr. Newt was a little too familiar when he flirted, and that his breath was offensive with spirituous fumes. He was noisy in the gentlemen's dressing-room. The stories he told there were of such a character, and he told them so loudly, that

more than once some husband, whose wife was in the neighboring room, had remonstrated with him. Sligo Moultrie,
during one of the winters that he passed in the city after his
marriage, had a fierce quarrel with Abel for that very reason.
They would have come to blows but that their friends parted
them. Mr. Moultrie sent a friend with a note the following
morning, and Mr. Newt acknowledged that he had been rude.

In the evening, at General Belch's, Abel was presented to
all the guests. Mr. Ele was happy to remember a previous occasion upon which he had had the honor, etc. Mr. Enos Slugby
(Chairman of our Ward Committee, whispered Belch, audibly,
as he introduced him) was very glad to know a gentleman
who bore so distinguished a name. Every body had a little
compliment, to which Abel bowed and smiled politely, while
he observed that the residence was much more comfortable
than the office of General Belch.

They went into the dining-room and sat down to what Mr.
Slugby called "a Champagne supper." They ate birds and
oysters, and drank wine. Then they ate jellies, blanc mange,
and ice-cream. Then they ate nuts and fruit, and drank coffee.
Then every thing was removed, and fresh decanters, fresh
glasses, and a box of cigars were placed upon the table, and
the servants were told that they need not come until summoned.

At this point a dry, grave, thin, little old man opened the
door. General Belch rose and rushed forward.

"My dear Mr. Bat, I am very happy. Sit here, Sir. Gentlemen, you all know Mr. Bat."

The company was silent for a moment, and bowed. Abel
looked up and saw a man who seemed to be made of parch
ment, and his complexion, of the hue of dried apples, suggested that he was usually kept in a warm green satchel.

After a little more murmuring of talk around the table,
General Belch said, in a louder voice,

"Gentlemen, we have a new friend among us, and a little
business to settle to-night. Suppose we talk it over."

There was a general filling of glasses and a hum of assent.

"I learn," said the General, whiffing the smoke from his mouth, "that our worthy friend and able representative, Watkins Bodley, is about resigning, in consequence of private embarrassments. Of course he must have a successor."

Every body poured out smoke and looked at the speaker, except Mr. Bat, who seemed to be undergoing a little more drying up, and looked at a picture of General Jackson, which hung upon the wall.

"That successor, I need not say, of course," continued General Belch, "must be a good man and a faithful adherent of the party. He must be the consistent enemy of a purse-proud aristocracy."

"He must, indeed," said Mr. Enos Slugby, whisking a little of the ash from his cigar off an embroidered shirt-bosom, in doing which the flash from a diamond ring upon his finger dazzled Abel, who had turned as he spoke.

"He must espouse the immortal cause of popular rights, and be willing to spend and be spent for the people."

"That's it," said Mr. William Condor, whose sinecure under government was not worth less than twenty thousand a year.

"He must always uphold the honor of the glorious flag of our country."

"Excuse me, General Belch, but I can not control my feelings; I must propose three cheers," interrupted Alderman Mac-Dennis O'Rourke; and the three cheers were heartily given.

"And this candidate must be equally the foe of class legislation and the friend of State rights."

Here Mr. Bat moved his head, as if he were assenting to a remark of his friend General Jackson.

"And I surely need not add that it would be the first and most sacred point of honor with this candidate to serve his party in every thing, to be the unswerving advocate of all its measures, and implicitly obedient to all its behests," said General Belch.

"Which behests are to be learned by him from the author-ized leaders of the party," said Mr. Enos Slugby.

"Certainly," said half of the gentlemen.

"Of course," said the other half.

During the remarks that General Belch had been making his eyes were fixed upon Abel Newt, who understood that this was a political examination, in which the questions asked in-cluded the answers that were to be given. When the Gener-al had ended, the company sat intently smoking for some time, and filling and emptying their glasses.

"Mr. Bat," said General Belch, "what is your view?"

Mr. Bat removed his eyes from General Jackson's portrait, and cleared his throat.

"I think," he said, closing his eyes, and rubbing his fingers along his eyebrows, "that the party holding to the only con-stitutional policy is to be supported at all hazards, and I think the great party to which we belong is that party. Our principles are all true, and our measures are all just. Specu-lative persons and dreamers talk about independent political action. But politics always beget parties. Governments are always managed by parties, and parties are always managed by—"

The dried-apple complexion at this point assumed an ashy hue, as if something very indiscreet had been almost uttered. Mr. Bat's eyes opened and saw Abel's fixed upon him with a peculiar intelligence. The whole party looked a little alarmed at Mr. Bat, and apprehensively at the new-comer. Mr. Ele frowned at General Belch,

"What does he mean?"

But Abel relieved the embarrassment by quietly completing Mr. Bat's sentence—

—"by the managers."

His black eyes glittered around the table, and Mr. Ele re-membered a remark of General Belch's about Mr. Newt's rid-ing upon the shoulders of his fellow-laborers.

"Exactly, by the managers," said every body.

"And now," said General Belch, cheerfully, "whom had we better propose to our fellow-citizens as a proper candidate for their suffrages to succeed the Honorable Mr. Bodley?"

He leaned back and puffed. Mr. Ele, who had had a little previous conversation with the host, here rose and said, that, if he might venture, he would say, although it was an entirely unpremeditated thing, which had, in fact, only struck him while he had been sitting at that hospitable board, but had impressed him so forcibly that he could not resist speaking— if he might venture, he would say that he knew a most able and highly accomplished gentleman—in fact, it had occurred to him that there was then present a gentleman who would be precisely the man whom they might present to the people as a candidate suitable in every way.

General Belch looked at Abel, and said, "Mr. Ele, whom do you mean?"

"I refer to Mr. Abel Newt," responded the Honorable Mr. Ele.

The company looked as companies which have been prepared for a surprise always look when the surprise comes.

"Is Mr. Newt sound in the faith?" asked Mr. William Condor, smiling.

"I answer for him," replied Mr. Ele.

"For instance, Mr. Newt," said Mr. Enos Slugby, who was interested in General Belch's little plans, "you have no doubt that Congress ought to pass the grant to purchase the land for Fort Arnold, which has been offered to it by the company of which our friend General Belch is counsel?"

"None at all," replied Abel. "I should work for it as hard as I could."

This was not unnatural, because General Belch had promised him an interest in the sale.

"Really, then," said Mr. William Condor, who was also a proprietor, "I do not see that a better candidate could possibly be offered to our fellow-citizens. The General Committee meet to-morrow night. They will call the primaries, and the

Convention will meet next week. I think we all understand each other. We know the best men in our districts to go to the Convention. The thing seems to me to be very plain."

"Very," said the others, smoking.

"Shall it be Abel Newt?" said Mr. Condor.

"Ay!" answered the chorus.

"I propose the health of the Honorable Abel Newt, whom I cordially welcome as a colleague," said Mr. Ele.

Bumpers were drained. It was past midnight, and the gentlemen rose. They came to Abel and shook his hand; then they swarmed into the hall and put on their hats and coats.

"Stay, Newt," whispered Belch, and Abel lingered.

The Honorable B. J. Ele also lingered, as if he would like to be the last out of the house; for although this distinguished statesman did not care to do otherwise than as General Belch commanded, he was anxious to be the General's chief butler, while the remark about riding on his companions' shoulders and the personal impression Abel had made upon him, had seriously alarmed him.

While he was busily looking at the portrait of General Jackson, General Belch stepped up to him and put out his hand.

"Good-night, my dear Ele! Thank you! thank you! These things will not be forgotten. Good-night! good-night!" And he backed the Honorable B. Jawley Ele out of the room into the hall.

"This is your coat, I think," said he, taking up a garment and helping Mr. Ele to get it on. "Ah, you luxurious dog! you're a pretty friend of the people, with such a splendid coat as this. Good-night! good-night!" he added, helping his guest toward the door.

"Hallo, Condor!" he shouted up the street. "Here's Ele —don't leave him behind; wait for him!"

He put him out of the door. "There, my dear fellow, Condor's waiting for you! Good-night! Ten thousand thanks! A pretty friend of the people, hey? Oh, you cunning dog! Good-night!"

General Belch closed the door and returned to the drawing-room. Abel Newt was sitting with one leg over the back of the chair, and a tumbler of brandy before him, smoking.

"God!" said Abel, laughing, as the General returned, "I wouldn't treat a dog as you do that man."

"My dear Mr. Representative," returned Belch, "you, as a legislator and public man, ought to know that Order is Heaven's first law."

CHAPTER LXVI.

MENTOR AND TELEMACHUS.

DRAWING his chair near to Abel's, General Belch lighted a cigar, and said:

"You see it's not so very hard."

Abel looked inquiringly.

"To go to Congress," answered Belch.

"Yes, but I'm not elected yet, thank you."

General Arcularius Belch blew a long, slow cloud, and gazed at his companion with a kind of fond superiority.

"What do you mean by looking so?" asked Abel.

"My dear Newt, I was not aware that you had such a soft spot. No, positively, I did not know that you had so much to learn. It is inconceivable."

The General smiled, and smoked, and looked blandly at his companion.

"You're not elected yet, hey?" asked the General, with an amused laugh.

"Not that I am aware of," said Abel.

"Why, my dear fellow, who on earth do you suppose does the electing?"

"I thought the people were the source of power," replied Abel, gravely.

The General looked for a moment doubtfully at his companion.

"Hallo! I see you're gumming. However, there's one thing. You know you'll have to speak after the election. Did you ever speak?"

"Not since school," replied Abel.

"Well, you know the cue. I gave it to you to-night. The next thing is, how strong can you come down?"

"You know I've failed."

"Of course you have. That's the reason the boys will expect you to be very liberal."

"How much?" inquired Abel.

"Let me see. There'll be the printing, halls, lights, ballots, advertisements— Well, I should say a thousand dollars, and a thousand more for extras. Say two thousand for the election, and a thousand for the committee."

"Devil! that's rather strong!" replied Abel.

"Not at all," said General Belch. "Your going to Washington secures the grant, and the grant nets you at least three thousand dollars upon every share. It's a good thing, and very liberal at that price. By-the-by, don't forget that you're a party man of another sort. You do the dancing business, and flirting—"

"Pish!" cried Abel; "milk for babes!"

"Exactly. And you're going to a place that swarms with babes. So give 'em milk. Work the men through their wives, and mistresses, and daughters. It isn't much understood yet; but it is a great idea."

"Why don't you go to Congress?" asked Abel, suddenly.

"It isn't for my interest," answered the General. "I make more by staying out."

"How many members are there for Belch?" continued Abel.

The General did not quite like the question, nor the tone in which it was asked. His fat nose glistened for a moment, while his mouth twisted into a smile, and he answered,

"They're only for Belch as far as Belch is for them—"

"Or as far as Belch makes them think he is," answered Abel, smiling.

The General smiled too, for he found the game going against him.

"We were speaking of your speech," said he. "Now, Newt, the thing's in your own hands. You've a future before you. With the drill of the party, and with your talents, you ought to do any thing."

"Too many rivals," said Abel, curtly.

"My dear fellow, what are the odds? They can't do any thing outside the party, or without the drill. Make it their interest not to be ambitious, and they're quiet enough. Here's William Condor—lovely, lovely William. He loves the people so dearly that he does nothing for them at twenty thousand dollars a year. Tell him that you will secure him his place, and he's your humble servant. Of course he is. Now I am more familiar with the details of these things, and I'm always at your service. Before you go, there will be a caucus of the friends of the grant, which you must attend, and make a speech."

"Another speech?" said Abel.

"My dear fellow, you are now a speech-maker by profession. Now that you are in Congress, you will never be free from the oratorical liability. Wherever two or three are gathered together, and you are one of them, you'll have to return thanks, and wave the glorious flag of our country. And you'll have to begin very soon."

CHAPTER LXVII.

WIRES.

GENERAL BELCH was right. Abel had to begin very soon. The committee met and called the meetings. The members of the committee, each in his own district, consulted with various people, whom they found generally at corner groceries. They were large, coarse-featured, hulking men, and were all named Jim, or Tom, or Ned.

JIM AND MR. SLUGBY.

" What'll you have, Jim ?"

" Well, Sir, it's so early in the day, that I can't go any thing stronger than brandy."

" Two cocktails—stiff," was the word of the gentleman to the bar-keeper.

The companions took their glasses, and sat down behind a heavy screen.

"Well, Sir, what's the word? I see there's going to be more meetin's."

"Yes, Jim. Bodley has resigned."

"Who's the man, Mr. Slugby?" asked Jim, as if to bring matters to a point.

"Mr. Abel Newt has been mentioned," replied the gentleman with the diamond ring, which he had slipped into his waistcoat pocket before the interview.

Jim cocked his eye at his glass, which was nearly empty.

"Here! another cocktail," cried Mr. Slugby to the bar-tender.

"Son of old Newt that bust t'other day?"

"The same."

"Well, I s'pose it's all right," said Jim, as he began his second tumbler.

"Oh yes; he's all right. He understands things, and he's coming down rather strong. By-the-by, I've never paid you that ten dollars."

And Mr. Slugby pulled out a bill of that amount and handed it to Jim, who received it as if he were pleased, but did not precisely recall any such amount as owing to him.

"I suppose the boys will be thirsty," said Mr. Enos Slugby.

"There never's nothin' to make a man thirsty ekal to a 'lection," answered Jim, with his huge features grinning.

"Well, the fellows work well, and deserve it. Here, you needn't go out of your district, you know, and this will be enough." He handed more money to his companion. "Have 'em up in time, and don't let them get high until after the election of delegates. It was thought that perhaps Mr. Musher and I had better go to the Convention. It's just possible, Jim, that some of Bodley's friends may make trouble."

"No fear, Mr. Slugby, we'll take care of that. Who do you want for chairman of the meeting?" answered Jim.

"Edward Gasserly is the best chairman. He understands things."

"Very well, Sir, all right," said Jim.

"Remember, Jim, Wednesday night, seven o'clock. You'll

want thirty men to make every thing short and sure. Gasserly, chairman; Musher and Slugby, delegates. And you needn't
say any thing about Abel Newt, because that will all be settled in the Convention; and the delegates of the people will
express their will there as they choose. I'll write the names
of the delegates on this."

Mr. Slugby tore off a piece of paper from a letter in his
pocket, and wrote the names. He handed the list, and, taking
out his watch, said,

"Bless my soul, I'm engaged at eleven, and 'tis quarter past.
Good-by, Jim, and if any thing goes wrong let me know."

"Sartin, Sir," replied Jim, and Mr. Slugby departed.

Mr. William Condor had a similar interview with Tom, and
Mr. Ele took a friendly glass with Ned. And other Mr.
Slugbys, and Condors, and Eles, had little interviews with
other red-faced, trip-hammer-fisted Jims, Toms, and Neds.
These healths being duly drunk, the placards were posted.
They were headed with the inspiring words "Liberty and
Equality," with cuts of symbolic temples and ships and lifted
arms with hammers, and summoned the legal voters to assem-
ble in primary meetings and elect delegates to a convention
to nominate a representative. The Hon. Mr. Bodley's letter
of resignation was subjoined:

"FELLOW-CITIZENS,—Deeply grateful for the honorable
trust you have so long confided to me, nothing but the imperative duty of attending to my private affairs, seriously injured
by my public occupations, would induce me to resign it into
your hands. But while his country may demand much of
every patriot, there is a point, which every honest man feels,
at which he may retire. I should be deeply grieved to take
this step did I not know how many abler representatives you
can find in the ranks of that constituency of which any man
may be proud. I leave the halls of legislation at a moment
when our party is consolidated, when its promise for the future was never more brilliant, and when peace and prosperity

seem to have taken up their permanent abode in our happy
country, whose triumphant experiment of popular institutions
makes every despot shake upon his throne. Gentlemen, in
bidding you farewell I can only say that, should the torch of
the political incendiary ever be applied to the sublime fabric
of our system, and those institutions which were laid in our
father's struggles and cemented with their blood, should tot-
ter and crumble, I, for one, will be found going down with the
ship, and waving the glorious flag of our country above the
smouldering ruins of that moral night.

"I am, fellow-citizens, your obliged, faithful, and humble
servant,   WATKINS BODLEY."

In pursuance of the call the meetings were held. Jim, Tom,
and Ned were early on the ground in their respective districts,
with about thirty chosen friends. In Jim's district Mr. Gasserly was elected chairman, and Messrs. Musher and Slugby
delegates to the Convention. Mr. Slugby, who was present
when the result was announced, said that it was extremely in-
convenient for him to go, but that he held it to be the duty
of every man to march at the call of the party. His private
affairs would undoubtedly suffer, but he held that every man's
private interest must give way to the good of his party. He
could say the same thing for his friend, Mr. Musher, who was
not present. But he should say to Musher—Musher, the people want us to go, and go we must. With the most respectful
gratitude he accepted the appointment for himself and Musher.

This brisk little off-hand speech was received with great favor. Immediately upon its conclusion Jim moved an adjournment, which was unanimously carried, and Jim led the way to
a neighboring corner, where he expended a reasonable propor-
tion of the money which Slugby had given him.

A few evenings afterward the Convention met. Mr. Slugby
was appointed President, and Mr. William Condor Secretary.
The Honorable B. J. Ele presented a series of resolutions,
which were eloquently advocated by General Arcularius Belch.

At the conclusion of his speech the Honorable A. Bat made a speech, which the daily *Flag of the Country* the next morning called "a dry disquisition about things in general," but which the *Evening Banner of the Union* declared to be "one of his most statesmanlike efforts."

After these speeches the Convention proceeded to the ballot, when it was found that nine-tenths of all the votes cast were for Abel Newt, Esquire.

General Belch rose, and in an enthusiastic manner moved that the nomination be declared unanimous. It was carried with acclamation. Mr. Musher proposed an adjournment, to meet at the polls. The vote was unanimous. Mr. Enos Slugby rose, and called for three cheers for "the Honorable Abel Newt, our next talented and able representative in Congress." The Convention rose and roared.

"Members of the Convention who wish to call upon the candidate will fall into line!" shouted Mr. Condor; then leading the way, and followed by the members, he went down stairs into the street. A band of music was at hand, by some thoughtful care, and, following the beat of drums and clangor of brass, the Convention marched toward Grand Street.

CHAPTER LXVIII.

THE INDUSTRIOUS APPRENTICE.

GOOD news fly fast. On the wings of the newspapers the nomination of Abel Newt reached Delafield, where Mr. Savory Gray still moulded the youthful mind. He and his boys sat at dinner.

"Fish! fish! I like fish," said Mr. Gray. "Don't you like fish, Farthingale?"

Farthingale was a new boy, who blushed, and said, promptly,

"Oh! yes, Sir."

"Don't you like fish, Mark Blanding? Your brother Gyles used to," asked Mr. Gray.

"Yes, Sir," replied that youth, slowly, and with a certain expression in his eye, "I suppose I do."

"All boys who are in favor of having fish dinner on Fridays will hold up their right hands," said Mr. Gray. He looked eagerly round the table. "Come, come! up, up, up!" said he, good-naturedly.

"That's it. Mrs. Gray, fish on Fridays."

"Mr. Gray," said Mark Blanding.

"Well, Mark?"

"Ain't fish cheaper than meat?"

"Mark, I am ashamed of you. Go to bed this instant."

Mark was unjust, for Uncle Savory had no thought of indulging his purse, but only his palate.

When the criminal was gone Mr. Gray drew a paper from his pocket, and said,

"Boys, attend! In this paper, which is a New York paper, there is an account of the nomination of a member of Congress — a member of Congress, boys," he repeated, slowly, dwelling upon the words to impress their due importance. "What do you think his name is? Who do you suppose it is who is nominated for Congress?"

He waited a moment, but the boys, not having the least idea, were silent.

"Well, it is Abel Newt, who used to sit at this very table. Abel Newt, one of Mr. Gray's boys."

He waited another moment, to allow the overwhelming announcement to have its due effect, while the scholars all looked at him, holding their knives and forks.

"And there is not one of you, who, if he be a good boy, may not arrive at the same eminence. Think, boys, any one of you, if you are good, may one day get nominated to Congress, as the Honorable Mr. Newt is, who was once a scholar here, just like you. Hurrah for Mr. Gray's boys! Now eat your dinners."

CHAPTER LXIX.

IN AND OUT.

"AND Boniface Newt has failed," said Mr. Bennet to his wife, in a low voice.

He was shading his eyes with his hand, and his wife was peacefully sewing beside him.

She made no reply, but her face became serious, then changed to an expression in which, from under his hands, for her husband's eyes were not weak, her husband saw the faintest glimmering of triumph. But Mrs. Bennet did not raise her eyes from her work.

"Lucia!" He spoke so earnestly that his wife involuntarily started.

"My dear," she replied, looking at him with a tear in her eye, "it is only natural."

Her husband said nothing, but shook his slippered foot, and his neck sunk a little lower in his limp, white cravat. They were alone in the little parlor, with only the portrait on the wall for company, and only the roses in the glass upon the table, that were never wanting, and always showed a certain elegance of taste in arrangement and care which made the daughter of the house seem to be present though she might be away.

"What a beautiful night!" said Mr. Bennet at last, as his eyes lingered upon the window through which he saw the soft illumination of the full moonlight.

His wife looked for a moment with him, and answered, "Beautiful!"

"How lovely those roses are, and how sweet they smell!" he said, after another interval of silence, and as if there were a change in the pleasant dreams he was dreaming.

"Yes," she replied, and looked at him and smiled, and, smiling, sewed on.

"Where is Ellen to-night?" he asked, after a little pause.

"She is walking in this beautiful moonlight."

"All alone?" he inquired, with a smile.

"No! with Edward."

"Ah! with Edward." And there was evidently another turn in the pleasant dream.

"And Gabriel—where is Gabriel?" asked he, still shaking the slippered foot.

His wife smoothed her work, and said, with an air of tranquil happiness,

"I suppose he is walking too."

"All alone?"

"No, with May."

Involuntarily, as she said it, she laid her work in her lap, as if her mind would follow undisturbed the happy figures of her children. She looked abstractedly at the window, as if she saw them both, the manly candor of her Gabriel, and the calm sweetness of May Newt—the loyal heart of her blue-eyed Ellen clinging to Edward Wynne. Down the windings of her reverie they went, roses in their cheeks and faith in their hearts. Down and down, farther and farther, closer and closer, while the springing step grew staid, and the rose bloom slowly faded. Farther and farther down her dream, and gray glistened in the brown hair and the black and gold, but the roses bloomed around them in younger cheeks, and the brown hair and the black and gold were as glossy and abundant upon those younger heads, and still their arms were twined and their eyes were linked, as if their hearts had grown together, each pair into one. Farther and farther—still with clustering younger faces—still with ever softer light in the air falling upon the older forms, grown reverend, until—until—had they faded in that light, or was she only blinded by her tears?

For there were tears in her eyes—eyes that glistened with happiness—and there was a hand in hers, and as she looked at her husband she knew that their hands had clasped each other because they saw the same sweet vision.

He looked at his wife, and said,

"Could I have been the rich man I one day hoped to be—the great merchant I longed to be, when I asked you to marry me—I could have owned nothing—no diamond—so dear to me as that very tear in your eye. I wanted to be rich—I felt as if I had cheated you, in being so poor and unsuccessful—you, who were bred so differently. For your sake I wanted to be rich." He spoke with a stronger, fuller voice. "Yes, and when Laura Magot broke my engagement with her because of my first failure, I resolved that she should see me one of the merchant princes she idolized, and that my wife should be envied by her as being the wife of a richer man than Boniface Newt. Darling, you know how I struggled for it—you did not know the secret spur—and how I failed. And I know who it was that made my failure my success, and who taught a man who wanted to be rich how to be happy."

While he spoke his wife's arm had stolen tenderly around him. As he finished, she said, gently,

"I am not such a saint, Gerald."

"If you are not, I don't believe in saints," replied her husband.

"No, I will prove it to you."

"I defy you," said Gerald, smiling.

"Listen! Why did you say Lucia in such a tone, a little while ago?" asked his wife.

Gerald Bennet smiled with arch kindness.

"Shall I answer truly?"

"Under pain of displeasure."

"Well," he began, slowly, "when I heard that Laura Magot's husband had failed, as I knew that Lucia Darro's husband had once been jilted by Laura Magot because he failed, I could not help wondering—now, Lucia dear, how could I help wondering?—I wondered how Lucia Darro would feel. Because—because—"

He made a full stop, and smiled.

"Because what?" asked his wife.

R 2

He lingered, and smiled.

"Because what?" persisted his wife, with mock gravity.

"Because Lucia Darro was a woman, and— well! I'll make a clean breast of it—and because, although a man and woman love each other as long and dearly as Lucia Darro and her husband have and do, there is still something in the woman that the man can not quite understand, and upon which he is forever experimenting. So I was curious to hear, or rather to see and feel, what your thoughts were; and, at the moment I spoke, I thought I saw them, and I was surprised."

"Exactly, Sir; and that surprise ought to have shown you that I was no saint. Listen again, Sir. Lucia Darro's husband was never jilted by Laura Magot, for the impetuous and ambitious young man who was engaged to that lady is an entirely different person from my husband. Do you hear, Sir?"

"Precisely; and who made him so entirely different?"

"Hush, Sir! I've no time to hear such folly. I, too, am going to make a clean breast of it, and confess that there was the least little sense of—of—of—well, justice, in my mind, when I thought that Laura Magot who jilted you, who were so unfortunate, and with whom she might have been so happy—"

Gerald Bennet dissented, with smiles and shaking head.

"Hush, Sir! Any woman might have been. That she should have led such a life with Boniface Newt, and have seen him ruined after all. Poor soul! poor soul!"

"Which?" asked her husband.

"Both—both, Sir. I pity them both from my heart."

"Thou womanest of women!" retorted her husband. "Art thou, therefore, no saint because thou pitiest them?"

"No, no; but because it was not an unmixed pity."

"At any rate, it is an unmixed goodness," said her husband.

The restless glance, the glimmering uncertainty, had faded from his eyes. He sat quietly on the sofa, swinging his foot, and with his head bent a little to one side over the limp cravat.

"Gerald," said his wife, "let us go out, and walk in the moonlight too."

CHAPTER LXX.

THE REPRESENTATIVE OF THE PEOPLE.

IN a few moments they were sauntering along the street. It was full and murmurous. The lights were bright in the shop windows, and the scuffling of footsteps, more audible than during the day, when it is drowned by the roar of carriage-wheels upon the pavement, had a friendly, social sound.

"Broadway is never so pleasant as in the early evening," said Mr. Bennet; "for then the rush of the day is over, and people move with a leisurely air, as if they were enjoying themselves. What is that?"

They were going down the street, and saw lights, and heard music and a crowd approaching. They came nearer; and Mr. Bennet and his wife turned aside, and stood upon the steps of a dwelling-house. A band of music came first, playing "Hail Columbia!" It was surrounded by a swarm of men and boys, in the street and on the sidewalk, who shouted, and sang, and ran; and it was followed by a file of gentlemen, marching in pairs. Several of them carried torches, and occasionally, as they passed under a house, they all looked up at the windows and gave three cheers. Sometimes, also, an individual in the throng shouted something which was received with loud hi-hi's and laughter.

"What is it?" asked Mrs. Bennet.

"This is a political procession, my dear. Look! they will not come by us at all; they are turning into Grand Street, close by. I suppose they are going to call upon some candidate. I never see any crowd of this kind without thinking how simple and beautiful our institutions are. Do you ever think of it, Lucia? What a majestic thing the popular will is!"

"Let's hurry, and we may see something," said his wife.

The throng had left Broadway, and had stopped in Grand

Street under a balcony in a handsome house. The music had stopped also, and all faces were turned toward the balcony. Mr. Bennet and his wife stood at the corner of Broadway. Suddenly a gentleman took off his hat and waved it violently in the air, and a superb diamond-ring flashed in the torch-light as he did so, while he shouted,

"Three cheers for Newt!"

There was a burst of huzzas from the crowd—the drums rolled—the boys shrieked and snarled in the tone of various animals—the torches waved—one excited man cried, "One more!"—there was another stentorian yell, and roll, and wave —after which the band played a short air. But the windows did not open.

"Newt! Newt! Newt!" shouted the crowd. The young gentleman with the diamond-ring disappeared into the house. with several others.

"Why, Slugby, where the devil is he?" said one of them to another, in a whisper, as they ran up the stairs.

"I'm sure I don't know. Musher promised to have him ready."

"And I sent Ele up to get here before we did," replied his friend, in the same hurried whisper, his fat nose glistening in the hall-light.

When they reached Mr. Newt's room they found him lying upon a sofa, while Musher and the Honorable B. J. Ele were trying to get him up.

"D—n it! stand up, can't you?" cried Mr. Ele.

"No, I can't," replied Abel, with a half-humorous maudlin smile.

At the same moment the impetuous roar of the crowd in the street stole in through the closed windows.

"Newt! Newt! Newt!"

"What in —— shall we do?" gasped Mr. Enos Slugby, walking rapidly up and down the room.

"Who let him get drunk?" demanded General Belch, angrily.

Nobody answered.

"Newt! Newt! Newt!" surged in from the street.

"Thunder and devils, there's nothing for it but to prop him up on the balcony!" said General Belch. "Come now, heave to, every body, and stick him on his pins."

Abel looked sleepily round, with his eyes half closed and his under lip hanging.

"'Tain't no use," said he, thickly; "'tain't no use."

And he leered and laughed.

The perspiring and indignant politicians grasped him—Slugby and William Condor under the arms, Belch on one side, and Ele ready to help any where. They raised their friend to his feet, while his head rolled slowly round from one side to the other, with a maudlin grin.

"'Tain't no use," he said.

Indeed, when they had him fairly on his feet nothing further seemed to be possible. They were all holding him and looking very angry, while they heard the loud and imperative—"Newt! Newt! Newt!" accompanied with unequivocal signs of impatience in an occasional stone or chip that rattled against the blinds.

In the midst of it all the form of the drunken man slipped back upon the sofa, and sitting there leaning on his hands, which rested on his knees, and with his head heavily hanging forward, he lifted his forehead, and, seeing the utterly discomfited group standing perplexed before him, he said, with a foolish smile,

"Let's all sit down."

There was a moment of hopeless and helpless inaction. Then suddenly General Belch laid his hands upon the sofa on which Abel was lying, and moved it toward the window.

"Now," cried he to the others, "open the blinds, and we'll make an end of it."

Enos Slugby raised the window and obeyed. The crowd below, seeing the opening blinds and the lights, shouted lustily.

"Now then," cried the General, "boost him up a moment and hold him forward. Heave ho! all together."

They raised the inert body, and half-lifted, half-slid it forward upon the narrow balcony.

"Here, Slugby, you prop him behind; and you, Ele and Condor, one on each side. There! that's it! Now we have him. I'll speak to the people."

So saying, the General removed his hat and bowed very low to the crowd in the street. There was a great shout, "Three cheers for Newt!" and the three cheers rang loudly out.

"'Tain't Newt," cried a sharp voice; "it's Belch."

"Three cheers for Belch!" roared an enthusiastic somebody.

"D— Belch," cried the sharp voice.

"Hi! hi!" roared the chorus; while the torches waved and the drums rolled once more.

During all this time General Arcularius Belch had been bowing profoundly and grimacing in dumb show to the crowd, pointing at Abel Newt, who stood, ingeniously supported, his real state greatly concealed by the friendly night.

"Gentlemen!" cried Belch, in a piercing voice.

"H'st! h'st! Down, down! Silence," in the crowd.

"Gentlemen, I am very sorry to have to inform you that our distinguished fellow-citizen, Mr. Newt, to compliment whom you have assembled this evening, is so severely unwell (oh! gum! from the sharp-voiced skeptic below) that he is entirely unable to address you. But so profoundly touched is he by your kindness in coming to compliment him by this call, that he could not refuse to appear, though but for a moment, to look the thanks he can not speak. At the earliest possible moment he promises himself the pleasure of addressing you. Let me, in conclusion, propose three cheers for our representative in the next Congress, the Honorable Abel Newt. And now—" he whispered to his friends as the shouts began, "now lug him in again."

The crowd cheered, the Honorable Mr. Newt was lugged in, the windows were closed, and General Belch and his friends withdrew.

"I tell you what it is," said he, as they passed up the street at a convenient distance behind the crowd, "Abel Newt is a man of very great talent, but he must take care. By Jove! he must. He must understand times and seasons. One thing can not be too often repeated," said he, earnestly, "if a man expects to succeed in political life he must understand when not to be drunk."

The merry company laughed, and went home with Mr. William Condor to crack a bottle of Champagne.

Mr. and Mrs. Bennet had stood at the street corner during the few minutes occupied by these events. When they heard the shouts for Newt they had looked inquiringly at each other. But when the scene was closed, and the cheers for the Honorable Abel Newt, our representative in Congress, had died away, they stood for a few moments quite stupefied.

"What does it mean, Gerald?" asked his wife. "Is Abel Newt in Congress?"

"I didn't know it. I suppose he is only a candidate."

He moved rapidly away, and his wife, who was not used to speed in his walking, smiled quietly, and, could he have seen her eye, a little mischievously. She said presently,

"Yes, our institutions are very simple and beautiful."

Mr. Bennet said nothing. But she relentlessly continued,

"What a majestic thing the election of Abel Newt by the popular will will be!"

"My dear," he answered, "don't laugh until you know that it *is* the popular will; and when you do know it, cry."

They walked on silently for some little distance further, and then Gerald Bennet turned toward St. John's Square. His wife asked:

"Where are you going?"

"Can't you guess?"

"Yes; but we have never been there before."

"Has he ever failed before?"

"No, you dear soul! and I am very glad we are going."

CHAPTER LXXI.

RICHES HAVE WINGS.

THEY rang at the door of Boniface Newt. It was quite late in the evening, and when they entered the parlor there were several persons sitting there.

"Why! father and mother!" exclaimed Gabriel, who was sitting in a remote dim corner, and who instantly came forward, with May Newt following him.

Mrs. Newt rose and bowed a little stiffly, and said, in an excited voice, that really she had no idea, but she was very happy indeed, she was sure, and so was Mr. Newt. When she had tied her sentence in an inextricable knot, she stopped and seated herself.

Boniface Newt rose slowly and gravely. He was bent like a very old man. His eye was hard and dull, and his dry voice said:

"How do you do? I am happy to see you."

Then he sat down again, while Lawrence went up and shook hands with the new-comers. Boniface drummed slowly upon his knees with the long, bony white fingers, and rocked to and fro mechanically, as he sat.

When Lawrence had ended his greetings there was a pause. Mrs. Newt seemed to be painfully conscious of it. So did Mr. Bennet, whose eyes wandered about the room, resting for a few instants upon Boniface, then sliding toward his wife. Boniface himself seemed to be entirely unconscious of any pause, or of any person, or of any thing, except some mysterious erratic measure that he was beating with the bony fingers.

"It is a great while since we have met, Mrs. Newt," said Mrs. Bennet.

"Yes," returned Mrs. Nancy Newt, rapidly; "and now that

we are to be so very nearly related, it is really high time that we became intimate."

She looked, however, very far off from intimacy with the person she addressed.

"I am glad our children are so happy, Mrs. Newt," said Gerald Bennet, in a tremulous voice, with his eyes glimmering.

"Yes. I am glad Gabriel's prospects are so good," returned Mrs. Newt. "I've no doubt he'll be a very rich man very soon."

When she had spoken, Boniface Newt, still drumming, turned his face and looked quietly at his wife. Nobody spoke. Gabriel only winced at what May's mother had said; and they all looked at Boniface. The old man gazed fixedly at his wife as if he saw nobody else, and as if he were repeating the words to which the bony fingers beat time. He said, in a cold, dry voice, still beating time,

"Riches have wings! Riches have wings!"

"I'm sure, Boniface, I know that, if any body does," said his wife, pettishly, and in a half-whimpering voice. "I think we've all learned that."

"Riches have wings! Riches have wings!" he said, beating with the bony fingers.

"Really, Boniface," said his wife, with an air of offended propriety, "I see no occasion for such pointed allusions to our misfortunes. It is certainly in very bad taste."

"Riches have wings! Riches have wings!" persisted her husband, still gazing at her, and still beating time with the white bony fingers.

Mrs. Newt's whimpering broadened into crying. She sat weeping and wiping her eyes, in the way which used to draw down a storm from her husband. There was no storm now. Only the same placid stare—only the same measured refrain.

"Riches have wings! Riches have wings!"

Lawrence Newt laid his hand gently on his brother's arm.

"RICHES HAVE WINGS!"

"Boniface, you did your best.   We all did what we thought
best and right."

The old man turned his eyes from his wife and went on silently drumming, looking at the wall.

"Nancy," said Lawrence, "as Mr. and Mrs. Bennet are about
to be a part of the family, I see no reason for not saying to
them that provision is made for your husband's support.   His
affairs are as bad as they can be; but you and he shall not
suffer.   Of course you will leave this house, and—"

"Oh dear! What will people say? Nobody'll come to see us in a small house. What will Mrs. Orry say?" interrupted Mrs. Newt.

"Let her say what she chooses, Nancy. What will honest people say to whom your husband owes honest debts, if you don't try to pay them?"

"They are not my debts, and I don't see why I should suffer for them," said Mrs. Newt, vehemently, and crying. "When I married him he said I should ride in my carriage; and if he's been a fool, why should I be a beggar?"

There was profound silence in the room.

"I think it's very hard," said she, querulously.

It was useless for Lawrence to argue. He saw it, and merely remarked,

"The house will be sold, and you'll give up the carriage and live as plainly as you can."

"To think of coming to this!" burst out Mrs. Newt afresh.

But a noise was heard in the hall, and the door opened to admit Mr. and Mrs. Alfred Dinks.

It was the first time they had entered her father's house since her marriage. May, who had been the last person Fanny had seen in her old home, ran forward to greet her, and said, cheerfully,

"Welcome home, Fanny."

Mrs. Dinks looked defiantly about the room. Her keen black eyes saw every body, and involuntarily every body looked at her—except her father. He seemed quite unconscious of any new-comers. Alfred's heavy figure dropped into a chair, whence his small eyes, grown sullen, stared stupidly about. Mrs. Newt merely said, hurriedly, "Why Fanny!" and looked, from the old habit of alarm and apprehension, at her husband, then back again to her daughter. The silence gradually became oppressive, until Fanny broke it by saying, in a dull tone,

"Oh! Uncle Lawrence."

He simply bowed his head, as if it had been a greeting.

Mr. Bennet's foot twitched rather than wagged, and his wife turned toward him, from time to time, with a tender smile. Mrs. Newt, like one at a funeral, presently began to weep afresh.

"Pleasant family party!" broke in the voice of Fanny, clear and hard as her eyes.

"Riches have wings! Riches have wings!" repeated the gray old man, drumming with lean white fingers upon his knees.

"Will nobody tell me any thing?" said Fanny, looking sharply round. "What's going to be done? Are we all beggars?"

"Riches have wings! Riches have wings!" answered the stern voice of the old man, whose eyes were still fixed upon the wall.

Fanny turned toward him half angrily, but her black eyes quailed before the changed figure of her father. She recalled the loud, domineering, dogmatic man, insisting, morning and night, that as soon as he was rich enough he would be all that he wanted to be—the self-important, patronizing, cold, and unsympathetic head of the family. Where was he? Who was this that sat in the parlor, in his chair, no longer pompous and fierce, but bowed, gray, drumming on his thin knees with lean white fingers?

"Father!" exclaimed Fanny, involuntarily, and terrified.

The old man turned his head toward her. The calm, hard eyes looked into hers. There was no expression of surprise, or indignation, or forgiveness—nothing but a placid abstraction and vagueness.

"Father!" Fanny repeated, rising, and half moving toward him.

His head turned back again—his eyes looked at the wall— and she heard only the words, "Riches have wings! Riches have wings!"

As Fanny sank back into her chair, pale and appalled, May took her hand and began to talk with her in a low, murmuring tone. The others fell into a fragmentary conversation, constantly recurring with their eyes to Mr. Newt. The talk went on in broken whispers, and it was quite late in the evening when a stumbling step advanced to the door, which was burst open, and there stood Abel Newt, with his hat crushed, his clothes soiled, his jaw hanging, and his eyes lifted in a drunken leer.

"How do?" he said, leaning against the door-frame and nodding his head.

His mother, who had never before seen him in such a condition, glanced at him, and uttered a frightened cry. Lawrence Newt and Gabriel rose, and, going toward him, took his arms and tried to lead him out. Abel had no kindly feeling for either of them. His brow lowered, and the sullen blackness shot into his eyes.

"Hands off!" he cried, in a threatening tone.

They still urged him out of the room.

"Hands off!" he said again, looking at Lawrence Newt, and then in a sneering tone:

"Oh! the Reverend Gabriel Bennet! Come, I licked you like — like — like hell once, and I'll — I'll — I'll — do it again. Stand back!" he shouted, with drunken energy, and struggling to free his arms.

But Gabriel and Lawrence Newt held fast. The others rose and stood looking on, Mrs. Newt hysterically weeping, and May pale with terror. Alfred Dinks laughed, foolishly, and gazed about for sympathy. Gerald Bennet drew his wife's arm within his own.

The old man sat quietly, only turning his head toward the noise, and looking at the struggle without appearing to see it.

Finding himself mastered, Abel swore and struggled with drunken frenzy. After a little while he was entirely exhausted, and sank upon the floor. Lawrence Newt and Gabriel stood panting over him; the rest crowded into the hall. Abel looked about stupidly, then crawled toward the staircase, laid

his head upon the lower step, and almost immediately fell into
a deep, drunken slumber.

"Come, come," whispered Gerald Bennet to his wife.

They took Mrs. Newt's hand and said Good-by.

"Oh, dear me! isn't it dreadful?" she sobbed. "Please
don't say any thing about it. Good-night."

They shook her hand, but as they opened the door into the
still moonlight midnight they heard the clear, hard voice in
the parlor, and in their minds they saw the beating of the
bony fingers.

"Riches have wings! Riches have wings!"

CHAPTER LXXII.

GOOD-BY.

THE happy hours of Hope Wayne's life were the visits of
Lawrence Newt. The sound of his voice in the hall, of his
step on the stair, gave her a sense of profound peace. Often,
as she sat at table with Mrs. Simcoe, in her light morning-
dress, and with the dew of sleep yet fresh upon her cheeks,
she heard the sound, and her heart seemed to stop and listen.
Often, as time wore on, and the interviews were longer and
more delayed, she was conscious that the gaze of her old
friend became curiously fixed upon her whenever Lawrence
Newt came. Often, in the tranquil evenings, when they sat
together in the pleasant room, Hope Wayne cheerfully chatting, or sewing, or reading aloud, Mrs. Simcoe looked at her
so wistfully—so as if upon the point of telling some strange
story—that Hope could not help saying, brightly, "Out with
it, aunty!" But as the younger woman spoke, the resolution
glimmered away in the eyes of her companion, and was succeeded by a yearning, tender pity.

Still Lawrence Newt came to the house, to consult, to in-
spect, to bring bills that he had paid, to hear of a new utensil

for the kitchen, to see about coal, about wood, about iron, to look at a dipper, at a faucet—he knew every thing in the house by heart, and yet he did not know how or why. He wanted to come—he thought he came too often. What could he do?

Hope sang as she sat in her chamber, as she read in the parlor, as she went about the house, doing her nameless, innumerable household duties. Her voice was rich, and full, and womanly; and the singing was not the fragmentary, sparkling gush of good spirits, and the mere overflow of a happy temperament—it was a deep, sweet, inward music, as if a woman's soul were intoning a woman's thoughts, and as if the woman were at peace.

But the face of Mrs. Simcoe grew sadder and sadder as Hope's singing was sweeter and sweeter, and significant of utter rest. The look in her eyes of something imminent, of something that even trembled on her tongue, grew more and more marked. Hope Wayne brightly said, "Out with it, aunty!" and sang on.

Amy Waring came often to the house. She was older than Hope, and it was natural that she should be a little graver. They had a hundred plans in concert for helping a hundred people. Amy and Hope were a charitable society.

"Fiddle diddle!" said Aunt Dagon, when she was speaking of his two friends to her nephew Lawrence. "Does this brace of angels think that virtue consists in making shirts for poor people?"

Lawrence looked at his aunt with the inscrutable eyes, and answered slowly,

"I don't know that they do, Aunt Dagon; but I suppose they don't think it consists in *not* making them."

"Phew!" said Mrs. Dagon, tossing her cap-strings back pettishly. "I suppose they expect to make a kind of rope-ladder of all their charity garments, and climb up into heaven that way!"

"Perhaps they do," replied Lawrence, in the same tone. "They have not made me their confidant. But I suppose that

even if the ladder doesn't reach, it's better to go a little way
up than not to start at all."

"There! Lawrence, such a speech as that comes of your
not going to church. If you would just try to be a little better man, and go to hear Dr. Maundy preach, say once a year,"
said Mrs. Dagon, sarcastically, "you would learn that it isn't
good works that are the necessary thing."

"I hope, Aunt Dagon," returned Lawrence, laughing—"I
do really hope that it's good words, then, for your sake. My
dear aunt, you ought to be satisfied with showing that you
don't believe in good works, and let other people enjoy their
own faith. If charity be a sin, Miss Amy Waring and Miss
Hope Wayne are dreadful sinners. But then, Aunt Dagon,
what a saint you must be!"

Gradually Mrs. Simcoe was persuaded that she ought to
speak plainly to Lawrence Newt upon a subject which profoundly troubled her. Having resolved to do it, she sat one
morning waiting patiently for the door of the library—in which
Lawrence Newt was sitting with Hope Wayne, discussing the
details of her household—to open. There was a placid air of
resolution in her sad and anxious face, as if she were only
awaiting the moment when she should disburden her heart of
the weight it had so long secretly carried. There was entire
silence in the house. The rich curtains, the soft carpet, the
sumptuous furniture—every object on which the eye fell,
seemed made to steal the shock from noise; and the rattle of
the street—the jarring of carts—the distant shriek of the belated milkman—the long, wavering, melancholy cry of the
chimney-sweep—came hushed and indistinct into the parlor
where the sad-eyed woman sat silently waiting.

At length the door opened and Lawrence Newt came out.
He was going toward the front door, when Mrs. Simcoe rose
and went into the hall, and said, "Stop a moment!"

He turned, half smiled, but saw her face, and his own settled into its armor.

Mrs. Simcoe beckoned him toward the parlor; and as he

went in she stepped to the library door and said, to avoid in-
terruption,

"Hope, Mr. Newt and I are talking together in the parlor."

Hope bowed, and made no reply. Mrs. Simcoe entered the
other room and closed the door.

"Mr. Newt," she said, in a low voice, "you can not wonder that I am anxious."

He looked at her, and did not answer.

"I know, perhaps, more than you know," said she; "not,
I am sure, more than you suspect."

Lawrence Newt was a little troubled, but it was only evident in the quiet closing and unclosing of his hand.

They stood for a few moments without speaking. Then
she opened the miniature, and when she saw that he observed
it she said, very slowly,

"Is it quite fair, Mr. Newt?"

"Mrs. Simcoe," he replied, inquiringly.

His firm, low voice reassured her.

"Why do you come here so often?" asked she.

"To help Miss Hope."

"Is it necessary that you should come?"

"She wishes it."

"Why?"

He paused a moment. Mrs. Simcoe continued:

"Lawrence Newt, at least let us be candid with each other.
By the memory of the dead—by the common sorrow we have
known, there should be no cloud between us about Hope
Wayne. I use your own words. Tell me what you feel as
frankly as you feel it."

There was simple truth in the earnest face before him.
While she was speaking she raised her hand involuntarily to
her breast, and gasped as if she were suffocating. Her words
were calm, and he answered,

"I waited, for I did not know how to answer—nor do I
now."

"And yet you have had some impression—some feeling—

some conviction. You know whether it is necessary that you should come—whether she wants you for an hour's chat, as an old friend—or—or"—she waited a moment, and added—" or as something else."

As Lawrence Newt stood before her he remembered curiously his interview with Aunt Martha, but he could not say to Mrs. Simcoe what he had said to her.

" What can I say ?" he asked at length, in a troubled voice.

" Lawrence Newt, say if you think she loves you, and tell me," she said, drawing herself erect and back from him, as in the twilight of the old library at Pinewood, while her thin finger was pointed upward—" tell me, as you will be judged hereafter—me, to whom her mother gave her as she died, knowing that she loved you."

Her voice died away, overpowered by emotion. She still looked at him, and suspicion, incredulity, and scorn were mingled in her look, while her uplifted finger still shook, as if appealing to Heaven. Then she asked abruptly, and fiercely,

" To which, in the name of God, are you false—the mother or the daughter ?"

" Stop !" replied Lawrence Newt, in a tone so imperious that the hand of his companion fell at her side, and the scorn and suspicion faded from her eyes. " Mrs. Simcoe, there are things that even you must not say. You have lived alone with a great sorrow; you are too swift; you are unjust. Even if I had known what you ask about Miss Hope, I am not sure that I should have done differently. Certainly, while I did not know—while, at most, I could only suspect, I could do nothing else. I have feared rather than believed—nor that, until very lately. Would it have been kind, or wise, or right to have staid away altogether, when, as you know, I constantly meet her at our little Club? Was I to say, ' Miss Hope, I see you love me, but I do not love you?' And what right had I to hint the same thing by my actions, at the cost of utter misapprehension and pain to her ? Mrs. Simcoe, I do love Hope Wayne too tenderly, and respect her too truly, not to try to protect her against the sting of her own womanly pride. And so I have not staid away. I have not avoided a woman in whom I must always have so deep and peculiar an interest. I have been friend and almost father, and never by a whisper even, by a look, by a possible hint, have I implied any thing more."

His voice trembled as he spoke. He had no right to be silent any longer, and as he finished Mrs. Simcoe took his hand.

"Forgive me! I love her so dearly—and I too am a woman."

She sank upon the sofa as she spoke, and covered her face for a little while. The tears stole quietly down her cheeks. Lawrence Newt stood by her sadly, for his mind was deeply perplexed. They both remained for some time without speaking, until Mrs. Simcoe asked,

"What can we do?"

Lawrence Newt shook his head doubtfully.

They were silent again. At length Mrs. Simcoe said:

"I will do it."

"What?" asked Lawrence.

"What I have been meaning to do for a long, long time," replied the other. "I will tell her the story."

An indefinable expression settled upon Lawrence Newt's face as she spoke.

"Has she never asked?" he inquired.

"Often; but I have always avoided telling."

"It had better be done. It is the only way. But I hoped it would never be necessary. God bless us all!"

He moved toward the door when he had finished, but not until he had shaken her warmly by the hand.

"You will come as before?" she said.

"Of course, there will not be the slightest change on my part. And, Mrs. Simcoe, remember that next week, certainly. I shall meet Miss Hope at Miss Amy Waring's. Our first meeting had better be there, so before then please—"

He bowed and went out. As he passed the library door

"GOOD-BY, MR. NEWT, GOOD-BY!"

he involuntarily looked in. There sat Hope Wayne, reading;
but as she heard him she raised the head of golden hair, the
dewy cheeks, the thoughtful brow, and as she bowed to him
the clear blue eyes smiled the words her tongue uttered—

"Good-by, Mr. Newt, good-by!"

The words followed him out of the door and down the
street. The air rang with them every where. The people he

passed seemed to look at him as if they were repeating them. Distant echoes caught them up and whispered them. He heard no noise of carriages, no loud city hum; he only heard, fainter and fainter, softer and softer, sadder and sadder, and ever following on, " Good-by, Mr. Newt, good-by!"

CHAPTER LXXIII.

THE BELCH PLATFORM.

"My dear Newt, as a friend who has the highest respect for you, and the firmest faith in your future, I am sure you will allow me to say one thing."

"Oh! certainly, my dear Belch; say two," replied Abel, with the utmost suavity, as he sat at table with General Belch.

"I have no peculiar ability, I know," continued the other, "but I have, perhaps, a little more experience than you. We old men, you know, always plume ourselves upon experience, which we make do duty for all the virtues and talents."

"And it is trained for that service by being merely a synonym for a knowledge of all the sins and rascalities," said Abel, smiling, as he blew rings of smoke and passed the decanter to General Belch.

"True," replied the other; "very true. I see, my dear Newt, that you have had your eyes and your mind open. And since we are going to act together—since, in fact, we are interested in the same plans—"

"And principles," interrupted Abel, laying his head back, and looking with half-closed eyes at the vanishing smoke.

"Oh yes, I was coming to that—in the same plans and principles, it is well that we should understand each other perfectly."

General Belch paused, looked at Abel, and took snuff.

"I think we do already," replied Abel.

"Still there are one or two points to which I would call

your attention. One is, that you can not be too careful of what you say, in regard to its bearing upon the party; and the other is, a general rule that the Public is an ass, but you must never let it know you think so. If there is one thing which the party has practically proved, it is that the people have no will of their own, but are sheep in the hands of the shepherd."

The General took snuff again.

"The Public, then, is an ass and a sheep?" inquired Abel.

"Yes," said the General, "an ass in capacity, and in preference of a thistle diet; a sheep in gregarious and stupid following. You say 'Ca, ca, ca,' when you want a cow to follow you; and you say 'Glorious old party,' and 'Intelligence of the people,' and 'Preference of truth to victory,' and so forth, when you want the people to follow you."

"An ass, a sheep, and a cow," said Abel. "To what other departments of natural history do the people belong, General?"

"Adders," returned Belch, sententiously.

"How so?" asked Abel, amused.

"Because they are so cold and ungrateful," said the General.

"As when, for instance," returned Abel, "the Honorable Watkins Bodley, having faithfully served his constituency, is turned adrift by—by—the people."

He looked at Belch and laughed. The fat nose of the General glistened.

"No, no," said he, "your illustration is at fault. He did not faithfully serve his constituency. He was not sound upon the great Grant question."

The two gentlemen laughed together and filled their glasses.

"No, no," resumed the General, "never forget that the great thing is drill—discipline. Keep the machinery well oiled, and your hand upon the crank, and all goes well."

"Until somebody knocks off your hand," said Abel.

"Yes, of course—of course; but that is the very point.

The fight is never among the sheep, but only among the shepherds. Look at our splendid system, beginning with Tom, Jim, and Ned, and culminating in the President—the roots rather red and unsightly, but oh! such a pretty flower, all broadcloth, kid gloves, and affability—contemplate the superb machinery," continued the General, warming, "the primaries, the ward committees, the—in fact, all the rest of it—see how gloriously it works—the great result of the working of the whole is—"

"To establish justice, insure domestic tranquillity, promote the general welfare, and secure the blessings of liberty to ourselves and our posterity," interrupted Abel, who had been scanning the Constitution, and who delivered the words with a rhetorical pomp of manner.

General Belch smiled approvingly.

"That's it—that's the very tone. You'll do. The great result is, who shall have his hand on the crank. And there are, therefore, always three parties in our beloved country."

Abel looked inquiringly.

"First, the *ins*, who are in two parties—the clique that have, and the clique that haven't. They fight like fury among themselves, but when they meet t'other great party they all fight together, because the hopes of the crank for each individual of each body lie in the party itself, and in their obedience to its discipline. These are two of the parties. Then there is the great party of the *outs*, who have a marvelous unanimity, and never break up into quarrelsome bodies until there is a fair chance of their ousting the *ins*. I say these things not because they are not pretty obvious, but because, as a man of fashion and society, you have probably not attended to such matters. It's dirty work for a gentleman. But I suppose any of us would be willing to pick a gold eagle out of the mud, even if we did soil our fingers."

"Of course," replied Abel, in a tone that General Belch did not entirely comprehend—"of course no gentleman knows any thing of politics. Gentlemen are the natural governors of a country; and where they are not erected into a hereditary governing class, self-respect forbids them to mix with inferior men—so they keep aloof from public affairs. Good Heavens! what gentleman would be guilty of being an alderman in this town! Why, as you know, my dear Belch, nothing but my reduced circumstances induces me to go to Congress. By-the-by—"

"Well, what is it?" asked the General.

"I'm dreadfully hard up," said Abel. "I have just the d—est luck you ever conceived, and I must raise some money."

The fat nose glistened again, while the General sat silently pondering.

"I can lend you a thousand," he said, at length.

"Thank you. It will oblige me very much."

"Upon conditions," added the General.

"Conditions?" asked Abel, surprised.

"I mean understandings," said the General.

"Oh! certainly," answered Abel.

"You pledge yourself to me and our friends that you will at the earliest moment move in the matter of the Grant; you engage to secure the votes somehow, relying upon the pecuniary aid of our friends who are interested; and you will repay me out of your first receipts. Ele will stand by you through thick and thin. We keep him there for that purpose."

"My dear Belch, I promise any thing you require. I only want the money."

"Give me your hand, Newt. From the bottom of my soul I do respect a man who has no scruples."

They shook hands heartily, and filling their glasses they drank "Success!" The General then wrote a check and a little series of instructions, which he gave to Abel, while Abel himself scribbled an I.O.U., which the General laid in his pocket-book.

"You'll have an eye on Ele," said the General, as he buttoned his coat.

"Certainly—two if you want," answered Abel, lazily, repeating the joke.

"He's a good fellow, Ele is," said Belch; "but he's largely interested, and he'll probably try to chouse us out of something by affecting superior influence. You must patronize him to the other men. Keep him well under. I have a high respect for cellar stairs, but they mustn't try to lead up to the roof. Good-by. Hail Newt! Senator that shall be!" laughed the General, as he shook hands and followed his fat nose out of the door.

Left to himself, Abel walked for some time up and down his room, with his hands buried in his pocket and a sneering smile upon his face. He suddenly drew one hand out, raised it, clenched it, and brought it down heavily in the air, as he muttered, contemptuously,

"What a stupid fool! I wonder if he never thinks, as he looks in the glass, that that fat nose of his is made to lead him by."

For the sagacious and fat-nosed General had omitted to look at the little paper Newt handed to him, thinking it would be hardly polite to do so under the circumstances. But if he had looked he would have seen that the exact sum they had spoken of had been forgotten, and a very inconsiderable amount was specified.

It had flashed across Abel's mind in a moment that if the General subsequently discovered it and were disposed to make trouble, the disclosure of the paper of instructions which he had written, and which Abel had in his possession, would ruin his hopes of political financiering. "And as for my election, why, I have my certificate in my pocket."

CHAPTER LXXIV.

MIDNIGHT.

GRADUALLY the sneer faded from Abel's face, and he walked up and down the room, no longer carelessly, but fitfully; stopping sometimes—again starting more rapidly—then leaning against the mantle, on which the clock pointed to midnight—then throwing himself into a chair or upon a sofa; and so, rising again, walked on.

His head bent forward—his eyes grew rounder and harder, and seemed to be burnished with the black, bad light; his step imperceptibly grew stealthy—he looked about him carefully—he stood erect and breathless to listen—bit his nails, and walked on.

The clock upon the mantle pointed to half an hour after midnight. Abel Newt went into his chamber and put on his slippers. He lighted a candle, and looked carefully under the bed and in the closet. Then he drew the shades over the windows and went out into the other room, closing and locking the door behind him.

He glided noiselessly to the door that opened into the entry, and locked that softly and bolted it carefully. Then he turned the key so that the wards filled the keyhole, and taking out his handkerchief he hung it over the knob of the door, so that it fell across the keyhole, and no eye could by any chance have peered into the room.

He saw that the blinds of the windows were closed, the windows shut and locked, and the linen shades drawn over them. He also let fall the heavy damask curtains, so that the windows were obliterated from the room. He stood in the centre of the room and looked to every corner where, by any chance, a person might be concealed.

Then, moving upon tip-toe, he drew a key from his pocket

and fitted it into the lid of a secretary. As he turned it in the lock the snap of the bolt made him start. He was haggard, even ghastly, as he stood, letting the lid back slowly, lest it should creak or jar. With another key he opened a little drawer, and involuntarily looking behind him as he did so, he took out a small piece of paper, which he concealed in his hand.

Seating himself at the secretary, he put the candle before him, and remained for a moment with his face slightly strained forward with a startling intentness of listening. There was no sound but the regular ticking of the clock upon the mantle. He had not observed it before, but now he could hear nothing else.

Tick, tick — tick, tick. It had a persistent, relentless, remorseless regularity. Tick, tick—tick, tick. Every moment it appeared to be louder and louder. His brow wrinkled and his head bent forward more deeply, while his eyes were set straight before him. Tick, tick—tick, tick. The solemn beat became human as he listened. He could not raise his head—he could not turn his eyes. He felt as if some awful shape stood over him with destroying eyes and inflexible tongue. But struggling, without moving, as a dreamer wrestles with the nightmare, he presently sprang bolt upright—his eyes wide and wild—the sweat oozing upon his ghastly forehead—his whole frame weak and quivering. With the same suddenness he turned defiantly, clenching his fists, in act to spring.

There was nothing there. He saw only the clock—the gilt pendulum regularly swinging—he heard only the regular tick, tick—tick, tick.

A sickly smile glimmered on his face as he stepped toward the mantle, still clutching the paper in his hand, but crouching as he came, and leering, as if to leap upon an enemy unawares. Suddenly he started as if struck—a stifled shriek of horror burst from his lips—he staggered back — his hand opened—the paper fell fluttering to the floor. Abel Newt had unexpectedly seen the reflection of his own face in the mirror that covered the chimney behind the clock.

THE FACE IN THE MIRROR.

He recovered himself, swore bitterly, and stooped to pick up the paper. Then with sullen bravado, still staring at his reflection in the glass, he took off the glass shade of the clock, touched the pendulum and stopped it; then turning his back, crept to his chair, and sat down again.

The silence was profound, not a sound was audible but the creaking of his clothes as he leaned heavily against the edge of the desk and drew his agitated breath. He raised the candle and bent his gloomy face over the paper which he held before him. It was a note of his late firm indorsed by Lawrence Newt & Co. He gazed at his uncle's signature intently, studying every line, every dot—so intently that it seemed as if his eyes would burn it. Then putting down the candle and spreading the name before him, he drew a sheet of tissue paper from a drawer and placed it over it. The writing was perfectly legible—the finest stroke showed through the thin tissue. He filled a pen and carefully drew the lines of the signature upon the tissue paper—then raised it—the fac-simile was perfect.

Taking a thicker piece of paper, he laid the note before him, and slowly, carefully, copied the signature. The result was a resemblance, but nothing more. He held the paper in the flame of the candle until it was consumed. He tried again. He tried many times. Each trial was a greater success.

Tearing a check from his book he filled the blanks and wrote below the name of Lawrence Newt & Co., and found, upon comparison with the indorsement, that it was very like. Abel Newt grinned; his lips moved: he was muttering "Dear Uncle Lawrence."

He stopped writing, and carefully burned, as before, the check and all the paper. Then covering his face with his hands as he sat, he said to himself, as the hot, hurried thoughts flickered through his mind,

"Yes, yes, Mrs. Lawrence Newt, I shall not be master of Pinewood, but I shall be of your husband, and he will be master of your property. Practice makes perfect. Dear Uncle Lawrence shall be my banker."

His brain reeled and whirled as he sat. He remembered the words of his friend the General: "Abel Newt was not born to fail."

"No, by God!" he shouted, springing up, and clenching his hands.

He staggered. The walls of the room, the floor, the ceiling, the furniture heaved and rolled before his eyes. In the wild tumult that overwhelmed his brain as if he were sinking in gurgling whirlpools—the peaceful lawn of Pinewood—the fight with Gabriel—the running horses—the "Farewell forever, Miss Wayne"—the shifting chances of his subsequent life—Grace Plumer blazing with diamonds—the figure of his father drumming with white fingers upon his office-desk—Lawrence and Gabriel pushing him out—they all swept before his consciousness in the moment during which he threw out his hands wildly, clutched at the air, and plunged headlong upon the floor, senseless.

CHAPTER LXXV.

REMINISCENCE.

On the very evening that General Belch and Abel Newt were sitting together, smoking, taking snuff, sipping wine, and discussing the great principles that should control the action of American legislators and statesmen, Hope Wayne and Mrs. Simcoe sat together in their pleasant drawing-room talking of old times. The fire crackled upon the hearth, and the bright flames flickering through the room brought out every object with fitful distinctness. The lamp was turned almost out— for they found it more agreeable to sit in a twilight as they spoke of the days which seemed to both of them to be full of subdued and melancholy light. They sat side by side; Hope leaning her cheek upon her hand, and gazing thoughtfully into the fire; Mrs. Simcoe turned partly toward her, and occasionally studying her face, as if peculiarly anxious to observe its expression.

It might have happened in many ways that they were speaking of the old times. The older woman may have intentionally led the conversation in that direction for some ulterior purpose she had in view. Or what is more likely than that the young woman should constantly draw her friend and guardian to speak of days and people connected with her own life, but passed before her memory had retained them ?

After a long interval, as if, when she had once broken her reserve about her life, she must pour out all her experience, Mrs. Simcoe began :

"When I was twenty years old, living with my father, a poor farmer in the country, there came to pass the summer in the village a gentleman, a good deal older than I. He was handsome, graceful, elegant, fascinating. I saw him at church, but he did not see me. Then I met him sometimes upon the road, idly sauntering along, swinging a little cane, and looking as if village life were fatiguing. He seemed at length to observe me. One day he bowed. I said nothing, but hurried on. When I was a little beyond him I turned my head. He also was turning and looking at me.

"I was old enough to know why I turned. Yes, and so was he. How well I remember the peaceful western light that fell along the fields and touched the trees so kindly! Every thing was still. The birds dropped hurrying homeward notes, and the cows were coming in from the pasture. I was going after our cow, but I leaned a long time on the bars and looked at the new moon timidly showing herself in the west. Then I looked at my clumsy gown, and thick shoes, and large hands, and thought of the graceful, elegant man, who had not bowed to me insolently. I imagined that a gentleman used to city life must find our country ways tiresome. I pitied him, but what could I do ?

"Once in the meadows I was following up the brook to find cardinal flowers. The brook wound through a little wood; and as I was passing, looking closely among the flags and pickerel-wood, I suddenly heard a voice close to me— 'The lobelia blossoms are further on, Miss Jane.' I knew instantly who it was, and I was conscious of being more scarlet than the flowers I was seeking.

"Well, dear," said Mrs. Simcoe, after pausing for a few moments, "I can not repeat every detail. The time came when

COLONEL WAYNE'S FIRST LOVE.

I was not afraid to speak to him—when I cared to speak to no one else—when I thought of him all day and dreamed of him all night—when I wore the ribbons he praised, and the colors he loved, and the flowers he gave me; when he told me of the great life beyond the village, of lofty and beautiful women he had known, of wise men he had seen, of the foreign countries he had visited—when he twined my hair around his finger and said, 'Jane, I love you!'"

Her eyes were excited, and her voice was hurried, but inexpressibly sad. Hope sat by, and the tears flowed from her eyes.

"A long, long time. Yet it was only a few months—it was only a summer. He came in May, and was gone again in November. But between his coming and going the roses in our garden blossomed and withered. So you see there was time enough. Time enough! Time enough! I was heavenly happy.

"One day he said that he must go. There was some frightful trouble in his eye. 'Will you come back?' I asked. I tremble to remember how sternly I asked it, and how cold and bloodless I felt. 'So help me God!' he answered, and left me. Left me! 'So help me God!' he murmured, as his tears fell upon my cheek and he kissed me. 'So help me God!'—and he left me. Not a word, not a look, not a sign had he given me to suppose that he would not return; not a thought, not a wish had he breathed to me that you might not hear. His miniature hung in a locket around my neck, even as my whole heart and soul hung upon his love. 'So help me God!' he whispered, and left me.

"He did not come back. I thought my heart was frozen. My mother sighed as she went on with her hard, incessant work. My father tried to be cheerful. 'Cry, girl, cry,' my mother said; 'only cry, and you'll be better.' I could not cry; I could not smile. I could do nothing but help her silently in the long, hard work, day after day, summer and winter. I read the books he had given me. I thought of the things he had said. I sat in my chamber when the floor was scrubbed, and the bread baked, and the dishes washed, and the flies buzzed in the hot, still kitchen. I can hear them now. And there I sat, looking out of my window, straining my eyes toward the horizon—sometimes sure that I heard him coming, clicking the gate, hurrying up the gravel, with his eager, handsome, melancholy face. I started up. My heart stood still. I was ready to fall upon his breast and say,

'I believe 'twas all right.' He did not come. 'So help me God!' he said, and did not come.

"My father brought me to New York to change the scene. But God had brought me here to change my heart. I heard one Sunday good old Bishop Asbury, and he began the work that Summerfield sealed. My parents presently died. They left nothing, and I was the only child. I did what I could, and at last I became your grandfather's housekeeper."

As her story proceeded Mrs. Simcoe looked more and more anxiously at Hope, whose eyes were fixed upon her incessantly. The older woman paused at this point, and, taking Hope's face between her hands, smoothed her hair, and kissed her.

"Your grandfather had a daughter Mary."

"My mother," said Hope, earnestly.

"Your mother, darling. She was as beautiful but as delicate as a flower. The doctors said a long salt voyage would strengthen her. So your grandfather sent her in the ship of one of his friends to India. In India she staid several weeks, and met a young man of her own age, clerk in a house there. Of course they were soon engaged. But he was young, not yet in business, and she knew the severity of your grandfather and his ambition for her. At length the ship returned, and your mother returned in it. Scarcely was she at home a month than your grandfather told me that he had a connection in view for his daughter, and wanted me to prepare her to receive the addresses of a gentleman a good deal older than she, but of the best family, and in every way a desirable husband. He was himself getting old, he said, and it was necessary that his daughter should marry. Your mother loved me dearly, as I did her. Gentle soul, with her soft, dark, appealing eyes, with her flower-like fragility and womanly dependence. Ah me! it was hard that your grandfather should have been her parent.

"She was stunned when I told her. I thought her grief was only natural, and I was surprised at the sudden change in her. She faded before our eyes. We could not cheer her.

But she made no effort to resist. She did not refuse to see her suitor; she did not say that she loved any one else. I think she had a mortal fear of her father, and, dear soul! she could not do any thing that required resolution.

"One day your grandfather said at dinner, 'To-morrow, Miss Mary, your new friend will be here.'

"All night she lay awake, trembling and tearful; and at morning she rose like a spectre. The stranger arrived. Mary kept her room until dinner-time. Then we both went down to see the new-comer. He was in the library with your grandfather, and was engaged in telling him some very amusing story when we came in, for your grandfather was laughing heartily. They both rose upon seeing us.

"'Colonel Wayne, my daughter,' said your grandfather, waving his hand toward her. He bowed—she sank, spectre-like, into a chair.

"'Mrs. Simcoe, Colonel Wayne.'

"Our eyes met. It was my lover. He was too much amazed to bow. But in a moment he recovered himself, smiled courteously, and seated himself; for he saw at once what place I filled in the household. I said nothing. I remember that I sank into a chair and looked at him. He was older, but the same charm still hovered about his person. His voice had the same secret music, and his movement that careless grace which seemed to spring from the consciousness of power. I was conscious of only two things—that I loved him, and that he was unworthy the love of any woman. ·

"During dinner he made two or three observations to me. But I bowed and said nothing. I think I was morally stunned, and the whole scene seemed to me to be unreal. After a few days he made a formal offer of his hand to Mary Burt. Poor child! Poor child! She trembled, hesitated, fluttered, delayed. 'You must; you shall!' were the terrible words she heard from her parent. She dreaded to tell the truth, lest he should force a summary marriage. Hope, my child, you could have resisted—so could I; she could not. 'Only, dear father,'

she said, 'I am so young. Let me not be married for a year.'
Her father laughed and assented, and I think she instantly
wrote to her lover in India.

"People came driving out to congratulate. 'Such a reasonable connection!' every body said; 'a military man of fine old
family. It is really delightful to have a union sometimes take
place in which all the conditions are satisfactory.'

"All the time his miniature hung round my neck. Why?
Because, in the bottom of my soul, I still believed him. I had
heard him say, 'So help me God!'

"He went away, and sometimes returned for a week. I
was comforted by seeing that he did not love your mother,
and by the confidence I had that she would not marry him. I
was sure that something would happen to prevent.

"The year was coming round. One night your mother appeared in my room in her night-dress; her face was radiant,
and she held a note in her hand. It was from her lover. He
had thrown himself upon a ship when her letter reached him,
and here he was close at hand. Full of generous ardor, he
proposed to marry her privately at once; there was no other
way, he was sure.

"'Will you help us?' she said, after she had told me every
thing.

"'But you are two such children,' I said.

"'Then you will not help. You will make me marry Colonel Wayne.'

"I tried to see the matter calmly. I sought the succor of
God. I do not say that I did just what I should have done,
but I helped them. The heart is weak, and perhaps I was the
more willing to help, because the fulfillment of her plan would
prevent her becoming the wife of Colonel Wayne. The time
was arranged when she was to go away. I was to accompany her, and she was to be married.

"The lover came. It was a June night; the moon was full.
We went quietly along the avenue. The gate was opened.
We were just passing through when your grandfather and

Colonel Wayne suddenly stepped from the shadow of the wall and the trees.

"Your mother and her lover stood perfectly still. She gave a little cry. Your grandfather was furious.

"'Go, Sir!' he shrieked at the young man.

"'If your daughter commands it,' he replied.

"Your grandfather seized him involuntarily.

"'Sir, my daughter is the betrothed wife of Colonel Wayne.'

"The young man looked with an incredulous smile at your mother, who had sunk senseless into my arms, and said, in a low voice,

"'She was mine before she ever saw him.'

"Your grandfather actually hissed at him with contempt.

"'Go—before I strike you!'

"The young man hesitated for a few moments, saw that it was useless to remain longer at that time, and went.

"The next day Mr. Burt sent for Dr. Peewee.

"The moment I knew what he intended to do I ran to your grandfather and told him that Colonel Wayne was not a fit husband for his daughter. But when I told him that the Colonel had deserted me, Mr. Burt laughed scornfully.

"'You, Mrs. Simcoe? Why, you have lost your wits. Remember, Colonel Wayne is a gentleman of the oldest family, and you are—you were—'

"'I was a poor country girl,' said I, 'and Colonel Wayne loved me, and I loved him, and here is the pledge and proof of it.'

"I drew out his miniature as I spoke, and held it before your grandfather's eyes. He fairly staggered, and rang the bell violently.

"'Call Colonel Wayne,' he said, hastily, to the servant.

"In a moment the Colonel came in. I saw his color change as his eye fell upon me, holding the locket in my hand, and upon your grandfather's flushed face.

"'Colonel Wayne, have you ever seen Mrs. Simcoe before?'

"He was very pale, and there were sallow circles under his eyes as he spoke; but he said, calmly,

"'Not to my knowledge.'

"Scorn made me icily calm.

"'Who gave me that, Sir?' said I, thrusting the miniature almost into his face.

"He took it in his hand and looked at it. I saw his lip work and his throat quiver with an involuntary spasm.

"'I am sure I do not know.'

"I was speechless. Your grandfather was confounded. Colonel Wayne looked white, but resolute.

"'God only is my witness,' said I, slowly, as if the words came gasping from my heart. 'So help me God, I loved him, and he loved me.'

"A quiver ran through his frame as I spoke, but he preserved the same placidity of face.

"'There is some mistake, Mrs. Simcoe,' said your grandfather, not unkindly, to me. 'Go to your room.'

"I obeyed, for my duty was done."

Mrs. Simcoe paused, and rocked silently to and fro. Hope took her hand and kissed it reverently. Presently the narration was quietly resumed:

"I told your mother my story. But she was stunned by her own grief, and I do not think she comprehended me. Dr. Peewee came, and she was married. Your mother did not say yes—for she could not utter a word—but the ceremony proceeded. I heard the words, 'Whom God hath joined together,' and I laughed aloud, and fell fainting.

"It was a few days after the marriage, when Colonel Wayne and his wife were absent, that your grandfather said to me,

"'Mrs. Simcoe, your story seems to be true. But think a moment. A man like Colonel Wayne must have had many experiences. We all do. He has been rash, and foolish, and thoughtless, I have no doubt. He may even have trifled with your feelings. I am very sorry. If he has done so, I think he ought to have acknowledged it the other day. But I hope sincerely that we shall all let by-gones be by-gones, and live happily together. Ah! I see dinner is ready. Good-day, Mrs. Simcoe. Dr. Peewee, will you ask a blessing?' "

It was already midnight, and the two women sat before the fire. It was the moment when Abel Newt was stealing through his rooms, fastening doors and windows. Hope Wayne was pale and cold like a statue as she listened to the voice of Mrs. Simcoe, which had a wailing tone pitiful to hear. After a long silence she began again:

"What ought I to have done? Should I have gone away? That was the easiest course. But, Hope, the way of duty is not often the easiest way. I wrote a long letter to the good old Bishop Asbury, who seemed to me like a father, and after a while his answer came. He told me that I should seek the Lord's leading, and if that bade me stay—if that told me that it would be for my soul's blessing that my heart should break daily—then I had better remain, seeing that the end is not here—that here we have no continuing city, and that our proud hearts must be bruised by grief, even as our Saviour's lowly forehead was pierced with thorns.

"So I staid. It was partly pity for your mother, who began to droop at once. It was partly that I might keep my wound bleeding for my soul's salvation; and partly—I see it now, but I could not then—because I believed, as before God I do now believe, that in his secret heart I was the woman your father loved, and I could not give him up.

"Your mother's lover wrote to me at once, I discovered afterward, but his letters were intercepted, for your grandfather was a shrewd, resolute man. Then he came to Pinewood, but he was not allowed to see your mother. The poor boy was frantic; but before he could effect any thing your mother was the wife of Colonel Wayne. Then, in the same ship in which he had come from India, he returned; and after he was gone all his letters were given to me. I wrote to him at once. I told him every thing about your mother, but there was not much to tell. She never mentioned his name after her marriage. There were gay parties given in honor of the wedding, and her delicate, drooping, phantom-like figure hung upon the arm of her handsome, elegant husband. People said that her maidenly shyness was beautiful to behold, and that she clung to her husband like the waving ivy to the oak.

"She did not cling long. She was just nineteen when she was married—she was not twenty when you were born—she was just twenty when they buried her. Oh! I did not think of myself only, but of her, when I heard the saintly youth breathe that plaintive prayer, 'Draw them to thee, for they wearily labor: they are heavily laden, gracious Father! oh, give them rest!'

> " 'No chilling winds or pois'nous breath
> Can reach that healthful shore:
> Sickness and sorrow, pain and death,
> Are felt and fear'd no more.' "

"And my father?" asked Hope, in a low voice.

"He went abroad for many years. Then he returned, and came sometimes to Pinewood. His life was irregular. I think he gambled, for he and your grandfather often had high words in the library about the money that he wanted. But your grandfather never allowed you to leave the place. He rarely spoke of your mother; but I think he often thought of her, and he gradually fell into the habit you remember. Yet he had the same ambition for you that he had had for your mother. He treated me always with stately politeness; but I know that it was a dreary home for a young girl. Hope," said Mrs. Simcoe, after a short pause, "that is all—the end you yourself remember."

"Yes," replied Hope, in the same low, appalled tone, "my father went out upon the pond, one evening, with a friend to bathe, and was drowned. Mr. Gray's boys found him. My grandfather would not let me wear mourning for him. I wore a blue ribbon the day Dr. Peewee preached his funeral sermon; and I did not care to wear black. Aunty, I had seen him too little to love him like a father, you know."

She said it almost as if apologizing to Mrs. Simcoe, who merely bowed her head.

It was past midnight. It was the very moment when Abel Newt was starting with horror as he saw his own reflection in the glass.

Something yet remained to be said between those two women. Each knew it—neither dared to begin.

Hope Wayne closed her eyes with an inward prayer, and then said, calmly, but in a low voice,

"And, aunty, the young man?"

Mrs. Simcoe took Hope's face between her caressing hands. She smoothed the glistening golden hair, and kissed her upon the forehead.

"Aunty, the young man?" said Hope, in the same tone.

"Was Lawrence Newt," answered Mrs. Simcoe.

—It was the moment when Abel sat at his desk writing the name that Mrs. Simcoe had pronounced.

Hope Wayne was perfectly sure it was coming, and yet the word shot out upon her like a tongue of lightning. At first she felt every nerve in her frame relaxed—a mist clouded her eyes—she had a weary sense of happiness, for she thought she was dying. The mist passed. She felt her cheeks glowing, and was preternaturally calm. Mrs. Simcoe sat beside her, weeping silently.

"Good-night, dearest aunty!" said Hope, as she rose and bent down to kiss her.

"My child!" said the older woman, in tones that trembled out of an aching heart.

Hope took her candle, and moved toward the door. As she went she heard Mrs. Simcoe repeating, in the old murmuring sunset strain,

> "Convince us first of unbelief,
> And freely then release;
> Fill every soul with sacred grief,
> And then with sacred peace."

T

CHAPTER LXXVI.

A SOCIAL GLASS.

THE Honorable Abel Newt was elected to Congress in place of the Honorable Watkins Bodley, who withdrew on account of the embarrassment of his private affairs. At a special meeting of the General Committee, Mr. Enos Slugby, Chairman of the Ward Committee, introduced a long and eloquent resolution, deploring the loss sustained by the city and by the whole country in the resignation of the Honorable Watkins Bodley—sympathizing with him in the perplexity of his private affairs—but rejoicing that the word "close up!" was always faithfully obeyed—that there was always a fresh soldier to fill the place of the retiring—and that the Party never summoned her sons in vain.

General Belch then rose and offered a resolution:

"*Resolved*—That in the Honorable Abel Newt, our representative, just elected by a triumphant majority of the votes of the enlightened and independent voters of the district—a constituency of whose favor the most experienced and illustrious statesmen might be proud—we recognize a worthy exemplar of the purest republican virtues, a consistent enemy of a purse-proud aristocracy, the equally unflinching friend of the people; a man who dedicates with enthusiasm the rare powers of his youth, and his profoundest and sincerest convictions, to the great cause of popular rights of which the Party is the exponent.

"*Resolved*—That the Honorable Abel Newt be requested, at the earliest possible moment, to unfold to his fellow-citizens his views upon State and National political affairs."

Mr. William Condor spoke feelingly in support of the resolutions:

"Fellow-citizens!" he said, eloquently, in conclusion, "if

there is one thing nobler than another, it is an upright, down-right, disinterested, honest man. Such I am proud and hap-py to declare my friend, your friend, the friend of all hon-est men, to be; and I call for three cheers for Honest Abel Newt!"

They were given with ardor; and then General Belch was called out for a few remarks, "which he delivered," said the *Evening Banner of the Union*, "with his accustomed humor, keeping the audience in a roar of laughter, and sending every body happy to bed."

The Committee-meeting was over, and the spectators retired to the neighboring bar-rooms. Mr. Slugby, Mr. Condor, and General Belch tarried behind, with two or three more.

"Shall we go to Newt's?" asked the General.

"Yes, I told him we should be round after the meeting," replied Mr. Condor; and the party were presently at his rooms.

The Honorable Abel had placed several full decanters upon the table, with a box of cigars.

"Mr. Newt," said Enos Slugby, after they had been smok-ing and drinking for some time.

Abel turned his head.

"You have an uncle, have you not?"

Abel nodded.

"A very eminent merchant, I believe. His name is very well known, and he commands great respect. Ahem!"

Mr. Slugby cleared his throat; then continued:

"He will naturally be very much interested in the career and success of his nephew."

"Oh, immensely!" replied Abel, in a thick voice, and with a look and tone which suggested to his friends that he was rapidly priming himself. "Immensely, enormously!"

"Ah, yes," said Mr. Slugby, with an air of curious medita-tion. "I do not remember to have heard the character of his political proclivities mentioned. But, of course, as the brother of Boniface Newt and the uncle of the Honorable Abel Newt"
—here Mr. Slugby bowed to that gentleman, who winked at

him over the rim of his glass—" he is naturally a friend of the people."

"Yes," returned Abel.

"I think you said he was very fond of you?" added Mr. Slugby, while his friends looked expectantly on.

"Fond? It's a clear case of apple of the eye," answered Abel, chuckling.

"Very good," said William Condor; "very good, indeed!"

"Capital!" laughed Belch; and whispered to his neighbor Condor, "In vino veritas."

As they whispered, and smiled, and nodded together, Abel Newt glanced around the circle with sullen, fiery eyes.

"Uncle Lawrence is worth a million of dollars," said he, carelessly.

The group of political gentlemen shook their heads in silent admiration. They seemed to themselves to have struck a golden vein, and General Belch could not help inwardly complimenting himself upon his profound sagacity in having put forward a candidate who had a bachelor uncle who doated upon him, and who was worth a million. He perceived at once his own increased importance in the Party. To have displaced Watkins Bodley—who was not only an uncertain party implement, but poor—by an unhesitating young man of great ability and of enormous prospects, he knew was to have secured for himself whatever he chose to ask. The fat nose reddened and glistened as if it would burst with triumph and joy. General Arcularius Belch was satisfied.

"Of course," said William Condor, "a man of Mr. Lawrence Newt's experience and knowledge of the world is aware that there are certain necessary expenses attendant upon elections —such as printing, rent, lighting, warming, posting, etc.—"

"In fact, sundries," said Abel, smiling with the black eyes.

"Yes, precisely; sundries," answered Mr. Condor, "which sometimes swell to quite an inordinate figure. Your uncle, I presume, Mr. Newt, would not be unwilling to contribute a certain share of the expense of your election; and indeed, now that you are so conspicuous a leader, he would probably expect to contribute handsomely to the current expenses of the Party. Isn't it so?"

"Of course," said General Belch.

"Of course," said Enos Slugby.

"Of course," echoed the two or three other gentlemen who sat silently, assiduously smoking and drinking.

"Oh, clearly, of course," answered Abel, still thickly, and in a tone by no means agreeable to his companions. "What should you consider to be his fair share?"

"Well," began Condor, "I should think, in ordinary times, a thousand a year; and then, as particular occasion demands."

At this distinct little speech the whole company lifted their glasses that they might more conveniently watch Abel.

With a half-maudlin grin he looked along the line.

"By-the-by, Condor, how much do you give a year?" asked he.

There was a moment's silence.

"Hit, by G—!" energetically said one of the silent men.

"Good for Newt!" cried General Belch, thumping the table.

There was another little burst of laughter, with the least possible merriment in it. William Condor joined with an entirely unruffled face.

"As for Belch," continued Abel, with what would be called in animals an ugly expression—" Belch is the clown, and they left him off easy. The Party is like the old kings, it keeps a good many fools to make it laugh."

His tone was threatening, and nobody laughed. General Belch looked as if he were restraining himself from knocking his friend down. But they all saw that their host was mastered by his own liquor.

"Squeeze Lawrence Newt, will you? Why, Lord, gentlemen, what do you suppose he thinks of you—I mean, of fellows like you?" asked Abel.

He paused, and glared around him. William Condor daintily knocked off the ash of his cigar with the tip of his little finger, and said, calmly,

"I am sure I don't know."

"Nor care," said General Belch.

"He thinks you're all a set of white-livered sneaks!" shouted Abel, in a voice harsh and hoarse with liquor.

The gentlemen were silent. The leaders wagged their feet nervously; the others looked rather amused.

"No offense," resumed Abel. "I don't mean he despises you in particular, but all bar-room bobtails."

His voice thickened rapidly.

"Of all mean, mis-mis-rabble hounds, he thinks you are the dirt-est."

Still no reply was made. The honorable gentleman looked at his guests leeringly, but found no responsive glance.

"In vino veritas," whispered Condor to his neighbor Belch. William Condor was always clean in linen and calm in manner.

"Don't be 'larmed, fel-fel-f'-low cit-zens! Lawrence Newt's no friend of mine. I guess his G— d— pride 'll get a tumble some day; by G— I do!" Abel added, with a fierce hiss.

The guests looked alarmed as they heard the last words. Abel ceased, and passed the decanter, which they did not decline; for they all felt as if the Honorable Abel Newt would probably throw it at the head of any man who said or did what he did not approve. There was a low anxious murmur of conversation among them until Abel was evidently very intoxicated, and his head sank upon his breast.

"I'm terribly afraid we've burned our fingers," said Mr. Enos Slugby, looking a little ruefully at the honorable representative.

"Oh, I hope not," said General Belch; "but there may be some breakers ahead. If we lose the Grant it won't be the first cause or man that has been betrayed by the bottle. Condor, let me fill your glass. It is clear that if our dear friend Newt has a weakness it is the bottle; and if our enemies at

Washington, who want to head off this Grant, have a strength,
it is finding out an adversary's soft spot. We may find in this
case that it's dangerous playing with edged tools. But I've
great faith in his want of principle. We can show him so
clearly that his interest, his advance, his career depend so entirely upon his conduct, that I think we can keep him straight.
And, for my part, if we can only work this Grant through, I
shall retire upon my share of the proceeds, and leave politics
to those who love 'em. But I don't mean to have worked for
nothing—hey, Condor?"

"Amen," replied William, placidly.

"By-the-by, Condor," said Mr. Enos Slugby.

Mr. Condor turned toward him inquiringly.

"I heard Jim say t'other day—"

"Who's Jim?" asked Condor.

"Jim!" returned Slugby, "Jim—why, Jim's the party in
my district."

"Oh yes—yes; I beg pardon," said Condor; "the name
had escaped me."

"Well, I heard Jim say t'other day that Mr. William Condor was getting 'too d—d stuck up,' and that he'd yank him
out of his office if he didn't mind his eye. That's you, Condor; so I advise you to look out. It's easy enough to manage Jim, if you take care. He'll go as gently as a well-broke
filly; but if he once takes a lurch—if he thinks you're too
'proud' or 'big,' it's all up with you. So mind how you treat
Jim."

"Well, well," said Belch, impatiently; "we've other business on hand now."

"Exactly," said Condor; "we are the Honorable Abel's
Jim. Turn about is fair play. Jim makes us go; we make
Abel go. It's a lovely series of checks and balances."

He said it so quietly and airily that they all laughed. Then
the General continued:

"We're going to send Newt to look after Ele, and I rather
think we shall have to send somebody to look after Newt.

However, we'll see. Let's leave this hog to snore by him-self."

They rose as he spoke.

"What were the words of your resolution, Belch?" asked William Condor, with his eyes twinkling. "I don't quite re-member. Did you say," he added, looking at Abel, who lay huddled, dead drunk, in his chair, "that he dedicated to his country his profoundest and sincerest, or sincerest and pro-foundest convictions?"

"And you, Condor," said Enos Slugby, smiling, as he light-ed a fresh cigar, "did you say that you were proud and hap-py, or happy and proud, to call him your friend?"

"Lord! Lord! what an old hum it is—isn't it?" said Gen-eral Belch, cheerfully, as he smoothed his hat with his coat-sleeve, and put it on.

They went down stairs laughing and chatting; and the Honorable Abel Newt, the worthy exemplar of the purest re-publican virtues—as the resolution stated when it appeared in the next morning's papers—was left snoring amidst his con-stituency of empty decanters and drained glasses.

CHAPTER LXXVII.

FACE TO FACE.

"Signor Pittore! what brings a bird into the barn-yard?" said Lawrence Newt as Arthur Merlin entered his office.

"The hope of some crumb of comfort."

"Do you dip from your empyrean to the cold earth—from the studio to a counting-room—to find comfort?" asked Law-rence Newt, cheerfully.

Arthur Merlin looked only half sympathetic with his friend's gayety. There was a wan air on his face, a piteous look in his eyes, which touched Lawrence.

"Why, Arthur, what is it?"

"Do you remember what Diana said?" replied the painter. "She said, 'I am sure that that silly shepherd will not sleep there forever. Never fear, he will wake up. Diana never looks or loves for nothing.'"

Lawrence Newt gazed at him without speaking.

"Come," said Arthur, with a feeble effort at fun, "you have correspondence all over the world. What is the news from Latmos? Has the silly shepherd waked up?"

"My dear Arthur," said Mr. Newt, gravely, "I told you long ago that he was dead to all that heavenly splendor."

The two men gazed steadfastly at each other without speaking. At length Arthur said, in a low voice,

"Dead?"

"Dead."

As Lawrence Newt spoke the word the air far off and near seemed to him to ring again with that pervasive murmur, sad, soft, infinitely tender, "Good-by, Mr. Newt, good-by!"

But his eye was calm and his face cheerful.

"Arthur, sit down."

The young man seated himself, and the older one drawing a chair to the window, they sat with their backs to the outer office and looked upon the ships.

"I am older than you, Arthur, and I am your friend. What I am going to say to you I have no right to say, except in your entire friendship."

The young man's eyes glistened.

"Go on," he said.

"When I first knew you I knew that you loved Hope Wayne."

A flush deepened upon Arthur's face, and his fingers played idly upon the arm of the chair.

"I hoped that Hope Wayne would love you. I was sure that she would. It never occurred to me that she could—could—"

Arthur turned and looked at him.

"Could love any body else," said Lawrence Newt, as his

eyes wandered dreamily among the vessels, as if the canvas were the wings of his memory sailing far away.

"Suddenly, without the least suspicion on my part, I discovered that she did love somebody else."

"Yes," said Arthur, "so did I."

"What could I do?" said the other, still abstractedly gazing; "for I loved her."

"You loved her?" cried Arthur Merlin, so suddenly and loud that Thomas Tray looked up from his great red Russia book and turned his head toward the inner office.

"Certainly I loved her," replied Lawrence Newt, calmly, and with tender sweetness; "and I had a right to, for I loved her mother. Could I have had my way Hope Wayne's mother would have been my wife."

Arthur Merlin stole a glance at the face of his companion.

"I was a child and she was a child—a boy and a girl. It was not to be. She married another man and died; but her memory is forever sacred to me, and so is her daughter."

To this astonishing revelation Arthur Merlin said nothing. His fingers still played idly on the chair, and his eyes, like the eyes of Lawrence, looked out upon the river. Every thing in Lawrence Newt's conduct was at once explained; and the poor artist was ready to curse his absurd folly in making his friend involuntarily sit for Endymion. Lawrence Newt knew his friend's thoughts.

"Arthur," he said, in a low voice, "did I not say that, if Endymion were not dead, it would be impossible not to awake and love her? Do you not see that I was dead to her?"

"But does she know it?" asked the painter.

"I believe she does now," was the slow answer. "But she has not known it long."

"Does Amy Waring know it?"

"No," replied Lawrence Newt, quietly, "but she will tonight."

The two men sat silently together for some time. The junior partner came in, spoke to Arthur, wrote a little, and went out again. Thomas Tray glanced up occasionally from his great volume, and the melancholy eyes of Little Malacca scarcely turned from the two figures which he watched from his desk through the office windows. Venables was promoted to be second to Thomas Tray on the very day that Gabriel was admitted a junior partner. They were all aware that the head of the house was engaged in some deeply interesting conversation, and they learned from Little Malacca who the stranger was.

The two men sat silently together, Lawrence Newt evidently tranquilly waiting, Arthur Merlin vainly trying to say something further.

"I wonder—" he began, at length, and stopped. A painful expression of doubt clouded his face; but Lawrence turned to him cheerfully, and said, in a frank, assuring tone,

"Arthur, speak out."

"Well," said the artist, with almost a girl's shyness in his whole manner, "before you, at least, I can speak, and am not ashamed. I want to know whether—you—think—"

He spoke very slowly, and stopped again. Before he resumed he saw Lawrence Newt shake his head negatively.

"Why, what?" asked Arthur, quickly.

"I do not believe she ever will," replied the other, as if the artist had asked a question with his eyes. He spoke in a very low, serious tone.

"Will what?" asked Arthur, his face burning with a bright crimson flush.

Lawrence Newt waited a moment, to give his friend time to recover, before he said,

"Shall I say what?"

Arthur also waited for a little while; then he said, sadly,

"No, it's no matter."

He seemed to have grown older as he sat looking from the window. His hands idly played no longer, but rested quietly upon the chair. He shook his head slowly, and repeated, in a tone that touched his friend to the heart,

" No—no—it's no matter."

" But, Arthur, it's only my opinion," said the other, kindly.

" And mine too," replied the artist, with an inexpressible sadness.

Lawrence Newt was silent. After a few moments Arthur Merlin rose and shook his hand.

" Good-by !" he said. " We shall meet to-night."

CHAPTER LXXVIII.

FINISHING PICTURES.

ARTHUR MERLIN returned to his studio and carefully locked the door. Then he opened a huge port-folio, which was full of sketches—and they were all of the same subject, treated in a hundred ways—they were all Hope Wayne.

Sometimes it was a lady leaning from an oriel window in a medieval tower, listening in the moonlight, with love in her eyes and attitude, to the music of a guitar, touched by a gallant knight below, who looked as Arthur Merlin would have looked had Arthur Merlin been a gallant medieval knight.

Then it was Juliet, pale and unconscious in the tomb; superb in snow-white drapery ; pure as an angel, lovely as a woman ; but it was Hope Wayne still—and Romeo stole frightened in, but Romeo was Arthur.

Or it was Beatrice moving in a radiant heaven; while far below, kneeling, and with clasped hands, gazing upward, the melancholy Dante watched the vision.

Or the fair phantom of Goëthe's ballad looked out with humid, passionate glances between the clustering reeds she pushed aside, and lured the fisherman with love.

There were scores of such sketches, from romance, and history, and fancy, and in each the beauty was Hope Wayne's ; and it was strange to see that in each, however different from all the others, there was still a charm characteristic of the woman he loved; so that it seemed a vivid record of all the impressions she had made upon him, and as if all heroines of poetry or history were only ladies in waiting upon her. In all of them, too, there was a separation between them. She was remote in sphere or in space; there was the feeling of inaccessibility between them in all.

As he turned them slowly over, and gazed at them as earnestly as if his glance could make that beauty live, he suddenly perceived, what he had never before felt, that the instinct which had unconsciously given the same character of hopelessness to the incident of the sketches was the same that had made him so readily acquiesce in what Lawrence Newt had hinted. He paused at a drawing of Pygmalion and his statue. The same instinct had selected the moment before the sculptor's prayer was granted; when he looks at the immovable beauty of his statue with the yearning love that made the marble live. But the statue of Arthur's Pygmalion would never live. It was a statue only, and forever. He asked himself why he had not selected the moment when she falls breathing and blushing into the sculptor's arms.

Alone in his studio the artist blushed, as if the very thought were wrong; and he felt that he had never really dared to hope, however he had longed, and wished, and flattered his fancy.

He looked at each one of the drawings carefully and long, then kissed it and turned it upon its face. When he had seen them all he sat for a moment; then quietly tore them into long strips, then into small pieces; and, lifting the window, scattered them upon the air. The wind whirled them over the street.

"Oh, what a pretty snow-storm!" said the little street children, looking up.

Then Arthur Merlin turned to his great easel, upon which stood the canvas of the picture of Diana and Endymion. Through the parted clouds the face of the Queen and huntress —the face of Hope Wayne—looked tenderly upon the sleep-

THE SOLITARY GRAVE ON THE HILL-TOP.

ing figure of the shepherd on the bare top of the grassy hill—
the face and figure of Lawrence Newt.

The painter took his brushes and his pallet, and his maul-
stick. He paused for some time again, as he stood before the
easel, then he went quietly to work. He touched it here and
there. He stepped back to mark the effect—rubbed with his

finger — sighed — stepped back — and still worked on. The hours glided away, and daylight began to fade, but not until he had finished his work.

Then he scraped his pallet and washed his brushes, and seated himself upon the sofa opposite the easel. There was no picture of Diana or of Endymion any longer. In the place of Diana there was a full summer moon shining calmly in a cloudless heaven. Its benignant light fell upon a solitary grave upon a hill-top, which filled the spot where Endymion had lain.

Arthur Merlin sat in the corner of the sofa with folded arms, looking at the picture, until the darkness entirely hid it from view.

CHAPTER LXXIX.

THE LAST THROW.

WHILE Arthur and Lawrence were conversing in the office of the latter, Abel Newt, hat in hand, stood in Hope Wayne's parlor. His hair was thinner and grizzled; his face bloated, and his eyes dull. His hands had that dead, chalky color in which appetite openly paints its excesses. The hand trembled as it held the hat; and as the man stood before the mirror, he was straining his eyes at his own reflection, and by some secret magic he saw, as if dimly traced beside it, the figure of the boy that stood in the parlor of Pinewood—how many thousand years ago?

He heard a step, and turned.

Hope Wayne stopped, leaving the door open, bowed, and looked inquiringly at him. She was dressed simply in a morning dress, and her golden hair clustered and curled around the fresh beauty of her face—the rose of health.

"Did you wish to say something to me?" she asked, observing that Abel merely stared at her stupidly.

He bowed his head in assent.

"What do you wish to say?"

Her voice was as cold and remote as if she were a spirit.

Abel Newt was evidently abashed by the reception. But he moved toward her, and began in a tone of doubtful familiarity.

"Miss Hope, I—"

"Mr. Newt, you have no right to address me in that way."

"Miss Wayne, I have come to—to—"

He stopped, embarrassed, rubbing his fingers upon the palms of his hands. She looked at him steadily. He waited a few moments, then began again in a hurried tone:

"Miss Wayne, we are both older than we once were; and once, I think, we were not altogether indifferent to each other. Time has taught us many things. I find that my heart, after foolish wanderings, is still true to its first devotion. We can both view things more calmly, not less truly, however, than we once did. I am upon the eve of a public career. I have outgrown morbid emotions, and I come to ask you if you would take time to reflect whether I might not renew my addresses; for indeed I love, and can love, no other woman."

Hope Wayne stood pale, incredulous, and confounded while Abel Newt, with some of the old fire in the eye and the old sweetness in the voice, poured out these rapid words, and advanced toward her.

"Stop, Sir," she said, as soon as she could command herself. "Is this all you have to say?"

"Don't drive me to despair," he said, suddenly, in reply, and so fiercely that Hope Wayne started. "Listen." He spoke with stern command.

"I am utterly ruined. I have no friends. I have bad habits. You can save me—will you do it?"

Hope stood before him silent. His hard black eye was fixed upon her with a kind of defying appeal for help. Her state of mind for some days, since she had heard Mrs. Simcoe's story, had been one of curious mental tension. She was inspired by a sense of renunciation—of self-sacrifice. It seemed to her that some great work to do, something which should occupy every moment, and all her powers and thoughts, was her only hope of contentment. What it might be, what it ought to be, she had not conceived. Was it not offered now? Horrible, repulsive, degrading—yes, but was it not so much the worthier? Here stood the man she had loved in all the prime and power of his youth, full of hope, and beauty, and vigor—the hero that satisfied the girl's longing—and he was bent, gray, wan, shaking, utterly lost, except for her. Should she restore him to that lost manhood? Could she forgive herself if she suffered her own feelings, tastes, pride, to prevent?

While the thought whirled through her excited brain:

"Remember," he said, solemnly—"remember it is the salvation of a human soul upon which you are deciding."

There was perfect silence for some minutes. The low, quick ticking of the clock upon the mantle was all they heard.

"I have decided," she said, at last.

"What is it?" he asked, under his breath.

"What you knew it would be," she answered.

"Then you refuse?" he said, in a half-threatening tone.

"I refuse!"

"Then the damnation of a soul rest upon your head for, ever," he said, in a loud coarse voice, crushing his hat, and his black eyes glaring.

"Have you done?" she asked, pale and calm.

"No, Hope Wayne, I have not done; I am not deceived by your smooth face and your quiet eyes. I have known long enough that you meant to marry my Uncle Lawrence, although he is old enough to be your father. The whole world has known it and seen it. And I came to give you a chance of saving your name by showing to the world that my uncle came here familiarly because you were to marry his nephew. You refuse the chance. There was a time when you would have flown into my arms, and now you reject me. And I shall have my revenge! I warn you to beware, Mrs. Law-

"THE DOOM OF MY SOUL BE UPON YOURS!"

rence Newt! I warn you that my saintly uncle is not beyond
misfortune, nor his milksop partner, the Reverend Gabriel
Bennet. I am a man at bay; and it is you who put me there;
you who might save me and won't. You who will one day
remember and suffer."

He threw up his arms in uncontrollable rage and excitement. His thick hoarse voice, his burning, bad, black eyes,
his quivering hands, his bloated body, made him a terrible
spectacle.

"Have you done?" asked Hope Wayne, with saintly dignity.

"Yes, I have done for this time," he hissed; "but I shall cross you many a time. You and yours," he sneered, "but never so that you can harm me. You shall feel, but never see me. You have left me nothing but despair. And the doom of my soul be upon yours!"

He rushed from the room, and Hope Wayne stood speechless. Attracted by the loud tone of his voice, Mrs. Simcoe had come down stairs, and the moment he was gone she was by Hope's side. They seated themselves together upon the sofa, and Hope leaned her head upon her aunty's shoulder and wept with utter surprise, grief, indignation, and weariness.

CHAPTER LXXX.

CLOUDS BREAKING.

THE next morning Amy Waring came to Hope Wayne radiant with the prospect of her Aunt Martha's restoration to the world. Hope shook her hand warmly, and looked into her friend's illuminated face.

"She is engaged to Lawrence Newt," said Hope, in her heart, as she kissed Amy's lips.

"God bless you, Amy!" she added, with so much earnestness that Amy looked surprised.

"I am very glad," said Hope, frankly.

"Why, what do you know about it?" asked Amy.

"Do you think I am blind?" said Hope.

"No; but no eyes could see it, it was so hidden."

"It can't be hidden," said Hope, earnestly.

Amy stopped, looked inquiringly at her friend, and blushed —wondering what she meant.

"Come, Hope, at least we are hiding from each other. I came to ask you to a family festival."

"I am ready," answered Hope, with an air of quiet knowl-

edge, and not at all surprised. Amy Waring was confused,
she hardly knew why.

"Why, Hope, I mean only that Lawrence Newt—"

Hope Wayne smiled so tenderly and calmly, and with such
tranquil consciousness that she knew every thing Amy was
about to say, that Amy stopped again.

"Go on," said Hope, placidly; "I want to hear it from
your own lips."

Amy Waring was in doubt no longer. She knew that Hope
expected to hear that she was engaged. And not with less
placidity than Hope's, she said:

"Lawrence Newt wants us all to come and dine with him,
because my Aunt Martha is found, and he wishes to bring
Aunt Bennet and her together."

That was all. Hope looked as confusedly at the calm Amy
as Amy, a moment since, had looked at her. Then they both
smiled, for they had, perhaps, some vague idea of what each
had been thinking.

The same evening the Round Table met. Arthur Merlin
came early—so did Hope Wayne. They sat together talking
rapidly, but Hope did not escape observing the unusual sadness of the artist—a sadness of manner rather than of expression. In a thousand ways there was a deference in his treatment of her which was unusual and touching. She had been
very sure that he had understood what she meant when she
spoke to him with an air of badinage about his picture. And
certainly it was plain enough. It was clear enough; only he
would not see what was before his eyes, nor hear what was
in his ears, and so had to grope a little further until Lawrence
Newt suddenly struck a light and showed him where he was.

While they were yet talking Lawrence Newt came in.
He spoke to Amy Waring, and then went straight up to Hope
Wayne and put out his hand with the old frank smile breaking over his face. She rose and answered his smile, and laid
her hand in his. They looked in each other's eyes; and Lawrence Newt saw in Hope Wayne's the beauty of a girl that

long ago, as a boy, he had loved; and in his own, Hope felt that tenderness which had made her mother's happiness.

It was but a moment. It was but a word. For the first time he said,

"Hope."

And for the first time she answered,

"Lawrence."

Amy Waring heard them. The two words seemed sharp: they pierced her heart, and she felt faint. The room swam, but she bit her lip till the blood came, and her stout heart preserved her from falling.

"It is what I knew: they are engaged."

But how was it that the manner of Lawrence Newt toward herself was never before more loyal and devoted? How was it that the quiet hilarity of the morning was not gone, but stole into his conversation with her so pointedly that she could not help feeling that it magnetized her, and that, against her will, she was more than ever cheerful? How was it that she knew it was herself who helped make that hilarity—that it was not only her friend Hope who inspired it?

They are secrets not to be told. But as they all sat around the table, and Arthur Merlin for the first time insisted upon reading from Byron, and in his rich melancholy voice recited

"Though the day of my destiny's over,"

it was clear that the cloud had lifted—that the spell of constraint was removed; and yet none of them precisely understood why.

"To-morrow, then," said Lawrence Newt as they parted.

"To-morrow," echoed Amy Waring and Hope Wayne.

Arthur Merlin pulled his cap over his eyes and sauntered slowly homeward, whistling musingly, and murmuring,

"A bird in the wilderness singing,
That speaks to my spirit of thee."

His Aunt Winnifred heard him as he came in. The good

old lady had placed a fresh tract where he would be sure to see it when he entered his room. She heard his cautious step stealing up stairs, for the painter was careful to make no noise; and as she listened she drew pictures upon her fancy of the scenes in which her boy had been mingling. It was Aunt Winnifred's firm conviction that society — that is, the great world of which she knew nothing—languished for the smile and presence of her nephew, Arthur. That very evening her gossip, Mrs. Toxer, had been in, and Aunt Winnifred had discussed her favorite theme until Mrs. Toxer went home with a vague idea that all the young and beautiful unmarried women in the city were secretly pining away for love of Arthur Merlin.

"Mercy me, now!" said Aunt Winnifred as she lay listening to the creaking step of her nephew. "I wonder what poor girl's heart that wicked boy has been breaking to-night;" and she turned over and fell asleep again.

That young man reached his room and struck a light. It flashed upon a paper. He took it up eagerly, then smiled as he saw that it was a tract, and read, "A word to the Unhappy."

"Dear Aunt Winnifred!" said he to himself; "does she think a man's griefs are like a child's bumps and bruises, to be cured by applying a piece of paper?"

He smiled sadly, with the profound conviction that no man had ever before really known what unhappiness was, and so tumbled into bed and fell asleep. And as he dreamed, Hope Wayne came to him and smiled, as Diana smiled in his picture upon Endymion.

"See!" she said, "I love you; look here!"

And in his dream he looked and saw a full moon in a summer sky shining upon a fresh grave upon a hill-top.

CHAPTER LXXXI.

MRS. ALFRED DINKS AT HOME.

A NEW element had forced itself into the life of Hope Wayne, and that was the fate of Abel Newt. There was something startling in the direct, passionate, personal appeal he had made to her. She put on her bonnet and furs, for it was Christmas time, and passed the Bowery into the small, narrow street where the smell of the sewer was the chief odor and the few miserable trees cooped up in perforated boxes had at last been released from suffering, and were placidly, rigidly dead.

The sloppy servant girl was standing upon the area steps with her apron over her head, and blowing her huge red fingers, staring at every thing, and apparently stunned when Hope Wayne stopped and went up the steps. Hope rang, entered the little parlor and seated herself upon the hair-cloth sofa. Her heart ached with the dreariness of the house; but while she was resolving that she would certainly raise her secret allowance to her Cousin Alfred, whether her good friend Lawrence Newt approved of it or not, she saw that the dreariness was not in the small room or the hair sofa, nor in the two lamps with glass drops upon the mantle, but in the lack of that indescribable touch of feminine taste, and tact, and tenderness, which create comfort and grace wherever they fall, and make the most desolate chambers to blossom with cheerfulness. Hope felt as she glanced around her that money could not buy what was wanting.

Mrs. Alfred Dinks presently entered. Hope Wayne had rarely met her since the season at Saratoga when Fanny had captured her prize. She saw that the black-eyed, clever, resolute girl of those days had grown larger and more pulpy, and was wrapped in a dingy morning wrapper. Her hair was not smooth, her hands were not especially clean; she had that dull carelessness, or unconsciousness of personal appearance, which seemed to Hope only the parlor aspect of the dowdiness that had run entirely to seed in the sloppy servant girl upon the area steps.

Hope Wayne put out her hand, which Fanny listlessly took. There was nothing very hard, or ferocious, or defiant in her manner, as Hope had expected—there was only a weariness and indifference, as if she had been worsted in some kind of struggle. She did not even seem to be excited by seeing Hope Wayne in her house, but merely said, " Good-morning," and then sank quietly upon the sofa, as if she had said every thing she had to say.

" I came to ask you if you know any thing about Abel?" said Hope.

" No; nothing in particular," replied Fanny; " I believe he's going to Congress; but I never see him or hear of him."

" Doesn't Alfred see him?"

" He used to meet him at Thiel's; but Alfred doesn't go there much now. It's too fine for poor gentlemen. I remember some time ago I saw he had a black eye, and he said that he and my ' d— brother Abel,' as he elegantly expressed it, · had met somewhere the night before, and Abel was drunk and gave him the lie, and they fought it out. I think, by-the-way, that's the last I've heard of brother Abel."

There was a slight touch of the old manner in the tone with which Fanny ended her remark; after which she relapsed into the previous half-apathetic condition.

" Fanny, I wish I could do something for Abel."

Fanny Dinks looked at Hope Wayne with an incredulous smile, and said,

" I thought once you would marry him; and so did he, I fancy."

" What does he do? and how can I reach him?" asked Hope, entirely disregarding Fanny's remark.

" He lives at the old place in Grand Street, I believe; the

Lord knows how; I'm sure I don't. I suppose he gambles when he isn't drunk."

"But about Congress?" inquired Hope.

"I don't know any thing about that. Abel and father used to say that no gentleman would ever have any thing to do with politics; so I never heard any thing, and I'm sure I don't know what he's going to do."

Fanny apparently supposed her last remark would end the conversation. Not that she wished to end it—not that she was sorry to see Hope Wayne again and to talk with her—not that she wanted or cared for any thing in particular, no, not even for her lord and master, who burst into the room with an oath, as usual, and with his small, swinish eyes heavy with drowsiness.

The master of the house was evidently just down. He wore a dirty morning-gown, and slippers down at the heel, displaying his dirty stockings. He came in yawning and squeezing his eyes together.

"Why the h— don't that slut of a waiter have my coffee ready?" he said to his wife, who paid no more attention to him than to the lamp on the mantle, but, on the contrary, appeared to Hope to be a little more indifferent than before.

"I say, why the h—" Mr. Dinks began again, and had advanced so far when he suddenly saw his cousin.

"Hallo! what are you doing here?" he said to her abruptly, and in the half-sycophantic, half-bullying tone that indicates the feeling of such a man toward a person to whom he is under immense obligation. Alfred Dinks's real feeling was that Hope Wayne ought to give him a much larger allowance.

Hope was inexpressibly disgusted; but she found an excitement in encountering this boorishness, which served to stimulate her in the struggle going on in her own soul. And she very soon understood how the sharp, sparkling, audacious Fanny Newt had become the inert, indifferent woman before her. A clever villain might have developed her, through admiration and sympathy, into villainy; but a dull, heavy brute merely crushed her. There is a spur in the prick of a rapier; only stupidity follows the blow of a club.

After sitting silently for some minutes, during which Alfred Dinks sprawled in a chair, and yawned, and whistled insolently to himself, while Fanny sat without looking at him, as if she were deaf and dumb, Hope Wayne said to the husband and wife:

"Abel Newt is ruining himself, and he may harm other people. If there is any thing that can be done to save him we ought to do it. Fanny, he is your own flesh and blood."

She spoke with a kind of despairing earnestness, for Hope herself felt how useless every thing would probably be. But when she had ended Alfred broke out into uproarious laughter,

"Ho! ho! ho! Ho! ho! ho!"

He made such a noise that even his wife looked at him with almost a glance of contempt.

"Save Abel Newt!" cried he. "Convert the Devil! Yes, yes; let's send him some tracts! Ho! ho! ho!"

And he roared again until the water oozed from his eyes.

Hope Wayne scarcely looked at him. She rose to go; but it seemed to her pitiful to leave Fanny Newt in such utter desolation of soul and body, in which she seemed to her to be gradually sinking into idiocy. She went to Fanny and took her hand. Fanny listlessly rose, and when Hope had done shaking hands Fanny crossed them before her inanely, but in an unconsciously appealing attitude, which Hope saw and felt. Alfred still sprawled in his chair, laughing at intervals; and Hope left the room, followed by Fanny, who shuffled after her, her slippers, evidently down at the heel, pattering on the worn oil-cloth in the entry as she shambled toward the front door. Hope opened it. The morning was pleasant, though cool, and the air refreshing after the odor of mingled grease and stale tobacco-smoke which filled the house.

As they passed out, Fanny quietly sat down upon the step, leaned her chin upon one hand, and looked up and down

the street, which, it seemed to Hope, offered a prospect that
would hardly enliven her mind. There was something more
touching to Hope in this dull apathy than in the most positive
grief.

"Fanny Newt!" she said to her, suddenly.

Fanny lifted her lazy eyes.

"If I can do nothing for your brother, can I do nothing for
you? You will rust out, Fanny, if you don't take care."

Fanny smiled languidly.

"What if I do?" she answered.

Thereupon Hope sat down by her, and told her just what
she meant, and what she hoped, and what she would do if she
would let her. And the eager young woman drew such pleasant pictures of what was yet possible to Fanny, although she
was the wife of Alfred Dinks, that, as if the long-accumula-
ting dust and ashes were blown away from her soul, and it began to kindle again in a friendly breath, Fanny felt herself
moved and interested. She smiled, looked grave, and finally
laid her head upon Hope's shoulder and cried good, honest
tears of utter weariness and regret.

"And now," said Hope, "will you help me about Abel?"

"I really don't see that you can do any thing," said Fanny,
"nor any body else. Perhaps he'll get a new start in Congress, though I don't know any thing about it."

Hope Wayne shook her head thoughtfully.

"No," she said, "I see no way. I can only be ready to be-
friend him if the chance offers."

They said no more of him then, but Hope persuaded Fanny to come to Lawrence Newt's Christmas dinner, to which
they had all been bidden. "And I will make him understand
about it," she said, as she went down the steps.

Mrs. Dinks sat upon the door-step for some time. There
was nobody to see her whom she knew, and if there had been
she would not have cared. She did not know how long she
had been sitting there, for she was thinking of other things,
but she was roused by hearing her husband's voice:

AFTER THE CALL.

"Well, by G—! that's a G— d— pretty business—squat-
ting on a door-step like a servant girl! Come in, I tell you,
and shut the door."

From long habit Fanny did not pay the least attention to
this order. But after some time she rose and closed the door,
and clattered along the entry and up stairs, upon the worn
and ragged carpet. Mr. Alfred Dinks returned to the parlor,
pulled the bell violently, and when the sloppy servant girl appeared, glaring at him with the staring eyes, he immediately

damned them, and wanted to know why in h— he was kept
waiting for his boots. The staring eyes vanished, and Mr.
Dinks reclined upon the sofa, picking his teeth. Presently
there was the slop—slop—slop of the girl along the entry.
She opened the door, dropped the boots, and fled. Mr. Dinks
immediately pulled the bell violently, walking across the room
a greater distance than to his boots. Slop—slop again. The
door opened.

"Look here! If you don't bring me my boots, I'll come
and pull the hair out of your head!" roared the master of the
house.

The cowering little creature dashed at the boots with a wo-
begone look, and brought them to the sofa. Mr. Dinks took
them in his hand, and turned them round contemptuously.

"G—! You call those boots blacked?"

He scratched his head a moment, enjoying the undisguised
terror of the puny girl.

"If you don't black 'em better—if you don't put a brighter
shine on to 'em, I'll—I'll—I'll put a shine on your face, you
slut!"

The girl seemed to be all terrified eye as she looked at him,
and then fled again, while he laughed.

"Ho! ho! ho! I'll teach 'em how—insolent curs! G—
d— Paddies! What business have they coming over here?
Ho! ho! ho!"

Leaving his slippers upon the parlor floor, Mr. Dinks mount-
ed to his room and changed his coat. He tried the door of
his wife's room as he passed out, and found it locked. He
kicked it violently, and bawled,

"Good-morning, Mrs. Dinks! If Miss Wayne calls, tell her
I've gone to tell Mr. Abel Newt that she repents, and wants
to marry him; and I shall add that, having been through the
wood, she picks up a crooked stick at last. Ho! ho! ho!
(Kick.) Good-morning, Mrs. Dinks!"

He went heavily down stairs and slammed the front door,
and was gone for the day.

When they were first married, after the bitter conviction that there was really no hope of old Burt's wealth, Fanny Dinks had carried matters with a high hand, domineering by her superior cleverness, and with a superiority that stung and exasperated her husband at every turn. Her bitter temper had gradually entirely eaten away the superficial, stupid good-humor of his younger days; and her fury of disappointment, carried into the detail of life, had gradually confirmed him in all his worst habits and obliterated the possibility of better. But the sour, superior nature was, as usual, unequal to the struggle. At last it spent itself in vain against the massive brutishness of opposition it had itself developed, and the re-action came, and now daily stunned her into hopeless apathy and abject indifference. Having lost the power of vexing, and beyond being really vexed by a being she so utterly despised as her husband, there was nothing left but pure passivity and inanition, into which she was rapidly declining.

Mr. Dinks kicked loudly and roared at the door, but Mrs. Dinks did not heed him. She was sitting in her dingy wrapper, rocking, and pondering upon the conversation of the morning—mechanically rocking, and thinking of the Christmas dinner at Uncle Lawrence's.

CHAPTER LXXXII.

THE LOST IS FOUND.

It was a whim of Lawrence's to give dinners; to have them good, and to ask only the people he wanted, and who he thought would enjoy themselves together.

"How much," he said, quietly, as he conversed with Mrs. Bennet, while his guests were assembling, "Edward Wynne looks like your sister Martha!"

It was the first time Mrs. Bennet had heard her sister's name mentioned by any stranger for years. But Lawrence spoke as calmly and naturally as if Martha Darro had been the subject of their conversation.

"Poor Martha!" said Mrs. Bennet, sadly; "how mysterious it was!"

Her husband saw her as she spoke, and he was so struck by the mournfulness of her face that he came quietly over.

"What is it?" he said, gently.

"For my son who was dead is alive again. He was lost and is found," said Lawrence Newt, solemnly.

Mrs. Bennet looked troubled, startled, almost frightened. The words were full of significance, the tone was not to be mistaken. She looked at Lawrence Newt with incredulous eagerness. He shook his head assentingly.

"Alive?" she gasped rather than asked.

"And well," he continued.

Mrs. Bennet closed her eyes in a silent prayer. A light so sweet stole over her matronly face that Lawrence Newt did not fear to say,

"And near you; come with me!"

They left the room together; and Amy Waring, who knew why they went, followed her aunt and Lawrence from the room.

The three stopped at the door of Lawrence Newt's study.

"Your sister is here," said he; and Amy and he remained outside while Mrs. Bennet entered the room.

It was more than twenty years since the sisters had met, and they clasped each other silently and wept for a long time.

"Martha!"

"Lucia!"

It was all they said; and wept again quietly.

Aunt Martha was dressed in sober black. Her face was very comely; for the hardness that came with a morbid and mistaken zeal was mellowed, and the sadness of experience softened it.

"I have lived not far from you, Lucia, all these long years."

"Martha! and you did not come to me?"

"I did not dare. Listen, Lucia. If a woman who had always gratified her love of admiration, and gloried in the power of gratifying it—who conquered men and loved to conquer them—who was a woman of ungoverned will and indomitable pride, should encounter—as how often they do?—a man who utterly conquered her, and betrayed her through the very weakness that springs from pride, do you not see that such a woman would go near to insanity—as I have been—believing that I had committed the unpardonable sin, and that no punishment could be painful enough?"

Mrs. Bennet looked alarmed.

"No, no; there is no reason," said her sister, observing it.

"The man came. I could not resist him. There was a form of marriage. I believed that it was I who had conquered. He left me; my child was born. I appealed to Lawrence Newt, our old friend and playmate. He promised me faithful secrecy, and through him the child was sent where Gabriel was at school. Then I withdrew from both. I thought it was the will of God. I felt myself commanded to a living death—dead to every friend and kinsman—dead to every thing but my degradation and its punishment; and yet consciously close to you, near to all old haunts and familiar faces—lost to them all—lost to my child—" Her voice faltered, and the tears gushed from her eyes. "But I persevered. The old passionate pride was changed to a kind of religious frenzy. Lawrence Newt went and came to and from India. I was utterly lost to the world. I knew that my child would never know me, for Lawrence had promised that he would not betray me; and when I disappeared from his view, Lawrence gradually came to consider me dead. Then Amy discovered me among the poor souls she visited, and through Amy Lawrence Newt; and by them I have been led out of the valley of the shadow of death, and see the blessed light of love once more."

She bowed her head in uncontrollable emotion.

"And your son?" said her sister, half-smiling through her sympathetic tears.

"Will be yours also, Amy tells me," said Aunt Martha. "Thank God! thank God!"

"Martha, who gave him his name?" asked Mrs. Bennet.

Aunt Martha paused for a little while. Then she said:

"You never knew who my—my—husband was?"

"Never."

"I remember—he never came to the house. Well, I gave my child almost his father's name. I called him Wynne; his father's name was Wayne."

Mrs. Bennet clasped her hands in her lap.

"How wonderful! how wonderful!" was all she said.

Lawrence Newt knocked at the door, and Amy and he came in. There was so sweet and strange a light upon Amy's face that Mrs. Bennet looked at her in surprise. Then she looked at Lawrence Newt; and he cheerfully returned her glance with that smiling, musing expression in his eyes that was utterly bewildering to Mrs. Bennet. She could only look at each of the persons before her, and repeat her last words:

"How wonderful! how wonderful!"

Amy Waring, who had not heard the previous conversation between her two aunts, blushed as she heard these words, as if Mrs. Bennet had been alluding to something in which Amy was particularly interested.

"Amy," said Mrs. Bennet.

Amy could scarcely raise her eyes. There was an exquisite maidenly shyness overspreading her whole person. At length she looked the response she could not speak.

"How could you?" asked her aunt.

Poor Amy was utterly unable to reply.

"Coming and going in my house, my dearest niece, and yet hugging such a secret, and holding your tongue. Oh Amy, Amy!"

These were the words of reproach; but the tone, and look, and impression were of entire love and sympathy. Lawrence Newt looked calmly on.

"Aunt Lucia, what could I do?" was all that Amy could say.

"Well, well, I do not reproach you; I blame nobody. I am too glad and happy. It is too wonderful, wonderful!"

There was a fullness and intensity of emphasis in what she said that apparently made Amy suspect that she had not correctly understood her aunt's intention.

"Oh, you mean about Aunt Martha!" said Amy, with an air of relief and surprise.

Lawrence Newt smiled. Mrs. Bennet turned to Amy with a fresh look of inquiry.

"About Aunt Martha? Of course about Aunt Martha. Why, Amy, what on earth did you suppose it was about?"

Again the overwhelming impossibility to reply. Mrs. Bennet was very curious. She looked at her sister Martha, who was smiling intelligently. Then at Lawrence Newt, who did not cease smiling, as if he were in no perplexity whatsoever. Then at Amy, who sat smiling at her through the tears that had gathered in the thoughtful womanly brown eyes.

"Let me speak," said Lawrence Newt, quietly. "Why should we not all be glad and happy with you? You have found a sister, Aunt Martha has found herself and a son, I have found a wife, and Amy a husband."

They returned to the room where they had left the guests, and the story was quietly told to Hope Wayne and the others.

Hope and Edward looked at each other.

"Little Malacca!" she said, in a low tone, putting out her hand.

"Sister Hope," said the young man, blushing, and his large eyes filling with tenderness.

"And my sister, too," whispered Ellen Bennet, as she took Hope's other hand.

CHAPTER LXXXIII.

MRS. DELILAH JONES.

Mr. Newt's political friends in New York were naturally anxious when he went to Washington. They had constant communication with the Honorable Mr. Ele in regard to his colleague; for although they were entirely sure of Mr. Ele, they could not quite confide in Mr. Newt, nor help feeling that, in some eccentric moment, even his interest might fail to control him.

"The truth is, I begin to be sick of it," said General Belch to the calm William Condor.

That placid gentleman replied that he saw no reason for apprehension.

"But he may let things out, you know," said Belch.

"Yes, but is not our word as good as his," was the assuring reply.

"Perhaps, perhaps," said General Belch, dolefully.

But Belch and Condor were forgotten by the representative they had sent to Congress when he once snuffed the air of Washington. There was something grateful to Abel Newt in the wide sphere and complicated relations of the political capital, of which the atmosphere was one of intrigue, and which was built over the mines and countermines of selfishness. He hoodwinked all Belch's spies, so that the Honorable Mr. Ele could never ascertain any thing about his colleague, until once when he discovered that the report upon the Grant was to be brought in within a day or two by the Committee, and that it would be recommended, upon which he hastened to Abel's lodging. He found him smoking as usual, with a decanter at hand. It was past midnight, and the room was in the disorder of a bachelor's sanctum.

Mr. Ele seated himself carelessly, so carelessly that Abel

saw at once that he had come for some very particular purpose. He offered his friend a tumbler and a cigar, and they talked nimbly of a thousand things. Who had come, who had gone, and how superb Mrs. Delilah Jones was, who had suddenly appeared upon the scene, invested with mystery, and bringing a note to each of the colleagues from General Belch.

"Mrs. Delilah Jones," said that gentleman, in a private note to Ele, "is our old friend, Kitty Dunham. She appears in Washington as the widow of a captain in the navy, who died a few years since upon the Brazil station. She can be of the greatest service to us; and you must have no secrets from each other about our dear friend, who shall be nameless."

To Abel Newt, General Belch wrote: "My dear Newt, the lady to whom I have given a letter to you is daughter of an old friend of my family. She married Captain Jones of the navy, whom she lost some years since upon the Brazil station. She has seen the world; has money; and comes to Washington to taste life, to enjoy herself—to doff the sables, perhaps, who knows? Be kind to her, and take care of your heart. Don't forget the Grant in the arms of Delilah! Yours, Belch."

Abel Newt, when he received this letter, looked over his books of reports and statistics.

"Captain Jones—Brazil station," he said, skeptically, to himself. But he found no such name or event in the obituaries; and he was only the more amused by his friend Belch's futile efforts at circumvention and control.

"My dear Belch," he replied, after he had made his investigations, "I have your private note, but I have not yet encountered the superb Delilah; nor have I forgotten what you said to me about working 'em through their wives, and sisters, etc. I shall not begin to forget it now, and I hope to make the Delilah useful in the campaign; for there are goslings here, more than you would believe. Thank you for such an ally. *You*, at least, were not born to fail. Yours, A. Newt."

"Goslings, are there? I believe you," said Belch to himself, inwardly chuckling as he read and folded Abel's letter.

"Ally, hey? Well, that *is* good," he continued, the chuckle rising into a laugh. "Well, well, I thought Abel Newt was smart; but he doesn't even suspect, and I have played a deeper game than was needed."

"I guess that will fix him," said Abel, as he looked over his letter, laughed, folded it, and sent it off.

Mr. Ele by many a devious path at length approached the object of his visit, and hoped that Mr. Newt would flesh his maiden sword in the coming fray. Abel said, without removing his cigar, "I think I shall speak."

He said no more. Mr. Ele shook his foot with inward triumph.

"The Widow Jones will do a smashing business this winter, I suppose," he said, at length.

"Likely," replied Newt.

"Know her well?"

"Pretty well."

Mr. Ele retired, for he had learned all that his friend meant he should know.

"Do I know Delilah?" laughed Abel Newt to himself, as he said "Good-night, Ele."

Yes he did. He had followed up his note to General Belch by calling upon the superb Mrs. Delilah Jones. But neither the skillful wig, nor the freshened cheeks, nor the general repairs which her personal appearance had undergone, could hide from Abel the face of Kitty Dunham, whom he had sometimes met in other days when suppers were eaten in Grand Street and wagons were driven to Cato's. He betrayed nothing, however; and she wrote to General Belch that she had disguised herself so that he did not recall her in the least.

Abel was intensely amused by the espionage of the Honorable Mr. Ele and the superb Jones. He told his colleague how greatly he had been impressed by the widow—that she was really a fascinating woman; and, by Jove! though she was a widow, and no longer twenty, still there were a good many worse things a man might do than fall in love with her.

'Pon honor, he did not feel altogether sure of himself, though he thought he was hardened if any body was.

Mr. Ele smiled, and said, in a serious way, that she was a splendid woman, and if Abel persisted he must look out for a rival.

"For I thought it best to lead him on," he wrote to his friend Belch.

As for the lady herself, Abel was so dexterous that she really began to believe that she might do rather more for herself than her employers. He brought to bear upon her the whole force of the fascination which had once been so irresistible; and, like a blowpipe, it melted out the whole conspiracy against him without her knowing that she had betrayed it. The point of her instructions from Belch was that she was to persuade him to be constant to the Grant at any price.

"To-morrow, then, Mr. Newt," she said to him, as they stood together in the crush of a levee at the White House— "to-morrow *our* bill is to be reported, and favorably."

Mrs. Delilah Jones was a pretty woman, and shrewd. She had large eyes, languishing at will—at will, also, bright and piercing. Her face was a smiling, mobile face; the features rather coarse, the expression almost vulgar, but the vulgarity well concealed. She was dressed in the extreme of the mode, and drew Mr. Newt's arm very close to her as she spoke. She observed that Mr. Newt was more than usually disposed to chat. The honorable representative had dined.

"*Our* bill, Lady Delilah? Thank you for that," said Abel, in a low voice, and almost pressing the hand that lay upon his close-held arm.

The reply was a slow turn of the head, and a half languishment in the eyes as they sought his with the air of saying, "Would you deceive a woman who trusts in you utterly?"

They moved out of the throng a little, and stood by the window.

"I wish I dared to ask you one thing as a pure favor," said

THE SUPERB DELILAH.

the superb Mrs. Delilah Jones, and this time the eyes were firm and bright.

"I hoped, by this time, that you dared every thing," replied Abel, with a vague reproach in his tone.

Mrs. Jones looked at him for a moment with a look of honest inquiry in her eyes. His own did not falter. Their expression combined confidence and respect.

"May I then ask," she said, earnestly, and raising her other hand as if to lay it imploringly upon his shoulder, but somehow it fell into his hand, which was raised simultaneously, and which did not let it go—

"For my sake, will you speak in favor of it?" she asked, casting her eyes down.

"For your sake, Delilah," he said, in a musical whisper, and under the rouge her cheeks tingled—"for your sake I will make a speech—my maiden speech."

There was more conversation between them. The Honorable Mr. Ele stood guard, so to speak, and by incessant chatter warded off the company from pressing upon them unawares. The guests smiled as they looked on; and after the levee the newspapers circulated rumors (it was before the days of "Personal") that were read with profound interest throughout the country, that the young and talented representative from the commercial emporium had not forfeited his reputation as a squire of dames, and gossip already declared that the charming and superb Mrs. D–li–h J–nes would ere long exchange that honored name for one not less esteemed.

When Abel returned from the levee he threw himself into his chair, and said, aloud,

"Isn't a man lucky who is well paid for doing just what he meant to do?"

For Abel Newt intended to get all he could from the Grant, and to enjoy himself as fully as possible while getting it; but he had his own work to do, and to that his power was devoted. To make a telling speech upon the winning side was one of his plans, and accordingly he made it.

When the bill was reported as it had been drafted by his friends in New York, it had been arranged that Mr. Newt should catch the speaker's eye. His figure and face attracted attention, and his career in Washington had already made him somewhat known. During the time he had been there his constant employment had been a study of the House and of its individual members, as well as of the general character and influence of the speeches. His shrewdness showed him the shallows, the currents, and the reefs. Day after day he saw a great many promising plans, like full-sailed ships, ground upon the flats of dullness, strike rocks of prejudice, or whirl in the currents of crudity, until they broke up and went down out of sight.

He rose, and his first words arrested attention. He treated the House with consummate art, as he might have treated a woman whom he wished to persuade. The House was favorably inclined before. It was resolved when he sat down. For he had shown so clearly that it was one of the cases in which patriotism and generosity—the finer feelings and only a moderate expense—were all one, that the majority, who were determined to pass the Grant in any case, were charmed to have the action so imposingly stated; and the minority, who knew that it was useless to oppose it, enjoyed the rhetoric of the speech, and, as it was brief, and did not encroach upon dinner-time, smiled approval, and joined in the congratulation to Mr. Newt upon his very eloquent and admirable oration.

In the midst of the congratulations Abel raised his eyes to Mrs. Delilah Jones, who sat conspicuous in the gallery.

CHAPTER LXXXIV.

PROSPECTS OF HAPPINESS.

The Honorable Abel Newt was the lion of the hour. The days of dinner invitations and evening parties suddenly returned. He did not fail to use the rising tide. It helped to float him more securely to the fulfillment of his great work. Meanwhile he saw Mrs. Jones every day. She no longer tried to play a game.

The report of his speech was scattered abroad in the papers. General Belch rubbed his hands and expectorated with an energy that showed the warmth of his feeling. Far away in

quiet Delafield, when the news arrived, Mr. Savory Gray lost
no time in improving the pregnant text. The great moral
was duly impressed upon the scholars that Mr. Newt was a
great man because he had been one of Mr. Gray's boys. The
Washington world soon knew his story, the one conspicuous
fact being that he was the favorite nephew of the rich merchant, Lawrence Newt. All the doors flew open. The dinner invitations, the evening notes, fell upon his table more
profusely than ever.

He sneered at his triumph. Ambition, political success, social prestige had no fascination for a man who was half im-
bruted, and utterly disappointed and worn out. One thing
only Abel really wanted. He wanted money—money, which
could buy the only pleasures of which he was now capable.

"Look here, Delilah—I like that name better than Kitty, it
means something—you know Belch. So do I. Do you suppose a man would work with him or for him except for more
advantage than he can insure? Or do you think *I* want to
slave for the public—*I* work for the public? God! would I
be every man's drudge? No, Mrs. Delilah Jones, emphatically not. I will be my own master, and yours, and my re-
vered uncle will foot the bills."

The woman looked at him inquiringly. She was a willing
captive. She accepted him as master.

"It isn't for you to know how he will pay," said Abel,
"but to enjoy the fruits."

The woman, in whose face there were yet the ruins of a
coarse beauty, which pleased Abel now as the most fiery liquor gratified his palate, looked at him, and said,

"Abel, what are we to do?"

"To be happy," he answered, with the old hard, black light
in his eyes.

She almost shuddered as she heard the tone and saw the
look, and yet she did not feel as if she could escape the spell
of his power.

"To be happy!" she repeated. "To be happy!"

Her voice fell as she spoke the words. Her life had not been a long one. She had laughed a great deal, but she had never been happy. She knew Abel from old days. She saw him now, sodden, bloated—but he fascinated her still. Was he the magician to conjure happiness for her?

"What is your plan?" she asked.

"I have two passages taken in a brig for the Mediterranean. We go to New York a day or two before she sails. That's all."

"And then?" asked his companion, with wonder and doubt in her voice.

"And then a blissful climate and happiness."

"And then?" she persisted, in a low, doubtful voice.

"Then Hell—if you are anxious for it," said Abel, in a sharp, sudden voice.

The poor woman cowered as she sat. Men had often enough sworn at her; but she recoiled from the roughness of this lover as if it hurt her. Her eyes were not languishing now, but startled—then slowly they grew dim and soft with tears.

Abel Newt looked at her, surprised and pleased.

"Kitty, you're a woman still, and I like it. It's so much the better. I don't want a dragon or a machine. Come, girl, are you afraid?"

"Of what?"

"Of me—of the future—of any thing?"

The tone of his voice had a lingering music of the same kind as the lingering beauty in her face. It was a sensual, seductive sound.

"No, I am not afraid," she answered, turning to him. "But, oh! my God! my God! if we were only both young again!"

She spoke with passionate hopelessness, and the tears dried in her eyes.

Later in the evening Mrs. Delilah Jones appeared at the French minister's ball.

"Upon the whole," said Mr. Ele to his partner, "I have never seen Mrs. Jones so superb as she is to-night."

She stood by the mantle, queen-like—so the representatives from several States remarked—and all the evening fresh comers offered homage.

"*Ma foi!*" said the old Brazilian embassador, as he gazed at her through his eye-glass, and smacked his lips.

"*Tiens!*" responded the sexagenarian representative from Chili, half-closing one eye.

CHAPTER LXXXV.

GETTING READY.

HOPE WAYNE had not forgotten the threat which Abel had vaguely thrown out; but she supposed it was only an expression of disappointment and indignation. Could she have seen him a few evenings after the ball and his conversation with Mrs. Delilah Jones, she might have thought differently.

He sat with the same woman in her room.

"To-morrow, then?" she said, looking at him, hesitatingly.

"To-morrow," he answered, grimly.

"I hope all will go well."

"All what?" he asked, roughly.

"All our plans."

"Abel Newt was not born to fail," he replied; "or at least General Belch said so."

His companion had no knowledge of what Abel really meant to do. She only knew that he was capable of every thing, and as for herself, her little mask had fallen, and she did not even wish to pick it up again.

They sat together silently for a long time. He poured freely and drank deeply, and whiffed cigar after cigar nervously away. The few bells of the city tolled the hours. Ele had come during the evening and knocked at the door, but Abel did not let him in. He and his companion sat silently, and heard the few bells strike.

"Well, Kitty," he said at last, thickly, and with glazing eye. "Well, my Princess of the Mediterranean. We shall be happy, hey? You're not afraid even now, hey?"

"Oh, we shall be very happy," she replied, in a low, wild tone, as if it were the night wind that moaned, and not a woman's voice.

He looked at her for a few moments. He saw how entirely she was enthralled by him.

"I wonder if I care any thing about you?" he said at length, leering at her through the cigar-smoke.

"I don't think you do," she answered, meekly.

"But my—my—dear Mrs. Jones—the su-superb Mrs. Delilah Jo-Jones ought to be sure that I do. Here, bring me a light: that dam—dam—cigar's gone out."

She rose quietly and carried the candle to Abel. There was an inexpressible weariness and pathos in all her movements: a kind of womanly tranquillity that was touchingly at variance with the impression of her half-coarse appearance. As Abel watched her he remembered the women whom he had tried to marry. His memory scoured through his whole career. He thought of them all variously happy.

"I swear! to think I should come to you!" he said at length, looking at his companion, with an indescribable bitterness of sneering.

Kitty Dunham sat at a little distance from him on the end of a sofa. She was bowed as if deeply thinking; and when she heard these words her head only sank a little more, as if a palpable weight had been laid upon her. She understood perfectly what he meant.

"I know I am not worth loving," she said, in the same low voice, "but my love will do you no harm. Perhaps I can help you in some way. If you are ill some day, I can nurse you. I shall be poor company on the long journey, but I will try."

"What long journey?" asked Abel, suddenly and angrily.

"Where we are going," she replied, gently.

"D— it, then, don't use such am-am-big-'us phrases. A man would think we were go-going to die."

She said no more, but sat, half-crouching, upon the sofa, looking into the fire. Abel glanced at her, from time to time, with maudlin grins and sneers.

"Go to bed," he said at length; "I've something to do. Sleep all you can; you'll need it. I shall stay here 'till I'm ready to go, and come for you in the morning."

"Thank you," she answered, and rose quietly. "Good-night!" she said.

"Oh! good-night, Mrs. De-de-liah—superb Jo-Jones!"

He laughed as she went—sat ogling the fire for a little while, and then unsteadily, but not unconsciously, drew a pocket-book from his pocket and took out a small package. It contained several notes, amounting to not less than a hundred thousand dollars signed by himself, and indorsed by Lawrence Newt & Co.—at least the name was there, and it was a shrewd eye that could detect the difference between the signature and that which was every day seen and honored in the street.

Abel looked at them carefully, and leered and glared upon them as if they had been windows through which he saw something—sunny isles, and luxury, and a handsome slave who loved him to minister to every whim.

"'Tis a pretty game," he said, half aloud; "a droll turn-about is life. Uncle Lawrence plays against other people, and wins. I play against Uncle Lawrence, and win. But what's un-dred—sousand—to—him?"

He said it drowsily, and his hands unconsciously fell. He was asleep in his chair.

He sat there sleeping until the gray of morning. Kitty Dunham, coming into the room ready-dressed for a journey, found him there. She was frightened; for he looked as if he were dead. Going up to him she shook him, and he awoke heavily.

"What the h—'s the matter?" said he, as he opened his sleepy eyes.

"Why, it's time to go."

"To go where?"

"To be happy," she said, standing passively and looking in his face.

He roused himself, and said:

"Well, I'm all ready. I've only to stop at my room for my trunk."

His hair was tangled, his eyes were bloodshot, his clothes tumbled and soiled.

"Wouldn't you like to dress yourself?" she asked.

"Why, no; ain't I dressed enough for you? No gentleman dresses when he's going to travel."

She said no more. The carriage came as Abel had ordered, a private conveyance to take them quite through to New York. All the time before it came Kitty Dunham moved solemnly about the room, seeing that nothing was left. The solemnity fretted Abel.

"What are you so sober about?" he asked, impatiently.

"Because I am getting ready for a long journey," she answered, tranquilly.

"Perhaps not so long," he said, sharply—"not if I choose to leave you behind."

"But you won't."

"How do you know?"

"Because you will want somebody, and I'm the only person in the world left to you."

She spoke in the same sober way. Abel knew perfectly well that she spoke the truth, but he had never thought of it before. Was he then going so long a journey without a friend, unless she went with him? Was she the only one left of all the world?

As his mind pondered the question his eye fell upon a newspaper of the day before, in which he saw his name. He took it up mechanically, and read a paragraph praising him and his speech; foretelling "honor and troops of friends" for a young man who began his public career so brilliantly.

"There; hear this!" said he, as he read it aloud and looked at his companion. "'Troops of friends,' do you see? and yet you talk of being my only dependence in the world! Fie! fie! Mrs. Delilah Jones."

It was melancholy merriment. He did not smile, and the woman's face was quietly sober.

"For the present, then, Mr. Speaker and fellow-citizens," said Abel Newt, waving his hand as he saw that every thing was ready, and that the carriage waited only for him and his companion, "I bid these scenes adieu! For the present I terminate my brief engagement. And you, my fellow-members, patterns of purity and pillars of truth, farewell! Disinterested patriots, I leave you my blessing! Pardon me that I prefer the climate of the Mediterranean to that of the District, and the smiles of my Kitty to the intelligent praises of my country. Friends of my soul, farewell! I kiss my finger tips! Boo—hoo!"

He made a mock bow, and smiled upon an imaginary audience. Then offering his arm with grave ceremony to his companion as if a crowd had been looking on, he went down stairs.

CHAPTER LXXXVI.

IN THE CITY.

It was a long journey. They stopped at Baltimore, at Philadelphia, and pushed on toward New York. While they were still upon the way Hope Wayne saw what she had been long expecting to see—and saw it without a solitary regret. Amy Waring was Amy Waring no longer; and Hope Wayne was the first who kissed Mrs. Lawrence Newt. Even Mrs. Simcoe looked benignantly upon the bride; and Aunt Martha wept over her as over her own child.

The very day of the wedding Abel Newt and his companion arrived at Jersey City. Leaving Kitty in a hotel, he crossed the river, and ascertained that the vessel on which he had taken two berths under a false name was full and ready, and would sail upon her day. He showed himself in Wall Street, carefully dressed, carefully sober — evidently mindful, people said, of his new position; and they thought his coming home showed that he was on good terms with his family, and that he was really resolved to behave himself.

For a day or two he appeared in the business streets and offices, and talked gravely of public measures. General Belch was confounded by the cool sobriety, and superiority, and ceremony of the Honorable Mr. Newt. When he made a joke, Abel laughed with such patronizing politeness that the General was frightened, and tried no more. When he treated Abel familiarly, and told him what a jolly lift his speech had given to their common cause—the Grant—the Honorable Mr. Newt replied, with a cold bow, that he was glad if he had done his duty and satisfied his constituents; bowing so coldly that the General was confounded. He spat into his fire, and said, "The Devil!"

When Abel had gone, General Belch was profoundly conscious that King Log was better than King Stork, and thought regretfully of the Honorable Watkins Bodley.

After a day or two the Honorable Mr. Newt went to his Uncle Lawrence's office. Abel had not often been there. He had never felt himself to be very welcome there; and as he came into the inner room where Lawrence and Gabriel sat, they were quite as curious to know why he had come as he was to know what his reception would be. Abel bowed politely, and said he could not help congratulating his uncle upon the news he had heard, but would not conceal his surprise. What his surprise was he did not explain; but Lawrence very well knew. Abel had the good sense not to mention the name of Hope Wayne, and not to dwell upon any subject that involved feeling. He said that he hoped by-gones would be by-gones; that he had been a wild boy, but that a career now opened upon him of which he hoped to prove worthy.

"There was a time, Uncle Lawrence," he said, " when I despised your warning; now I thank you for it."

Lawrence held out his hand to his nephew:

"Honesty is the best policy, at least, if nothing more," he said, smiling. "You have a chance; I hope, with all my heart, you will use it well."

There was little more to say, and of that little Gabriel said nothing. Abel spoke of public affairs; and after a short time he took leave.

"Can the leopard change his spots?" said Gabriel, looking at the senior partner.

"A bad man may become better," was all the answer; and the two merchants were busy again.

Returning to Wall Street, the Honorable Abel Newt met Mr. President Van Boozenberg. They shook hands, and the old gentleman said, warmly,

"I see ye goin' into your Uncle Lawrence's a while ago, as I was comin' along South Street. Mr. Abel, Sir, I congratilate ee, Sir. I've read your speech, and I sez to ma, sez I, I'd no idee of it; none at all. Ma, sez she, Law, pa! I allers knowed Mr. Abel Newt would turn up trumps. You allers did have the women, Mr. Newt; and so I told ma."

"I am very glad, Sir, that I have at last done something to deserve your approbation. I trust I shall not forfeit it. I have led rather a gay life, and careless; and my poor father and I have met with misfortunes. But they open a man's eyes, Sir; they are angels in disguise, as the poet says. I don't doubt they have been good for me. At least I'm resolved now to be steady and industrious; and I certainly should be a great fool if I were not."

"Sartin, Sir, with your chances and prospects, yes, and your talents, coz, I allers said to ma, sez I, he's got talent if he hain't nothin' else. I suppose your Uncle Lawrence won't be so shy of you now, hey? No, of course not. A man who has a smart nevy in Congress has a tap in a good barrel."

And Mr. Van Boozenberg laughed loudly at his own humor.

"Why, yes, Sir. I think I may say that the pleasantest part of my new life—if you will allow me to use the expression—is my return to the friends best worth having. I think I have learned, Sir, that steady-going business, with no nonsense about it, is the permanent thing. It isn't flopdoddle, Sir, but it's solid food."

"Tonguey," thought old Jacob Van Boozenberg, "but vastly improved. Has come to terms with Uncle Lawrence.' Sensible fellow!"

"I think he takes it," said Abel to himself, with the feeling of an angler, as he watched the other.

Just before they parted Abel took out his pocket-book and told Mr. Van Boozenberg that he should like to negotiate a little piece of paper which was not altogether worthless, he believed.

Smiling as he spoke, he handed a note for twenty-five thousand dollars, with his uncle's indorsement, to the President. The old gentleman looked at it carefully, smiled knowingly, "Yes, yes, I see. Sly dog, that Uncle Lawrence. I allers sez so. This ere's for the public service, I suppose, eh! Mr. Newt?" and the President chuckled over his confirmed conviction that Lawrence Newt was "jes' like other folks."

He asked Abel to walk with him to the bank. They chatted as they passed along, nodded to those they knew, while some bowed politely to the young member whom they saw in such good company.

"Well, well," said Mr. Zephyr Wetherley as he skimmed up Wall Street from the bank, where he had been getting dividends, "I didn't think to see the day when Abel Newt would be a solid, sensible man."

And Mr. Wetherley wondered, in a sighing way, what was the secret of Abel's success.

The honorable member came out of the bank with the money in his pocket. When the clock struck three he had the amount of all the notes in the form of several bills of foreign exchange.

He went hastily to the river side and crossed to Jersey City.

"They have sent to say that the ship sails at nine in the morning, and that we must be on board early," said Kitty Dunham, as he entered the room.

"I am all ready," he replied, in a clear, cold, alert voice. "Now sit down."

His tone was not to be resisted. The woman seated herself quietly and waited.

"My affectionate Uncle Lawrence has given me a large sum of money, and recommends travelling for my health. The money is in bills on London and Paris. To-morrow morning we sail. We post to London—get the money; same day to Paris—get the money; straight on to Marseilles, and sail for Sicily. There we can take breath."

He spoke rapidly, but calmly. She heard and understood every word.

"I wish we could sail to-night," she said.

"Plenty of time—plenty of time," answered Abel. "And why be so anxious for so long a journey?"

"It seems long to you, too?"

"Why, yes; it will be long. Yes, I am going on a long journey."

He smiled with the hard black eyes a hard black smile. Kitty did not smile; but she took his hand gently.

Abel shook his head, mockingly.

"My dear Mrs. Delilah Jones, you overcome me with your sentimentality. I don't believe in love. That's what I believe in," said he, as he opened his pocket-book and showed her the bills.

The woman looked at them unmoved.

"Those are the delicate little keys of the Future," chuckled Abel, as he gloated over the paper.

The woman raised her eyes and looked into his. They were busy with the bills. Then with the same low tone, as if the wind were wailing, she asked,

"Abel, tell me, before we go upon this long journey, don't you love me in the least?"

Her voice sank into an almost inaudible whisper.

Abel turned and looked at her, gayly.

"Love you? Why, woman, what is love? No, I don't love you. I don't love any body. But that's no matter; you shall go with me as if I did. You know, as well as I do, that I can't whine and sing silly. I'll be your friend, and you'll be mine, and this shall be the friend of both," said he, as he raised the bills in his hands.

She sat beside him silent, and her eyes were hot and dry, not wet with tears. There was a look of woe in her face so touching and appealing that, when Abel happened to see it, he said, involuntarily,

"Come, come, don't be silly."

The evening came, and the Honorable Mr. Newt rose and walked about the room.

"How slowly the time passes!" he said, pettishly. "I can't stand it."

It was nine o'clock. Suddenly he sprang up from beside Kitty Dunham, who was silently working.

"No," said he, "I really can not stand it. I'll run over to town, and be back by midnight. I do want to see the old place once more before that long journey," he added, with emphasis, as he put on his coat and hat. He ran from the room, and was just going out of the house when he heard a muffled voice calling to him from up stairs.

"Why, Kitty, what is it?" he asked, as he stopped.

There was no answer. Alarmed for a moment, he leaped up the stairs. She stood waiting for him at the door of the room.

"Well!" exclaimed he, hastily.

"You forgot to kiss me, Abel," she said.

He took her by the shoulders, and looked at her before him. In her eyes there were pity, and gentleness, and love.

"Fool!" he said, half-pleased, half-vexed—kissed her, and rushed out into the street.

CHAPTER LXXXVII.

A LONG JOURNEY.

ABEL NEWT ran to the ferry and crossed. Then he gained Broadway, and sauntered into one of the hells in Park Row. It was bright and full, and he saw many an old friend. They nodded to him, and said, "Ah! back again!" and he smiled, and said a man must not be too virtuous all at once.

So he ventured a little, and won; ventured a little more, and lost. Ventured a little more, and won again; and lost again.

Then came supper, and wine flowed freely. Old friends must pledge in bumpers.

To work again, and the bells striking midnight. Win, lose; lose, win; win, win, lose, lose, lose, lose, lose, lose.

Abel Newt smiled: his face was red, his eyes glaring.

"I've played enough," he said; "the luck's against me!"

He passed his hands rapidly through his hair.

"Cash I can not pay," he said; "but here is my I O U, and a check of my Uncle Lawrence's in the morning; for I have no account, you know."

His voice was rough. It was two o'clock in the morning; and the lonely woman he had left sat waiting and wondering: stealing to the front door and straining her eyes into the night: stealing softly back again to press her forehead against the window: and the quiet hopelessness of her face began to be pricked with terror.

"Good-night, gentlemen," said Abel, huskily and savagely.

There was a laugh around the table at which he had been playing.

"Takes it hardly, now that he's got money," said one of his old cronies. "He's made up with Uncle Lawrence, I hear. Hope he'll come often, hey?" he said to the bank.

The bank smiled vaguely, but did not reply.

It was after two, and Abel burst into the street. He had been drinking brandy, and the fires were lighted within him. Pulling his hat heavily upon his head, he moved unsteadily along the street toward the ferry. The night was starry and still. There were few passers in the street; and no light but that which shone at some of the corners, the bad, red eye that lures to death. The night air struck cool upon his face and into his lungs. His head was light. He reeled.

"Mus ha' some drink," he said, thickly.

He stumbled, and staggered into the nearest shop. There was a counter, with large yellow barrels behind it; and a high blind, behind which two or three rough-looking men were drinking. In the window there was a sign, "Liquors, pure as imported."

The place was dingy and cold. The floor was sanded. The two or three guests were huddled about a stove—one asleep upon a bench, the others smoking short pipes; and their hard, cadaverous faces and sullen eyes turned no welcome upon Abel when he entered, but they looked at him quickly, as if they suspected him to be a policeman or magistrate, and as if they had reason not to wish to see either. But in a moment they saw it was not a sober man, whoever he was. Abel tried to stand erect, to look dignified, to smooth himself into apparent sobriety. He vaguely hoped to give the impression that he was a gentleman belated upon his way home, and taking a simple glass for comfort.

"Why, Dick, don't yer know him?" said one, in a low voice, to his neighbor.

"No, d— him! and don't want to."

"I do, though," replied the first man, still watching the new-comer curiously.

"Why, Jim, who in h— is it?" asked Dick.

"That air man's our representative. That ain't nobody else but Abel Newt."

"Well," muttered Jim, sullenly, as he surveyed the general appearance of Abel while he stood drinking a glass of brandy —"pure as imported"—at the counter—"well, we've done lots for him: what's he going to do for us? We've put that man up tremendious high; d'ye think he's going to kick away the ladder?"

He half grumbled to himself, half asked his neighbor Dick. They were both a little drunk, and very surly.

"I dunno. But he's vastly high and mighty—that I know; and, by ——, I'll tell him so!" said Dick, energetically clasp ing his hands, bringing one of them down upon the bench on which he sat, and clenching every word with an oath.

"Hallo, Jim! let's make him give us somethin' to drink!"

The two constituents approached the representative whose election they had so ardently supported.

"Well, Newt, how air ye?"

Abel Newt was confounded at being accosted in such a place at such an hour. He raised his heavy eyes as he leaned unsteadily against the counter, and saw two beetle-browed, square-faced, disagreeable-looking men looking at him with half-drunken, sullen insolence. .

"Hallo, Newt! how air ye?" repeated Jim, as he confront-ed the representative.

Abel looked at him with shaking head, indignant and scornful.

"Who the devil are you?" he asked, at length, blurring the words as he spoke, and endeavoring to express supreme contempt.

"We're the men that made yer!" retorted Dick, in a shrill, tipsy voice.

The liquor-seller, who was leaning upon his counter, was in-stantly alarmed. He knew the signs of impending danger. He hurried round, and said,

"Come, come; I'm going to shut up! Time to go home; time to go home!"

The three men at the counter did not move. As they stood facing each other the brute fury kindled more and more fierce-ly in each one of them.

"We're Jim and Dick, and Ned's asleep yonder on the bench; and we're come to drink a glass with yer, Honorable Abel Newt!" said Dick, in a sneering tone. "It's we what did your business for ye. What'yer going to do for us?"

There was a menacing air in his eye as he glanced at Abel, who felt himself quiver with impotent, blind rage.

"I dun—dun—no ye!" he said, with maudlin dignity.

The men pressed nearer.

"Time to go home! Time to go home!" quavered the liquor-seller; and Ned opened his eyes, and slowly raised his huge frame from the bench.

"What's the row?" asked he of his comrades.

"The Honorable Abel Newt's the row," said Jim, pointing at him.

There was something peculiarly irritating to Abel in the pointing finger. Holding by the counter, he raised his hand and struck at it.

Ned rolled his body off the bench in a moment.

"For God's sake!" gasped the little liquor-seller.

Jim and Dick stood hesitatingly, glaring at Abel. Jim struck his teeth together. Ned joined them, and they sur-rounded Abel.

"What in —— do you mean by striking me, you drunken pig?" growled Jim, but not yet striking. Conscious of his strength, he had the instinctive forbearance of superiority, but it was fast mastered by the maddening liquor.

"Time to go home! Time to go home!" cried the thin piping voice of the liquor-seller.

"What the —— do you mean by insulting my friend?" half hiccuped Dick, shaking his head threateningly, and stiff-ening his arm and fist at his side as he edged toward Abel.

The hard black eyes of Abel Newt shot sullen fire. His rage half sobered him. He threw his head with the old defiant air, tossing the hair back. The old beauty flashed for an instant through the ruin that had been wrought in his face, and, kindling into a wild, glittering look of wrath, his eye swept them all as he struck heavily forward.

"Time to go home! Time to go home!" came the cry again, unheeded, unheard.

There was a sudden, fierce, brutal struggle. The men's faces were human no longer, but livid with bestial passion. The liquor-seller rushed into the street, and shouted aloud for help. The cry rang along the dark, still houses, and startled the drowsy, reluctant watchmen on their rounds. They sprang their rattles.

"Murder! murder!" was the cry, which did not disturb the neighbors, who were heavy sleepers, and accustomed to noise and fighting.

"Murder! murder!" It rang nearer and nearer as the watchmen hastened toward the corner. They found the little man standing at his door, bareheaded, and shouting,

"My God! my God! they've killed a man—they've killed a man!"

"Stop your noise, and let us in. What is it?"

The little man pointed back into his dim shop. The watchmen saw only the great yellow round tanks of the liquor pure as imported, and pushed in behind the blind. There was no one there; a bench was overturned, and there were glasses upon the counter. No one there? One of the watchmen struck something with his foot, and, stooping, touched a human body. He started up.

"There's a man here."

He did not say dead, or drunk; but his tone said every thing.

One of them ran to the next doctor, and returned with him after a little while. Meanwhile the others had raised the body. It was yet warm. They laid it upon the bench.

"Warm still. Stunned, I reckon. I see no blood, except about the face. Well dressed. What's he doing here?" The doctor said so as he felt the pulse. He carefully turned the body over, examined it every where, looked earnestly at the face, around which the matted hair clustered heavily:

"He has gone upon his long journey!" said the young doctor, in a low, solemn tone, still looking at the face with an emotion of sad sympathy, for it was a face that had been very handsome; and it was a young man, like himself. The city bells clanged three.

"Who is it?" he asked.

Nobody knew.

"Look at his handkerchief."

They found it, and handed it to the young doctor. He unrolled it, holding it smooth in his hands; suddenly his face turned pale; the tears burst into his eyes. A curious throng of recollections and emotions overpowered him. His heart ached as he leaned over the body; and laying the matted hair away, he looked long and earnestly into the face. In that dim moment in the liquor-shop, by that bruised body, how much he saw! A play-ground loud with boys—wide-branching elms —a country church—a placid pond. He heard voices, and summer hymns, and evening echoes; and all the images and sounds were soft, and pensive, and remote.

The doctor's name was Greenidge—James Greenidge, and he had known Abel Newt at school.

CHAPTER LXXXVIII.

WAITING.

THE woman Abel had left sat quivering and appalled. Every sound started her; every moment she heard him coming. Rocking to and fro in the lonely room, she dropped into sudden sleep—saw him—started up—cried, "How could you stay so?" then sat broad awake, and knew that she had dozed but for a moment, and that she was alone.

WAITING.

"Abel, Abel!" she moaned, in yearning agony. "But he kissed me before he went," she thought, wildly—"he kissed me—he kissed me!"

Lulled for a moment by the remembrance, she sank into another brief nap—saw him as she had seen him in his gallant days, and heard him say, I love you. "How could you stay so?" she cried, dreaming—started—sprang up erect, with her head turned in intense listening. There was a sound this time; yes, across the river she heard the solemn city bells strike three.

Wearily pacing the room—stealthily, that she might make no noise—walking the hours away, the lonely woman waited for her lover. The winter wind rose and wailed about the windows and moaned in the chimney, and in long, shrieking sobs died away.

"Abel! Abel!" she whispered, and started at the strangeness of her voice. She opened the window softly and looked out. The night was cold and calm again, and the keen stars twinkled. She saw nothing—she heard no sound.

She closed it again, and paced the room. There were no tears in her eyes; but they were wide open, startled, despairing. For the first time in her terrible life she had loved.

"But he kissed me before he went," she said, pleadingly, to herself; "he kissed me—he kissed me!"

She said it when the solemn city bells struck three. She said it when the first dim light of dawn stole into the chamber. And when the full day broke, and she heard the earliest footfalls in the street, her heart clung to it as the only memory left to her of all her life:

"He kissed me! he kissed me!"

CHAPTER LXXXIX.

DUST TO DUST.

SCARCELY had Abel left the bank, after obtaining the money, than Gabriel came in, and, upon seeing the notes which Mr. Van Boozenberg had shown him, in order to make every thing sure in so large a transaction, announced that they were forged. The President was quite beside himself, and sat down in his room, wringing his hands and crying; while the messenger ran for a carriage, into which Gabriel stepped with Mr.

Van Boozenberg, and drove as rapidly as possible to the office of the Chief of Police, who promised to set his men to work at once; but the search was suddenly terminated by the bills found upon the body of Abel Newt.

The papers were full of the dreadful news. They said they were deeply shocked to announce that a disgrace had befallen the whole city in the crime which had mysteriously deprived his constituency and his country of the services of the young, talented, promising representative, whose opening career had seemed to be in every way so auspicious. By what foul play he had been made way with was a matter for the strictest legal investigation, and the honor of the country demanded that the perpetrators of such an atrocious tragedy should be brought to condign punishment.

The morning papers followed next day with fuller details of the awful event. Some of the more enterprising had diagrams of the shop, the blind, the large yellow barrels that held the liquor pure as imported, the bench, the counter, and the spot (marked O) where the officer had found the body. In parlors, in banks, in groceries and liquor-shops, in lawyers' rooms and insurance offices, the murder was the chief topic of conversation for a day. Then came the report of the inquest.

There was no clew to the murderers. The eager, thirsty-eyed crowd of men, and women, and children, crushing and hanging about the shop, gradually loosened their gaze. The jury returned that the deceased Abel Newt came to his death by the hands of some person or persons unknown. The shop was closed, officers were left in charge, and the body was borne away.

General Belch was in his office reading the morning paper when Mr. William Condor entered. They shook hands. Upon the General's fat face there was an expression of horror and perplexity, but Mr. Condor was perfectly calm.

"What an awful thing!" said Belch, as the other sat down before the fire.

"Frightful," said Mr. Condor, placidly, as he lighted a cigar, "but not surprising."

"Who do you suppose did it?" asked the General.

"Impossible to tell. A drunken brawl, with its natural consequences; that's all."

"Yes, I know; but it's awful."

"Providential."

"What do you mean?"

"Abel Newt would have made mince-meat of you and me and the rest of us if he had lived. That's what I mean," replied Mr. Condor, unruffled, and lightly whiffing the smoke. "But it's necessary to draw some resolutions to offer in the committee, and I've brought them with me. You know there's a special meeting called to take notice of this deplorable event, and you must present them. Shall I read them?"

Mr. Condor drew a piece of paper from his pocket, and, holding his cigar in one hand and whiffing at intervals, read:

"Whereas our late associate and friend, Abel Newt, has been suddenly removed from this world, in the prime of his life and the height of his usefulness, by the hand of an inscrutable but all-wise Providence, to whose behests we desire always to bow in humble resignation; and

"Whereas, it is eminently proper that those to whom great public trusts have been confided by their fellow-citizens should not pass away without some signal expression of the profound sense of bereavement which those fellow-citizens entertain; and

"Whereas we represent that portion of the community with whom the lamented deceased peculiarly sympathized; therefore be it resolved by the General Committee,

"*First*, That this melancholy event impressively teaches the solemn truth that in the midst of life we are in death;

"*Second*, That in the brilliant talents, the rare accomplishments, the deep sagacity, the unswerving allegiance to principle which characterized our dear departed brother and associate, we recognize the qualities which would have rendered the progress of his career as triumphant as its opening was auspicious;

" *Third*, That while we humble ourselves before the mysterious will of Heaven, which works not as man works, we tender our most respectful and profound sympathy to the afflicted relatives and friends of the deceased, to whom we fervently pray that his memory may be as a lamp to the feet;

" *Fourth*, That we will attend his funeral in a body; that we will wear crape upon the left arm for thirty days; and that a copy of these resolutions, signed by the officers of the Committee, shall be presented to his family."

"I think that'll do," said Mr. Condor, resuming his cigar, and laying the paper upon the table.

"Just the thing," said General Belch. "Just the thing. You know the Grant has passed and been approved?"

"Yes, so Ele wrote me," returned Mr. Condor.

"Condor," continued the General, "I've had enough of it. I'm going to back out. I'd rather sweep the streets."

General Belch spoke emphatically, and his friend turned toward him with a pleasant smile.

"Can you make so much in any other way?"

"Perhaps not. But I'd rather make less, and more comfortably."

"I find it perfectly comfortable," replied William Condor. "You take it too hard. You ought to manage it with less friction. The point is, to avoid friction. If you undertake to deal with men, you ought to understand just what they are."

Mr. Condor smoked serenely, and General Belch looked at his slim, clean figure, and his calm face, with curious admiration.

"By-the-by," said Condor, "when you introduce the resolutions, I shall second them with a few remarks."

And he did so. At the meeting of the Committee he rose and enforced them with a few impressive and pertinent words.

"Gratitude," he said, "is instinctive in the human breast.

When a man does well, or promises well, it is natural to regard him with interest and affection. The fidelity of our departed brother is worthy of our most affectionate admiration and imitation. If you ask me whether he had faults, I answer that he was a man. Whoso is without sin, let him cast the first stone."

On the same day the Honorable B. Jawley Ele rose in his place in Congress to announce the calamity in which the whole country shared, and to move an adjournment in respect for the memory of his late colleague—"a man endeared to us all by the urbanity of his deportment and his social graces; but to me especially, by the kindness of his heart and the readiness of his sympathy."

Abel Newt was buried from his father's house. There were not many gathered at the service in the small, plain rooms. Fanny Dinks was there, sobered and saddened—the friend now of Hope Wayne, and of Amy, her Uncle Lawrence's wife. Alfred was there, solemnized and frightened. The office of Lawrence Newt & Co. was closed, and the partners and the clerks all stood together around the coffin. Abel's mother, shrouded in black, sat in a dim corner of the room, nervously sobbing. Abel's father, sitting in his chair, his white hair hanging upon his shoulders, looked curiously at all the people, while his bony fingers played upon his knees, and he said nothing.

During all the solemn course of the service, from the gracious words, "I am the resurrection and the life," to the final Amen which was breathed out of the depth of many a soul there, the old man's eyes did not turn from the clergyman. But when, after a few moments of perfect silence, two or three men entered quietly and rapidly, and, lifting the coffin, began to bear it softly out of the room, he looked troubled and surprised, and glanced vaguely and inquiringly from one person to another, until, as it was passing out of the door, his face was covered with a piteous look of appeal: he half-rose from his chair, and reached out toward the door, with the

THE FUNERAL.

long white fingers clutching in the air; but Hope Wayne
took the wasted hands in hers, placed her arm behind him
gently, and tenderly pressed him back into the chair. The
old man raised his eyes to her as she stood by him, and holding one of her hands in one of his, the spectral calmness returned into his face; while, beating his thin knee with the
other hand, he said, in the old way, as the body of his son

was borne out of his house, " Riches have wings! Riches have wings !" But still he held Hope Wayne's hand, and from time to time raised his eyes to her face.

CHAPTER XC.

UNDER THE MISLETOE.

THE hand which held that of old Boniface Newt was never placed in that of any younger man, except for a moment; but the heart that warmed the hand henceforward held all the world.

We have come to the last leaf, patient and gentle reader, and the girl we saw sitting, long ago, upon the lawn and walking in the garden of Pinewood is not yet married! Yes, and we shall close the book, and still she will be Hope Wayne.

How could we help it? How could a faithful chronicler but tell his story as it is? It is not at his will that heroes marry, and heroines are given in marriage. He merely watches events and records results; but the inevitable laws of human life are hidden in God's grace beyond his knowledge.

There is Arthur Merlin painting pictures to this day, and every year with greater beauty and wider recognition. He wears the same velvet coat of many buttons—or its successor in the third or fourth remove—and still he whistles and sings at his work, still draws back from the easel and turns his head on one side to look at his picture, and cons it carefully through the tube of his closed hand; still lays down the pallet and, lighting a cigar, throws himself into the huge easy-chair, hanging one leg over the chair-arm and gazing, as he swings his foot, at something which does not seem to be in the room. Cheerful and gay, he has always a word of welcome for the loiterer who returns to Italy by visiting the painters; even if the loiterer find him with the foot idly swinging and the cigar musingly smoking itself away.

Nor is the painter conscious of any gaping, unhealed wound that periodically bleeds. There are nights in mid-summer when, leaning from his window, he thinks of many things, and among others, of a picture he once painted of the legend of Latmos. He smiles to think that, at the time, he half persuaded himself that he might be Endymion, yet the feeling with which he smiles is of pity and wonder rather than of regret.

At Thanksgiving dinners, at Christmas parties, at New Year and Twelfth Night festivals, no guest so gay and useful, so inventive and delightful, as Arthur Merlin the painter. Just as Aunt Winnifred has abandoned her theory it has become true, and all the girls do seem to love the man who respects them as much as the younger men do with whom they nightly dance in winter. He romps with the children, has a perfectly regulated and triumphant sliding-scale of gifts and attentions; and only this Christmas, although he is now—well, Aunt Winnifred has locked up the Family Bible and begins to talk of Arthur as a young man—yet only this Christmas, at Lawrence Newt's family party, at which, so nimbly did they run round, it was almost impossible to compute the actual number of Newt, and Wynne, and Bennet children — Arthur Merlin brought in, during the evening, with an air of profound secrecy, something covered with a large handkerchief. Of course there could be no peace, and no blindman's-buff, no stage-coach, no twirling the platter, and no snap-dragon, until the mystery was revealed. The whole crowd of short frocks and trowsers, and bright ribbons, and eyes, and curls, swarmed around the painter until he displayed a green branch.

A pair of tiny feet, carrying a pair of great blue eyes and a head of golden curls, scampered across the floor to Lawrence Newt.

"Oh, papa, what is that green thing with little berries on it?"

"That's a misletoe bough, little Hope."

"But, papa, what's it for?"

The painter was already telling the children what it was

for; and when he had hung it up over the folding-doors such
a bubbling chorus of laughter and merry shrieks followed,
there was such a dragging of little girls in white muslin by
little boys in blue velvet, and such smacking, and kissing, and
happy confusion, that the little Hope's curiosity was immediately relieved. Of all the ingenious inventions of their
friend the painter, this of the misletoe was certainly the most
transcendent.

But when Arthur Merlin himself joined the romp, and,
chasing Hope Wayne through the lovely crowd of shouting
girls and boys, finally caught her and led her to the middle of
the room and dropped on one knee and kissed her hand under
the misletoe, then the delight burst all bounds; and as Hope
Wayne's bright, beautiful face glanced merrily around the
room—bright and beautiful, although she is young no longer
—she saw that the elders were shouting with the children,
and that Lawrence Newt and his wife, and his niece Fanny,
and papa and mamma Wynne, and Bennet, were all clapping
their hands and laughing.

She laughed too, and Arthur Merlin laughed; and when
Ellen Bennet's oldest daughter (of whom there are certain sly
reports, in which her name is coupled with that of her cousin
Edward, May Newt's oldest son) sat down to the piano and
played a Virginia reel, it was Arthur Merlin who handed out
Hope Wayne with mock gravity, and stepped about and bowed
around so solemnly, that little Hope Newt, sitting upon her
papa's knee and nestling her golden curls among his gray hair,
laughed all the time, and wished that Christmas came every
day in the year, and that she might always see Mr. Arthur
Merlin dancing with dear Aunt Hope.

When the dance was over and the panting children were
resting, Gabriel Newt, Lawrence's youngest boy, said to Arthur,

"Mr. Merlin, what game shall we play now? What game
do you like best?"

"The game of life, my boy," replied Arthur.

UNDER THE MISLETOE.

" Oh, pooh !" said Gabriel, doubtfully, with a vague feeling that Mr. Merlin was quizzing him.

But the painter was in earnest; and if you are of his opinion, patient and gentle reader, it is for you to say who, among all the players we have been watching, held Trumps.

THE END.